FIRESIDE:
The Wes Lyons Story

A Novel

DEE BRITT

Quill Hawk Publishing

Manufactured in the United States of America

ISBN: 978-1-7372037-9-7 Paperback

ISBN: 979-8-9850905-0-5 Large Print

Cover design: Virginia McKevitt & Ava Wood

This book is a work of fiction. Any references to historical events, real people, or real places are used fictitiously. Other names, characters, places, and events are products of the author's imagination, and any resemblance to actual events, places, or persons, living or dead, is entirely coincidental.

Content warning: contains scenes with sex, hate, violence, homosexuality, and homophobia.

Edmond, Oklahoma

This book is dedicated to all who lift people up, the lifter of heads and the binder of broken spirits.

"It is not the critic who counts: not the man who points out how the strong man stumbles or where the doer of deeds could have done better. The credit belongs to the man who is actually **in the arena,** whose face is marred by dust and sweat and blood, who strives valiantly, who errs and comes up short again and again... (because) who spends himself in a worthy cause; at the best, knows, in the end, the triumph of high victory and who, at the worst, if he fails, at least he fails while daring greatly."

—Theodore Roosevelt

Speech in the Sorbonne, Paris, April 23, 1910

ACKNOWLEDGEMENTS

So many people have made this sophomore effort a success. My family has supported me through thick and thin, and without this foundation of love supporting me, I would not be the same person today. Donna, Mom (Janna,) Brenda, Kent, Esther, JoAnna, Justin, John, Anita, Rhonda, Robert, Craig, Les, Kandi, cousins, old friends, and new... you have made my life richer. I would like to especially thank Imogene for showing me how a strong woman's resolve is tougher than mere situations. At 98, she had the will of an army, and the last year I spent with her, she taught me lessons I would not have learned anywhere else. Imo, I love you; see you on the other side. (Donna, you are a chip off the ole block. Your love and perseverance have taught me a lot about resilience.)

To Amy M. Le, Founder of Quill Hawk Publishing, thanks for all I have learned from you and for always being there to help me drag these books across the finish line.

Mighty 7 Critique Group, our sessions always got down to the brass tacks, and you guys know you absolutely made my book better. Thank you.

Thanks to Alicia Dean for editing, Virginia McKevitt, and Ava Wood of Fins and Feathers Designs for the sweet cover. Thanks to Tamara Dragseth for my final beta reader feedback.

I would like to thank Joy Neilson, a retired Oklahoma City Police Officer and detective, for being an accuracy consultant for police culture.

Thanks to my family/friends who gave good (honest) critiques when I asked. This includes Brenda, Mom, Esther, and Joy.

Lastly, Thanks, Mom, for asking regularly how the book was going. Without your gentle encouragement and genuine interest, it is possible that no one would be reading this page right now. Thanks, I love you.

"When you are using the gifts God gives you, it creates energy and flow in your life."

—Loretta Lyons,

Mother of Wes Lyons

Atlanta, Georgia

"No one reaches their purpose without the talents of others. Embrace the talents of those around you, and they will embrace you, walking you to the finish line."

—Wes Lyons,

Atlanta, Georgia

Chapter 1

Present Day

Pastor Wes Lyons closed his Bible, glanced left and right, and then whispered, "Amen." Sitting in the ornate vestibule of Fireside Assisted Living Center, in Atlanta Georgia, Wes felt like he was being welcomed to one of his church services from the past. Fragrant, fresh flowers were placed on a credenza at the entryway, by a full-length mirror with filigree around the frame. Wes arrived a little early for his appointment with Erma, the Fireside Administrator. Wes believed ten minutes early was professional and punctual. It showed respect for those you met and had long been a practice of his while leading one of the largest churches in the country.

Taking in his surroundings, Wes breathed deeply and, like a dry sponge in a baptismal bowl, soaked in where his life's journey had left him. With this thought, he closed his eyes and clenched his jaw. He had gone from living a premier life in a mansion on a hill, to waiting for his turn to tour a facility for elders, with all his earthly possessions in the suitcase by his feet. Seventy-five years of life shouldn't fit nicely in a single suitcase. He opened his eyes in a startle as the click of high heels on vinyl flooring marched toward him like a metronome, getting louder the closer she got.

As she approached within talking range, Erma, the Fireside Administrator, reached out her hand to welcome Wes. "I have joined you for worship many times by television. You are somewhat of a celebrity around here, Pastor Wes." Erma beamed, her expression one of starstruck adoration, as if she were meeting a movie star.

Wes hated that look. It was a reminder that the public knew 'Pastor Wes,' a man who was far from the real Wesley Lyons. He fidgeted and mumbled under his breath, *here we go again.* "Good morning. Isn't your name Erma?" Wes struggled to stand, extending his hand for introductions with a smile like a car salesman. Wes always researched anyone he was going to meet. He felt like it gave him the upper hand. Wearing slacks, Kenneth Cole shoes, and a dress shirt with French cuffs rolled to the elbow, he presented as if he had just stepped out of his pastoral study while preparing for the next sermon.

"Well, yes, my name is Erma." Anticipation oozed from her being. She was buffed and polished to the best version of herself. "Let me give you a tour of the place, and then we can sit down to talk in my office, if that is agreeable to you."

"Any woman who has been the administrator of a fine facility like this for twelve years has my undivided attention. That sounds good to me, Erma." Wes nodded and smiled. There. He had her right where he wanted her. Wes expected her to talk freely. That was exactly what he wanted, someone who was in charge and willing to let him into her circle of privilege. Wes reached for his suitcase and twisted his facial expression into one of discomfort and concern.

Erma took the suitcase. "Let me take that. I'll stow it away under my desk."

Wes outwardly showed a resistance to being taken care of, but inside he was thinking, *Wes, set the hook and reel her in.*

As Erma was setting Wes's suitcase under her desk, she bumped the Bible still in his hand. "Here, let me set that on the desk by your suitcase." She reached for it and turned to walk away, but he didn't let go. She paused a beat. "You don't want to carry that around, do you?" She quizzed with raised eyebrows.

Wes sputtered, "Uh, I just like to keep it with me. I carry it with me always. You know what they say, if you keep the word of God with you, uh, it sinks in." He turned around and started down the hall, leaving her behind in silence.

Wes grinned as he turned just enough to see Erma had spun around to see him slowly saunter away. She quickened her steps to get back in line with the pied piper. "Oh, I think I *have* heard of that saying. I just didn't realize it was a literal thing." She was now keeping pace beside him, pointing out selling features of Fireside.

They continued talking and slowly strolled down the hall when a nurse with red hair cut around the corner. To avoid a collision, she had to quickly sidestep, like a bull-fighter stepping to the side with her cape. She shouted, "Sorry, in a hurry!" and continued walking with a purpose toward an exit door. She shouted, "Smoke break," as she pushed the bar on the door.

"Who *was* that?" Pastor Wes's full attention was immediately on the redheaded blur that had shed her steamy lab coat on the way to the exit door by the kitchen. Her tank top and jeans framed a variety of colorful tattoos on her athletic body. The only article identifying her as a nurse was the stethoscope hanging around her neck.

Erma rolled her eyes and instinctively let out a muted growl. "Oh, that would be Ginger. She is the director of nursing here. She is a handful and dresses like she is always on her way to a rock concert. You don't see all 'that' when she keeps on her lab coat." She put her hand up to her eyes as if she were shielding them from the abhorrent sight. "The only problem is, she almost never keeps it on."

Wes laughed in view of the juxtaposition of the unortho-dox nurse and watched Ginger all the way out the back door and shook his head. "Interesting." Wes detected jeal-ousy on Erma's face and leaned toward her. "The Lord al-ways considers the heart, but it is hard not to see all those tattoos." He raised his Bible in the form of an exclamation point.

Leaning into his last comment, Erma explained, "I know. Those tattoos are hideous and, if it were up to me, she would be out of here. When I give tours, I try to steer clear of Ginger. She does not represent what we are all about. I know you can't judge a book by its cover, but I am a pretty good judge of character. I can tell you I know integrity when I see it. Our *other* nurses are professional."

While Erma professed to know how to pick a person with character out of a line-up, Wes was a master. Over decades in the ministry, reading people came naturally and, like-wise, finding others' Achilles heel was like a skip through the park. He questioned Erma's naivety, but she was standing on a platform and announcing it to the world herself, like the barker at a circus. In a fifteen-minute tour around the facility, he had won Erma's confidence and found the true pulse of Fireside, Ginger, the rebellious nurse.

Turning the last corner, having explored the entire facility, they came full circle to Erma's office. Erma clasped both hands in front of her well-endowed bosoms, drawing attention to her loud, floral, knit dress with a plunging neckline. She stepped aside and invited Pastor Wes into her office. "Can I offer you some coffee while we sit to discuss arrangements?" She held out her arm to direct him into the office clearly in front of them.

"That would be wonderful. A little pick-me-up sounds great." He stepped into her office and made himself comfortable in the leather wingback chair in front of her desk, while Erma excused herself to get the coffee.

As Erma left, he checked over his shoulder. His smile dissolved as he dropped his head with a loud exhale. He closed his eyes and gave himself a little pep talk. "So far so good, Wes. Almost there."

The last few years had been hard on him. He had pastored a megachurch, and his family had a home on both coasts, staying connected to build the nationwide Kingsridge Church brand.

Wes pulled out his wallet and flipped through the pictures, now old and faded. His heart ached as he saw snippets from his life, his wife, the pool outside on his property in California, and his son, Jordan. He stared at Jordan and his heart felt as if it were in a vise. Gone, all gone. He realized he had been mesmerized by the pictures for quite some time and scurried to get his billfold back in his pocket before Erma returned with the coffee.

Stepping away from the pulpit and the limelight a short time ago, few knew it, but he had no family and no home left. He still dressed like a million bucks, but his clothes were from his prior years of preaching, and all he had left was literally in the suitcase beside him.

Wes startled as Erma zipped back into her office with a tray of two coffees, cream, and sugar. She smiled and lifted the tray to show her handiwork. "Coffee is served. I didn't ask you if you take cream or sugar, so I brought both, just in case." She put the tray on the desk and waited for him to take his cup first.

As they prepared their coffee, Erma stirred the sugar and cream and started the business end of the conversation. "We are so pleased you visited us today. I am sure that we are competing with multiple homes, but I want you to know that we would consider it an honor to have someone of your position staying here." She lifted the cup to her lips and let out a loose, healthy slurp. She returned the cup to her saucer and waited for his reply.

"Erma, it has been a wonderful morning strolling through these well-kept halls and talking to you. I feel as if I made a new friend."

Erma beamed with these words.

He leaned forward toward Erma and sat his coffee to the side, focusing totally on Erma's face. He wanted her to feel an intimate connection with him. Under his breath he coached himself, "Less is more. Keep it simple and emotional." He cleared his throat, "Erma, Fireside just might be the place for me. This place has such a homey atmosphere and I only walked in thirty minutes ago." As he reached out to momentarily touch her hand, Erma blushed. He continued, "I'm in a bit of a jam and was wondering if you could help me out." He cleared his throat from a nervous tickle. "I am in the process of selling some property and my assets are a little tied up right now. I have investments that cannot be disturbed and I am only days away from closing on a sizable property deal. If I pay for a full year up front, do you think we could write the contract allowing me to move in now and pay the full year upon closing on this property?" He continued with lies, "I don't want to be a burden on my family. I recently had some health issues and may not need to stay here longer than a year or so. I have already done the math. After the sale of my property, I will have enough to pay for a full year. If agreeable, I would like to continue paying year by year." He returned volley, raising his cup for a slow, smooth sip.

Erma kept a smile on her face but reached for a sip of her coffee, giving herself time to think for a moment. "When do you think you could have the money?" She returned the cup to its saucer.

Wes shrugged casually. "A few days. I expect to get a closing date anytime now."

Erma left an uncomfortable silence.

He felt her hesitation, showing a hint of suspicion. He blurted out, "I hate to even ask, but I am literally between homes. For about a week or so, I don't have a place to stay." His voice cracked and he covered it by clearing his throat again. "All my other assets are tied up here and there and literally, all I have right now, is my suitcase and my Bible."

Erma started, "Well, I would like—"

"I noticed the small rooms on the other side of the building. Some of them are furnished. It seems some of them have been vacant for a while. I can slip in there and be out of the way and we can settle up when my assets are freed. I would appreciate your servant's heart meeting my need at this turning point in my life. And it should be noted that not only would you be helping out a friend but, also, you would get an entire year of rent up front, in one lump sum. Just receive it like God is blessing you-in a week or two." He smiled a tranquil smile.

Erma agreed under her breath and already trusted him. He was *the* Pastor Wes... *from TV!* Although this was years ago, he appeared and sounded the same. She could use a little extra cash in the till and he was promising a year's advance in only a few days.

Erma gazed into the eyes of Pastor Wes and she could not refuse him. It was only a delay in paperwork, she would get a little cushion in the Fireside bank account, and the famous Pastor Wes would live at Fireside. Erma stood and extended her hand across the table. "Welcome to the Fireside family."

He stood to meet her. "Erma I really appreciate this. Thank you. I will love living here."

Erma held out her arm in the direction of the hallway. "Let's go find you the perfect room." She escorted him to the other side of the building where a furnished room was waiting. The room was sparsely furnished, but it had a warm bed and a hot shower. He couldn't wait to try both.

Erma apologized. "It is not very—"

"It is perfect. I love it and appreciate your hospitality."

Erma beamed from ear to ear and gave notice. "Lunch is at 11:30. Today is rotisserie chicken and mashed potatoes. Please enjoy yourself. I will contact you next week concerning the paperwork and payment that need to be finished."

"You will never know how much this means to me," Wes finished.

Erma smiled and turned her body while keeping eye contact with him as long as possible. She returned to her office with a little spring in her step, feeling good about the good turn she just extended.

Wes wiped away a tear from his eye. He had food and shelter for a few nights; the pressure was gone. He could relax for the moment.

He researched Erma and picked Fireside because he thought it was a soft target. She had no idea of all the twists and turns he had experienced over recent years. He was homeless, financially decimated, alone, and addicted.

Wes was truly thankful for this stroke of luck in his life. He reached for the door, shut, and locked it. He sat on the twin bed and opened his Bible to Titus, where one of his favorite passages was found. He preached from this text many times, "Everything is pure to those whose hearts are pure. But nothing is pure to those who are corrupt and unbelieving, because their minds and consciences are corrupt. Such people say they know God, but they deny Him by the way they live." These words that prophesied his life over the past several years had never been truer than that moment.

At this book-marked page in Titus, through tears and pain, he wiped sweat from his forehead and then dug into a hidden compartment for a couple of little pills. He chewed and swallowed them, closed the Bible, bowed his head, and whispered, "Amen."

He flipped to the back cover to open a piece of paper that was wrinkled and well-worn. He took his pen from his shirt pocket and marked off a goal achieved; he now had a room at Fireside. Next on his list of goals was to find a way to *stay* at Fireside. No property sale was on the horizon; this would become evident in the upcoming days. He would take the evening to celebrate a warm bed and a good meal. Tomorrow, he would go about finding a way to stay in this community forever.

Chapter 2

Present Day

Ginger combed her hand through her long, red hair once more and paused with her palm resting on her forehead. The notebook on her desk, decorated with a variety of colorful pen marks, a few underlines, strike-throughs, and exclamation marks, revealed the conflict in her thoughts. Wads of paper scattered across her desk exposed the obvious; Ginger had been working on the staffing schedule a good bit of the day. She was reaching her simmering point. As she wadded up another piece of paper to throw at the toy wastepaper basketball goal, Rob stepped through the door as he knocked. The wad of paper hit him squarely in the face.

Rob squinted his eyes and put up his arm to deflect the blur of an object. "Is that any way to treat the guy who covers your tracks at work and maintains a flavor of style and professionalism in this place? Dad may be our boss, but when he hired me as the marketing director, he chose the best-dressed, well-spoken guy in Atlanta." Rob scanned the room to see a graveyard of wadded-up papers covering the floor. "What the heck are you doing?" He popped his elbow to expose his large-faced watch and shook his head. "Girl, we have a Zoom meeting with Dad in three minutes, and I would rather be positioned and in place when it starts. I don't want to draw any more attention than your rebellious reputation already attracts. You created a target on both our backs, and I would like to, just once, blend into the background."

Ginger focused her eyes on the wall clock and grumbled, "Well, shit. Get your chair over here and put your Gucci butt in it. Can you connect us to Zoom while I clean up this office?"

Rob took the driver's seat behind the desk and started pecking on her computer keyboard. Another glance at his watch, and he raced to enter the meeting on time.

Ginger grabbed her lab jacket, and as she put it on, noticed cans behind Rob on the credenza. In one smooth sweep of her arm, she knocked all the empty soda cans onto the floor. She then turned photos face down that she chose not to share with corporate Fireside attending the Zoom call.

Rob's finger strikes on the keyboard got louder as seconds ticked. "We are waiting to join the conference; you better get in place." Ginger turned around, put a fake smile on her face, and leaned against the credenza. Now, she was ready for the meeting to start... but more ready for it to conclude. Rob's phone lit up with a message from Dr. Remington. Ginger was in a perfect position to see his screen.

Ginger teased, "Well, well, well, looks like you and Dr. Remington are on-again, in your on-again, off-again world. He's so handsome. How did you score a guy—" She ruffled his hair and raised up to see the Zoom participants all watching and listening to her. She continued, "Guy...uh, guidance Coach for Medical Marketing." Ginger flashed a smile to the computer camera that gave the false impression that she loved interacting in this meeting. She gave a firm slap on Rob's back, still smiling, yet telling Rob she was perturbed he failed to tell her the meeting had started.

Rob swatted her hand away. "Good morning, all. Ginger and I are here and accounted for." Rob was a pro at working on the fly and had become accustomed to covering Ginger's wild side. They needed each other. Rob Miles was the owner's son. Mr. Miles, who held status in the community and led several committees at church, loved his son deeply. Although many across America were accepting of the gay community, many parts of the South still found homosexuality taboo. Open acceptance of the gay community could be costly to Mr. Miles's status at church and his business at Fireside. He loved his son, but he would rather leave his son's gayness in the closet. The collective church was a funnel for new residents at Fireside. Mr. Miles made sure Rob remembered; word of mouth traveled fast when people bragged on you, but traveled faster when accompanied with gossip. When Rob needed a beard, Ginger was his date. When Ginger needed someone to run interference when she colored outside the lines, Rob was an expert and happy to do so. They both got what they needed.

Ginger appeared to be taking notes on the meeting; however, she was still working on the nursing schedule, a thorn in every charge nurse's side. Everybody *can't enjoy Christmas at home, drinking eggnog in an ugly sweater, and kissing under the mistletoe.*

Still focused on the schedule, Ginger eventually heard Mr. Miles. "Right, Ginger? Ginger, do we have your support?"

Ginger snapped to reality. With a tilt of her head and a disingenuous smile, she responded, "Of course, Mr. Miles. I'm your girl."

Rob had been nursing his cup of coffee. But, with that surprising endorsement, he choked on his morning elixir, causing him to reach for a tissue to cover his mouth. In this moment of confusion, while hustling to clean up the coffee, Ginger took the opportunity to disconnect the Zoom meeting quickly.

"What the hell?" Rob sharply questioned as he brushed coffee off his favorite tie.

Ginger patted her jeans pocket to find her lighter and motioned toward the door as she stepped out to her second office outside, by the dumpster behind the kitchen.

Rob, as always, dropped what he was doing and followed her for a smoke. As he sneaked through the facility back door, Ginger had already fired up and sat on a milk crate, leaning on the brick wall across from the dumpster that smelled of soured milk and old grease.

Rob reached out. "Can I bum one?" He sniffed repeatedly and shook his head. "You know, the stench out here is always shocking, even though we escape to this place at least once a day. I don't know if it is worth it."

Ginger tapped ash from the tip of her cigarette. "The stench is sour, but the solace is sweet. It is worth the smell to have peace and quiet." She twitched a half-smile. "Smoke your own." Ginger took a long draw of nicotine.

"I won't. You created this mess. The least you can do is give me one of your cigarettes. Hand it over." He glared at her with his hand still extended. "What is going on? You usually are not a bundle of joy in the morning, but that was weird." As he flicked his lighter, the smell of the initial burn of the cigarette was soothing and familiar.

"This staffing schedule is impossible. Each nurse wants to select her work schedule like she is ordering off a menu. Well, this isn't Burger King, and you can't have it your way." Ginger drew another drag from her cigarette and tilted her head back as she blew controlled puffs of smoke like an old-fashioned locomotive.

She took a moment to reflect and added, "It's not that we don't have enough breathing bodies to put on the schedule. I can hire a few more nurses tomorrow, but are they just breathing bodies that want to stay on social media and get a paycheck? Or, are they a person who puts the patient before TikTok and texting their friends? I want caring nurses who will treat Gertrude, in room 201, like she was their grandma."

Rob sat against the building with knees bent and one arm draped over his knee. He peeked at Ginger and then turned away, afraid of the backlash he was sure was coming his way. "I hate to rain on your parade a little more, but have you any idea what you agreed to in the Zoom meeting?"

"I have no idea, Rob, but your coffee-spitting episode allowed me to exit that gallery of closed-minded socialite stiff-shirts." She smiled at the thought of her quick exit.

Rob braced for the reaction. "Well... my dad, the owner and lead stiff-shirt of Fireside, asked us to represent Fireside at the annual black-tie gala at the Country Club. It celebrates business growth in Atlanta."

Ginger's eyes glazed over into a blank stare as she dropped her burning cigarette onto her t-shirt. She brushed the cigarette off her shirt with the back of her hand. "Damn, shit, hell, fu..." She stood up with her hands on her hips and started pacing. "Can today get any worse?"

Rob tried to show the bright side. "I know it sounds terrible, but it is only for one night, and this ought to be the only event for at least a year—"

"Stop it; just stop it," Ginger snapped. "I have to get out of here. I am pulling a freaking double tonight; short-staffed also means a screwed supervisor. I will be covering staffing gaps until I find more nurses that have the skill and heart."

Ginger left without waiting for a response from Rob. She approached Erma while on her way to her office.

Erma held up her finger. "Ginger, I just had the best idea," Erma envied the positive attention that Ginger often generated. She hated Ginger's rebellious nature but wouldn't mind having some of the limelight and would enjoy a ride along on Ginger's coattails for the evening, "I will be attending the gala, too. Let's coordinate our gowns. We can sit together and be twins. I am envisioning a dusty rose-colored tulle fabric with puff sleeves."

Without changing expression or acknowledging Erma, Ginger stomped toward her office. Tulle, freaking tulle? I would rather have a tooth extraction. At least you get good drugs. "I already have plans for that night, Erma. I forgot." She stepped into her office and shut the door on her refuge and the conversation with Erma.

Chapter 3

Present Day

"I will not let go." Mr. Epstein held onto his favorite pants. "Why are you doing this? Those are my pants, and I want them back." For a little man in his late nineties, he could put up quite a scuffle. Mr. Epstein's hook nose nearly met his chin, and without his teeth, it was even more pronounced. His receding gray hair was slicked back with Vaseline and the nape of his neck sported a curly fringe while in wait for a good haircut. Amanda, his certified nursing assistant, bribed, "Just let me sew the hole in the knee. I will bring you some extra bacon with breakfast tomorrow morning. What do you say?"

Mr. Epstein's grip tightened as his speech rose an octave. "What do I want with bacon? I am Jewish. I am an Auschwitz survivor, and you will not outlast me. This, I know. I have the favor of Abraham and the fight of David. I will spend my last breath holding on to these pants."

Amanda scanned the area to see who was listening. "Mr. Epstein, my boss told me not to come back to the break room till I get these pants. After I sew them, I will bring them right back. Can you help me out?"

Mr. Epstein knew who was behind this, Erma. Directly or indirectly, Erma was everyone's boss, and she had been trying to throw his pants in the trash for over a year now. Mr. Epstein knew what he had to do. "Ginger! Where are you? Ginger!" Mr. Epstein held onto his pants with white knuckles in one hand and banged on his wheelchair with his cane with the other.

Ginger heard Epstein's yells and knew what was going on. Of course, those idiots tried to take his pants, again. That was the ultimate icing on her crappy cake. She grabbed her lab coat and put it on as she stomped down the hall. When she approached Mr. Epstein, he raised his cane and exclaimed, "Sweetie, tell this little girl these are my pants, and I will not throw them away. She says she will give them back, but I know the drill. My property is my property, whether it is a toothpick or my pants. I still wear those pants almost every day. It was wash-day, and I took them off for the laundry and this girl, here Alisha—"

Amanda exhaled. "Amanda. My name is Amanda, Mr. Epstein."

"Like I said, Samantha is trying to take my favorite pants. I know it is not her fault. That battle-ax, Erma, is behind this; she has to be."

Ginger held both palms up and shrugged. "What's up, Amanda?" Ginger knew Amanda. She was dependable and good-hearted; in fact, she wished most of her nurses had the same integrity and work ethic as this young C .N.A. She knew Erma forced Amanda to confront Mr. Epstein, but she had to hear it from Amanda's lips.

Amanda struggled to hold back her tears. "I need this job, Ginger. My family depends on me. I don't want to offend Mr. Epstein, but Erma said that my work hours would be cut back if I don't get his pants and sew up the hole in the knee."

Ginger squatted by Mr. Epstein's wheelchair. "If Amanda promises to return your pants, washed and with the holes mended, will you let her take them? I can vouch for her, Mr. Epstein. She is good people."

Mr. Epstein glared at Amanda. "Do you promise me? Look me in the eye. I know a liar when I look them in the eye." Mr. Epstein still held tight to his pants.

Amanda apologized, "Yes sir. Just let me wash and mend them, and I will bring them directly back. And, I promise not to bring you bacon."

"You were going to bring him bacon?" Ginger quizzed. Mr. Epstein loosened his grasp and let the pants slip through his fingers.

Amanda gazed down like she should know better. "Erma told me he liked bacon."

"Go take care of Mr. Epstein and take care of his pants as he directs," Ginger instructed. "I'm going to go have a coffee with Erma."

Mr. Epstein straightened his spine and carried himself with the respect Ginger recognized.

Ginger stopped by the dining room on the way to Erma's office and picked up a couple of coffees with cream and sugar packets. Ginger knocked and waited.

Erma recognized her knock and waved her in. "What a surprise, Ginger. What's on your mind?"

Ginger simply said, "Mr. Epstein." She started dressing up her coffee with cream and sugar. As she stirred the cream and sugar, some coffee slopped out on Erma's antique desk. It was all Ginger could do to leave the spilled coffee right there, but this was in her plan.

Erma immediately noticed the coffee spill and, without mentioning it, handed Ginger some tissue to wipe up the mess and a coaster to protect the wooden desktop.

Ginger took the tissue, blew her nose, and threw it away. She left the coaster right where Erma placed it. Ginger leaned back in her chair and put her feet up on Erma's desk. Ginger saw Erma's brow furrow as Ginger's nasty boots slid across the heirloom.

Erma scolded Ginger, "Why did you come in here? And, get your boot-stomping feet off my desk."

Ginger swung both feet off the desk in one motion and cleaned away the spilled coffee with a remaining tissue. Ginger leaned forward. "Bacon? You told Amanda to give Mr. Epstein bacon?"

"Ah, I see what this is about, those hideous, stained, worn-out pants. I just told Amanda that little nugget of information to try to give her a little leverage. Everybody loves bacon." Erma smiled, delighted in her tricky thinking.

Ginger pleasantly agreed, but her volume grew as her comment progressed, "Yes, everyone loves bacon unless you practice a religion that rejects pork! Mr. Epstein is Jewish."

Erma squinted and tilted her head. "Really? Huh, I didn't know he was Jewish," demonstrating Erma's focus for the residents was all about the money. Her connection with them revolved around the Fireside bank statement. "Mr. Epstein, I'm sure is a nice man, but his worn-out pants are offensive when I give facility tours. He has better; he should wear better." Erma gathered stacks of paper on her desk. She straightened them into piles by lightly tapping groups of paper vertically to align the edges.

Ginger knew if she raised her voice, Erma would disengage. She continued with measured tone and volume, "If Mr. Epstein had any trust in you, he might listen. But you have not done anything to instill that trust. The primary interaction you have initiated revolves around two things, timely payments and getting your hands on his prized possession, his pants. Get to know him, learn what is important to him, and meet his needs where you can. He will then listen to you without suspicion."

Erma defended herself, "How could those pants be important... in any way?"

Ginger saw her chance. "Why did you give a shit that I spilled coffee on this old banged-up desk? It is easy to see it has seen better days. I see several coffee rings on that corner and the decorative carving on the front has a large chunk pulled completely off. I see you have built up that rear leg with a folded piece of cardboard because the desk is wobbly. There is a proper desk in the nurses' lounge. Have maintenance bring that down here. It would make a much better impression on the prospective residents taking a tour."

Erma briefly turned her head to the window so Ginger couldn't see her lower eyelids filling with tears. "All those things give this desk character. It is an heirloom from my mother. She got it from her dad, my grandpa." She returned her eyes to Ginger once she gained composure. "The coffee rings on the corner are from long midnight sessions when Mom poured over bills while I was sleeping. The decorative carving was ripped off the front when I tied the dog's toy to it. Whitey sunk his teeth in it and ran, ripping the carving off the desk. I have lugged this desk around with every move I have made since my mom died. It gives me comfort when times get tough."

Ginger leaned back in her chair, glad she gave Erma space to talk. "That, Erma, is why Mr. Epstein holds on to those hideous pants. They are his pants. He survived Auschwitz, where his clothes today would pass for dress clothes. He learned to live on so little in the concentration camp. He learned everything he values has nothing to do with material gains: freedom, integrity, and faith, to name just a few. Your desk is your desk. His pants are his pants. Leave him alone."

Erma put both hands on her desk as she pushed away from it. "Thanks, Ginger. I think you would agree we are generally quite different people. In the midst of all our dislikes and differences, we manage to find a way to tolerate each other. You intrigue me, but I have never felt I understood you and all your tattoos. You live your truth, and I will live mine."

Ginger stood. "Just like you reflected on your past, these residents remember days of glory and suffering. Give them the space and respect to do so gracefully." As Ginger turned to return to her office, her steps were a bit lighter.

As the door closed, Erma pulled out a can of furniture polish and a soft rag she kept in her drawer. She took time to polish her desk and remember her dear mom in the process. She then exited for the kitchen for another cup of coffee and a pocket full of all the fixings. This was something she did when feeling down.

Erma sat at her desk with a sigh of solace. She smiled as she added enough cream to make the coffee change to the color of her taupe pantyhose. She closed her eyes and thought of her dear mother. *Mamma, no one understands my connection to this old desk, the only true connection I still have to my childhood and you. Kids teased me because of my dirty hair and clothes as I walked to school.* She paused and looked up for a moment, as if someone was really sitting across the desk. *They followed behind me, throwing sticks or rocks while taunting me all the way to the playground. It took me a while to figure out that your cough medicine was really whiskey, and many of those long nights, you weren't sick, you were simply passed out from an all-day drunk. Still, to this day, no matter how much I try to fix my issues from the past, you are still the only person I can say has ever really loved me. You may not have been perfect, but I was never the same after they made me go to foster care, Mamma. Missed you every day and still do. Thanks for our little talks.* Her mood and expression softened to a smile; *it reminds me of a time that others thought was a disgrace, but it was actually the happiest time of my life. My mother loved me, and that is something not all kids could say.* She stacked her saucer, cup, and spoon and placed them behind her on the credenza for the moment. *Now, on to my fun-filled day.* She turned her focus to her computer and focused on the corporate emails waiting in her inbox.

Chapter 4

1950s

Little Wesley tiptoed past his father's study, with his shoes in one hand and his comic book in the other. The summer heat in Atlanta was stifling as Wesley made his way through the house like a soldier working his way through enemy territory. He dodged their barking dog and eluded his mom on a regular basis en route to his hideout. Today, his dad was preparing a sermon for Sunday, so that put one more obstacle in the mix. Wesley's big toe was fully exposed through a hole in his sock, and the wood floor was cool against it as he skillfully made his way past his dad's study door.

Wes was supposed to be doing homework, but he had grander ideas for the hot day, immersing himself in the world of Superman while chewing Super Bubble. Success! He made it to the kitchen undetected and slid on the linoleum with delight! As he scrambled out the screen door, he ran into his mom face-to-face. She was carrying a wicker basket with clothes she had just taken off the line. He squinted his eyes and put his comic book over his backside awaiting her response.

"Wesley Lyons, you better have your homework done, *all* of it." She put her laundry basket on the ground, grabbed his wrist and held it over his head, awaiting his answer. This was their usual stance, almost like dancing positions, every time Wesley got caught misbehaving.

"Mom..." Wesley paused and gazed up to the sky, like a plane were going to write an answer for him. "I just have a little bit left, but I was getting so droopy and floppy, just laying on my bed trying to keep my eyes open." He put on his sweetest face, but kept his comic book to his backside for protection. "I am totally awake now. I will hurry to my room and finish it, okay?" He started trying to gently turn as if she had already agreed.

"Not so fast, son. You know our rules: homework first and comic books later."

"Oh, but Mom, I'm sorry." He closed his eyes, knowing what was in store.

She turned her eyes to the willow tree and then to Wesley. "Put on your shoes and go get me a switch. We will get this over with."

Over the years, Wesley tried to discover which switches were easier on the behind; his conclusion thus far: they all hurt as much as the last. Wesley tied his laces and dragged his feet with slumped shoulders. He was already misty-eyed when he handed the switch to his mom.

"Grab your ankles," she said with no emotion.

Wesley grabbed his ankles and just as she was in her back-swing, he had an idea and stood slightly trying to hold her attention.

She continued with her follow through, "One... two... three." She always counted each one out loud and it was always three licks. In a weird way, it made things a little better. At least he knew what was coming and how many. Wesley wasn't a bad kid; he was a free-spirited boy with an imagination. Superman comics were much more his style than mathematics.

"Now, go to your bedroom and study... your *homework*. Leave that comic book alone." Loretta had to make it sound good, but she understood Wesley's difficulty with sitting still.

Wesley ran to his room, shut the door, and flopped on his bed. He pulled out his Big Chief tablet and worked through the problems from his textbook. It wasn't that he couldn't do it, but it was like harnessing a tornado for him to sit still. Structured problem-solving just seemed to suck the very life out of his wildly imaginative brain, but after three licks, he always seemed to find a measure of discipline and focus.

Pastor Lyons liked a quiet house when he was composing a sermon. His office wasn't really an "office space," but a transformed bedroom down the hall from the kitchen. He and Loretta had planned to have another child, but the Lord had other plans, so until God blessed them with another child, it would remain his office. Before he wrote a sermon, he would get on his knees in the adjoining closet and pray, asking for God to forgive him of his sins and give him words of value for his flock. He learned this habit from his father, who was also a pastor. Pastor Lyons often said, "If it was good enough for Daddy, it is good enough for me." Sometimes it took five minutes; sometimes it took fifty minutes to get his heavenly inspiration, but he always waited on the Lord.

Inside his office, Pastor Lyons kept his desk neat and organized. His small frame was styled with coal-black hair, slicked back with Brylcreem, and pressed slacks with a white starched shirt Loretta meticulously ironed. He truly had a heart for God and a calling to serve people. He dressed every day ready to leave at a moment's notice to pray for the sick and comfort the dying. He was just as driven to serve the community and his God, as Wesley was to read comic books and create entertaining stories.

Pastor Lyons put down his pen and shifted toward the open window to get a breath of fresh air. The glass of sweet tea Loretta fixed earlier had condensation on the outside and made his hand wet when he raised it to his lips. He hungered to reach more people for the Lord, but there was something missing. He prayed, studied the Word, and worked hard every day, yet his little church stayed the same. The same twenty-five people came every Sunday. They sang, they prayed, they put an envelope in the offering plate, and smiled as they shook his hand on their way out. Most went home to enjoy a meal at the kitchen table. Some had more than others, but they all had enough. Despite all his efforts, he saw no fire for the Lord, no passion in his congregation. He bowed his head at his desk and prayed for guidance.

###

Wesley bounced his leg at the dinner table, waiting not so patiently for his mom to dollop a spoonful of mashed potatoes on his plate. He waited quietly with his fork in hand, ready to shovel food in his mouth.

"Your father is washing up, Wesley, be patient." She moved about the table putting serving spoons in each dish.

Pastor Lyons shuffled in and patted Wesley on the back as he turned for his chair. "Let us pray."

They all closed their eyes as Harold led them, "Thank you, oh God, for the bounty we are about to receive and bless the hands that have prepared it—"

"Amen," they all replied.

"How's it going, son?" Harold looked toward Wesley.

Wesley smiled. "Just fine, Dad." He begged his mom with pleading eyes as Pastor Lyons hit the side of the bottle of ketchup, encouraging it to come out on his meatloaf. *Please don't tell Dad about my licks.*

Loretta inspected her plate and then changed the subject. "How's your sermon coming along, Harold?" She put a spoonful of pea salad in her mouth.

Pastor Lyons was encouraged to hear her interest in his writing. "Oh," he nodded several times as he readied his fork with meatloaf, "it is coming along. 1 Corinthians 12:12 is the text. 'For as the body is one, and hath many members, and all the members of that one body, being many, are one body, so also is Christ.'"

Loretta agreed, "Amen."

Wesley sneaked his comic book to his thigh at the table and caught a glance when his parents were distracted.

The pastor beamed with Loretta's approval. "What do *you* think about it, Wesley?"

Uh, oh. Wesley was not prepared. "Yes, sir. I like it."

"What about it do you like?" Pastor Lyons took a swig of sweet tea and cleared his throat.

"I like all of it, because you like it, Dad; but really, I don't get most of it. Those words are hard to understand." Wesley sopped up his plate with the remaining white bread by his plate and slid his comic book up his shirt as his dad closed his eyes and clenched his jaw momentarily.

Harold searched for the right words to say and glared at Wesley. "What verse *do* you like?"

Wesley was exploding with energy and had to get out of there. He quoted the only verse he remembered, "John 11:35, 'Jesus wept'... John 11:35, may I be excused, please?" He slowly scooted out the side of his chair, waiting to dart outside the second he was given the green light.

"Okay, son, go outside and play." Pastor Lyons's exasperated eyes found Loretta's, pleading for an explanation.

Loretta reached her hand across the table. "He's young, Harold. Give him time. You have to give him some credit; he gave reference and verse in the proper format, just like the older kids when they have a Bible quiz. He just happened to give the shortest verse in the Bible. But it *is* a verse and it probably *is* his favorite because it's the shortest."

Loretta strolled around the table and put her arms around him from behind in a lingering hug. She whispered in his ear. The pastor's eyes widened with surprise as he turned toward her.

"Loretta! It is still daylight outside. Are you sure?"

Loretta lingered and lightly stroked his arm. "Song of Solomon 8:3 'His left hand should be under my head and his right hand should embrace me.' Song of Solomon 8:3. That is one of *my* favorite verses. I need your touch, Harold. Wesley will be outside till we make him come inside." She unbuttoned the top button of her dress and slowly backed away without losing eye contact with Harold. He followed her to the bedroom, and they lost track of time in each other's arms.

Chapter 5

1950s

Wesley fidgeted with a flash of grimace on his face, sitting on a pallet offstage in the wings. Waiting for his cue to enter stage right, he couldn't get comfortable. "Why couldn't Peter Pan wear a cape like Superman?" Wesley joked with his classmate as he stood, shifted his weight, and removed a wedgie from the backside of his leotard costume. Wesley relished his lead role in the school play, and he was finding that the leotard was not as comfortable as it appeared. He shook his arms and hands and bounced from his left foot to his right, like a fighter warming up before his entrance. He filled his lungs with three deep breaths, readying himself for his entry.

Wendy Darling, his co-star character in the play, stood at center stage. She put her hand above her eyes, as if peering into the sun, "Where is that boy from Neverland?"

Wesley embodied his character and entered from stage right. He was a natural on stage. He was the only kid in the cast who was more nervous in the stillness of the wings than when he was in front of an audience of five hundred people.

Loretta arrived early so she could get a seat on the aisle. Waiting for his entrance, she clicked a few pictures with her Kodak Brownie and nudged the woman next to her while never taking her eyes off the stage, "Peter Pan is my son." Loretta saw Wesley improve with each performance. His capacity to maintain focus and stay connected with his environment was noticeably better when he was performing than it was when he was studying. He demonstrated a natural ability to resonate with the audience and found a knack for improvisation. Sitting in math class for forty minutes was a near impossible situation, but creative activity held his attention for hours. Loretta supported Wesley's acting, as it was a source of pride and confidence for him.

The woman next to Loretta tapped her on the arm. "Are you Pastor Lyons's wife? If he is coming, I'll scoot down a seat."

Loretta slid back in her seat and whispered, "He had church work, maybe next time." She returned her attention to the stage, hoping there would be no further questions. Loretta hated covering for Harold. He acknowledged little benefit in the performing arts, viewing it as "only entertainment" and felt his own time was better served studying for an upcoming sermon series on The Sermon on the Mount.

Wesley was electric that night. He exercised precise timing and kept the attention of the entire audience, causing them to laugh and applaud spontaneously. He was a natural performer and lifted the mood of the entire auditorium. Loretta saw the power and value in his acting and was praying that her husband would see the same importance. She understood that his success on the stage counterbalanced his struggles in the classroom. Wesley needed the arts as they gave him expression and success that he found nowhere else.

At the end of the performance, the drama teacher introduced each actor. The audience gave a polite, distracted applause to each child as he worked through the roster of actors. Then the lead actors were introduced. "Playing Peter Pan, we have Wesley Lyons." Wesley bowed and ran to his place with the others. The audience turned and gave a hearty applause with a few hoots and hollers in addition. Wesley naturally felt their connection and spontaneously ran back to the center for a second bow, recognizing their appreciation. The cast assembled for a team bow and the curtain was dropped.

The cast buzzed with energy and hugged each other with congratulations. Parents were waiting for their kids in the auditorium as they raised the house lights. They visited with each other, getting caught up on each other's lives.

Wesley ran out to Loretta's side and gave her a big hug while she was making small talk with another parent. As their conversation came to a close, she turned to face Wesley. "You were fabulous, son! You had the attention of the full crowd. I am so proud of you."

"Is Dad in the bathroom?" He leaned to search behind her and then scanned the room for a sign of his dad.

"He had to work, Wesley. Maybe next time." She ruffled his hair and offered, "Let's go to the A&W Drive-In and get some ice cream to celebrate." She opened her purse and located her keys, then turned to see his disappointed face.

Wesley put his hands in his pockets and shrugged. "Sure." He would never turn down ice cream, but he would have traded the ice cream for his dad's presence.

As they left, Loretta put her hand around his shoulder. Other kids ran down the aisle and shouted, "Good job, Wesley."

"Thanks, guys. See y'all tomorrow."

It took two hands for Wesley to open the door of their 1957 Chevy Bel Air. Harold bought it at a great price from a guy who had wrecked the front end. All it needed was a once-over from his mechanic. Harold felt blessed to have found such a great car at such a discount. He would drive it while he saved the money to have the front bumper and hood fixed. Even though it wasn't new, he still kept his car in pristine condition. The aqua and white paint with accents of chrome shined like a diamond. As Wesley crawled into the front seat, his feet didn't quite touch the floor. Wesley mumbled, "I wish Dad cared about me as much as he cares about this stupid car."

"What did you say, honey? I could barely hear you." Loretta checked her lipstick in the rearview mirror.

"Mom, why doesn't Dad come to see my plays?" He looked at the floorboard, clearly dejected in spite of his outstanding performance.

Loretta tried to defend Harold, although it was difficult. "Wesley, he was working and I guess he couldn't break away. He loves you very much. Maybe next time."

"That's what you said *last* time. I'll take a banana split with double chocolate. Gotta get it while I can." Wesley smiled, knowing she would always be his biggest fan. He glanced out the window and changed the subject.

Harold sat in his office and smiled at his great progress on the new series. He pushed away from his desk, stood, and paced to and fro in his office, holding a stack of papers and preaching to the furniture as if it was the congregation. Harold prided himself in precise research and Biblical references. No one gave a better-referenced sermon, nobody.

Loretta pulled in the driveway, and Wes couldn't wait for the car to completely stop. He jumped out and ran directly to his room. His mind shifted gears and he made a beeline to lay on the floor and draw army guys and airplanes.

After cleaning her face and combing her hair, Loretta tucked little Wesley into bed. As she sat on the edge of the bed and brushed the disheveled hair from his face, she smiled and planted a loud, puckering kiss right in the middle of his forehead. "Love you. You are the bee's knees."

"Bee's knees? That is silly. Where did you get that?"

"Oh, your grandma used to tell me that when she was tucking me in. It means you are a winner. You are top-notch, and you are."

"Mom, I can't explain it, but I feel like I can fly when I am on stage. Maybe I really am Peter Pan." He laughed with a genuine joy he rarely tapped into.

"I love you, son. Oatmeal tomorrow morning for breakfast?"

"How about chocolate cake? I saw it in the kitchen." He flashed his enticing grin.

She caved. "Okay. This time; this time only."

"Thanks. You're the best."

###

Loretta spoke in a monotone. "Harold, you said you were coming. What happened this time?"

"I know, I know, but I had a breakthrough with this research and I couldn't get free. See what I found." He flipped a few pages deeper into his pile of papers, scanning line after line for his newly found topic.

Loretta turned and left his office, without saying a word, leaving him talking to himself as he was engrossed in his sermon. He became aware he was alone a few lines later and raised his hands in wonder.

Harold went to their bathroom and interrupted Loretta brushing her teeth. "Why did you leave me high and dry? I think you would really enjoy my new findings."

"Harold, your son admires you and wants to please you. Why can't you show up for him... just once?"

"It would be different if he was making good grades, or scoring a touchdown, or mowing someone's yard-doing good deeds. But he is just playing, fun and games. What worth is there in fun and games?"

"The arts feed his soul, Harold. Acting breathes life into his being. I might add that he lifts the spirits of everyone in the auditorium. Surely you find value in serving other people." She paused for him to interject, but it was met with silence. "He may never be successful as a scholar. He is too small and uncoordinated to excel in sports, but he has a natural talent for acting, and he is still just a boy. He will get better with time. When I tucked him in, he was still talking about the performance and the exhilaration he felt from playing Peter Pan."

"There are so many other things he could invest his time into other than playing make believe. Make believe... my son is talented in pretending." Harold shook his head. "I will come to bed in a minute, honey."

He returned the papers to his office and stopped by the kitchen for a snack before bedtime. He opened the fridge and spied the buttermilk. He crumbled yesterday's corn-bread into a Tupperware glass and soaked it with the tangy, thick buttermilk. He sat at the kitchen table, eating a snack he watched his father eat many times. Spoonful by spoonful, he wrestled with the idea that his son was not what he had hoped for. He prayed. *God, please teach my son Your ways and give him the strength and talent to find success in a more suitable pastime.* Harold tipped the glass to get the last drops of buttermilk and made his way to his bedroom that was already dark with Loretta making audible puffs with each exhale as she slept.

###

Wesley crawled out of his bed, still amped up from his exciting night. He grabbed a piece of newspaper used as a liner in his trash can and folded it into a Peter Pan hat. He sat his stuffed animals in little rows and performed the last scene again. When he ended his lines with a flurry of expression, he gave sweeping bows to his new audience and imagined their applause. He crawled into bed with the hat still on his head.

###

Loretta came to his room the next morning to tell him it was time for breakfast. She saw the newspaper hat and knew what he had been doing. She kissed him on the cheek to awaken him.

He smiled. "Mom, can I get a new comic book with my allowance today?"

Loretta smiled. "You bet, honey. You bet. Get dressed now and come out for breakfast."

Loretta sat at the kitchen table and wrote in her diary while she drank her coffee. *I don't know what Wesley will do for a living when he grows up, but this I do know, it will be the arts, stories, and drama that will make his life worthwhile. Can't wait to see where it will all take him.*

Chapter 6

Present Day

Wes leaned on the sink and inspected himself in the mirror. He saw the face of a used-up man and wondered how it all went wrong over the years. Gazing deep into his own eyes, he searched to recognize a trace of the man he used to be. His eyes seemed hollow like his heart, an arid wasteland void of love. He whispered, "The eye is the lamp of the body." He preached on this text from Mathew 6:22-23 many times and now he understood it much better. He felt worn out and used up, an old man with no purpose or impact on those around him.

Then, like shifting gears in his old Corvette, he switched personalities like a chameleon. His acting classes as a boy served him well over the years. He flashed his patented smile and tilted his head to the same position thousands of promo pictures used over the years. "It's showtime.

You live in the middle of an opioid gold mine; it's time to start digging."

He grabbed the towel on the rod nearby and turned the shower water on without taking one step. The small, efficient bathroom offered dignity to a man who had been stripped of it prior to moving to Fireside. A little soap, water, and Visine would fix a lot. Time to switch into performance mode.

Wes checked himself in the mirror again: hair combed, shaved, clean clothes, and a glint in his eye. "Not bad," he bragged, as he turned to view back and front to see his full presentation in the mirror. He took several long gulps of vodka, unwrapped a stick of Juicy Fruit and popped it into his mouth. He would be good for only a short while, so he stepped out of his room, locked it, and hunted for the med cart.

Wes started down the unusually quiet hall. His stomach ached, and sweat crept down the sides of his face, tingling his freshly shaved skin. He pulled out his monogrammed handkerchief and wiped off the evidence to his withdrawal. He didn't feel well, but the aches, sweats, and runny nose were more frequent than they used to be, and his cover-up became more natural.

He turned the corner and could see an unattended med cart right there. Just within his reach. As he slowly approached, he checked out his surroundings. He found himself truly alone in the hallway. Sweat beaded on his forehead again and he put his hands in his pockets, noticing the certified nursing assistant's leg clearly visible from outside the patient's room. Wes could almost smell the oxies stored under lock and key. While the C.N.A. talked to the resident in the room, with the turn of her head, she could see the entire med cart. He knew he would not score meds this time, but he decided to take advantage of this moment to gather information about her process. He sat in a hallway chair nearby with a good view of the med cart. Hunting for something to give him a purpose, he grabbed the closest magazine on a nearby table and used it as a decoy while he took mental notes of any Achilles heel that might present itself in the med pass process. Much to his disappointment, she had an iron-clad routine, noting all exchanges made in the flowsheets and locking the cart when she stepped away. The C.N.A. left the resident's door open while she handed off the pills to the resident. Wes quickly recognized the weak link to a quick score of meds waited elsewhere.

Nauseated, fatigued, and depressed, he closed the magazine and shuffled down the hall. He sat at the next intersection of halls for a moment and tried to clear his mind for another idea, when he saw what he called "a gift from God." Continuing to make a new plan, he kept watching the med pass C.N.A. He discovered an additional step with a few patients. An opportunistic smile grew across his face as he noticed she tore a corner off of a pad of paper. After she popped the pills out of a bubble pack, she took a long drink out of her insulated tumbler and stretched her arms as she glanced around. He sat in the distance, but close enough to guess her plan. Once the coast was clear, she quickly put a couple of pills in the paper, folded it, and shoved it into her pocket. She poured a small cup of water and continued with her routine.

The C.N.A. continued down the hall and Wes knew what he would do. He stood and approached her. As he got near, he gave her a gentleman's nod. "Hi, I am new around here. My name is Wes. I think I may have the flu. I have the sniffles, the sweats and just feel rotten all the way around. My room is just right around the corner. Do you think you could come by after you finish this person and take my temperature?"

The C.N.A. responded without distraction from her work. "My name is Skylar. I can't come by your room till I have finished passing meds, but lucky for you, I only have one room left." She grinned. "Nice to meet you, Mr. Wes. I will be with you shortly."

"Great. I appreciate it." Wes left and once he turned the corner, jogged to his room, hoping his plan would work. He unlocked his door, sat on his bed, and took another nip of vodka. As the familiar burn calmed him like an old friend, he unwrapped a fresh stick of gum. His old gum lost its flavor and became stiff to the chew.

In only moments, Skylar knocked on his door, "Nursing."

Wes cleared his throat and wiped his forehead. "Come in, Skylar."

Skylar had a temperature gun ready to use. As she stepped forward, she asked, "Do you have any nausea, vomiting, or body aches?"

"Most of those, I guess. I just feel crummy."

She pulled the trigger and read it. "97.8 degrees, cool as a cucumber, Mr. Wes."

"You can just call me Wes. It's Wes Lyons."

"Wes Lyons? The preacher, Wes Lyons?"

"Well, yes—"

"The 'Pastor Wes' my grandma watched every Sunday and saved her money to see in person across town, Pastor Wes?"

"I guess that would be me."

"You seem a lot different in person, sir. I can't call you Wes. My grandma wouldn't allow it. I am happy to help you in any way I can. Happy to meet you." She reached out her hand for a courteous handshake.

"Skylar, I guess maybe it is just allergies getting worse, thanks."

"No problem. It is such an honor to meet you. How'd you get—"

"I have a question for you," Wes diverted the conversation, "I bet you can help me out."

"Sure." Her eyes widened a bit and she stepped forward.

"I'll ask Ginger to see if she can get me some better allergy medicine, and I am due for some refills on other meds soon, like high blood pressure and medication for constipation. My pain meds prescription never made it here to Fireside and the pain is sometimes unbearable. I guess you heard about my bad car wreck a few years ago. Anyway, I still deal with terrible pain from that wreck." He rubbed the back of his neck and his lower back for a little extra emphasis. "If you have any ideas to help, I would try anything. Please give it some thought. I will try to find Ginger after I rest my back a bit." He grimaced in pain and searched her eyes to see if she was empathetic. "Ginger should be able to help me. Thank you so much."

Skylar became mesmerized with Wes. A dyed-in-the-wool church goer, her grandma would tell her about "Pastor Wes's" sermons each Sunday. She grinned. "I am happy to help you anytime, Pastor Wes, I will give it some thought."

Character assessment came easy to Wes. Over his years as a pastor, he had seen the good, the bad, and the ugly. He wanted to get close to her. He thought that maybe she peddled pills on the side, and he might leverage some oxies out of her. Now, his gut denied that explanation. He offered her a stick of gum. "Skylar, tell me about your grandma. Is she healthy? Does she suffer from ailments? I'll pray for her. I can tell you treasure her."

She hastily looked at her watch. "My grandma stepped in to raise me when the Department of Human Services planned to put me in foster care. My mom is bipolar and there were a lot of nights she never came home. I don't really know my mom all that well anymore. My grandma took me in years ago and I owe her everything. She worked hard all her life as a waitress, and she has terrible pain every day from back surgery that didn't do all they advertised." She showed a nervous flicker of a grin and gazed at the ground. She peeked at her watch again. "Hey, Pastor Wes, I gotta go. I am so pleased to meet you and, if you don't mind, I am gonna tell my grandma that I met you."

Wes had a hunch the meds were not for spending money or herself. The pain meds were for her grandma, and he presumed the new opioid laws were now taking away the medication they freely gave and encouraged when her grandma first had surgery. He pressed just a little longer. "Skylar, I will certainly pray for your grandma. I know what it is like to have pain that makes you cry in the night and beg for the next day. My wreck did the same thing to me. To make it worse, ten years ago when I had my surgery, they told me to take my pain medicine and encouraged me to take even more than I wanted to take. Now, the same doctors won't even give me enough to make it month to month. I am struggling and in pain, most of the time—"

"I know," She interjected with feeling, "those doctors kept telling Grandma to take more and more immediately following her surgery and then they cut her off. Boom. Not only did they cut her way back, but they made her feel like a criminal to ask for the medication they forced on her."

"I know how she feels. I cry myself to sleep many nights."

"She has, too." Skylar put her hands on her hips. "Pastor Wes. Can I tell you a secret?"

"Certainly."

"I mean, I could help you, if you promise to keep our secret. You have given inspiration and hope to my grandma over the years, and that has provided for me in more ways than I can count."

"You can count on me. I will not only listen and keep your confidence, but I will pray for you and your grandma.

Please bring your grandma up here and visit with me. It would be an inspiration to me, as well."

"I could get in trouble if anyone found this out, but I am doing it to help my grandma's pain, and only for that. When a patient gets their pain meds, usually the prescription is written with a variable dosage. They can take one or two pills every so many hours."

He nodded and he already knew where this was heading, help... from the most unlikely, sweet young girl.

"Many of these elderly patients don't take the maximum dosage. They don't need that much and they don't want to take two with every dose. Sometimes I mark on their med chart that they took two when they only took one, and I slip the extra one in a slip of paper in my pocket." She wrung her hands nervously, a bit ashamed.

By now, all the "help" he received from the vodka dwindled to nothing and the tremors and sweats were more prominent. He interlaced his hands in his lap to lessen the shaking. "You are helping your grandma, Skylar."

"I mostly do it when she has run out or when they try her on a new medicine that does not help at all."

"Oh, I know it so well. I am waiting on a script right now because they lost it in the shuffle with my arrival, and they will not write another script for another month. I am in agony." He lamented and captivated her by connecting with her eyes.

"Also, when patients die or leave for the hospital, there are ways I can gather a few pain pills without being noticed." She reached in her pocket and paused, knowing the risk, but she also wanted to help the man who gave her grandma and herself so much inspiration when they struggled over the years. She pulled out the folded paper and gave him half of the pills in her hand. "Half for you and half for my grandma. I hope this helps till they get your script straightened out." She held out the pills in her hand, an offering of momentary peace.

"Are you sure?" He asked, praying for relief. Knowing her grandma's position, however, he would not take the meds if she wavered. He found resources on a regular basis and would find another way.

"Please take them. I will never take a pill from a patient that they need or want. I will only take their scraps. Please take it." She handed him the slip of paper with the pills nestled safely inside.

"Bless you, sweet Skylar. Please bring your grandma to see me. Just let me know before you bring her, so I can be presentable. I will put on a fresh shirt for her."

"Thank you, Pastor Wes. You have made a regular day, a memorable one." She checked out her watch again. "I'm late. See you soon."

He felt the weight of the monkey on his back slowly lighten as he swallowed the pills and chugged a shot of vodka to kick-start the result. Now he only needed a few more small-time scores, like Skylar, to carry him through till he could find a more permanent, bigger source.

Chapter 7
1960s

Wesley and Jennifer sat on the last pew, holding hands and could keep their minds on nothing else except each other. Wesley's long hair, hunter green bell bottoms, and paisley, large collared shirt were a bit loud for his parents' taste, but Wesley dressed like a rockstar with a personality to match. Jennifer's blonde, straight hair, parted down the middle, shined like satin waving under the sun. Her pale blue dress boasted a short length modeled by most of the girls her age. Her mother wouldn't allow her skirt to be shorter than her arm length when Jennifer was standing with her arms hanging to her side. When Jennifer's mom sized-up the skirt length, she measured the tips of Jennifer's fingers against the hem of her dress. Jennifer often slumped her shoulders slightly, to give the go-ahead to a shorter dress, when she could get away with it.

Wesley's dad, Harold, was driving home the message to his Sunday sermon, "Search Me, Oh, God, and Know My Heart." Loretta was on the front pew and mouthing the words as Harold rallied in a flurry of scripture and emotion. Her eyes intently fixed on Harold, followed his every move. Loretta knew sections of his sermon by heart. She was his test audience at home and oftentimes knew the sermon as well as he did by the time Sunday rolled around. Loretta wore a respectable, mustard-yellow A-line dress with the hem hitting just below her knee. She wore a brown sweater over the dress, as the sanctuary was often too cold for her liking. Her brown pumps with one-inch heels complemented her sweater.

Apparent to everyone in the sanctuary but Harold, mothers were checking their watches and fathers were yawning. Soft muffled comments floated between family members, "There goes my roast again. It will be burned before we get home," or, "the game starts in ten minutes, I wish he could end on time for once." Harold had a passion for correct volumes of scripture. If two scriptures were good, ten would be better. He was always prepared, always correct with the references and usually boring. By the end of his services, those attending struggled to maintain their manners and planned for their opportunity to escape. Harold was a good pastor. He always presented a well-prepared sermon and visited people when sickness knocked at their door. The townspeople loved him; they just didn't love his preaching.

Wesley and Jennifer were also anxious to fly the coop. Jennifer just turned sixteen and had a car. Old, with battle scars, the Valiant offered no air conditioning and the passenger door had to be opened from the inside, but it gave freedom to two kids who itched to break free from the tethers of expected norms. They bowed their heads to pray as Harold began the altar call.

"Dear Lord, here we are once—"

Wesley tugged on Jennifer's hand, "Let's go." They tip-toed out the vestibule and ran down the front steps. As the fresh air hit Wesley's face, he threw both arms up in the air like he was breaking the tape at the end of the race. It was as if his thoughts, his brain, and body were being restrained, and the minute he raced outside, his whole being drank in the opportunity for expression. "Woo hoo." He turned and started running backward while keeping his eyes on Jennifer. "You are coming over for Sunday dinner, aren't you?"

"Sure. I love your mom's roast, potatoes, and carrots. Slow down. I can't keep up." She gave a poor effort to catch up as she trotted a few steps and started walking again. "You better slow down a little. Remember who has the keys." She pulled a set of keys out of her purse and held them up like holding a treat over a well-trained beagle.

"Guess you have me there." Wesley grinned a heart-felt smile that revealed his unmistakable, joyful, loving heart. "You had me anyway. I would follow you if we crawled all the way there."

Jennifer chuckled. Now she had the upper hand, with the keys resting safely in her palm. She gave the slightest shove to his shoulder and ran to the driver's seat. She locked his door and waited for him to say "please."

"C'mon, Jen! Pl-ease." He stretched it into two syllables. "I'll sing for you? I'll write a song for you?"

Jennifer unlocked the door. "You'll write a song for me?"

Wesley flopped into the car seat and rolled down the window. "Sure, can't be too hard."

Jennifer turned her entire body toward Wesley. "Have you ever written a song before?"

"No, but just think about it." He cleared his throat and sang, "'We All Live in a Yellow Submarine,'" and how about, "'Tutti Frutti?'" "That song is practically written in code. The next time I see you, I will sing you the song I wrote." He slapped his knee like he was saying, "Done deal."

Jennifer couldn't keep up with Wesley's energy, but she was drawn to his magnetism and his joyful soul. "I am holding you to it, Wesley. Let's go get a Coke, before your folks get home for lunch."

"Great. I'll take a Royal Crown Cola. It has more fizz." Wesley peeked out the window.

"Of course, the boy with the most pizzazz wants the soda with the most fizz." Jennifer teased, but that was the way it always was with Wesley, wanting more, hunting for fun, and pizzazz. She turned on the radio and they sang "California Dreamin'" at the top of their lungs, with Wesley holding his arm out the window surfing on the air as they cruised to the drive-in.

###

Loretta stomped straight into the kitchen before changing her clothes and pulled the roast out of the oven. She took a brief peek under the lid to check out the condition of the roast, but didn't want to let the moist air escape the roasting pan. "Burned ends, again," she spoke out loud, softly, in disappointment as her efforts for Julia Child quality sank to the level of the home economics student.

"That section I added at the end really gave the sermon more meaning, don't you think, sweetheart?" Harold spoke with pride as he entered the room.

"Yes, Harold. It added. It added dried roasts on dinner tables all across this town. While you were reveling in your additional ten minutes of preaching, you were ruining scads of housewives' dinners. Reducing a succulent, expensive cut of meat to something that could only be swallowed with a gallon of gravy." She opened the lid for him to get the full view of a roast overcooked.

He gawked at the roast and then back at Loretta. "Is that why we always get the roast with the gravy already ladled all over it? Huh. I never knew that. Well, the whole purpose is to get the message out, the *whole* message. A little dry roast is not a big deal when we are talking about giving them the full message of God."

"You know how much I love you. I support you and follow you around this town like I am physically attached to you, but I have to tell you the truth. When you extend your sermon on these rabbit-chasing tangents, the main message you are telling people is that your speaking is more important than the food they have on their table and the money they spent on that food. We need to hear the word of God, but we also need to see a pastor who thinks of others and sees others more important than himself. The next time you have the urge to extend your sermon, think of the mother who got up at 5:30 a.m. to put the roast or turkey in the oven, or the dad who put in a little extra overtime to put a nice cut of meat on the table for Sunday dinner. When you extend your preaching longer and longer on Sundays, you are telling everyone in that room, including me, that what you're doing is more important than what we are doing, and that just isn't so."

Harold stood and just listened. It had been a long time since Loretta stood up to him and told him what he needed to hear. "It really didn't add to the impact of the sermon, did it?"

"No, honey. They got your point after the first twenty minutes, and that part was good. After that, you lost them. When you yell louder and preach longer, it doesn't mean it is always better. God can talk to His people in one of your fifteen-minute sermons, just like He can in one of your forty-minute sermons. It is God doing the "touching." He is just using your words to reach them."

Harold leaned in to see the full roast. "You might make a little extra gravy." He loosened his tie and stepped into their bedroom to change into more comfortable clothes.

Loretta loved Harold, but when his focus was blurred and on himself, he sabotaged his own sermon. His lesson today, "Search Me, Oh, God and Know My Heart," was like a magnifying glass on his own heart. He told his congregation today that he was the most important person in the room and should be accommodated, rather than the intent of the original text: "*Search me, God, and find the imperfections of my heart. Lead me in the way everlasting, serving those around me.* All his words were overridden by his actions. Harold was a gifted scholar and had worthwhile teaching to share, but when a student didn't want to hear the teacher, it was wasted air and damaging prose. Actions spoke louder than words.

Wesley sat across from Jennifer at the dinner table. He reached his foot over to play with Jennifer's underneath.

At first, she thought she bumped into his foot and excused herself. "I'm sorry. I bumped your foot."

Wesley grinned. "That's okay." He scooped some potatoes with gravy into his mouth. He bumped her foot again.

"Oh, my goodness, I am so sorry. I don't know what has gotten into my feet. Please excuse me."

"Of course." He lightly squeezed her hand as if to say "That's okay." Wesley was having some fun with her.

This time, Wesley tapped her foot and gave her a little lingering nudge.

Jennifer then knew what was going on and she got an idea. She continued with his little prank. "Wes, my foot keeps slipping, please excuse me."

Wesley, feeling confident in his prank, spoke sweetly, "That's okay, Jennifer, it happens to all of us."

Then, Jennifer waited for Wesley to take a drink of his tea. She slipped her foot out of her shoe and starting at the wide bell of his hunter green pants, she worked her foot slowly all the way up past his knee and to his thigh, teasing and kneading his leg with her toes. All the while she kept her attention to her plate as she cut up her dry roast and potatoes.

Wes first took a big gulp of tea and then his eyes became as big as dinner plates as he was trying to hide his immediate hormone rush. He blurted out uncontrollably, spraying tea across the room. Jennifer stood and helped sop up the mess. As Wesley caught his breath and saw the havoc he created, it was one of the first times he had no words or antidotes of humor.

Jennifer bent down with her mouth by his ear and whispered, "There's more where that came from."

Loretta, busied around, got new napkins and refilled the tea around the table. She sat back down in a huff and glared at Harold. "It was the damn dry roast, Harold."

Harold dropped his carrots in disbelief. "Loretta, you will not—"

"Death by rump roast, Harold. Death by *dry*... rump... roast. Wes *choked* on it, for heaven's sake. I will not

"*WHAT*," Harold? *I* will tell you what I will not do again. I will not serve another dry, ruined roast on Sunday dinner again. Ever."

With that, the entire table froze. All that could be heard were the inspirations and exhalations of those surrounding it.

Wesley's eyes sparkled with an idea. "Well, it wasn't your fault, Mom. The roast had good flavor, but it *was* a bit dry." There, he did it. He shifted blame away from himself and Jennifer and scored yet another, unsolicited, request to shorten Sunday services all in one sweet turn of a sentence. Wesley and Jennifer finished their dinner and excused themselves like the angelic children they were.

They drove the Valiant to the lake and found a secluded spot with a shade tree. Jennifer pulled out the blanket they kept in the trunk and smoothed it on the ground. For quite some time, they used the blanket for long talks solving the world's problems, and planning their future lives of adventure and promise. Two dreamers, dreaming of a perfect world.

Wesley brushed the hair that fell covering her face as she focused on the blanket. "You said there was more where that came from; did you mean it?"

Wes was the kindest and most lighthearted boy Jennifer had ever met. He cared deeply and had a special place in his heart for Jennifer, but when it came to intimacy, he was extremely shy. He could get up in front of a classroom and keep them rolling with laughter when the teacher went to the office for supplies, but he was unable to initiate a kiss with the girl he dreamed about at night.

Jennifer leaned into him. "I have wanted to do this all day." She lightly brushed her lips across his, tickling his senses. Wesley closed his eyes and kept his lips poised for what he hoped would be another kiss.

"Now it's your turn." Jennifer took his hand and put it up to her face, and she felt what seemed to be a gravitational pull drawing them together.

They kissed and held each other, innocently and freely. All the while, Wesley thought to himself, *Thank you, God, for dry rump roast and footsie under the table.* This small but powerful act of affection gave their relationship a new level of intimacy.

Chapter 8

Present Day

Mr. Epstein stirred his coffee, watching the ice cube placed in the cup slowly shrink into nothing. Like many Jews, ceremony was woven into many normal activities for Mr. Epstein. Some he spoke eloquently about to others, educating them in the glory of the Jewish traditions. Other things were an unspoken self-meditative experience. His morning coffee was one of these things. These traditions gave a focus and a rhythm to the day and were in many ways a prayer of actions and remembrance of those who went before and taught these life lessons to the next generation.

As he prepared to take his first sip, he remembered his mother telling his father at the breakfast table, "May you have a light and sweet day, Benjamin. She would place the milk and sugar near his cup and saucer. The milk represented the 'light' and the sugar represented the 'sweet' in a sometimes, bitter world. Mr. Epstein preferred his coffee hot and black, but he always saved back the last few sips and would add a bit of milk and sugar in a prayerful recognition of those who went before and to ask God to bless his day.

Mr. Epstein did not rush his meals. He would whine to his tablemates, "It is not good for the digestion. Take your time." Even so, one by one, his tablemates would get up after scarfing down their food, a well-practiced American tradition, leaving a Jewish man with his thoughts and a cup of coffee in hand.

As he drank the last portion of the coffee, Mr. Epstein began to prepare for his morning ritual no one else under-stood. He ceremoniously and silently "introduced" the milk and sugar, placing them near the coffee cup. Then he poured a small amount of milk and sprinkled a bit of sugar from the packet and spoke his blessing softly as he stirred before drinking the last bit.

Unaware anyone was within a hundred yards of him, he lifted his cup and heard "Shalom" in a sweet tone from behind him. Mr. Epstein turned to find the voice who obviously understood his actions. "Who is that?" His stiff neck prevented him from seeing the woman standing behind him.

She stepped to the side. "May your heavy load be lightened, and the bitter words you hear be sweetened."

Mr. Epstein was flooded with a sense of belonging. She understood his ritual prayer. Mr. Epstein's fond memories of his father reciting this ritual covered his mind and emotions like a cozy blanket on a winter day. As he raised his first sip of coffee to his mouth, he would offer, "*Father, I don't know if today will be a light one or a sweet one, but I know it is a day you have given me, and I am thankful.*" It had become Mr. Epstein's ritual, too. "Ah, the sweet sound of a woman who understands the meaning of a proper cup of coffee. Please sit for just a moment." He reached to the adjacent chair and scooted it away from the table as an invitation to sit with him. His gestures were inviting, and he was already enamored with the woman who clearly knew her way around the Jewish table.

"Thank you. I will just stay a moment." She nodded with her hands folded in front of her waist, then reached for the chair back and scooted in toward the table and sat down to an eager Mr. Epstein.

"Would you like a cup of coffee?" Mr. Epstein scanned the room for kitchen staff that might grab her a cup.

"No, thank you. I had my one cup and usually that is my limit." She smiled and everything about her had clearly been thought out and put together. Her purse had a side pocket with a handkerchief folded over the edge for easy access. Her clothes were simple, but pressed. She wore a cotton button-up blouse and knit slacks with a crease sewn in the front and back for a crisp, tidy style. Her hair was fixed with combed out curls held in place with hairspray. "I was so taken in with your coffee routine. I must have seen similar rituals hundreds of times over the years." She pointed to the milk and sugar placed nearby the coffee cup. She smiled with an understanding of the meaning and importance behind a simple cup of Joe with milk and sugar.

"It is so nice to meet you. My name is Isaac. Isaac Epstein." Mr. Epstein had an unusual relaxed countenance about him. On a typical day, Mr. Epstein was already halfway pissed-off in a world that didn't take the time to help or understand him and his wonderful Jewish traditions. But she knew him. Even though she never met him before, she *knew* him.

"Oh, so pleased to meet a man who, I would guess, was raised with chicken soup on the stove and a kippah on his head at temple." She grinned like a friend hearing a familiar family story.

About that time, a kitchen worker hustled by and Mr. Epstein startled him with his loud, nasal request. "Please bring us another coffee, with milk and sugar. We have some catching up to do." He then glanced at his new friend, "You don't have to drink it if you don't want to."

As the worker returned with the steaming coffee, milk, and sugar. Mr. Epstein asked, "Did you just move here?

I don't think I have seen you here before, and I make a habit of knowing everyone who comes and goes in this joint." His eyes squinted with the widening smile spreading across his face.

With her forearms on the table, she leaned toward him, "I visit my brother often. He is down that hall." She nodded toward a hallway on the other side of the building. "He stays in his room most of the time, so that is where I am, when I come to visit. I didn't sleep well last night. So, honestly, maybe a little coffee will help perk up this old lady."

Mr. Epstein was already positioning the cups, milk, and sugar by the time she finished talking. "Here's to a great Jewish day." He scooted a cup in front of her. "You never said your name. You are..."

"I am Ruth, Ruth Miller."

"And, I am Isaac Epstein. Happy to serve you." He gave a brief bow of his head.

"Thank you for the extra care given to this cup of coffee." She took the coffee cup handle and waited as she knew he was not finished.

Mr. Epstein introduced the milk and sugar to the cups of coffee, moving them closer and positioning them just right. As he poured milk into Ruth's cup of coffee he began, "May our God lighten any burden, like the milk lightens the coffee." Then he reached for the sugar. "May the course of this day be sweetened like sugar mellows bitterness." He smiled and fixed his own coffee in the same manner. "Whether it is a bitter day, a light day, or a sweet day, the Lord has given us *another* day and we shall be grateful for it." He raised his cup in a gesture toward Ruth and she did the same. Mr. Epstein was given a wonderful gift in the middle of a usual, boring day at Fireside. He was given understanding and connection in the midst of people who accepted him, from a distance.

"What a wonderful prayer, Isaac. It takes me back to my days at home when father would bless the food, and those gathered, before each meal. Those were the days." She raised her cup and slurped a gracious sip, drinking in, not only the coffee, but the sentiment with which it was given.

Mr. Epstein sat at the table, forgetting he was in the middle of a facility. The tension that was typically easily seen on his face had vanished and he was not only smiling with his mouth, but with his eyes and his whole being. Who would have ever thought that coffee, milk, and sugar could bring such a connection?

"Isaac, I have to be going, but I am so pleased to meet you. I visit my brother at least once a week. Maybe I can visit with you again when I come to Fireside. I would suggest you go find my brother, but he is not a mixer. He prefers to stay to himself and I don't force him to do otherwise. Thank you for the hospitality you have shown."

This, too, made Mr. Epstein feel at home, the recognition of his hospitality. The demonstration of hospitality was taught to all Jewish children from a young age. He was particularly thankful that on this typical bitter coffee day, God chose to pour a little milk and sugar into the bitterness, lightening his load, at least for the day. *I will be looking for you in the halls, Ruth.*

Chapter 9

Present Day

Ginger had mixed feelings about her date with Eric tonight. With every brush of her long red hair, she dreaded seeing him more and more. She already had a beer going and might have another before he got there. How did things get so complicated? She asked herself that question a thousand times since he returned from the Oklahoma City interview to join the police department there.

Rose knocked on the door frame of Ginger's bedroom. "Hannah and I are heading out so you can have the place to yourself. I will keep her tonight and you can get her tomorrow morning if you like. You know I enjoy my 'Hannah time' so don't feel like you need to rush to get her."

Hannah bobbed her head to Lady Gaga's "The Edge of Glory." The volume of Hannah's headphones was so loud Ginger could hear the song clearly.

"Hannah, turn that down. You'll go deaf."

"What, Mom? Can't hear. Gaga is amazing, isn't she?" Her head kept bouncing to the pulsing beat.

Ginger was losing her patience and removed the headphones from Hannah's ears with Hannah now singing at the top of her lungs. "Now that I have your undivided attention."

"Mom, C'mon, give'em back." She reached for the headphones and Ginger put them behind her back. Hannah was full of vinegar and Ginger couldn't help but smile as she recognized herself in her young daughter.

"I will see you tomorrow, baby. Don't give your granny a hard time, okay?" Ginger tossed the headphones on the couch. "Leave these at home, you little Gaga Monster. Mom doesn't want to spend an evening with a set of headphones." Ginger was actually pleased that Hannah was a Gaga fan; her inclusion of all her fans helped to shine a good light on those who were different.

"Oh, Mom. Grandma and I are B.F.F.s. By the end of the night, I will have *her* dancing to Gaga."

Ginger knew her daughter. "*Still,* love her or not, don't give her a hard time. Love you, Hannah."

"You, too." Hannah planted a big wet kiss on Ginger's cheek and ran to pick up her headphones while Ginger spoke with Rose."

"Thanks, Mom. I'll let you know how it goes."

"Ginger," Rose counseled. "Eric is a good man. Even if things don't work out right now, don't break his spirit."

"Oh, Mamma, I will be the one crushed, but I will remember your words."

As they left, Rose and Hannah discussed their wonderful plans, "What do you want for supper, sweetie? Liver and onions?" Rose teased Hannah.

Hannah pretended she was choking, "Uh, no, that's not what I want. I want a double cheese pizza... thin crust... with ranch on the side. And a red soda pop, A *large* red soda pop."

"Okay, okay, you win." Rose basked in the replica of Ginger, her energetic, strong-willed Hannah. "Actually, I don't like liver, Hannah. Just a secret between you and me. There are a lot of adults who hate liver, too. I am one of them."

"Awesome, I can taste that pizza right now!" Hannah said.

Eric nervously knocked on the door and Ginger paused on the other side. She almost didn't want to open it. Things weren't settled yet, but at least at this point, it wasn't "over." Almost all relationships come to an intersection like this at some point. Eric is the only man she has been with who did not try to change her... not even little bit. He loved her and he wanted her "as is." He considered her feisty nature, her free spirit, and intelligent humor all as a benefit. At the end of the night, would she be able to say the same? Tonight, it would likely be settled one way or the other. She painted on a fake smile and opened the door.

"Hi. I always think you deserve flowers." He handed her a casual bouquet of daisies.

Ginger took them and smiled. "You shouldn't have, but they are really pretty. Come in. I'll put them in some water." Eric stepped in and Ginger had a simple roast and potatoes in the oven, one of Eric's favorites.

Ginger proceeded to the shelf near the sink and picked out the perfect vase. *Would it be the old jelly glass or salsa jar? Decisions, decisions.*

"I have been thinking, Ginger. I think for me... *and* you, I need to move to Oklahoma City, and join their police department by myself." Eric spoke softly and firmly.

"Wow." Ginger took a beat, then turned around. Instantly reverting back to that high school girl left on the fringes at coronation. "Okay, Eric. I thought we would at least talk about it, but if you are done, you are done."

"I am not "done" with us. I just need to become the man that would make you think twice about moving. I want to see you on the weekends and try a long-distance relationship. It will either draw us together—"

"Or it will push us apart." Ginger crossed her arms in insecurity and quickly locked eyes with Eric. "So that is it? You're not even going to eat the roast I made?"

Eric gazed into her eyes with so much passion it pulled her toward him like a magnet, even though her mind told her to step away.

Eric touched her soft porcelain cheek and gently brushed the few hairs that fell in front of her face. "I know how much I love you, Ginger. I'm just not sure how much you love me. If you are honest with yourself, you would say the same thing."

Ginger closed her eyes as if it would make this conversation automatically go away.

Eric gave her a whisper of a kiss, so soft and brief, she almost thought she imagined it. She opened her eyes to find Eric so close, she could feel his breath on her face.

Eric kissed her again with a little more caress and Ginger froze, her eyes closed, and her mouth anticipating what would come next. Eric nibbled on her ear and whispered, "I still love you. Don't let go of us." He continued kissing down her neck and slid her shirt to the side, exposing her shoulder.

As he kissed down her neck and to her silky soft shoulder, she placed two fingers on his lips, "If we do this, not a word is to be spoken. You show me what you want to say with your touch. I will do the same."

Eric backed away a step and waited for her to step towards him. He had to know she wanted him. As he slowly stepped away, she locked eyes with his and knew that she would have to show him what she wanted. She wanted him.

Ginger stepped forward and kissed Eric gently on the lips, then softly bit his lower lip in a tease. Then Ginger stepped away, not saying a word, letting him know that she too wanted to see what he wanted.

Eric stepped over to her and took her open hands and led her to unbutton her own blouse. Ginger lifted his t-shirt over his head. Eric took his phone out of his pocket and pulled up his music. He selected, "Wonderful Tonight," by Eric Clapton. He set his phone on the table and held out his hand, asking her to dance.

Ginger loved that song and loved even more that he picked it. She melted, letting down her guard. They danced to the rhythm of their hearts. Eric guided the dance to the hallway and Ginger turned and took his hand, leading him to her bed. She jumped into his arms and showered him with passionate kisses.

Eric laid her down gently and expressed all his love through touching, kisses, and desire. Without words, they expressed their love with repeated calls and refrains, giving each other what they craved. As they lay in quiet repose after their passionate lovemaking, they both knew in the center of their souls, they belonged together. They drifted into a brief nap and Ginger was awakened by a rustling sound. She rolled over to find Eric dressing.

"What are you doing?" Ginger straightened the covers and sat up.

"I love you with all my heart, Ginger and I think you love me. We just experienced something really special, almost spiritual. I woke up and knew I had to go now. We just gave each other the best goodbye we could ever give. I don't want you to move to Oklahoma with me if you don't want to go, and I think the only way you will know what *you* want is for me to move away on my own. Call me *anytime* you want to talk. I love you, Ginger. I will come back as often as I can. I hope you will come to see me as well."

Ginger stood with her beautiful green eyes brimmed with tears that fell like a waterfall as she blinked. "What will I tell Hannah? What will I tell Mom?" She crossed her arms as she stared at the floor. She couldn't bear to look him in the face. "I will listen to "Wonderful Tonight" often and think of you." Ginger conjured a smile, "I love you."

With that, Eric kissed Ginger with a lingering gentleness and vanished out the door.

Ginger waited until she could hear his steps fade away in the distance and slumped to the floor, in the grief of being separated from her love. She wailed and sobbed in surges of heartbreak that echoed down the hall of her humble home. *Here I am in the energized city of Atlanta, and I feel as though I am isolated on a desert island, separated from all that matters. Well, Ginger, find those bootstraps and pull them up, sister. You have been through heartbreak before.* She got up, washed her face, and shifted gears, like she has so many times when facing disappointment. *Pivot and compartmentalize, Ginger. You know it well.*

Chapter 10

1970s

Wes slipped into the back row pew during a prayer. He was late for Wednesday evening services and knew he would hear about it after church.

"In Jesus' name we pray. Amen." His dad closed the prayer by the pulpit and turned to catch his son's eye. He gave a double take, as if to say, *oh, there you are... late and disinterested.*

Wes flashed a flicker of a smile and raised his eyebrows in a sentiment of, *it's all okay, Dad.*

Harold just pivoted and stayed on point with his service. "Now, while you give from your hearts as the Lord would lead, my son, Wesley Lyons, will sing the offertory special."

Wes stood and strutted to the front of the sanctuary. As he moved through the audience, heads turned as he passed each row on his way to the piano. He was as calm as a cucumber and eager to sit behind the keyboard of black and white keys. He was a natural musician, playing by ear and singing from the heart. He was more comfortable behind the piano than he was sitting in the pew. He was a unique fellow when it came to performance. He felt a connection with the audience and a steadiness in his gut. When he began to play and sing, he felt both an energy and a peace. He started with full, choppy chords, up… then down the keyboard. "Lean on me, when you're not strong…" There was a soulful tone in his voice as he closed his eyes and let the music take control of his body.

Children scooted to the front of the pews and held to the pew in front of them, trying to get a better view. Elderly wives were nudging their husbands, "Wake up. It's the Lyons kid singing, again."

He could feel the connection thickening between himself and the congregation. He saw a teenager near the back start clapping in rhythm with the song, then another stood and joined in. Before he knew it, people were joining in, singing the popular song "Lean on Me," was known by everyone. Wes stood from the piano and took the mic out of the mic stand. He moved to the center of the room and encouraged everyone to sing the chorus again. As the people sang louder, he took the mic away from his own mouth and reached it out toward the congregation, letting them know they were taking the lead. As the song was coming to a close, he moved back behind the piano and slowed the song a bit, closing the piece with a prayerful last line. As he finished, he closed his eyes at the piano, "Thank you, God." He knew that something special had just happened, and he was thanking God for using him in a powerful way.

Pastor Harold stepped back to the pulpit. "Well, if I knew we were coming to a rock concert tonight, I would have put some flowers in my hair." The congregation chuckled, but still felt the glow from a young man pouring out his heart and allowing the Lord to move through him.

He slipped back into the congregation and sat on a nearby pew. He knew his father was not pleased. He was supposed to sing a hymn tonight. Keeping his head bowed, he lifted his eyes to see his father. His father was sweating and showing an anxious, forced smile, trying to gain control of the congregation again. Spontaneity made Harold nervous. He felt he had lost control of the service... and he had.

Wes crept out the back of the church while Harold was giving the benediction. The reaction of the congregation to his song was invigorating. He was inspired and in the groove for writing. He drove home and ran into his old childhood room. He grabbed his guitar and sat on the corner of his bed. He began playing what he felt in his heart. It was joyful. The rhythm of the guitar was revealing the heartbeat of a new song. Songwriting was invigorating to him. He felt closest to God when he was writing and allowing his heart to be revealed in words and melodies of emotion.

Harold pulled in the driveway. As he came closer to the house, he could hear the guitar and marched straight to Wes's old room. He knocked on the door and entered. "What was that, son? I asked you to sing the offertory, not perform the encore of a rock concert. Son, you have to get a hold of yourself. The sanctuary demands a certain level of decorum."

"Dad, I just felt an overwhelming connection with the congregation. It was like they were hungry and I was feeding them." Wes couldn't help but smile as he remembered the people taking in his offering of song. "I know you said the scripture for the sermon was James 1:27. I picked out that song because it talks about serving others, like that scripture says to visit the orphans and widows."

"Next time, "Amazing Grace" will do just fine." Harold gave a heavy-handed pat on Wes's back and left the room.

Deflated, Wes flopped back on the bed, with his feet still on the floor, exasperated with the conflict he felt. When he was singing, he felt closer to God, and far, far away from his dad. This was a polarity he wished was different in his life. How could something that brought him closer to God and brought joy to others be so irritating to his father? He was torn by the strange way these things pulled in opposite directions.

Loretta walked to Wes's room. "Son, can I come in?"

"Sure, Mom."

She sat on the bed next to him and he sat up and leaned into her. "Did you hear my song, Mom? The emotion and love I felt from the people carried me like I was riding a ten-foot wave in Hawaii." He jumped up, stood sideways, and held his hands out, acting as if he were surfing on a killer wave.

Loretta knew her son was talented and was uniquely connected to people and to God. He sensed things other people didn't and had a soft heart for the struggles of others. He understood heartache and defeat. At such a young age, many others haven't experienced such feelings. She knew that this was one of the reasons he connected so well to people when he performed. He had a special gift and she wanted to encourage him. She tousled his hair. "Son, when you took the mic out of the stand, I knew you were gonna bring down the house." She stood and mimicked his performance, as if she were a mime, singing into a non-existent microphone and then holding it out for the "audience" to take the lead. "You have a God given talent. You should use the talent for good."

He sat up in disbelief. "Mom, I didn't know you had it in ya!" He saw a side of his mother that he had never seen before. "If I didn't know better, I would think you had been on a stage before?" He was half-way asking a question and half-way making a statement, waiting for her response.

Loretta leaned into him. "I never talked about it, but I was quite the drama ham in school. Oh, and musicals...they were my thing."

He slowly nodded like he had just been introduced to a very hip, cool stranger. "Wow, you never said anything, all this time."

"Your father didn't want me to encourage your performances, but I couldn't keep myself from attending every single performance and living the excitement through you, again. I just wanted you to know that I 'get it.' I feel the surge of the emotion with you, and I know how it feels to get lost in the energy of a performance. The give and take exchange with people sitting in the audience is powerful. There is nothing like the feeling of knowing that when people are low and discouraged, you can lift them and give them new hope. It is a very powerful talent and should be regarded as such."

Wes sat on the edge of his childhood bed and saw his mother, fully, for the first time. It was mind-blowing to hear her speak these words and realize that not only did she have other talents and interests than being a great mom, but she was a drama geek, too. "You mean, I got this from you?"

"Well, my family and I are a motley crew of performers from way back. Give me a minute; I want to show you something." Loretta got up and hurried to her bedroom.

Wes sat on his bed, sensing his mom was divulging secrets, intended to remain in the shadows. He ran his hand through his hair, which mirrored his hero, Mick Jagger, loose full hair, with a random part and feather-like layers resting dangerously close to his collar. It was a rule that his hair would not grow beyond his collar. If it did, Harold would cut off all cash support at the local community college. His low-riding, wide bell-bottoms were brown and orange striped with patch pockets on the front and back. He had a wide, brown leather belt, which was unnecessary due to his tight-fitting pants. His brown and green shirt with large collar and cuffs finished off his style. At a glance, he could be Mick's younger brother.

Loretta came back through the door carrying a large, old Bible he had never seen before. She was clutching it to her chest, as if it were worthy of protection. She sat next to Wes and rested the Bible on her lap, face up. She placed both hands on the book as if she were saying hello to an old friend. "I think you should know about your family. The other side of your family you never met."

He squinted his eyes. "Huh? Other family?"

Loretta continued, "Your father never wanted you to know about some things from the past. He thought it might lead you down a dark, difficult path. I never said anything, as I didn't want to rock the boat, and it didn't seem important, especially when you were very young.

Take a look." She opened the old Bible and pulled out some newspaper clippings. She carefully unfolded the yellowed paper and watched Wes's eyes as he took it and began to read.

He leaned forward as he held the paper,his eyes quickly scanning left to right, devouring every word with locked focus. "'Getting Gertie's Garter' a Broadway Smash, Captures the hearts of New Yorkers." He glanced at his mom and kept reading. "Hazel Dawn dazzles the audience in yet another box office sell-out, taking them on a journey of laughter and tears." He shuffled the clippings one-by-one to find notice upon notice of the superior performance of this Hazel Dawn.

"My mother, Wes. Hazel Dawn was my mother." She smiled like a child boasting that her mom was better than everyone else's mom. "You come from a long line of talented actors and singers."

Wesley was excited and confused. He looked up with a face of puzzled wonder. "Why? Why haven't I heard of her before?"

"That is the $20,000 question, son. It started with us feeling you were too young to really grasp the complicated layers of the past."

Wes dug a little deeper and found a clipping that caused him to tune out all the surrounding noises. He stared at the headlines as he read aloud, "Loretta Dawn Dazzles in Local Performance of *Carousel*." He read on to find more. "Harold Lyons gave an unforgettable performance as Jigger Craigin and left us wanting more." Wes lowered the clippings, and a vacant, hurt face questioned his mother for an explanation.

Loretta eyed her folded hands resting on top of the family Bible. *God, give me the words to say, and may the tenderness of my words bring healing to Wes.* At first, still gazing at her lap, she started to tell a story of love, rejection, and redemption. "I grew up in a house full of music, laughter, theatre, and art. It was a period of my life that allowed unique thinking and growth. I met your father on the set of *Carousel* and we fell in love. He was such a sweet boy and treated me like a queen. We were inseparable. As a child, my parents encouraged free expression and the exploration of ideas. Harold grew up, the son of a conservative preacher. As time passed and we fell helplessly in love, we devoted ourselves to each other as teenagers. We thought we had been careful, but I got pregnant… with you." She put her hand on his knee with a genuine smile only a mother can give. "Your father dropped out of school and married me. We started our family and then he went back to school and ontinued in his father's footsteps to carry on the ministry and later went to college to study the Word of God in depth. As time went on, we both became devoted to God and serving people in our community. Your father didn't want you to take the same road we took. He didn't want you to get mixed up in crowds that encouraged free love and 'expanding your mind' through drugs. To him, those were the groups associated with the arts. He wanted you to associate with groups who appreciated the discipline and clean living of the church. So, there you have it. Your talents are both a family trait and a gift from God. It is in your blood, Wes, and you should be using your talents to serve people, lift their spirits, and give the gift of joy. People need those who have the gift of encouragement. Son, you have that gift. If you don't use it, your vibrant spirit will wither. When you are using the gifts God gives you, it creates energy and flow in your life. Like riding that wave you described from the *Lean on Me* performance. I could see it in your being. You were in that zone."

"You were an actress?"

"Yes, and a good one."

"Dad was an actor?"

"And had a voice that could draw you in like a moth to a flame. Mesmerizing."

With tears running down his face, he held the clippings like valuable artifacts. "So, I am not a weak, sissy wash-out, like Dad has insinuated? I am a chip off the ole block... a chip off of *his* block. How dare he make me feel 'less than' when I am walking in his very footsteps."

"We had some very rough times as a young family. We almost didn't make it. It was with the guidance of the church and our commitment to God that pulled us both through. That is the most important facet of our lives, our relationship with God. I will tell you that as much as I love the theatre and the arts, without God they are all meaningless. Although I never agreed with guiding you away from the arts, I did agree with leading you to God. You have a unique opportunity to combine the two: the arts and your faith."

He stood and kissed his mom on the cheek. He stomped to his father's study and entered without an invitation. He was channeling his Mick Jagger attitude with his hair flowing behind him. "Carousel, huh? How about you sing me a few bars, Dad?"

Harold turned toward Wes, keeping a stone-cold face, "That was a long time ago, and a mistake."

"Are you saying the play was a mistake, or that *I* was a mistake?" He slowly stepped toward his father with innocence and painful exasperation saturating his young face.

"Your mother spoke with you, didn't she—" He yelled, "Loretta, come in here...now!" Harold stood, showing his dominance over Wes, "It was all for your own good. Playing in the devil's playground will only hurt you."

"The devil's playground? I sang "Lean on Me," Dad, not some deranged nasty song. I sang a song about reaching out to our fellow man, something you will find is a primary theme of the Bible."

Loretta approached with a confidence she rarely showed. "Harold, you are the head of this household and I respect all that entails; however, I am the neck that turns the head on the shoulders. I am directing you to look in another direction. Your son is very talented, just like you were years ago. He is in college now and has opportunities knocking on his door. Don't limit him. Let God take him where his talents can be used. God's hand is on him, Harold. The spirit of God used him tonight, long hair, rock song and all." She put her hands on her hips and continued, "He knows it all. I told him about my mom and all the talented family, *his* talented family, that brought joy to thousands of people. He knows why we got married and I am proud to have told him how he was conceived in the greatest love story I have ever known, ours. Give him wings! Give him your blessings."

"The theatre and the arts lead to debauchery, drinking, drugs, and wild sex. I won't have it in my house." Harold threw down the gauntlet.

Wes was not shaken. He stood with great resolve. "This all explains so much, Dad…why you couldn't support my third-grade play, with the role of a cowboy riding a stick horse. I now understand that level of moral degradation is below you. Also, I assume my critically acclaimed role as Peter Pan was a role that could sway the staunchest Christian from their holy beliefs. Give me a break! Those were innocent children's stories. You crushed my spirit each time you tore apart my performance or just didn't consider it important enough to attend. Writing the fourth draft of your sermon was far more important than your son's play. Did you know that Jimmy told me you attended his basketball games? Jimmy, the choir director's son, enjoyed more support from you than I did."

Loretta huffed, "Harold, you never told me."

"They were midday games and he was working so hard. I wanted him to know I appreciated his effort."

"*I was working hard too, Dad. I* was working hard." Wes was slipping into the submissive personality his father preferred.

"You were playing make-believe. You weren't working. You were playing games—"

"I am going to go back to my dorm. I have early classes tomorrow and need some time to clear my brain." He gathered his composure and preached to his father, a sermon Harold needed to hear. "I have always sensed that you didn't want me around. Now that I know the full picture, I see that what you really are turning away from is the part of yourself that you don't like. You look at me and you see the part of you that you loathe. Despite your attempts to squelch my talents, they have risen to the top, and I am ever grateful for what the Lord has given me and the people who encouraged me to use my talents. You have taught me well, Dad. You taught me to never bow down to the level of other people I don't want to become. We all rub off on each other, if we allow it. I have lived by this principle and others you taught me from the Bible. I never thought these lessons I have adopted as my own would lead me to turn away from my own father. I will not bow down to the level you are trying to drag me. I will use my talents and in doing so, bring glory and honor to God and you, whether you recognize it or not." Wes came over and kissed his mom on the cheek. "Thank you for being honest with me and giving me wings of understanding tonight. I love you." He shook the long hair from his face. A confident, changed, and talented young man, determined to make the most of all his opportunities, walked out of Harold's study. Before he left, he saw the face of a woman who, he knew, understood his heart. She stood with a free-spirited smile that told him, *I am with you all the way, regardless of the twists and turns in your life.* She gave the briefest nod that assured him, *you are going to be fine.* Her eyes glistened with tears she held back, showing him that she was strong and beside him, come what may.

###

He walked out to his car and heard the Lynyrd Skynyrd song "Give Me Back My Bullets," blasting in his head. He felt as if he were in some kind of war. He just wanted to blaze out of there. He opened the door of his '63 Rambler American and dropped into the seat, punched in the clutch with his left foot, and pumped the gas a few times before turning the key. Nothing. He pumped it some more and rolled his eyes. Not exactly the scene he saw in his head. He felt like dropping into a shining blue '68 Mustang and peeling rubber as he turned donuts when he left. Instead, he sat in that old jalopy that was now flooded and smelling of gas. He sat for a moment and rested his forehead against the huge steering wheel. He put both hands up on the dash and took a deep breath. *God, I know you are there, but I can't see you and I can't feel you. My life feels like a cruel joke sometimes. Please start this car and please just get me out of here.* He gave the car a moment to clear the gas from the carburetor, crossed his fingers, and held his breath. He turned the key again, and with a cough, a sputter, and a puff of smoke, the car started. "Woo hoo," he shouted as he turned up the radio and combed his hand through his hair. *Now off to find Jennifer.*

###

Jennifer sat on her twin bed inside her dorm room painting her toenails for the next day. She was listening to Bobby Sherman's "Easy Come Easy Go." *Click.* She heard something hit the window. She turned toward the window, thinking it was a branch of a tree or a bug. She returned her attention to her ragamuffin toes and slowly dragged the polish brush across the middle of the next toe. Then a spray of clicks hit at once. She looked at the second-story window, then back at her toes. She carefully put the polish brush back in the small bottle and, with cotton balls between her toes, she stood and walked on her heels to the window. Once she peered out through the curtains, her heart skipped a beat. She raised the window and saw Wes holding up two sodas.

"Hey, come out and see me. The moon is out and maybe we can chill for a bit." He held the sodas up and shrugged his shoulders as if to say, *what do you have to lose?*

Jennifer leaned through the window with her hands on the windowsill. "I can't. The dorm mother is on the loose, and if she catches me down the hall, it will mean big trouble. I wish I could."

He got an idea. He went back to the car and turned out the lights. He turned the car around and drove it quietly under Jennifer's second-story window. "Jump!"

"Jump? Are you serious?" she whispered, trying not to wake up the other girls in the room below her.

Wes opened one of the sodas and took a long, enticing chug, then wiped the corners of his mouth. He held the other bottle in her direction.

Jennifer inspected her toes and then considered his offer. She thought, *well, they are dry, now.* She held up one finger, telling him to wait a minute. She pulled the cotton out from between her toes and put on some sneakers. She grabbed a jacket and ran over to the window. It was not a long distance to the top of his car.

Wes scooted out of the passenger side of the car and had already gathered up the blanket they used for star gazing and dreaming of their future lives. He put it on top of the car for a bit of cushion and to muffle the sound of her landing on the top of the car. He stood nearby waiting patiently.

Jennifer loved it. He was the most thoughtful person she knew. She sat on the windowsill and slipped down to the roof of the car not far below her feet. With a sneaky move that would have made a burglar proud, she lay still for a moment before scurrying off the car with the blanket in hand.

Wes slid into the car from the passenger side and scooted behind the wheel. Jennifer was close behind him. They pulled it off and giggled like second graders. He slowly drove away, in the dark, and pulled the light-switch knob for headlights as they got closer to the road.

Jennifer turned up the radio and bounced in the seat. She raised both hands in the air, shook her hair loose and sang at the top of her lungs with the radio.

He automatically felt at peace again. Jennifer always helped him find his way after a clash with his dad. She knew him best and she *knew* he wasn't a derelict or lazy, as his dad tried to tell him. When he was with Jennifer, he knew he was going to be okay.

Wes pulled up to their favorite spot by the lake and turned off the ignition while reaching for the blanket in the back seat. "C'mon, the stars are exploding; they are so bright tonight."

He spread out the blanket and they both lay down, taking in the wonders of the sky. They just lay there in silence for the longest time. Wes grabbed her hand. "Guess what I just found out? My dad and I got into another fight and afterward, my mom told me that they were both into acting when they were my age, *and* I have a relative that performed on *Broadway*."

Jennifer rolled in toward Wes and put one hand on his chest. "Wes, that is the absolute last thing I ever expected to hear out of your mouth." Jennifer's romantic feelings were growing. They had been buddies and sweethearts since grade school. She was falling in love, and she could see the pain in his face as he winced while telling his story.

He closed his eyes as the memory still stung in his mind. He felt a whisper of hair fall on his arm. Jennifer's long blonde hair tickled his skin as she leaned in to give him a gentle kiss.

Wes kept his eyes closed, hoping the kiss would linger. He slowly opened his eyes to see the most beautiful blue eyes and smooth, suntanned face looking right at him. "Wow. That was groovy." He reached up to gently brush her hair from her face. Jennifer closed her eyes and rolled to her back, maintaining hold of his hand.

He rolled to his side and for once felt free to show his attraction toward Jennifer. All the conflicts with his dad over the years caused him to have terrible anxieties about showing love to others, afraid he would be rejected. When he was on the stage, he felt the love of others through applause. It was quite different with face-to-face interactions. As he turned her way, it was like he was in a movie. His eyes drank in her beauty, and everything else surrounding them went into a blur. The noisy crickets and bullfrogs beside the lake were suddenly not noticeable. He was drawn to the scent of her hair and the invitation of her smile. Nothing else mattered right then. He was connected to Jennifer in a way that he could only describe as a magnet that was pulling them both together. Wes lightly touched her lips as she turned her head toward his touch. "I am going to kiss you, okay?"

"Okay."

Wes put his arm under her head to make her more comfortable and kissed her with a soft, long kiss that thrilled his soul. He pulled away with his eyes still closed. "Dentyne. You are chewing Dentyne." He smiled, then laughed and combed her hair back. "I suddenly love the taste of Dentyne chewing gum."

They both laughed and exchanged innocent, wonderful kisses in the night. They fell asleep keeping each other warm and awakened with the sun peeking over the horizon.

"Jennifer, Jennifer. We have to go. It is morning."

"What?" Jennifer opened her eyes to see the boy she was falling in love with and an impressive sunrise behind him. "I have class at nine o'clock. I gotta go."

They hustled back and went to a well-known doughnut shop on campus. He bought them a doughnut and they said their goodbyes. Jennifer walked back to her dorm, avoiding potential prying questions.

Wes cranked up the radio in his Rambler and grinned from ear to ear. What an amazing night.

Chapter 11
1970s

Wes eyed the powder blue tuxedo hanging over his bathroom door. He smoothed the velvet navy trim on the wide lapels and removed the navy velvet bow tie to hold it to his neck in the mirror. *Sweet. It was money well spent.*

Loretta knocked on his door and waited. "Can I come in?"

He put the bow tie back over the hanger. "Sure, come on in."

As she opened the door, she was already speaking, "I just wanted to get a look at your—"

He turned to her, "My what?"

Her head tilted to the side as she pointed to the powder blue tux. "Is that the tuxedo you were so excited about? Light blue?"

"Oh, yeah, Mom. Isn't it great? I mowed extra lawns and got my order submitted before all the other guys. I got one of the last ones. All the others are boring black." He beamed with pride and turned to see his mom with her head still tilted and her mouth slightly open, trying to understand his choice.

"Wow! Powder blue. Just, Wow!" Loretta was expecting a simple dashing black tux with matching cummerbund. She didn't want to rain on his parade, but it was quite a shock.

"Exactly, Mom. Mine is different; mine is unique. It is beautiful." Wes combed his feathered, long hair with his long-handled, wide-toothed comb and shook it loose. "I love it."

"Tell me all about how you decided on this one," she looked it up and down and tried to downplay her surprise, "the powder puff color with huge lapels and two-inch cuffed, bell-bottomed pants."

"Mom, this is the cutting edge of fashion. I am gonna make quite a splash! You didn't expect me to stroll in like everyone else, did you?"

"Is Jennifer aware of the great deal you got on your tuxedo?"

"No, it's gonna be a surprise." He giggled and shimmied with excitement.

"I love you, son. Please don't ever change. Don't forget, I am taking pictures before you two leave the house. I know in college, most may not get their pictures made before the dance, but you didn't get to go to your prom because your dad wouldn't allow it. So ... I am taking your pic at your first college dance." She noted under her breath, *not missing a chance to pull out these photos in about twenty-five years and get a few good laughs.*

"Fine with me. I'm not afraid of the camera." He flashed his Pepsodent smile as Loretta turned to leave.

Loretta smiled. *Why did it surprise me that he was sporting a powder blue tux?*

###

Jennifer stood at the bathroom sink preparing for the big date. Her hair shined like a mirror from a fresh shampoo with Wella Balsam. She parted it down the middle and used old frozen orange juice cans as rollers, to eliminate any creases or curls. She patted her torso with body powder and spritzed Chanel, her mother's perfume, around her neck.

She turned to take her dress off the hanger; pink chiffon covered the white satin full skirt beneath. The off the shoulder neckline accented the fitted waist, which flowed into a full skirt. She wanted to look like a southern belle from Georgia.

###

Wes waited by the driveway in his powder blue tux, platform blue patent shoes, and his perfect hair.

Jennifer pulled into the driveway, where he was waiting. "Jennifer, would you allow me to escort you to the Spring Dance?" He gave a slight bow and offered his arm to grab.

Her smile was the biggest he had ever seen and this made him even more excited.

"Of, course, you would look *this* cool, Wes. I absolutely love the tux." She stood from the driver's seat.

"Well, the least I can do is escort you into the house, since we are taking your car. One day I will have that ole Rambler fixed, and we won't have to worry if it will start every time we take it. Not gonna take a chance on a night like tonight. Thanks for taking your car." He wasn't prepared for her unique beauty. He dropped the corsage from his hand and batted it two or three times before it ultimately hit the ground. She looked like Cinderella, with long, straight, blonde hair. "I, I, I ... you, you, you. I mean, wow, Jennifer, you are so beautiful tonight." As she took his elbow, he held it securely in place with his other hand.

The two lovebirds walked to the front door, and Loretta was ready with her Polaroid. "Oh, my! What a handsome couple. How are you doing, Jennifer? Thanks for meeting at the house so I could get pics. Your dress is lovely."

"Oh, thanks, Mrs. Lyons. I'm great."

"You kids go stand by the curtains over there." She pointed them out with her Polaroid still in hand.

She didn't have to ask them to say cheese; they were already thrilled with the night ahead of them. Loretta took several photos, one of which was while he was trying to figure out how to put the corsage on Jennifer's dress. They giggled while he fumbled and squirmed, finally getting it right.

"Okay, Mom, we are off to the dance." He grabbed Jennifer's hand and they ran to the car, excited about the night before them. On their way, he reached out his hand, knowing Jennifer would slide her hand snugly into his. It was their routine every time they got into the car. Jennifer turned on the radio with her right hand and tuned it perfectly to their favorite station.

The D.J. crooned, "Outta sight, groovy cats and kittens, put on your dancin' shoes. Spinnin' now, Earth, Wind and Fire; *September*! Can you dig it?" The horns started layering in. Wes and Jennifer looked at each other and came in, right on beat. They bounced and danced in their seats all the way to the dance, singing at the top of their lungs. Some of the lyrics were correct and some... not so much, but sung with enthusiasm.

Once they arrived at the gym, He found a parking spot and threw the car into first gear, up and in on the steering column, then held up his hand, signaling Jennifer to wait. He scrambled out of the driver's seat and hustled around the car to open her door. "Let's go dance our shoes off," he exclaimed while opening the door. Jennifer grabbed the hem of her dress and they ran to the gym.

When they walked in, it was like being caught up in a scene from a movie. Those who had dates were sitting, standing, or dancing together. The students who went stag were gathered up in little bunches, girls on one side and boys on the other, talking to each other and trying to get up the nerve to ask their crush for a dance. The football players without dates were at the punch bowl, clearly guarding it from the sponsors. They had one punch bowl for the students, flavored with vodka, and another bowl they secretly designated for the old folks. The sponsors remarked how mature the football boys were to man the punch bowl.

Then, the band slowed down and the guitar player started an emotional lead introduction for "Wonderful Tonight." Even though they found their friends and had started toward their direction, when the music started, Wes changed direction and led Jennifer by the hand onto the dance floor. "We *have* to dance to this one. It is perfect for my beautiful girl." He led her to the center of the floor and interlaced his fingers behind her low back. Jennifer then wrapped her arms around his shoulders and neck. They danced that song... then the next... then the next. They may have been at a dance, but they were in their own little world. The night was a blur of music, laughs, and dancing. As The Bee Gee's "Stayin' Alive" was coming to an end, the gym lights abruptly flipped on, and sponsors started mixing about the room. "Last song, people," they announced. Wes and Jennifer looked around to find half of the kids had already left for other after-parties across town.

"Oh, wow!" Jennifer spun around, looking at the sparse room, "I guess I got lost in the music and dancing."

"Well, sweetheart, you may feel lost, but I feel totally found tonight, submerged in music and the arms of the truest love I have known. Thank you for a wonderful night."

Jennifer squeezed his hand. "It really was magical, wasn't it?"

"It doesn't have to be over. Let's get some soda and go to our favorite spot at the lake. What do you say? I actually also got a bottle of wine to celebrate. If you want a bit of it, Boone's Farm Wild Berry.

"Wow. Maybe a little. I really am not into drinking, but, yes! Absolutely!"

Wes drove to the Top Hat drive-in and ordered a large RC Cola, 7 Up, and large fries. They drove to the lake. He spread the blanket on the ground, and they lay in their formal attire kissing, talking, eating, and alternating small swigs of wine occasionally with their soda. They were making plans for the future. They innocently fell asleep in each other's arms. He rustled to roll over, and Jennifer peeked at her watch, "Get up, Get up! It is 12:20! We are gonna miss curfew. Let's go!"

"That will be okay with me. This has been the most breathtaking night of my life. It was like a dream. I don't care if I get grounded. No one ever meets curfew after a dance, anyway. Everyone knows that."

They laughed while they folded the blanket and stowed it in the trunk, ready for their next trip to the lake.

Chapter 12

Present Day

Ginger wadded up another scrap of notes and shot it like a basketball toward the toy basketball goal over her office door. She missed the basket by about a foot, which perfectly expressed how close she was to fixing her staffing problem. She searched her contact list and her brain; both were empty. She slumped in her chair with her backside barely remaining on the edge and her head draped over the back, like Jennifer Beal's character, Alex Owens, in *Flashdance*, but a lot less sexy. She exhaled with closed eyes, attempting to relieve the stress from scheduling her staff on the calendar. *Calgon, take me away.* Her thoughts were almost a prayer requesting rescue from this thorn in her side.

Where have all the caring, disciplined nurses gone? Literally, where have they gone? She was not above competing for good staff and would try to entice any good nurse to leave their current situation to join the Fireside team. The healthcare staff of any assisted living center sustained the very heartbeat of the facility. Without caring nurses, nursing assistants, housekeeping, and kitchen staff, an assisted living center was just a warehouse for humans. The staff made all the difference.

Rob stuck his head around the corner of her doorway with his eyes crossed and his hair ruffled, trying to bring a smile to her face. "How's the nurse search going? You have been searching for these nurses for months." Frustration was evident with Diet Coke cans lining her desk and wads of paper littering the floor.

Ginger straightened up in her chair as Rob plopped into the guest chair. "Rob, I refuse to run a place with half-ass nurses. I *refuse.* The nurses are the lifeblood of any assisted living center. I've got to do better. I *will* do better." She closed her eyes and shot another paper wad toward the toy goal. She opened her eyes to see the paper slide through the cords of the net. *Swish.* "Really? I close my eyes and *then* I get nothing but net. Maybe I am trying too hard.

Maybe I should just let it come to me, like shooting that blind shot."

"No, Ginger. No. No. *No.* You have got to stay in the mix and keep pounding the pavement. It can always get worse. The assisted living centers that are the armpit of humanity adopt the philosophy of shooting blind shots. You are better than that and so is Fireside."

"See these applications?" A stack of resumes scattered as Ginger slid them across her desk. "I only printed off the best ones. Take a good analysis."

Rob straightened the papers and shuffled through to find one with promise. He flipped from page to page and peeked up at Ginger. "How many have you interviewed?"

"Zero. Zip. Nada. Why interview *that*?" She pointed to the stack of applicants.

"Because you have to start somewhere," Rob bantered.

"Let me have those again." Ginger picked up the first page. "This one has no steady transportation." She flipped it over on her desk to keep the pages in proper order. "Oh, here's one, credentials are okay, but she takes a vacation to Hawaii for two weeks every Christmas and she lists this as a prerequisite for employment. Really? We can't all go to Hawaii during Christmas; nobody but Oprah and the president do that. Who does she think she is?" She turned another page over. "Here's one. This guy seems promising. He is a brand-new graduate, but check out the spelling and the freaking emojis on his resume. I refuse to hire anyone who thinks it is appropriate to put emoticons on a professional resume. I *refuse.*" She picked up her remaining Diet Coke can and raised it to take a drink... empty, just like her options. "I have got to do something. Our residents deserve better."

"Well," Rob cleared his throat, "why don't you get some help from a marketer."

"Help from a marketer? Are you crazy? We don't have money to hire a marketer to bring in top prospects." Ginger grew more frustrated the further this conversation progressed. She pushed away from her desk and stood, hoping it would invite Rob out of her office.

Rob remained seated. "Yes, goofball. Rob, your friend and marketer reporting for duty, ma'am."

"Oh, you?"

"Well, I am a damn good marketer… and dancer, but let's focus on the marketing aspect for now."

Finally, Ginger flashed a flicker of a grin. "I guess you *are* a good marketer. Give me a bit and I will get back to you on that offer. I have to get a few things done on the floor because the last nurse I hired called in "sore" today. I am not kidding; she called in because she was sore from water skiing over the weekend. She won't last. I won't have a nurse around here who does not have enough pride in her work to hustle through a little bit of soreness."

Ginger shrugged her shoulders. "Here we go again." She stepped out of her office door and bumped directly into Skylar, the nursing assistant.

"Ginger, I was looking for you." She paused a moment for Ginger to say something in response, but it was met with silence and Ginger glancing at her watch. Skylar picked up the non-verbal communication. "Oh, it won't take long, I just wanted to tell you that Mrs. Klinger's blood pressure has been slowly creeping up over the past few days. Thought you would want to know." Skylar flashed a quick smile and glanced down out of reflex. "Have a good one." She turned and went down the hall to her next resident's room.

"There. Did you hear that, Rob? She wanted me to know Mrs. Klinger's status. Why can't we have more *nurses* like that?"

"Well, you can. Why don't you—"

"I've got it. I will start some kind of program to develop promising nursing assistants into licensed nurses." Ginger stood with her hands on her hips and a fling of her hair over her shoulder.

Rob spoke through his laughter, "I was just going to say, find the people with the character and attributes you want and teach them how to be the nurses you want."

"Great minds think alike." Ginger had her snap back. She shook her red, long hair loose and bumped her hip into his like she was dancing to the Commodores in the seventies.

"Nice to have you back, Ginger." He stepped quickly to the side to maintain his balance, not expecting the bump from her hip.

Ginger took off down the hall and everyone knew that Ginger was in the area. Her Dingo boots measured long and steady strides, like a drummer keeping a solid beat. With this liberating thought, she grabbed onto the idea that she had options and could create the world she wanted to live and work in at Fireside.

Chapter 13

Present Day

Ginger's mind saw signs of hope. She was gathering her thoughts when she turned the corner and saw Mr. Epstein visiting with his new friend, Ruth, in the commons area. Mr. Epstein was wearing his nice "just in case" pants and his socks matched, so Ginger knew that he took time to put his ensemble together. Ruth, who was visiting her brother again, was dressed in a crisply ironed cotton floral blouse and her signature knit slacks with creases sewn in, to ensure a polished look.

As Ginger approached them, she noticed Mr. Epstein pulled his hand away from Ruth's and returned it to his lap. They had been holding hands. In his recognizable whine, Mr. Epstein initiated conversation. "Ginger, dear, how are you? Allow me to introduce you to my new friend, Ruth. Ruth Miller." His smile was as genuine as the sunrise in the morning. It could not be stopped, and it could not be changed.

"Hello, Ruth, how are you?" Ginger downshifted her internal motor, nodded, and waited for a cordial response.

"I am just fine, thank you for asking." Ruth smiled with an inner glow that made Ginger want to slow down and just be around her. That was something that didn't happen very often to Ginger.

During this sweet exchange, Ginger got an idea. "Let me ask your opinions on something."

Mr. Epstein lit up like a menorah. "Anything for you, sweetie. What's on your mind." He grinned and leaned in to hear every word from Ginger's mouth.

"I want your opinion," Ginger made eye contact with Mr. Epstein and Ruth. "If you were the boss, what would you search for in a new employee."

"If I were the boss... if *I were* the boss. Hmmmm." Mr. Epstein savored the question and scratched his chin while he pondered. "Sweetie, I have seen both sides of that coin.

I saw what *not* to do while I was in the concentration camp, observing the monsters running that joint." Even after all these years, he wrung his hands remembering the treatment he received from the Germans. "It all starts and ends with respect. Once the respect is broken by anyone in any relationship, even in a boss and subordinate relationship, the respect must be repaired before proper function can be restored. The employee must understand the importance of respect, but so must the boss."

Ruth added, "You also have to find someone with a positive attitude. Without a positive attitude, there will be days when it is difficult to give the respect required to make it work. I would pursue someone who sees the glass half-full."

Ginger patted her lab coat pocket to find a pad and pen, but found none, so she pulled out her phone to take notes. She wanted to remember their perspective.

Mr. Epstein turned to Ruth. "Oh, she is going to take a picture. That is how the young people do it these days." Mr. Epstein straightened his shirt and ran his hand across the top of his head to smooth the sparse remaining hair he had left. He leaned into Ruth and put his arm around her back. "Okay, I guess we are important enough to get a picture. That's Epstein, spelled with an "e-i-n."

Ginger glanced up from her phone to see the cutest couple smiling back at her. Mr. Epstein had more hair coming out of his ears and nose than he had just smoothed on the top of his head and with his smile, his eyes became little crescent-shaped slits. Ruth's smile showed her overflowing, spontaneous joy, while she tilted her head toward Mr. Epstein and giggled softly.

"Oh, Mr. Epstein, I wasn't—"

He raised his eyebrows as he talked through his perfect smiling pose. "Yes, sweetie?"

"I wasn't going to... uhhh ... *miss this perfect moment.*" Ginger found herself snapping several shots with her phone. She quickly saw that she had stumbled onto something precious. With each shot, Mr. Epstein and Ruth changed their pose, like a real photo shoot.

"Thank you for the information and thank you for the pics. I will get you some copies once they are ready."

As Ginger stepped away, she wondered, *how long has it been since somebody asked their opinion? Perhaps even more remote, how long has it been since someone asked to take their picture?* Ginger knew she had just made their day, maybe their week. She saw a tangible demonstration that everybody longed to be heard and seen. She had just experienced a masterclass in the importance of noticing and recognizing one's value.

As Ginger rambled down the hall, she knew what she had to do. She just had to get her routine work done and carve out some time during tomorrow's schedule. This was going to be fun.

Ginger had a new attitude. It was a new day and her coffee cup was full. Ginger had a list of people she wanted to visit. Her plan was to conduct a brief interview and photo shoot of these people and then give all residents the opportunity to participate after lunch on an upcoming afternoon.

Ginger knocked on Mrs. Klinger's door. "Mrs. Klinger, may I come in?"

"Oh, yes, Ginger. Please come in." She lowered her *National Geographic* magazine as Ginger approached. "Is everything okay, Ginger?"

Ginger's heart sank for just a moment. It was apparent from her response that Mrs. Klinger was expecting to discuss a problem, making it obvious that this was typically when Ginger came by to talk.

"Oh, yes, everything is just fine. Do you have a moment to visit?"

"Visit? Oh, sure. I was just trying to keep myself entertained by reading this ole magazine. The teacher in me wants to stay current on things." She laid the magazine to the side to give Ginger her full attention. "Now, what is on your mind."

Ginger had her pad and pen ready this time. "If you were the boss, what would you seek in a new employee?"

"What an intriguing question. Hmmmm." She crossed her arms and gazed upward, while still maintaining a level head position. "I would say, find someone with proper preparation, knowledge, and dedication to improvement." She clapped her hands together and held them in this pose, reviewing her statement. "Yes, that's it. If someone has no desire to learn and improve, they will fall by the wayside. This is a 'must have'."

Ginger took notes as Mrs. Klinger watched her and checked her spelling. "Awesome, thank you. I think you have something there; preparation is key. May I take your picture?"

"Take my picture? Really? Well, what will you do with it?"

Ginger should have known she would be asked that, especially from a retired schoolteacher. "I will give you a copy and I will keep one for myself."

"Well, I think that is a grand idea, Ginger, but I am not my best today. Maybe I should pass on the picture."

"How about we get a picture of both of us, together. I am not having a great hair day, myself."

Mrs. Klinger inspected Ginger's hair. "Well, I guess that *is* true..."

Ginger looked across the room at the mirror. *Is it really that bad?* She shook off the mirror check and tried to coax Mrs. Klinger. "Oh, C'mon, it will be fun; like high school friends."

Mrs. Klinger reflected back. "We sure had some crazy pictures when we were younger. I remember when I was a newlywed, my husband got a brand-new hunting rifle. He was so proud of it, he wanted to get a picture of it. He stood me out in a field and asked me to hold it. So, I did and he took my picture with a good ole Polaroid. The only thing we didn't think through was the fact that I gained about twenty-five pounds when we first got married. I appeared pregnant; like I was gonna get a husband one way or another; a shotgun wedding photo."

She laughed at the memory and reached out her arm to bring Ginger into her hug. "Let's do it. I already took the worst photo I could ever take, holding that shotgun, big, fat, and appearing pregnant."

They both smiled as Ginger took several selfies. As Ginger finished and gathered up her things, Mrs. Klinger made eye contact with Ginger. "What a wonderful thing you just did. You took an old woman back to the days when we were all worthy of pictures. And... by the way... that was a selfie we just took. *National Geographic* did a piece called "The Psychology of the Selfie" last month. I am proud to say that I have now taken one."

Ginger got a lump in her throat. "I should have taken a selfie with you a long time ago." She nudged Mrs. Klinger's shoulder in a playful note of acknowledgment. "In fact, you are very photogenic." She scrolled through showing her the pics on her phone.

"Not bad for an old lady from the country. Thank you." Mrs. Klinger blushed.

"Do you want me to leave the door open or shut." Ginger lingered with her hand on the doorknob.

"Shut it, dear. I want to finish my article." She adjusted her reading light and glasses, and returned her attention to her magazine.

Ginger bounced to the next resident's door, having the time of her life. Who knew this could be so much fun? She knocked on the next door. "Mr. Johnson, may I come in?"

"Of, course, Ginger. I'd know that voice anywhere."

Mr. Johnson was a fairly new addition to their community. She enjoyed him a great deal and was anxious to get his perspective.

"How can I help you, Ginger." Mr. Johnson was finishing his regular soap opera, *The Love of a Lifetime.* He sat in his wheelchair, impeccably groomed and ready for anything that might happen that day. His crisp, light blue shirt and khakis contrasted nicely against his dark skin. The pant leg on his amputated side was rolled up to avoid tangling in the wheel of the wheelchair.

"I want your opinion on something." Ginger locked eyes with him and smiled.

"You want a black, sharecropper's son's opinion?"

"Yes, that is precisely what I want. You are one of the most successful people I know. I want to hear your thoughts."

"It's about time *somebody* does." Mr. Johnson's shoulders lifted slightly as he chuckled, entertained with his own comment.

"Mr. Johnson, if you were the boss, what would you look for in a new employee?"

"Oh...that is a good question." Without hesitation, he spoke more eloquently than a professor. "I would want someone who depended on that job for their livelihood, for their pride in self, and for their opportunity to help others, because through helping others we all find our truest calling. Once a person has found their calling, they will sacrifice everything they have to see it through."

Ginger sat in amazement. James Johnson just explained to her why she herself was such a fantastic nurse. She checked all those boxes.

James leaned toward her, "Are you okay, Ginger? I said—"

"Yeah, James, I got it. I got it..." She swallowed hard to clear the lump in her throat that seemed to keep appearing while talking to these amazing elders. "I have to say, James, you are one of the smartest men I know; and I know a lot of people."

"I have been around the block and I watched everything that was going on while I traveled." He laughed thinking back on his life and all the life lessons he learned.

"Can I get a picture with you, James?"

"You want a picture of me... with *you?*"

"Please. My day wouldn't be complete without it."

"Well, I don't want to be the cause of your incomplete day. Let me transfer over to the couch. People tend to stare at my wheelchair and don't even see my pretty face."

He held his hand up to his chin and put on the cheesiest smile.

Ginger came over to the couch, sat down, and made room for James. "I think that is a perfect idea."

They sat on the couch, and Ginger leaned into James's side for several pics. James held his head high, proud of who he was and the friend he knew would stand by him come hell or high water. They had an understanding, and they had each other's back.

"What are you gonna do with that, Ginger?"

"I am not totally sure yet, but I can guarantee you that you and your friends here at Fireside are making this a better place. Love you, man."

"Love you, too. Let me know what you have up your sleeve; I am happy to help if I can."

"You, bet. Thanks." Ginger walked away a changed woman. She escaped to her "second office," by the soured dumpster, and pulled a milk crate to the brick wall. She sat down, lit up a cigarette, and pulled out her notes.

Ginger thumbed through the list of attributes for potential new hires, and she could have been considering notes from a Fortune 500 company. According to the elders in her building, a new hire should be able to offer and receive respect; carry a positive attitude; be knowledgeable and prepared, with a desire to grow; see their job as their source of livelihood, pride, and their calling. Ginger knew she was sitting on a treasure chest of knowledge with all the experience of elders surrounding her. She could not get better advice from Bill Gates, himself.

Her process for hiring and training staff was about to change. She was now excited about the next hire she would choose because she would be comparing applicants a little differently from now on, and she would institute a hiring committee of volunteer residents that would give feedback on the applicants.

The first person she wanted to talk to for possible consideration was Skylar, the conscientious nursing assistant she bumped into only yesterday. *Skylar, your world is about to change.*

Chapter 14

Present Day

Ginger glanced at her watch. She nervously bounced her leg and snapped her gum on every other chew, something that would normally grate on her nerves if someone else were doing it, but she was not aware of her rude gum chewing.

Rob happened by her office and did a double take, grabbing her doorway as he passed by. "How ya doing, princess? You look like you are wound up tighter than a Tiffany clock."

Ginger snarled and rolled her eyes. "Number one, I am not a princess. Number two, what makes you think I am uptight?"

"Girl, you are chewing that gum like you are trying to kill it. What is going on?"

Ginger pushed away from her desk and stood with a huge exhale. She stepped to the door and closed it for privacy. "It's Eric. He is coming to town over the weekend and I am nervous. Imagine that. The girl who dropped *his* guard and many times left him speechless is now an emotional wreck." She crossed her arms in insecurity and glanced at the ground, waiting for Rob's response.

"Wow. I never thought I'd see this... Ginger Mahoney, a stumbling bundle of nerves... nervous over a man? There's a first for everything."

"Oh, shove it, Rob."

"Alrighty, then. You know this is kinda cute, don't you?"

"Rob, what do you want? Why are you here?" She turned toward Rob and her usual persona returned, hands on her hips and a sarcastic tone to her voice.

"Well, excuse me for caring. You have the best poker face in town, but even a child could read your face right now."

"Eric is picking up some things from his parents. He texted and said he would give me a shout when he got into town."

"How many times have you seen him since he moved to Oklahoma?"

Ginger flashed her eyes at Rob quickly and turned away.

"You haven't seen him in three weeks? Let's go talk outside."

Ginger grabbed her cigarettes from her desk. "Let's go." She opened her office door and sped down the hall, knowing Rob would be right behind her.

She pushed the bar on the heavy metal door and leaned into it to open. She ambled over to a milk crate and kicked it like a soccer ball into the parking lot. Selecting another milk crate, she nudged it with her foot to move it near the wall, so she could sit with a makeshift backrest. She shook a cigarette to the top of the pack and lit it with her trusty Zippo. Taking an initial draw on her cigarette, Ginger held up her lighter like a point of interest. "This

Zippo has seen all my ups and downs. I got it in high school when I first started smoking."

"We aren't out here to discuss your sentimental attachment to that Zippo. What the hell, Ginger? You haven't seen him for three weeks? You two are the perfect couple. What happened?"

"Well, when he left, he told me to call him."

"And..." Rob searched her eyes. "Did you?"

Ginger tapped ashes onto the pavement and gazed into the distance. Her expression unchanging. "Why do I have to call him? He left me."

"Whoa, whoa, whoa. Wait a minute here, Queen of Sheba. That math doesn't add up."

"What do you mean?" Ginger blew a steady stream of smoke to the side of Rob's head.

"Eric loves you, you goofball. He is trying to make himself successful so you will be effing proud of him. He didn't *leave* you."

"Really? Sure, felt like it." Ginger continued, avoiding Rob's eyes. Pouting.

"Ginger, let's review this. Ever since he was a boy, Eric's dream was to become a police officer. He tried to join every nearby police department, with no luck. This is who he is. It was in his D.N.A. Long before he met you, he was getting turned down by the local police department academy year after year. Then, he met you. From that moment on, not only did he want to do it for himself, but he wanted to do it for *you*. He loves you. He wants to feel worthy of you and hold down a job of status. He wants you to be proud of him, and being a security guard and 'police hopeful' was just not good enough. When he got accepted to the police academy in Oklahoma City, he felt like it was finally his turn to make it all happen, including taking the next step in his relationship with you. When he told you the great news that he had been accepted into the academy, he saw it as a step forward for both of you, never dreaming you wouldn't follow him to Oklahoma. *He felt like you left the relationship by not following him to Oklahoma.* When he told you to call him, he was searching your heart to see if you still had feelings for him. He's not going to call, but I can guarantee you… he is checking his phone every damn day for missed calls."

"Really?" Ginger finally started listening and was starting to feel like a spoiled child who had made a terrible mistake.

"You don't want a man who has no pride and no drive to achieve success."

Ginger leaned forward with her arms draped over her knees and the cigarette burning ash at least one inch long. "Well, I just felt threatened. I have worked hard for this life at Fireside and I don't want it to change."

Rob tapped the ash off her cigarette. "And he has worked hard for this opportunity. Don't ruin it. Don't break his spirit. Building a lasting relationship doesn't survive in spite of changes. It survives because both parties are willing to sacrifice for each other. Give and take, ebb and flow. If you want to hang on to this guy, you are in a season of 'give' and 'ebb.' Call him. You gotta call him."

"Maybe you are right." Ginger dropped the cigarette and smashed it with her boot.

"Just call him. That is how you make the first step, but you have to make the first move. If you don't, he is going to think you have moved on."

"Moved *on*? I can't sleep at night wondering how he is. Hannah asked me last night if Eric asked about *her*. I told her, 'Yes,' because I didn't want her to be heartbroken. What is wrong with me?"

"Nothing, princess. You are in love."

"Oh, my gosh. I feel like I have the flu."

"Yeah, sometimes it feels kinda like the flu." Rob smiled and lifted up her chin with his hand. "That's love."

Ginger strutted into D.J.'s and Dixie threw a coaster on the bar, followed by some trail mix.

"Oh, is that the new trail mix? I love that stuff."

"Well, I figured you hadn't eaten, again. That is my only way of ensuring you get a little protein along with those carbs you are drinking every night. You know, it has been nice seeing you more often, now that Eric is gone, but isn't it about time you spent more time at home with Hannah?"

"I'm doing alright. How about you?" Ginger sarcastically spoke. She grabbed the brown long-neck bottle and chugged several gulps. She closed her eyes for just a moment and returned the bottle to the bar-top, then started playing with the label. Returning to Ginger's usual tone, "Mom does great with Hannah, better than me, actually. Hannah gets a fantastic supper each evening I am not there and prayer-time every night. She is great."

"Alright, Ginger the smart ass, you are drinking a little earlier than usual. What's up?"

"Well, I needed a little liquid courage before I call him."

"Call who?" Dixie wiped the bar-top with a rag, just to give her something to do.

"Eric." Ginger raised her beer, as if proposing a toast and let a few more gulps slide down her throat.

"Oh, wow," Dixie reached in the cooler and popped a top for herself, "tell me more."

"Well, it's a long story, but after a long discussion with Rob, I think we figured out that I am not sick with the flu. I am in love with Eric."

"That's not a news flash," Dixie chuckled in disbelief. "Haven't you ever been—"

"No, Dear Abby. I haven't ever been in love before."

"Oh...my...gosh. Baby, you call that guy of yours. He is a good man. Give him a chance and *listen* more than you talk this time. Remember this, he is not trying to trick you or pull the wool over your eyes. Listen to him to *understand* him, not to plan your next jab."

Ginger relaxed a bit and trusted her lifelong friend. She started working on the beer label again. Her phone buzzed with a new text. Ginger's heart pounded as she pulled her phone out of her pocket. "Just letting you know I am in town," Ginger read out loud. She flipped the phone over with the screen down, as if it would make it all go away.

"Eric? Well, you gonna call him?" Dixie asked.

"Yeah, I just need to get my thoughts together." Ginger grabbed a cocktail napkin from the bar and a pen patrons used to write down phone numbers. She wrote notes and talked out loud, "Good to hear from you. How was your drive? Maybe we should grab a drink—"

"How about right now?" Eric had quietly entered the bar as Ginger was brainstorming. He slowly strolled toward Ginger from behind. His hair was cut shorter than usual, and his muscles were bragging on themselves through his t-shirt.

Ginger connected eyes with Dixie without lifting her head and whispered, "Is that ..."

"Yep. I have to clean out the storage room. You got it from here, Ginger. You can do this."

Dixie glanced Eric's way. "Sure is good to see you, Eric. Come here and give me a big hug." Dixie gave Eric a hug like a hug should be given, heart-felt. "I'll be in the storage room." She brushed her hands off on her jeans and left the church-key bottle opener on the bar.

"If anyone else comes in, Ginger, just take care of them like I would." Dixie gave her a wink and continued to the storage room.

Eric slowly took one step at a time, testing the water to see if he was welcome there. "I hoped I would see your car here when I pulled into town."

Ginger was trying to think of her next words when she remembered the advice, *listen to understand, not to plan your next move.* "I should have called before now. I didn't know what to say."

Eric stepped closer. "I just need to be with you and feel your presence. You don't even have to *say* a word." He took a deep breath. "Your hair still smells like honeysuckle. It is just so damn good to see you."

Like a tidal wave... gratitude, guilt, and devotion crashed down on Ginger's heart. She had essentially turned her back on Eric weeks ago, afraid of change and protecting her heart from what appeared to be isolation and rejection. "Well, what are you doing here?"

"I am fighting to stay connected to my heart. You. You, Ginger, are my heart. I can succeed as a police officer. I can grow and achieve my lifelong dreams, but it will be incomplete without you in my life. I just had to know the truth. Have you moved on?"

"Eric, you asked *me* to call *you*, didn't you?"

"Yeah, but—"

"Can we start this thing over? Really. Go back outside to your car. No joke."

"Really? Uh, okay. Well, this is uncomfortable." Eric scanned side to side as if maybe someone caught something he missed, but they were the only two in the bar. Eric took two slow steps backward and turned to slowly go back out to his car.

Eric sat in his car seat and draped his wrist over the wheel, wondering what happened, as his phone rang. He grabbed his phone; it was Ginger. "What are you doing?"

"I don't want to let you down. It may not be like you intended … me calling you while you were in Oklahoma City, but I *am* calling you *now*. I need you in my life. You are what makes me feel alive. You are what makes me fight to be a better person, a better mother, and nurse. It is time that I fight to be a better girlfriend. I felt alone, and I had been left holding the bag so many times with other men. I felt that I wasn't good enough…again. I felt that if I had more to offer, you would not have gone to Oklahoma in the first place. I know I am not the everyday girl, but I *do* need you. I want you in my life." Ginger waited for his response and closed her eyes, waiting for his words. "Eric … hello? Eric?"

The door opened and Eric entered the bar … again. Ginger shouted out to Dixie, "Hey, Dixie, can you get a cold brew for Eric. He's coming back in."

Dixie grabbed two beers in one hand and her church key opener in the other. "That is what I want to see, my two favorite people sitting at my bar top. Love it."

Eric appeared the same with a little bonus. The police training beefed up his arms and chest, and his hair was perfectly styled. The real difference was in his confidence and assertiveness. A quiet strength that was *so sexy,* like a new and improved, perfect Eric.

"Here's to the best evening I have had in a long time." Eric raised his stubby bottle of Jamaican beer and Ginger followed suit with her domestic. *Clink.*

"A great end to a mediocre day." Ginger agreed. Ginger felt an unusual peace and comfort in just 'being' with Eric.

"I don't know what to say or do." Ginger blurted out, breaking an uncomfortable silence.

"I have an idea. Let's start over. No expectations and no demands. I am graduating from the academy in about a week. I will be in Oklahoma for a while, but we don't have to give up on us. We have the weekends and we can make it happen. Don't shut me out."

Ginger gazed at Eric and she could see her future in his eyes. "Eric, I never did let go. I was afraid you found someone prettier, smarter, and richer."

"Whoa, there, little lady. There is not another woman like you... *anywhere.* I love your giving spirit, your "don't start with me" attitude, your Dingo boots, jeans, and tattoos, your family, and your commitment to the residents at Fireside. You are over the top." Eric stopped and turned his whole body toward Ginger with one foot on the bottom rung of the stool and one foot on the ground. "Ginger just be open, honest, and trust me with your heart. I will protect it with my life."

"I don't have a lot of words. You know me." She stepped away from the bar, danced to the jukebox, and plugged it with a few bucks. She pushed E9 and John Legend's "All of Me" began playing. She walked back over to Eric, who was watching every move she made. He had turned around on his stool, facing the center of the bar.

Ginger spread his knees farther apart so she could easily fit up close to him. She couldn't take her gaze off his perfect blue eyes that invited her to get closer. Ginger leaned in and lightly placed her cheek next to his and whispered, "Come on." She led him to the small linoleum dance floor by the jukebox. Ginger placed her cheek against his chest and her apprehensions melted away. It was as if the music gently orchestrated their dance, connecting their emotions, the lyrics and their bodies. Ginger could feel Eric's heartbeat beneath her ear. She didn't want the song to end. This was perfection. No words and no promises were exchanged, but the obvious commitment was palpable.

John Legend finished "All of Me" and as Nora Jones started singing "Come Away with Me" Ginger's eyes connected with Eric. "Hey, you want to go to Neon for just a brief bit? Rob is going there tonight, and I would love for him to see you. Well, since I am going to try to do better about expressing myself, I should tell you that Rob talked to me and explained *you* to *me*".

"Huh?" Eric pulled away briefly. "How did a gay man explain me to you?"

"I thought the same thing, but he *is* a man and he has had several long-term relationships. He really does have insight and helped me understand 'you' and 'me' and 'you and me.' I think that would be the beginning of a perfect night."

As they left the dance floor, Dixie dried beer glasses and swooned at the sight of true romance playing out before her eyes. "Y'all outta here?" Dixie felt that her job was done. It helped her believe in love to see them snuggle. If it could happen for Ginger, there was still hope for her.

They held hands and approached the bar top like high school kids at the prom. "We have some catching up to do." Ginger reached her arm around Eric and put her hand in his rear jeans pocket. "I'll talk to you soon, Dixie." Ginger smiled. "What? What is so funny, Dixie?"

Dixie was smiling from ear to ear and giggled a little. "You kids go have fun... and don't overthink things. Love y'all."

"Oh, wow, don't go getting all sentimental on me, Dix." Ginger and Eric turned toward the door. Ginger paused for a moment and looked to Dixie. "I know you had a hand in this, thanks." Ginger turned to go out with her left hand in Eric's left rear jeans pocket and her right hand on his chest. She was home ... at home in Eric's arms.

Chapter 15

Present Day

Ginger flipped down the sun visor to check out her hair in the mirror. "Give me just a minute. I feel like my lipstick is smeared from ear to ear."

"Well, sorry, but I couldn't just give you a little peck on the cheek. I have been starved for those lips for over three weeks."

"Oh, believe me, not complaining. I just don't want to bounce in like a clown in a parade... a happy clown, but still a clown."

"I can feel the bass thumping already. Ah, man ... have I ever missed the music at Neon. Best dance club in Atlanta."

"I bet Rob is already cruising the upstairs loft. He and Dr. Remington are on a bit of a break." Ginger organized her credit cards, I.D. and money so she could put them in her pocket and leave her purse locked in the glove box of the car. "Eric, I am not one for long conversations about emotional stuff, but ... I am so glad you came by D.J.'s. I can see the changes you have made since going to the academy, and it has made you a more confident person. I always knew you were one who had a silent inner strength, an emotional strength. People always thought I was the stronger one, but I am a coward when it comes to feelings and emotions. I promise I will be a better communicator. My whole life, I have questioned and suspicioned the actions and motives of others, because I have been burned so many times. My first impulse is to question what others have to gain with their actions. I think the worst and make them prove me wrong, that way I don't get hurt. I will make one promise to you, Eric. I will automatically expect the best from you. I guess that means I trust you. Thank you for making the second effort. You probably saved 'us' because I don't know that I was a big enough person to make myself vulnerable to the potential heartache. Thanks."

Eric used his thumb to remove a smudge of lipstick on Ginger's chin. "Now, I think we are ready. Let's go dance our asses off." Eric escorted Ginger to the entrance with his hand along her waist. The bouncer gave them both hello hugs and stamped their hand with a red cherry symbol to prove admission.

Ginger caught the bouncer, Max, checking out Eric's backside. "Hands off, Mighty Max, he's all mine." Eric grinned at hearing those words, music to his ears.

"Okay, okay. You can't blame a guy for dreamin'."

"Well, dream from a distance." She playfully punched Max's shoulder as they entered the club.

The techno-pop music had a driving beat and was addictive. They both started scanning the room for their little buddy, Rob.

"Up here. Ginger...Eric...up here." Rob smiled and waved them down like a plane coming in for a landing.

Eric patted his pockets and realized he did not have his nicotine gum. He 'danced' Ginger up to Rob and his friends and then leaned into Ginger. "I left my nicotine gum in the car. No smoking is allowed in the bar, and I will have a headache in just a little bit if I don't go get it. When I come back, I'll bring you a beer and tequila shooter."

"Sounds great. Thanks." Ginger turned back around and started dancing in place, arms above her head and eyes closed. Ginger was in her element and was having the time of her life.

As Eric got near the entrance, the bouncer stepped inside for a bathroom break, "Be right back," he said reflexively. Eric started jogging to his car, not wanting to miss another minute he could spend with Ginger.

As he neared the corner where his car was parked, he noticed a few guys hanging out and burning time, leaning against and sitting on the tailgate of an old pickup. As he jogged past them, he heard one of the guys, "Swish, swish, swish. Check out the fairy running." They all laughed and mimicked an effeminate man running.

Eric ignored them, but was ever mindful of where they were and what they were doing. He felt they were up to no good.

Eric sat in his car and dug through his console, but couldn't seem to find his gum.

"Whatchoo diggin' for, sweetheart? You forget your tampons?" The boys had moved over by Eric's car, and he was now pinned in his car.

"Hi, guys. My girlfriend and I came out to dance and drink a little. Neon is the best dance club in Atlanta."

"You and your *girlfriend*, huh? We don't believe that for a minute," Bubba chided. "Look at that hair and your sissified clothes. You are one of them, all right." They were passing around a brown paper bag that clearly had whiskey nestled inside. They undoubtedly spilled as much on their clothes as they put in their bellies. The stench could be smelled from a block away. They could have been the cast from *The Dukes of Hazzard:* nasty, NASCAR t-shirts, unshaven, steel-toed boots, and Levi's sagging to their knees. "We know your kind, fairy-boy.

You wouldn't be down here if your pecker wasn't hurtin' for some action inside that den of devils over there." They pointed to Neon.

"I am not interested in men." Eric finally found the gum. He slid it in his pocket and gave a side glance toward the entrance to see if the bouncer was back at his station, but it was empty.

Eric felt that he was pretty safe, as long as he was in the car. So, he just waited.

Bubba wasn't going to be happy unless he was beating up some gay folks. It was the only reason these country guys came to town that night; find some gay guys and show them the error of their ways.

"I think I will head on home." Eric tried to divert their efforts. "Y'all have a good night." He grabbed the car door and acted like he was going to shut it, but Bubba was standing in the way and didn't even flinch.

"How ya gonna do that, girlie boy?"

"Don't call me that—"

"How you gonna stop me, Liberace?" His country mafia buddies laughed and closed in a little closer.

Eric peeked at the entrance again, hoping that Max was back at his post.

"What you doin,' princess? We slipped some 'medicine' in his drink; he will be tied up in the bathroom for quite a while." Bubba and his buddies all started taking off their belts and closing in on Eric. "It is PRIDE week, sweet cakes, you had to know that, right?"

"Uh, I had forgotten—"

"We have a family tradition around our parts. Every year while you fairies are celebrating your fairy-hood, my buddies and I celebrate our right to kick your feminine little asses. Grab him, boys." The country mafia grabbed Eric and he didn't have a chance. Initially, it was only Bubba slugging him, and Bubba was no match for Eric. Eric got in a couple of heavy blows and knocked Bubba to the ground. Then all hell broke loose. They dragged Eric into the shadows next to their run-down pick-up truck, and beat him unconscious. They continued, blow after blow, quoting Bible verses, shouting obscenities, and beating him until he was rendered unconscious, bleeding, and defenseless in the shadows of the industrial district. They robbed him and left Eric for dead.

An impatient Ginger glanced toward the entrance, again, and then to her watch. *Where is that beer and tequila shot?* She stood and danced her way to the front of the club, grabbing one stranger after another, for a few moments of a dance on her way to the door, staying in perfect step with the beat.

Rob noticed her working her way to the front door and chased her down to ask about the obvious hookup with Eric in private. "Hey, Ginger, wait up." He hustled down the loft stairs two at a time. "You didn't waste any time taking my advice," Rob gloated, "glad to see Eric, and by the way, he is looking delicious tonight."

Ginger rolled her eyes and scanned the bar top and the bartender. He was slinging drinks like a magician, tossing glasses in the air and catching them behind his back. "Dixie pulled a few strings, but I am glad she did." She searched from side to side. She saw nothing. Where did Eric *go*? She went to the front and asked the bouncer, "Hey, man, did you see Eric?"

The bouncer, Max, stood with his feet apart and hands clasped in front of him in a stance of 'don't try it, buddy.' His earpiece blinked blue every few seconds, showing he was connected... to something, probably a ballgame. "Oh, yeah, babe. He went out a while ago, haven't seen him come back in, but I had to step away for a bit."

Ginger turned toward Rob. "C'mon let's go check it out." As they got closer to Eric's car, they could see his car door was still open. Their pace quickened and Ginger shouted, "Eric... Eric... you okay?" They broke into a full run and saw the car ransacked with no Eric to be found.

Max heard the commotion and ran in their direction. "You need some help?"

Ginger started screaming, "Eric... Eric!" They all spread out and searched the area. "Max, you didn't hear *anything*?"

"No, Ginger. I run a tight ship around here. It has been peaceful all night. Two country guys even came up and offered me a cold sports drink. I was so parched; I took it in a flash. Not too long after that, I had to make an extended 'deposit' in the men's room. That was the only time I was away from my station."

Rob shouted, "I found him over here. Call an ambulance. He's still breathing."

Chapter 16

1970s

Wes ran up the church's front steps and checked his watch, knowing what it would reveal. *Damn, late again.* he grumbled under his breath. As he reached for the gold door pull on the opulent white front door, he noticed a coughing noise around the corner. He peered around the corner behind a half wall hiding the heat and air units. "Hello? Is someone back there?" Wes cautiously stepped closer to the seldom-seen area housing the church's heating and air system. Silence. He was about to turn back around when another cough drew his attention again. As he crept a bit closer, he was amazed at what he saw. On the other side of the HVAC units, an unusual ragamuffin boy hid, hoping Wes would not see him.

"I know, I know," the young man started with an apologetic tone, "I was told to be gone by 4:00 today, be-

fore people start showing up for church tonight. I have nowhere else to go. Crashing by the church is just so much safer than crashing in the park or on the downtown streets. It is a little noisy behind this brick half-wall, but I don't have to worry about being robbed, or worse, when I am here. I like it here."

Wes was mesmerized by what he saw. A stack of schoolbooks, a pallet of foam, blankets, and pillows. With a closer survey, he saw a t-shirt and jeans drying on a milk crate. Another nearby milk crate was being used as a table with a flashlight, paper, and pencils placed in an orderly fashion. The most sobering sight was the dichotomy of the open Bible he had been studying lying next to a jar of peanut butter and crackers. The vision of a hobo teen's food for the soul next to the food for his body framed a scene in Wes's brain that would never be erased. The young man had gathered old newspapers and saved pictures and articles of things that were beautiful and inspiring to him and taped them up wherever he could find a place to put them.

"Man, what are you doing back here?" He squatted down near the young man and offered him some gum.

"I am so sorry. Please don't tell Pastor Lyons. He will call the police again. I can be out of here in just a few minutes. I know what I was told. Just give me a little while." He smiled with a little effort and started rolling up his bedding before he waited for an answer.

"What are you talking about? And...what is your name?"

"My name?" The boy wiped his runny nose with the back of his hand and paused with the surprise of the question. *Cough, cough.* He squelched his coughs the best he could, but there was no suppressing them.

"My name is Thomas." He looked Wes in the eye momentarily, then returned his eyes to the ground. Thomas straightened his t-shirt. It was evident that he was rarely asked his name or shown any other kind of human interest other than pushing him down the road, landing on someone else's property, and becoming someone else's problem.

"You have quite a pad here. Where are you from? What is your last name? You feel so familiar to me."

Thomas returned to his packing. "I am from these parts. My parents are Fred and Mary Franks. I am one of the Franks boys."

"Franks ... Franks ... I know that name." Wes had totally forgotten about church at this point. He sat across from Thomas with his legs crisscrossed and leaning back on extended elbows. "Yes. I had one of your brothers in my class. Charlie Franks. He your brother?"

"Yep. He went into the Army. Mamma passed away last year from cancer, and Dad has had a hard time since then. Well, in fact, he left for California. I am on my own until I graduate and can enlist. I am the youngest kid in my family and plan to join the Army just like my brothers did, but I am still too young." He beamed momentarily with the pride he felt for his brothers' military service. "You know, when you join the Army, those guys become like your family. You don't have to worry about a roof over your head or food on your table."

"Or peanut butter on your milk crate?"

"Oh, that?" Thomas blushed with embarrassment. "Well, it is the best thing I can get for my time after school. I am on an adventure! Last year, about the time we had to read 'Gulliver's Travel,' Mom died and Dad flew the coop. He left me with my uncle and aunt, but they used me as a field hand. All I got to eat was their leftovers. I sat in class listening to the teacher talk about 'Gulliver's Travels' and I knew what I had to do. I ran away to a better situation, until I join the Army. I would rather live on my own, hustling for food, than live in a house with my relatives; unseen, unheard, and watching the family dog eat better than I did. Out here, I call my own shots."

Wes sat and listened to a young boy, matured by hard knocks, who clearly had not been given a chance to share his story for quite some time.

"What about school?" He was amazed at the level of satisfaction this boy displayed in the midst of his lack of support financially, emotionally, and materially.

Thomas sat up with pride. "I go to school. I also work at the Texaco gas station when old man Jenkins wants a little help. I use the bathroom there to clean up." He glanced downward in shame. I only have to make it another few months till I can join the Army and it will be a piece of cake after that."

Wes kept a smile on his face while he considered the statement that Thomas just made. His new friend was anticipating the life he would have in the Army, even though the Vietnam War was still in full combat. That put Thomas's situation in crystal clarity. He got an idea. "Well, it's Wednesday and you know church is starting in just a few minutes. Oh, did I mention there will be a potluck dinner after church for all those who attend? Why don't you come to church with me?"

"Are you serious? You want me to go to church with you? I need a shower and I dress like a hobo. Well... I guess I *am* a hobo. You want me to go in and sit on the clean pew cushions and drink out of the same water fountain that you use, not to mention break bread with you at supper?"

"In a word, yes." He smiled, got up off the ground, and held out his hand to give his new friend a little help. "C'mon, we can slip in on the back row ... my usual place because I am usually sliding in under the wire." They both laughed at his honesty.

Thomas and Wes connected on a basic level. They were both young and searching for their place in this world. As they stepped in the church entryway, Thomas noticed the bathroom. "Give me just a minute. I want to wash my face and hands."

"Sure. I'll wait right here." He dug into his pocket for his comb. "Hey, you know what? Why don't you take my comb? I have several at home."

"Really? Thanks." Thomas pushed through the swinging bathroom door. Wes leaned against the wall and listened to his dad from the pulpit.

Pastor Lyons had a certain tone when he was preaching. He wondered if they had a class in college for 'preacher voice 101.' "Our scripture reading is from 1 Samuel 16:7

this evening. Please get your Bibles and turn to this scripture."

Thomas came out and appeared ten times better with his face washed and hair combed, "I feel better about going into the sanctuary now." He smiled and was excited about joining the church service. "When my mom was alive, we attended church every week. This will be great."

As the boys crept into the sanctuary, they slipped into the last row without disrupting the congregation. As they sat there, Thomas ran his hand across the soft, pristine pew cushion and closed his eyes. "I love these pews. They're beautiful."

Pastor Lyons stood with every hair in place, and his shirt crisply starched and pressed, thanks to Loretta. Let's read the scripture lesson for today, 1 Samuel 16:7. Thomas grabbed the pew Bible and flipped right to the referenced scripture. "I love this scripture. It makes me feel more normal."

Wes heard his dad preach on this verse many times and never could find 1 Samuel easily. "Hey, can I read with you? I never can find that chapter."

"Sure." As Pastor Lyons read the text, Thomas mumbled the words with him, "1 Samuel 16:7. Don't look at his appearance or how tall he is, because I have rejected him. God does not see as humans see. Humans look at outward appearances, but the Lord looks into the heart."

Thomas closed the book. "Amen." He leaned forward with his elbows on his knees and was tuned in to every word that passed Pastor Lyons's lips.

Wes was surprised. That young kid was hanging on every word his dad had to say, truly as if Harold was sent by God to speak to Thomas. It made him pay a little more attention than usual, a difficult thing to accomplish for a kid with so much energy.

Pastor Lyons brought the fury, fire, and brimstone, asking each person to search their hearts and view people in a new light. Thomas had never felt so welcomed into a group. He listened to Pastor Lyons and felt a little less self-conscious about his clothes and hair.

The service came to a close. Pastor Lyons reminded the congregation that a potluck dinner was to follow and gave the benediction from Philippians 4:23. "The grace of our Lord Jesus Christ be with you *all*. Amen." Harold enjoyed his growing congregation. He felt as if all his hard work was finally paying off.

The boys went into the church parlor where the women of the church scurried around, putting serving spoons in the dishes and filling ice into glasses.

"The aroma of homemade meatloaf, fried chicken, and apple pie wafted through the room. Thomas was smitten with the whole experience. "Thank you, Lord." Thomas automatically searched for a spot in the corner of the room where he would not be noticed. He had become an expert in the art of blending in. "Hey, I'm gonna wait over here. I want to stay out of the wake of your dad. I will fill my plate once he starts eating. A little trick I learned when I was a kid."

Wes smiled. "Sure. I better make my appearance. Mom and Dad will come looking." He pulled up his bell-bottoms, re-tucked his shirt, and pushed his hair behind his ears again. It made his hair seem a little shorter.

He went over by the galley kitchen to find his dad considering the dishes and planning his path through the buffet line. Harold rose to see Wes. "Hi, Dad. I loved what you had to say tonight."

"Say, Wes, can you do me a favor? There is a bum who has been bedding down to the side of the church. He is dirty, has long shaggy hair, and wears shabby clothes. He might scare some of our new members. I told him yesterday that he better be gone by tonight. Can't have individuals like him visible to those around our church. Some of our new members are significant contributors.

His newly found pride in his father following his dynamic sermon suddenly slumped to disappointment, again. "What do you want me to do?"

"Well, just take care of it. If he is bedded down by the air conditioning unit, do what you have to do to get him out of there. He will ruin the perception of our church. Got it?"

"Okay, Dad. Got it." He was heartbroken. He automatically questioned the sincerity of his dad's heart. His dad just stood in the pulpit and challenged his flock to judge a person by his heart, not his appearance, obviously a practice Harold was not exercising himself.

Harold grabbed a serving spoon and an empty pot. He clanged the pot to get everybody's attention. "Welcome one and all. All are welcome at the Father's table. Let us pray. Father, God, make us the church you want us to become. Keep our hearts open and our hands reaching for those who need your love. In Jesus' name, Amen."

The congregation agreed, "Amen."

Wes rolled his eyes as he turned to join his new friend in the corner. "Let's go get in line, Thomas."

"Really? Right now?"

"You heard my dad; all are welcome at our Father's table." He held his arm out in the direction of the food line.

Thomas glanced at the food and then back at Wes. "Let's go. I am starving."

Thomas was a quiet kid and had learned the less you talk, the less people remember you. So, he smiled a lot and talked little, keeping his gaze low and making no eye contact with anybody.

The boys filled their plates, piled high with meatloaf, macaroni and cheese, mashed potatoes, and two desserts. It was a surreal evening for Thomas. The very man who had been so mean to him just preached a sermon of inclusion, and he was eating a wonderful meal. Thomas experienced so many hardships since his mother's death. One thing that gave him solace was his continued study in his Bible. It made him feel connected to his late mother. She took him to church and read the Bible to him every night. He was young, but well-versed in the scriptures.

"You want another piece of chocolate cake?" Wes wanted to ensure that Thomas had eaten all he wanted.

"Oh, I am full. Thanks. Thank you for taking a moment to peek around the corner when you entered the church, and thanks for taking a moment to listen to me. I will never, *ever* forget tonight. It has been magical."

Wes nervously grinned. He was in turmoil. Inside he was saying, *but that's not good enough. A night like tonight should not be the highlight of anyone's life. How can I do what my dad asked? How?*

His grin grew into a huge, infectious smile as an idea sparked a plan. "We have a little work to do, Thomas. I need your help."

"Okay. I have nothing else to do." They were sitting near the rear exit and gathering their things, getting ready to leave.

Harold slipped up behind the boys. "I didn't know you had a friend with you, Wes. Who do we have here?" Pastor Lyons reached out his hand, welcoming the 'visitor.'

Thomas's eyes opened as wide as basketballs, and he swallowed so hard he was sure it was audible to others. "Hi, great sermon, Preacher."

"Well, thank you, son. What is your name?"

"Thomas. My name is Thomas, sir." Thomas avoided eye contact, which was also welcoming to Harold, who craved feeling superior.

"Come back anytime. Maybe your manners will rub off on my son." Harold turned around to meet some other newcomers, unaware he had just welcomed the boy he had been persecuting.

"Follow me, Thomas." He had a plan.

Wes and Thomas sneaked back to Thomas's makeshift home by the air conditioner units.

They laughed and shared stories from school. Once it was twilight, Wes motioned to Thomas. "Let's gather up your things. I promised Dad I would make sure you gathered up your things and moved on down the road."

Thomas's face fell with disappointment. "Oh, I see. I didn't see that coming."

"I'm going to help you. I'm going to move you out of this outdoor space and help you find a real place that will give you shelter until you join the Army, or whatever else you might choose to do."

"You are going to do *that*, for *me*? Why?"

"Because it is the right thing to do. C'mon, pack this all up and follow me."

The boys packed Thomas's things and loaded them into Wes's car.

Wes drove to the back side of the church property, where the youth gym was. "Follow me; you're gonna flip out, man."

Wes led Thomas to a window behind a tree. He raised the window and they crawled in. "Okay, confession time. This is where I go when I am out too late and break curfew. The dorms lock up tighter than a jug at midnight. There is an abandoned office near the locker room. It has a sofa, a great place to crash for the night. The showers in the locker room still work. It should be a huge step up from camping out by the air conditioner."

The gym had a unique smell of sweat and fresh paint. The bleachers had just received their yearly fresh coat of paint. The gym was used for church league basketball and for church events in the winter. In spite of the smell, Thomas was thrilled. "Really? I can stay here?"

"Yep. I am doing exactly what Dad told me to do. He told me to 'take care' of you and move you away from the church building. I have done exactly that."

That small gesture changed Thomas's life. He got regular showers, washed his few clothes in the sink, and got protected sleep under the roof of that church gym. Thomas went to church to hear Pastor Lyons regularly, and with a haircut, shower, and newfound confidence, Pastor Lyons never caught on to the shenanigans of the boys. Thomas joined the Army, as he wanted, and acknowledged Wes as his angel who gave him hope.

Chapter 17

Present Day

Rob cleared his throat, trying to regain his composure, but his voice still quivered. Kneeling beside his friend, who was beaten and left for dead, he understood this better than most. "Almost every year during Pride Week, evil people crawl out from under their rocks and try to put us in our place. I heard about these beatings dished out by the Country Mafia Boys. The C.M.B. always leaves a 'calling card.' In fact, their signature 'calling card' is two cards; both queens, placed prominently on the victim. I guess they saw Eric leave Neon and assumed he was gay." There in plain sight were two playing cards on Eric's chest, fanned so that both queens were easily seen.

The police and paramedics arrived at the same time and a barrage of questions ensued. Ginger, Rob and others found themselves pushed away from the area as they strung up yellow crime scene tape.

Ginger pushed her way back through to the cops coordinating the investigation. "I'm Ginger, his girlfriend. His name is Eric. Eric Harrison."

A hard-nosed cop with the persona of a bulldog sneered at her with a facial expression that said, *who asked you?*

"Listen here." Ginger ducked under the yellow tape and ran around to get a view of his name plate, "Sergeant Winters. I am with him." She walked with a purpose and brushed shoulders with the cop as she strode past him. Eric *was* her purpose. She left the sergeant chasing her, with each step causing her wild, red hair to bounce with her cadence. "Rob, what are you waiting for?" Ginger barked as she continued on her way.

Rob stepped toward the cop. "We'll stay to the side and out of the paramedics' way. He needs us. Well, he needs Ginger and Ginger needs me. I'll keep her in line." He was clearly promising something he couldn't control.

Rob ran to catch up with Ginger. As he caught up and matched her stride-for-stride, Ginger glanced his way. "Keep who in line?"

"Oh, that? Had to figure out a way to get past him."

"Thought so." Ginger's pace slowed as they drew near Eric's limp body. Eric was still unconscious, his face swollen and bloody. The paramedics were still assessing him and scurrying about like army ants with a blood pressure cuff still velcroed in place and oxygen tubing draped across Eric's chest.

A paramedic turned to them. "You family? He can't hear you, but you might give him a few words..."

"I am an R.N. *and* family. Get out of my way. I will make sure he knows I am here and then I'll get out of *your* way. Where ya taking him?"

"Kaiser, downtown." The paramedics looked around asking. "Who is this chick?"

"Eric, I know you can hear me. You'll be fine. I am going to get out of these guys' way, so they can help you. Love you and I will be with you."

Ginger sat in silence with the exception of the occasional beep of the I.V. pump. Her bloodshot eyes reflected her fatigue and concern but they remained trained on the vital signs bleeping on Eric's bedside monitor.

"Go get some rest, I promise I'll call you when he wakes up." The nurse paused at the door to use hand cleaner before she entered farther. "Since I met you, I have taken your fella on as if he were my own brother." She crossed the room to view the medications hanging on the I.V. pole.

"Hey, who has the beets?" Eric mumbled, almost unintelligibly, with his eyes still closed.

"Eric! Eric! You're awake!" Ginger dropped her phone and ran to his bedside. "What did you say, babe? What do you want?"

He tried to smile, but the bruising around his mouth made him grimace in pain. "Beer. I want beer."

"You are in the hospital, Eric."

"What? No way." He looked all around and became instantly alarmed. "What happened?"

"Let me in here." The nurse elbowed her way through to see Eric up close. "What is your name, sir?"

"Eric Harrison."

"Can you tell me what day it is?"

"An unlucky day." Eric was becoming agitated.

"Okay. I get it. I will be back to do a full head-to-toe assessment, but I am going to message the doctor, so he can stop by. He is on the floor making rounds."

Ginger tried to keep her emotions muted so Eric wouldn't see how concerned she was. "We were at Neon celebrating, Eric. Do you remember anything else about that night?" Ginger traced a heart on the palm of his hand with the gentle touch of her finger.

"Well, not really. Maybe if you reminded me a little it would hawk me remember."

"Okay. Did you mean help you remember?" she started off with a smile.

"Yes." He glared at her like she was losing it.

The door bolted open. "I'm Dr. White. How are we doing here?" He continued to rub the hand sanitizer into his hands as he drew closer to Eric.

Ginger waited for Eric to speak. "Go ahead, Eric. He wants to hear it from you." She squeezed his hand in solidarity.

"Well, I'm just feather. I guess you will tell me how I really am." Eric spoke with little confidence and didn't shy from looking the doctor in the eye.

"Eric, did you mean to say feather, instead of fine?"

"No. Why would I do that?"

"One result of brain injury is aphasia. We will talk about that later. Let me continue." Dr. White asked Eric to follow a series of commands that sounded trivial, like, "Raise your arms. Don't let me push them down. Follow my pen with your eyes. Open your mouth… now, move your tongue side to side. Okay, I am going to write your orders. In brief, Mr. Harrison, you are a very lucky man. If you weren't in such good shape, the damage would have been worse. You have sustained a traumatic brain injury, which is causing you to switch words. Also, you sustained multiple orthopedic injuries, some of which are serious. I will stop back by tomorrow. Any questions?" He waited, barely, for a response and rushed out the door.

Ginger searched Eric's big, blue, scared eyes. "Eric, you know I want to spend the rest of my life—"

"I know… *I* want to spend the rest of *my* horse with you, too."

"Your *life* with me?" Ginger redirected him.

"Ginger, just go with it. Okay? I want to marry you. I think it is awesome that *you* proposed to *me.* And, no … I will *never* let you forget you did the shooting."

"Asking … I did the asking."

"Yes, the asking." He smiled and took a deep breath. "This is not going to be easy. Thanks, G."

"I need to let the Oklahoma City Police Academy know about all this." He scanned the room for his phone.

"They have been notified. You aren't due back until next week, anyway, but this will take more time than that. With a traumatic brain injury and broken bones, you won't be going anywhere next week." Ginger kissed him lightly on the cheek. "We will take it a step at a time. We can notify them and tell them we don't have all the answers yet. I am sure they will hold a place for you."

"Hold a *place* for me? We aren't talking about summer camp, Ginger. If I miss it, I miss it. I will have to start over ... applications, interviews, testing ... everything!" Eric threw his head back against the pillow as he thought about the impact this attack could have on his life. "Too much to toot about right now."

"You mean, 'talk' about, babe. Too much to talk about." Ginger gently corrected his word choice.

"I am not sure what I mean, but I am tired. I know you have my back. I think I will curtain my eyes for a bit. Babe, you want to crawl up in the bed with me?"

Ginger didn't say a word. She pulled back the blanket and started to climb into bed with him. "Move over a bit, babe."

When the covers were pulled back, Eric and Ginger were overcome by the stench of his leg "What is that smell?"

"The dressing needs to be changed." Ginger knew infection when she saw and smelled it. Green drainage was just beginning to seep through his right lower leg dressing and with the drainage, came the stench. Trying to not concern him, Ginger did her best to not show her hand, but she was worried. Any wound can get infected, but the parking lot where they found him was filthy.

"I don't think they have told you about your leg yet. Your lower leg is broken. From the marks on your leg, they think the thugs hit your lower leg with something like a brick. It was mud covered and created quite a gash in addition to the fractures. It will heal with time, but for now, let's just be happy with a dressing change. Are you okay for a minute, honey? Before we take a nap, I want to tell the nurse about your dressing."

"Yeah, sure. No guitars that I will be awake when you get back. I am so tired. Just take your chances."

"Okay that is a deal. I know… no guarantees." She flashed a grin and pulled the hand sanitizer lever as she left the room. Ginger stepped straight to the window at the end of the hall and gazed out over downtown Atlanta. Her heart was overwhelmed with what the future might hold. She felt a wave of emotion building from her innermost being. She felt out of control and had to find some relief.

Ginger saw a linen cart nearby. She grabbed a stack of towels and dashed into the stairwell around the corner. She ran down to the bottom landing, sat on the steps and buried her face in the towels. Her sobs came from her inner sanctum of emotion. She screamed a while, cried a while and hit the towels a while, taking out her anger on the stack of pristine, innocent bath towels. Ginger had never been on such an emotional roller coaster. The word-finding problems, the emotional scars and now, green drainage from his wound, which was most likely a pseudomonas infection.

Ginger slowed her breathing and tried to focus on the sounds and sights around her, an established technique to decrease anxiety. She sat in the corner of the stairwell landing and just breathed. *You have to get real with yourself, Ginger. You keep telling him he can do this and keep trying to lift him up, but you don't really know if you can do it. All the dreams you just now let yourself believe, again, could be up in smoke. One day at a time, G. One day at a time.*

The door swung open, and Ginger could hear someone trotting down the staircase. She stood and walked back up to Eric's floor. Ginger was one tough cookie. She was about to find out how tough.

Chapter 18

Present Day

Mr. Epstein sat at the entryway and waited for the next visitor. Wearing his usual threadbare pants and mismatched socks, he was in his element, keeping tabs on the comings and goings of Fireside. The door swung open, and Mr. Epstein greeted the unsuspecting visitor.

"Welcome to Fireside," Mr. Epstein whined in his famous Jewish brogue.

The young man scanned the room and back at Mr. Epstein, "How ya doin'?" He was wearing sunglasses, an Astros ball cap, and a black hoodie, with his hands in the hand-warming pouch.

"I am fine, young man. How can I help you?" Mr. Epstein observed the new acquaintance and felt a bit unsettled.

The receptionist sat listening at the nearby greeter's desk. She was interested in his answer, too.

"Oh, I am just looking for my good friend, Wes. You know him? Wes Lyons?"

Mr. Epstein volleyed, "Sure, I know him. How do you know—"

The receptionist cleared her throat. "Come sign the visitor book, and I can help you find him, Mr...."

"Pinky. My friends just call me Pinky."

"What do other people call you?" Mr. Epstein whined. Still unsure about this stranger who left on his sunglasses indoors.

The man adjusted his sunglasses. "Excuse me, but..."

The receptionist handed him a pen. "Pinky, sign your full name here, and I can help you." She smiled her best professional, plastic smile. She, too, was taking note of the new visitor.

Mr. Epstein pushed his wheelchair around the corner to Ginger's office. "Mischief just came in the door. I don't trust him. He left his sunglasses on when he came inside. He calls himself Pinky. *Pinky*. What kind of name is that?" He paused for a response. Ginger was focused on the employee schedule and glanced up in a bit of confusion. "Just thought you would want to know. If I learn anything else, I will keep you in the loop." He gave her a wink and turned his wheelchair around.

Ginger didn't have time to respond before he left, so she gave a little shout down the hall as he pushed his way back to the entry of the building. "Thanks, Mr. Epstein." She took a sip of coffee that was, at best, lukewarm and screwed up her face in disappointment of the temperature.

As he returned to his 'post,' the receptionist nodded in the direction of Pinky. "He is here to visit Wes. Some old friend from school."

"Yeah, and I am Lady Gaga in spandex," Mr. Epstein said a bit too loudly.

"How do you know who Lady Gaga is?" She quizzed.

"I know things. I stay informed. Well... My granddaughter showed me her picture and I thought she had a Jewish flair. She isn't, but she sings with Tony Bennett, so that makes her okay."

"Mr. Epstein, Tony Bennett isn't Jewish, either."

"What?" Mr. Epstein seemed almost offended.

"He is Italian and believes in God, but he is not Jewish," she continued.

"Well, he *should* be." Mr. Epstein seemed perturbed with a furrowed brow and squinted eyes. He spun his wheelchair around. "Well, if no one else is going to keep an eye on him, I will."

"Mr. Epstein, you can't just go around and spy on people."

"I am getting my morning exercise and who knows what I will see along the way. See you later." He waved goodbye with a dismissive flick of his hand, basically shooing her away, like a fly hovering over buttermilk pie.

As he rolled down the hall, he went straight toward Wes's room. The new intriguing resident had a strange visitor, and Mr. Epstein made it his business to ensure he was an actual visitor and not 'trouble.' Mr. Epstein pulled a magazine from behind his back. He kept it there to ensure he didn't lose it before reading all the good parts. He parked down the hall, where he had a good view. He locked his brakes and raised the magazine as if he were reading it, but his gaze was on Pinky.

Pinky waited for the door to open and glanced at his watch a couple of times. Otherwise, his hands stayed in the hoodie pouch.

Wes opened the door, and his eyes widened in a fight or flight reaction. He immediately tried to shut the door, but Pinky blocked it with his foot and pushed his way through with little trouble.

Mr. Epstein heard glass breaking and a scuffle. He pushed his wheelchair to the door and knocked with authority. "Wes, let me in. Let me in, now."

Things went still in the apartment. Wes opened the door, showing only his head. "Hi, Mr. Epstein. What's up?"

"Are you okay?" Mr. Epstein leaned to the side trying to see around the door without success.

"Oh, yeah. I'm good. Did you hear the lamp break? I tripped on the cord. I am so clumsy." He flashed a canned smile and tilted his head.

Mr. Epstein saw right through the attempted deflection. Wes appeared sick--dark circles under his eyes, stringy hair, unshaven, and skin glistening with sweat. "I didn't fall off the turnip truck yesterday. This, I know. I know trouble when I see it and *he* just stepped into your room. To be honest, you don't look much better." Mr. Epstein leaned so far to the side, trying to see around the door, that he almost slipped into the floor.

"I really need to hit the shower. I know I'm frazzled in the morning." He flashed his patented TV commercial smile. "This is a friend from my church years ago."

"He doesn't seem old enough to be a friend from years ago." Epstein questioned.

"Well, he is the son of a friend." Wes bantered, with his speech growing louder with a bit of a staccato delivery. *Since when is old man Epstein so smart?* Wes saw that he needed to be more careful. Mr. Epstein truly was the centurion of Fireside.

Mr. Epstein did what he came to do. He didn't like outsiders frequenting his home and, according to him, until proven differently, this guy with sunglasses and an Astros cap was outsider-trash. "All right, have it your way. Remember, we are a family here and family doesn't hurt family. Roots of the heart grow deep and my roots are here. Preacher or no preacher, keep riffraff away from my family here."

"Thank you for your concern, Mr. Epstein." He nodded and closed the door before Mr. Epstein could respond.

Wes spun around to face Pinky. "Okay. Stop throwing stuff around. I know I was late with payment last time, but you got your money and we are even now. Let's talk business."

Pinky never flinched and never smiled. He was a dealer with a robotic face. "Don't go getting all friend-zie and emotional here. This is business, period. What do you want?"

"That's right, Pinky. Like I said, let's talk business." He stayed turned so Pinky couldn't fully see his face. As he rubbed his hand across his facial stubble, it made a scratching sound, the coarse hair protesting against his smooth hand.

"I have an opportunity here. Sitting on a gold mine, but I need product."

"What are you saying, man? You want to service Grannyville? Is that what you are saying?"

Wes turned facing Pinky fully. "What do you care? Money is money... right?" Wes gave a smirk that showed his lack of scruples.

"What are you talking?"

"Oxy... Hydros... Their doctors got them hooked on painkillers and now they can't get them because they changed the laws. We would be doing them a favor. What do you say?"

Pinky's eyes couldn't be seen because he still had on his sunglasses. His face showed no expression. "What do I think about providing my service to defenseless old people who have already been screwed over by their doctors?"

"What?" Wes held up both hands and shrugged, his voice amplifying as his anger rose. "So, you won't service old people but you will service a preacher on TV? C'mon, man." Wes's forehead was sweating, and his hand showed the slightest tremor as he wiped his sweaty hands on his pants. He reached for a glass of water to soothe his parched throat.

"Let me tell you something. We became acquainted because you had friends. Just like a rock star, you were recognized on every TV in the U.S., and across most of the world. Your entourage had connections, and there I was, but make no mistake, I have my limits. I won't service children, and I won't service the elderly. I can't do this, man."

Wes had just seen a flicker of love in the stone-cold heart he knew as Pinky. "I can't believe it. Pinky, better known as 'The Coke Machine,' now has high standards. Geez." Wes scowled at Pinky in disbelief.

"My grandma is the closest thing to pure love I have ever known. She's the reason I don't use. I can't pull old folks down the rabbit hole. You dove down the rabbit hole headfirst. If it hadn't been me, you would have found someone else. I can't do that to these people."

"Well, how 'bout a little help for me?" He could feel the generosity dwindle in Pinky's voice and turned on his TV smile.

"Sure, you are my kind of guy, no backbone ... easily distracted ...with a drug problem. But... only enough for you, so no large scores."

"Yeah, yeah, yeah. Whatever. Did you bring some Hillbilly H. with you?"

"Now you are talking like the man I know. Yes. Yes, I did." Pinky smiled from behind his sunglasses. "You need to learn a lesson, Wes. A desperate man is not a good negotiator, and a user is a desperate man. Someday, if you quit using, I might put you under my wing, but until you get off the roller-coaster for good, you are just a customer. Got it? And leave these old folks alone. If I hear that you are servicing them with treats, I will come find you."

"Give me the stuff." Wes grabbed it from Pinky's hand and opened the bag. "Here's your money."

Pinky took the money and counted it, eyeing Wes periodically as he always did. "Take care of yourself, Wes. You're losing weight." Pinky tipped his Astros cap and strolled out the door.

Wes studied his hand and then the closed door. Those last three words stung. *You're losing weight.* The drug dealer who put money and power above all things just showed him that everybody has a limit, and everybody has a heart. Even a scumbag like Pinky. This was a bit scary for Wes. He had not yet found his own limit - a line he was not willing to cross, and he was recognizing less and less of a heart in himself. Was the drug dealer, Pinky, more of a human than he was? Wes knew that he had dropped to a new all-time low. He tossed a few pills in his mouth and chewed them for a quicker response.

Chapter 19
1970s

Wes rolled over to find his sheets tangled like spaghetti, and Jennifer lying by his side. He shook his head as if it would help him remember last night, but it was all a haze. He scanned his dorm room to see remnants of what must have been a great party. He sat on the edge of the bed, and Jennifer awakened with a smile, like a young child who had never experienced fear or hardship.

"Good morning, Wes, The Magnificent!" Jennifer threw out her arm as if she were introducing him to the stage.

"Huh?" He stared at Jennifer as if she were speaking a foreign language. He glanced down at his clothes and saw that all his clothes were on backwards and inside out. "Why—"

"You decided we would all have a race to see who could undress and put our clothes back on...backwards and inside-out the fastest. You won. You were the only one who competed. You were fast, though. You were really fast.”

“Oh, wow.” Wes continued to scrutinize the entire room. “Did you have a good time? I mean, it obviously seems like I did, but did you?”

Jennifer looked at Wes with the warmth of love and lightly stroked his back in loving tickles. “Yes, sweetie, we both had a great time, but you, dear, were the life of the party.”

“If I was the life of the party last night, why do I feel so crappy today?” Wes got up, looked at himself in the mirror and turned his head to the side as he rubbed the five facial hairs along his jawline.

“Wes, you gotta talk to your dad. Even if it isn’t pleasant. You have been hiding behind bottles and doobies for months. Just talk.”

“Thanks for the advice, Dear Abby, but *he* needs to talk to *me.*“ Wes pulled off his shirt and shorts only to find that his underwear was also inside out and backward. “Oh...my...gosh.” He held out his hands like *I am not believing this.*

"Oh, yes, I saw all that *and more,* last night."

"Maybe you are right. I am not settled in my soul. I just don't feel right; like my aura is off, ya know? My brain stays tied up in knots, and my thoughts are like the needle on a stereo turntable that has been left in place long after the album finished playing. It just keeps making the same noise over and over, making no sense and with no resolution." Wes was a soft-hearted, kind soul who hated conflict and found that a little weed mellowed his anxiety to a place where he could be more comfortable in his own skin. "For a guy who has always been a people-pleaser, how is it that I could be such a disappointment to my dad? All I have ever wanted to do is make him proud."

"C'mon. Get dressed... properly. We have places to go." Jennifer giggled and chunked a pillow at him.

"All right, all right," he winced as he stumbled toward the bathroom sink littered with beer cans. "How many people came to the party?"

"Well, it started with the two of us and a few others from the Freshman Welcoming Committee; about five people total. You then decided that we should 'welcome' the entire fourth floor of the dorm. You said, 'If we are a welcoming committee, we should be *welcoming* people.'" Jennifer crossed her arms and swung her feet while sitting on his bed. She scanned the ceiling and counted out loud, "Twenty-five, twenty-six... I would say about twenty-five to twenty-six people were 'welcomed' in style last night."

Wes took the trash can, walked to the bathroom sink and knocked all the dead soldiers in the can. They clanged as each hit the bottom of the aluminum trash receptacle. "Well, this won't hack it. I'll go find the janitor and get an industrial-sized trash sack for the rest of this." He zigzagged across the floor as if avoiding landmines, only these landmines were empty cans, bottles, and wrappers of snacks left scattered across the floor like the aftermath of a concert in the park. Several beer tab chains hung over the doorway, hanging like trophies as one entered and exited the dorm room. Each beer tab interlocked with the next, showcasing the numbers of beers consumed and the appropriate "welcoming" of the fourth floor.

Wes searched down the hall, looking for the janitor. He encountered a fourth-floor resident who promptly gave him some skin and blurted out, "Man, what a groovy party last night. You are crazy, man, but I love ya. How's your backside?"

"My backside? How's my ass? My ass is fine, how about yours?" Wes sized him up with a suspicious fish eye and afraid of what might be revealed. He paused for a moment and realized that his butt was a bit sore.

"You stood on a chair and gave a brief, but prolific speech about not changing your moral compass of love and peace for anybody or anything. Man, it was inspired... like Jack Kerouac after a few beers. Then, you asked everyone present to take a pledge with you, something like, 'Let me be an instrument of love. Where there is division, let me be a bridge, where there is hate, let me be healing love and understanding.' Then you dropped your pants and invited everyone who would join in the pledge to sign your bare ass. It was poetic, man. There you were, standing on that chair and person after person stepped up to sign your ass in solidarity to live a life of world-changing love. Then you fell off the chair when you started dancing to "Born to be Wild" as it started playing on the radio. You landed on a beer bottle, right where everyone was signing. You got a small cut and as the night went on, you commented several times that your ass was hurting, I bet you have one heck of a bruise back there."

Wes took in his words, amazed at the happenings and a little proud of himself for preaching love and understanding. He tried to appear like this was not a big deal. "Oh, that. Yeah, I'm okay. Thanks for asking." His eyes darted downward, halfway out of embarrassment and halfway out of humility.

"Well, glad you are okay. You really made an impact last night. Kids are calling it the Left Cheek Pledge. You have started a tiny revolution here on campus. Under the title *Be a Bridge of Love and Understanding,* you probably have twenty signatures, in permanent marker, on your ass. Beautiful, just beautiful, man." He offered a slow clap applause.

"Well, I gotta go. See you in class, later." Wes turned to find the janitor again and rubbed his left cheek as he rambled down the hall.

Jennifer stacked cans, ashtrays and trash into piles in his room. He came in with a mammoth trash bag and shook it loose into an open bag as he entered. "Did you forget to tell me about something?" He sauntered over to Jennifer and gave her the bag to hold open as he filled it with the evidence.

"Huh?" She tilted her head and scrunched up her nose in confusion.

He turned his back to her and dropped his pants. "What do you see?"

"Oh. Yeah. Well, it all happened so fast. One minute we were all dancing and living it up and then all of a sudden, you stand up in that chair and give a speech about love and understanding—"

"What do you *see*?"

"I see a great butt... with one, two, three, four ... twenty-one, twenty-two signatures. And a bruise... a big gnarly bruise ... and a small cut."

"And how do you leave that out?" He started with a bit of a scolding tone in his words, but it quickly turned to laughter and disbelief.

"Well, it started out like a big joke, but people started saying, 'Yeah, I'll do it.' I can tell you this, no one will forget the night they pledged themselves to live a life with more love and understanding. Those who were here last night will be eighty years old, telling their grandkids about the night a group of college kids vowed to live a life of love. It's really a beautiful thing. The fact that they all signed your backside will just make it unforgettable."

"Get a mirror. I have to see my ass."

Jennifer reached for her purse and dug to the bottom for her little mirror. Wes stood with his back to the bathroom mirror and held hers up to catch a reflection. "Wow. It *is* kind of impressive." At the top of the list was Jennifer's name written in huge letters. "Do you think you wrote your name big enough?"

"I wanted everyone to know that I would follow you any-where. I would build a bridge of understanding or travel the world over in search of a place where love ruled."

That was the day Wes knew that Jennifer really loved him. She supported him because of, and in spite of, his true self and she literally signed the dotted line.

Chapter 20

1970s

Harold scooted clothes to the left and right in his closet, giving him just enough room to kneel by his shoes on the floor. As he knelt in an attitude of humility, he cried out to God for a way to connect Wes to the church more closely. He was a good kid, but Harold worried for his son's salvation. "Show me the way, Lord. Amen." Harold had a new attitude about connecting with his son. He felt Wes drifting away from him and wanted to try to find some common ground.

###

Wes sat at the piano in the drama department. It was dark, near 9:00 p.m., and he was submerging himself in the consuming waters of *Jesus Christ Superstar*, his next play. He won the role of Judas and was throwing himself into the music of the play. He stayed behind the rest, after drama practice, uneasy and hoping some time with the piano could calm his anxiety and give him clarity of thought. He was playing and singing, "I Don't Know How to Love Him," and found himself connecting to the song as he sang it over and over. Such emotion simmered beneath the surface he could not quit singing it. The song was intended to be sung by Mary Magdalene in the play, but Wes was drawn to it and was taking it into his soul.

Harold drove by the college on his way home from a board meeting at the church. He saw Wes's car next to the auditorium and pulled into a parking spot nearby. He pushed open the back door of the auditorium, he heard the perfect tone and melody of "I Don't Know How to Love Him." The emotion coming from Wes's singing was magnetic, and it was evident that he was connecting to something deeper. Harold pulled down a seat to a chair on the last row and quietly listened to him sing it over and over. Harold was overcome with the talent of his son and the heartfelt expression of emotion that poured from his heart. Harold had a change of heart. He quietly stood and as he returned the chair seat to its folded position, the spring squeaked an alert.

Wes stopped and turned to see who it was. "Dad? What are you doing here?"

"Oh, I saw your car and wanted to stop by and say hi. Son, I heard your singing, and it is really good. Maybe you could sing it at church sometime. That would be great."

"Really? You think they would like it? Sure." He was up for a performance anywhere people would listen.

"Come to church on Sunday and you can sing it for the offertory song." Harold didn't want to sound pushy, because he knew that would turn him off.

"Okay, Dad. If you want me to." He had not performed in his dad's church since the last time the people gave such a resounding applause. Harold said it was distracting.

###

Jennifer sat next to Wes on their favorite, last row pew of the sanctuary. Loretta came back to welcome them both.

"Son, your dad told me you were singing tonight. I can't wait."

"I hope you enjoy it," he removed his arm from around Jennifer's shoulder and stood to hug his mom. "Love you."

"You could sing anything and I would like it. Knock it out of the park!"

As Harold started the service, people finished their conversations and returned to their seats.

Harold prepared well for the sermon and had recently taken the advice of Loretta. He timed his sermons to end promptly at 11:55 a.m. The congregation was starting to grow and the sermons were making an impact on the daily lives of the church members. Harold had finally found his groove, and his efforts were bearing fruit.

Harold gave a rousing lesson on tithing. Usually this was a sermon that fell flat on the ears of the congregation, but this time, Harold brought it home with emotion. As he concluded his sermon, he finished with a smile. "I think you all know my son, Wes. Please welcome him as he prepares our hearts for giving."

He stood and walked up to the piano. The congregation was quiet and anxious to hear him. He started playing chords and felt he should give a bit of context. As he played random chords in the background, he explained that the song was from the popular play, *Jesus Christ Superstar*. "I was rehearsing the other night and I found myself drawn to this song." He scooted a bit on the piano bench and turned to see their faces. "In the play, the song was meant to be sung by Mary Magdalene, Jesus' confidant and close friend. As I sang this the other night, I was drawn to the words and the statement, 'I don't know how to love Him ...'" As he continued playing the piano, he spoke the words to the beginning of the song. The congregation hung on his every word. "So, I can tell you, that if you, too, feel like you don't really know how to love Him, but you would like to try, sing this with me. Tell God you want to know Him."

Wes morphed the chords he was playing into the melody and began to sing. The words were personal to him; that was obvious. His words and melody were not perfect. He was growing so emotional it was hard to control his singing, but this gave even more impact behind his words. He was on the verge of tears himself as he was trying to sing this beautiful song as it should be sung.

"I'm just one more…" The last line rang out and he turned to sit on the end of the piano bench. "I came to realize over the last few days that this song was meant for me. Not meant for me to sing, but meant for me to hear. I have felt that something is missing. As I sang, 'I don't know how to love Him…' I realized that those were my words because I really don't know how to love Him. I know who Jesus is, but I don't know how to love Him, not like I should. If you are like me and know you really don't love God the way you should but you are willing to say it out loud, stand with others who feel the same way. Make your way down to the front, and we will sing the last line together."

Harold started getting nervous and stood to gain control of the congregation again. When he scanned over the congregation and saw almost half of the people rising and shuffling to the altar to sing, he understood the power of honest expression of weakness. Harold decided to just go down front with them. When he made his way to the front and bowed his head, these words rushed into his mind; *You asked me to help you get Wes into church. Suppose you can stay out of the way and take him as he is?*

The congregation started singing, and he started playing the song again. As they all became one, singing a song that simply acknowledged that they didn't know God as well as they should or wanted to know Him. Harold quietly stepped to the other side of the pulpit, where he could not be seen. He knelt down and thanked God for using his son to bring him closer to God.

Wes felt his spirit rise and knew that God was breathing life into his words. The sanctuary was staying in rhythm with Wes's words. He slowed the song and eventually stopped playing the piano, offering naked words of prayer, singing a cappella. The entire room followed his lead and softened their voices, waiting for what came next.

Wes spoke simple words that resonated with the people. "I want to know God better. Do you? Are you tired of your heavy load? I am so tired, myself." He stepped forward. "We are already standing. Join me and find a private place to sit... or kneel and talk to God. Dad, you got anything else for us before we go?"

Harold turned to his unorthodox, energetic son. "No, son, I think your song was the message we needed to hear tonight. Please, everyone, spend some time with the Lord, and excuse yourself as you are ready to leave." Harold held his arm out in an invitation to spread across the sanctuary. Some people left, but many found a quiet place to talk to God.

Loretta came over to Harold and took his hand. "I don't know what we just experienced here, but I think Wes has a heart for God, whether he recognizes it or not."

"Honey, you may just be right." Harold squeezed her hand. "But he is all over the place. How will we control him?"

"We won't. God will."

Chapter 21

Present Day

Erma closed the file with force and shook with anger. "Insufficient funds, again. Late on his payment and his account has no money." Erma glared at her computer screen, again in disbelief. She reached for the Tums and Excedrin, but the plastic Tums container was empty. She took the empty bottle and threw it at the trash can and gave a double take when she actually made it.

Erma knew where to find Ginger this time of morning. She hustled to the dumpster area behind the kitchen and bolted through the heavy push-bar door. Ginger was painting her fingernails, while her cigarette burned resting on the corner of an adjacent milk crate. "Don't you have some work to do, or something?" Erma was already perturbed, and seeing Ginger lollygag around just made it worse.

"I am taking my smoke break." Ginger never budged.

"Since when do you smoke fingernail polish?"

"Eric had a really rough night. He has excruciating pain in his foot, and I was trying to help him into the early morning. I am barely hanging on here. The nail painting is a nice diversion for a few minutes. Regardless of what I am doing, I am calling this my 'smoke break.'" Ginger lifted her head to find a frazzled Erma. She knew something had to be odd because Erma never searched for Ginger intentionally. She usually tried to avoid her.

Erma stepped closer and blurted out, "What do you know about Wes Lyons?"

"You mean Pastor Wes? The sweetest, good-looking preacher that used to be on TV, Wes Lyons?"

"Oh, okay. I know I have been a bit star-struck, but he has been a fixture in my living room every Sunday for years. What do you know about him?"

"Not much." Ginger held the back of her hand up in front of her face to inspect her brightly painted, red fingernails. Never making eye contact with Erma, she continued. "You having trouble with him?"

Erma put her hands on her hips and huffed with a large exhale. "Money. It seems he has none."

"What?" Ginger stared directly at Erma. "That can't be. A new resident has to have proof of payment up front before they ever move in, unless someone held his paperwork back for— Oh my gosh, you didn't—"

"All right, all right, so I held his paperwork back until some things cleared the bank. He told me he sold some property and he should have the money soon, but he needed a place to stay for a couple of days until his bank received the money. I put him in that old room at the end of the hall down there." She pointed toward his room. "He is not in the way, and we had other open rooms at the time, so it is not so noticeable, but I have several interested families coming to tour the building, and if they all want to move in, we will be in a jam."

"*We* will be in a jam? You got a frog in your pocket?" Ginger was now fully engaged in the conversation with

Erma. "I don't know, Erma, I hardly ever see him. In fact, I almost forgot he lived here. I know someone who can help us, though… James. He is a master of observation and human nature."

"You can't tell another resident about Wes's financial situation."

"No shit, Sherlock." Ginger rolled her eyes and thought for a minute, *and why do I want to help Battle Ax Erma?* "I won't have to say a word; I will just ask James what he knows about ole Wes. If there is anything strange going on, James will know about it." Ginger stood, brushed off her hands on her jeans, and as she entered the building, reassured Erma, "Give me a few days."

James sat at his usual spot in the dining room. He snapped his paper into place and slurped the hot coffee to cool it while he drank. His dark skin was in contrast with the white tablecloth and his powder blue crisply pressed shirt.

Ginger pulled up a chair and sat down with her coffee before James could offer an invitation. "James, we have had several new folks move into Fireside. Have you noticed?" She sipped her coffee, never taking her eyes off James, in case he showed some sort of facial reaction. Ginger reached over to steal the last bite of James's bacon.

"Well, sounds like you are fishing for a trouble report to me."

"Oh, no. I'm not asking for trouble. Lord knows I have enough of my own." Ginger held up her hand as if she were under oath. "I just know that you are very observant, that's all. If you notice anything, let me know, okay?"

"You bet, Ginger. You know I got you covered. I will keep an eye peeled."

Ginger reached for his plate again.

"Get your own, young lady." He smiled from ear to ear. "You know how long it has been since someone ate off my plate? Since Estelle and I lived in our old apartment. Thanks for the memory, Ginger. There is probably no one else in this place that I would let eat off my plate, but you are welcome to share my food anytime. I kinda feel like we are family, anyway."

Ginger gave him a quick wink. "I feel that way, too. I feel like you are an uncle. I would trust you with my life. Just let me know if you notice anything strange going on."

"You got it, Red." He raised his coffee cup like he was proposing a toast in agreement. As Ginger strode away, James reflected on his life. When he was a child, he would have *never* thought he would be friends and teammates with a red-headed, pale-skinned nurse. He smiled thinking that hopefully in another fifty years, maybe things will change even more.

James decided he would start pushing his wheelchair around the perimeter of Fireside's hallways, taking note of the environment. This would be his new routine over the next few weeks.

As James got close to the end of the hall, he noticed a man struggling to get in his door. "Let me help you with that." James held out his hand to assist the man with his keys.

"Oh, that's okay. I got it. This door gets jammed." Wes turned his back, shielding his bruised face so that James couldn't see it.

"Okay. Anyway, if you ever need help, I am happy to do so. You new around here?" James tried to push his chair to the side to offer a handshake and introduction, but Wes adjusted his position again. "My name is James. What's—"

The tumblers turned in the door lock just as James made it to a position where he could see a little better.

"There. Got it. Nice to meet you." Wes stepped inside his room and closed the door and his eyes in relief.

James took a pad and pencil from his pocket. He noted the nameplate near the door but saw 'resident' written on the nameplate. *That is interesting. Who is he?* James wrote a few notes for future reference and planned to frequent this end of the hall. He rolled back to his room and started planning his strategy for the detective work to come. James was smiling with anticipation.

Chapter 22

1980s

Wes peeked in the bassinet and fell hopelessly in love with his baby boy, Jordan. How could a man love this much? He now knew the depth of his love; it lay in a tiny bed, bundled up in warmth. He was scuffing along in a stupor of sleep deprivation and dreams. It was his turn to check on the boy and he never minded the chore. Little Jordan was mesmerizing. He knew Jennifer would make a beautiful baby, but he was not prepared for the emotional connection toward his son. He loved Jennifer with all his heart, but this was different. It was like beholding a tiny little Wes and he stood there considering a second opportunity to do better.

"Uh-hum…" Jennifer cleared her throat as she leaned against the doorway wearing one of his oversized t-shirts. "Are you coming back to bed, Mr. Lyons? Or have you decided to change roommates?" She leaned her head to the side as she crossed her arms waiting for an answer.

"Mrs. Lyons, I will *never* change roommates, but would you take a long, hard look at the boy in the bassinet? Isn't he perfect? It is like seeing yourself without all the scars, mistakes and blemishes."

"He *is* perfect. But, so are you, babe. Perfect *for me.*" She hugged Wes around the waist, while he gazed back at his new son. "We are so blessed. We are *so blessed.*"

He held her and spoke a simple prayer aloud, "Lord keep us a family like we are right here, right now. Bless us all and help us give you glory. In Jesus' name. Amen."

"Amen." Jennifer echoed. "Now... join me for some apple pie in the kitchen?"

"Apple pie? We still have some apple pie?"

"I put some back for tonight. It seems we have regular midnight meetings in the hall and I was thinking it might help us go back to sleep."

"I never turn down a beautiful girl ... or pie."

"Watch it, Romeo. You better turn down the other beautiful women."

"Oh, I was just teasing. You *are* beautiful, and I do love pie." He flashed an exaggerated, disingenuous smile and planted a big smooch right on her lips.

She giggled, turned and took off. "First one to the kitchen gets the biggest piece." She slid around the corner in her socks and missed the next corner toward the refrigerator.

Wes clipped her in the end and beat her to the refrigerator door, and the pie. "All mine; the big piece is all mine."

"I didn't want the large piece anyway," Jennifer chided. "I have got to get these last ten pounds off from my pregnancy. It was fun eating pickles and ice cream, but not nearly as much fun taking *off* the weight I gained."

"You are still beautiful to me, Jen." He took a slice out of the pie plate and served it to Jennifer, while he just kept the entire pie plate and the one remaining piece for himself. "C'mon, sit down a minute." He pulled out a chair for her at the table.

"Uh, oh. You've been thinking again."

"What is that supposed to mean?" His words were muffled as he stuffed another huge bite in his mouth. "I was just thinking that I needed to bring in more money. We have a family and I have to be thinking about the future."

Jennifer dropped her fork right in the plate and stared at a man she thought she knew. Funny, compassionate, smart, and talented were all what made Wes…Wes. But, conservative and cautious? Not so much. "You are probably right, but what sparked these thoughts?"

"I want to be a good daddy. I want to give our son *everything*. Well, at least I want to give him all he needs and some of what he wants. I better start making a plan."

"*We* better start making a plan." He tapped his fork with hers and they both laughed. Jennifer now mumbled through a mouthful of apple pie, "Watch out, world, the Lyons's are coming! Do you have any ideas?"

"Well, Dad has that opening for music director at the church." He glanced down at his pie and then back up to her. "You think I should talk to him about it? Apply for the job?"

"Wow, never saw that coming." Jennifer looked him in the eye and knew he was serious.

"Well, I am sure he wouldn't pay me like a guy who has his degree, but I will have a degree in a year or so, and it would be great on my resume. I was just thinking—"

"I think it is a great idea. Maybe it will help bring you two closer, too."

"Yeah, well, I'm not holding my breath on that one. But I do think he would like to help out his grandson, and he knows I need work. Maybe he will do it for his grandson."

"Uh, oh, did you hear that? There he goes again." Jennifer closed her eyes as solace slipped away.

"What..." Wes gazed into space, "oh, I hear it now. He *is* crying." Jordan started picking up the volume, "Waaaa-waaaa-waa."

Wes turned to Jen, "Let's rock, paper, scissors for it."

Jen agreed, "Okay, loser changes the diaper."

"You're on."

The two new parents slam their fist into their other palm twice and then Jen threw out scissors and Wes threw out paper."

"I have it, babe." He smiled. "I knew you would throw out scissors. I want to spend some more time with him anyway."

"Wes Lyons, you are a saint."

"Well, if he blew out his drawers like a poop volcano, I may come find you!" They both broke into uncontrolled laughter.

"I love you, Mr. Lyons."

"I love you, too, Mrs. Lyons."

They strolled down the hall hand-in-hand and as they approached their son's room, Wes kissed Jennifer's forehead and turned to give his crying son the attention he needed.

"I'll keep your spot warm, babe, thanks." Jennifer knew she had a keeper. Oh, there would always be the unexpected things like buying a library of records to learn Portuguese, or stepping into the kitchen to find more flour on the floor than in the mixing bowl, when he was trying to surprise her with a birthday cake. He was a spontaneous, unconventional, loving man and she knew she was lucky.

Wes sat in his car practicing his speech over and over. He turned the rear view mirror so he could see his delivery. *Here you go. Wes. Do your thing.* With papers in hand, he stood at the door of his childhood home. *Knock, knock, knock.*

Harold opened the door and was pleasantly surprised to see Wes standing before him. "Hi, son. How's the baby?"

"Jordan is great. Can I come in and talk with you a bit?" He poised himself to step into his childhood home.

"Sure, son. Absolutely. Come in."

Wes wasted no time. "I would like to apply for your open position, Dad. I know I have not graduated yet, but I will work hard and Jen and I could really use the extra money. Her little job at T. G. & Y. won't pay all the bills while I am still in school."

"Let's go to the kitchen." Harold directed.

Wes was glad they were going to the kitchen, a much more neutral territory than Harold's office.

"You want some coffee? Help yourself." Harold poured himself a cup and made himself comfortable at the table. He lifted his head from his coffee and searched his son's eyes. "Really? You want to work at Kingsridge? How did you find out about the job?"

"Like everyone else, I guess, I saw it in the 'Help Wanted' section of the paper." Wes decided he would take his dad up on the offer for coffee after all. He got up and poured a cup of Joe.

"You searched the paper for jobs."

"Yes, Dad. I need a job."

"My son looked in the paper—"

"Yes, I looked in the paper for jobs."

Pastor Lyons went on, "Well, I am just amazed you picked up a newspaper ... for anything."

"Dad, I am not the same ole screw-up I used to be. I am a man. I have a wife and a son. I need a real job."

"You don't have a degree." Harold pointed out.

"I graduate in May." Wes debated.

"You don't even really like the church." Harold noted.

"I don't like some of the repetitious, ceremonial routines, but I love God and I love music. And... the people love me, Dad. Every time I play and sing for your church, they love it."

"I don't know, Wes. I think you are too wild for our church."

"Dad, please. I need a job."

"Don't 'please, I need a job' me. You got your girlfriend pregnant and then eloped to some Justice of the Peace on the other side of town and got married to save face."

Filled with anger at the sight of the world's biggest hypocrite, Wes calmed his emotions, knowing his family was depending on him. He was making this decision to sustain his family, not to make his dad proud. "Wow, that is the pot calling the kettle black, isn't it, Dad? We got married because we love each other. That is all and that is enough. Having a baby does not change the fact that I love my wife. Back off." Wes stood, hurt and broken after stepping forward in humility to ask his condescending, self-righteous father for help.

"Ah, sit down. Are you sure you want this job? You will be placed in a position of recognition in the church. Do you want to be seen as a church guy?"

"I want to be a guy who uses his gifts and talents to serve people. No, I never thought I would be working with you, but I always wanted to use my talents to help and encourage people, and I would be doing that."

"I can't pay you like I would someone who has a degree. The deacons would think I was giving you special treatment."

"Do you really care what *they* think more than you care about helping your new grandson?"

"I have to care about appearances and perception; without it, neither one of us would have a job."

Wes swallowed his pride. "How much would you pay me for the job opening you posted in the paper?" He clasped his hands and steadied his eyes on his father's eyes, which was very hard to do. It took extra effort to keep eye contact with his father. Growing up, he always felt he didn't measure up in his dad's eyes and would glance at the ground when his dad looked him in the eye. Not today. Today, he was standing up for himself and his family.

"You really want this job, huh?"

"Yes, sir." Wes maintained his eye contact and waited for Harold's response, like a mature man in negotiations with his future employer.

"I will pay you $20.00 less per week because you have no degree. You must be on time, and you must not rock the boat. This is *my congregation,* and I will run the show."

"How about $15.00 less per week, and just a reminder, this is God's church, Dad. I would be thrilled to work in God's house, and I promise I will do all I can to glorify God."

"Yeah, yeah, it *is* God's house, but I am the boss. Deal. I will pay you $15.00 less per week and you will plan, perform, and educate the church in music."

"Thanks, Dad. I won't let you down." Wes got up, elated that he now had a better way to provide for his family. He ran over to hug his dad and found himself awkwardly reaching out to hug a man that had the warmth and expression of a chunk of wood. "Oh, yeah, when I graduate, I expect not only a raise but a promotion. That is if everything works out for both of us."

"Son, if we last a year working together, I will do exactly that."

"I will make it work. Thank you. I won't forget it."

###

Wes went through his house to a quiet place in the back-yard. He knelt by the oak tree and thanked God for blessing him with a job. *God, thank you for this opportunity. I will do my best for the congregation, my dad, and you, Lord. Please guide me and help me do the job as you would have me do it. In Jesus' name, Amen.*

Jennifer saw him out the window and saw a man changing before her eyes. He was a joyful kid filled with compassion, love, and spirit. She was watching Jordan, his baby, still unable to speak, teach Wes how to grow up and be a man of conviction and faith. Jennifer bowed her head. "Lord, I knew the man I loved was a good man, capable of insight, love, giving, and encouragement. I was not sure how a baby would change him. Thank you for being a heavenly Father who is teaching Wes how to be a man. In Jesus' name. Amen."

Wes got up off his knees and saw Jennifer by the window. "I got the job. I got the job," he shouted as he ran to hug her. "We will be alright, Jennifer. This job is the beginning of something big."

"That is awesome, sweetie. Always the optimist and always my knight in shining armor." She hugged him, and they strolled hand-in-hand back to the living room.

She had no idea how right Wes's comment was. *This job was the start of something big.* The world would hear from Wes Lyons.

Chapter 23

Present Day

Mr. Epstein sat at the entry of the activity room, his hair slicked back with Vaseline and a smile so big it seemed to close his eyes. He waited with anticipation as people could be seen approaching the room from down the hall. "Come to the bingo extravaganza!" He was the welcoming committee and the bouncer, all in one guy. He seemed harmless enough, but don't cross the ole codger! He could put you out the door, just like he could welcome you in.

Mrs. Klinger was slowly gliding to Bingo in her wheelchair. She was dressed in her gathered skirt and bright floral blouse.

Good morning, Mrs. Klinger! My, you are beautiful this morning. Please come in." He guided her into the activity room like an airport worker flagging a plane into the correct position.

"Good morning, Mr. Epstein. Is that a new shirt?"

Mr. Epstein peeked down at his shirt as if he forgot what he had put on that morning. "Oh, no, this is a shirt from a few Christmases back. Thought I would dust it off this morning." He grinned at the compliment.

As she entered the room, others started rounding the corner. Bingo had become a popular pastime. Many planned their entire day around the bingo tables of camaraderie and competition. "Prepare to get beat!" Mr. Epstein chuckled as he announced the demise of his competitors.

James rolled through the doors and gave Mr. Epstein a challenge. "Guess you're forgetting the competitive spirit of the Wii Grand Champion for 2024. Check your words, Mr. Epstein, while you check your bingo dauber." James won the yearlong Wii competition at Fireside, like the World Series of Wii, after months of regular play. There was no one more competitive than Mr. Epstein and Mr. Johnson. Both grew up having to outperform and outsmart others around them. It was almost as if all those years of competing for opportunity had led them to this opportunity for dominance and they both enjoyed the clash of wills.

James rolled up to his table and organized his three bingo cards to his liking. He tested his dauber on a scrap piece of paper to ensure it functioned properly. Once he was settled and his claim was staked at his table, he rolled over to get some iced tea and sweetener.

Erma clomped down the hall in heels that were a bit too tall, causing her to appear as graceful as an infantryman at war, lumbering down the hall with an expression of *why did I choose these shoes today?* "All right, all right. Settle in everybody; we need to get going. The Christian Church will take over the room in an hour for hymn singing."

Mr. Epstein snapped his head around. "We will give them the room when we are finished. First come first serve, Erma."

"We will comply with the facility schedule, Mr. Epstein. If you want to get finished, I would suggest we get started."

Mr. Epstein hated being put in his place in front of others. There was simply no need. He was an old man, with little to no political leverage in the assisted living center. "Attila, I mean Erma, what are you doing here?" The whole room swiveled their heads in his direction. Everyone wanted to ask, but only Mr. Epstein had the guts.

"Why Mr. Epstein, might I remind you that I am the administrator of this fine facility and I have an unwritten invitation to all activities at Fireside. Besides, the activity director is out sick, and the only way you will have bingo today is if I am the caller."

Erma was an eternal wet blanket on all that went on at Fireside. When residents gathered, if Erma showed up, the party fell apart in a matter of minutes. It was like she let the air out of the fun balloon. Erma clomped up to the front of the room, *Okay, how hard can this be? Turn the handle on the cage holding the numbered balls. Open the little door, pull out the ball, and read the number.*

Mr. Epstein continued his watch over the entry of the room, as if he was waiting on someone. He maintained his watch like a centurion and then examined left and right down the empty hallway. Then a smile spread across his face. Ruth turned the corner with a Walmart sack on one arm and her purse on the other. When she saw Mr. Epstein waiting at the entry, her pace quickened, and she couldn't help but give him a big wave.

"Okay, we are ready to start, now." Mr. Epstein grabbed Ruth's hand as she got near and they peered into each other's eyes, as if it had been months since they were together. "See the one in the back, that is our table." He gave a wink and motioned for her to step in front, while he rolled behind.

"Okay, keep the chatter down, y'all," Erma's voice grated on everyone's nerves. It wasn't that it was squeaky, or too loud, although she *was* loud. It was simply that most of the time when Erma showed up, the residents and employees already had things flowing smoothly, and in the course of Erma flexing her administrative muscles, she usually found a way to strip them of their humanity or expression. "I see that the caller's table is at the front of the room, near the drinks table. I think it would be better if I bring the calling station to the rear of the room, where there is more space."

Tuning her out, Mr. Epstein was giving Ruth all his attention. "It is so good to see you, Ruth. I have been counting the days till you returned." His cheeks blushed and he scooted closer to her chair.

Just behind him, Erma settled in with her microphone and bingo calling equipment. The rest of the room had adjusted their chairs to see her and were poised with dobbers in hand and hearing aids turned up.

Erma checked her watch and grimaced as bingo was starting late, and she wanted the hymn singing to be timely. Without doing a mic check, she plodded along to get bingo out of the way.

Her voice boomed across the small PA system and feedback screeched and hummed. "Good morning; let's get going."

Mr. Epstein reflexively covered his ears and yelled, "What? What? What are you doing?" He jerked so hard that his knees banged the bottom of the table, causing Ruth to instinctively turn to inspect for skin tears.

"No, no, my knees are just fine, it is my brain that is suffering, listening to that battle-ax run the show." He turned to Erma. "We like it the way *we* like it, and that is the way it has always been. We don't need you rearranging bingo or improving it to your subpar standards. You almost gave me a heart attack. Turn it down, move to the front, and give the mic to someone else."

"Who do you propose I hand the mic to? You?"

"No." He spun about quickly for an idea when Ginger clomped by. "Ginger will do it." He put his hand up to his mouth trying to amplify his shout. "Ginger. Ginger, come here. We need you."

Ginger knew his voice without seeing him. She also knew that she was usually called in this manner when Erma was on the loose. She peered in the room that held twenty elders, poised with dobbers similar to shoe polish bottles, all staring at her with the hope that she could get Erma down the hall and their game on the road. "Hi, everyone. What's up."

"I have it all under control, Ginger. You can move on down the hall." Erma stood with a stance that suggested she loved the spotlight and could have broken into a chorus of Cabaret.

"The only thing she has under control is her hair sprayed so heavy, it would break if anything brushed against it," Mr. Epstein blurted out before he even thought. The room tried to stifle a group chuckle. Erma's hair was always fixed and sprayed with enough lacquer to embalm her entire body.

"The activity director couldn't come, so I decided to fill in so that the inspiring hymn singing can stay on schedule." Erma reported with an agitated tone.

Ginger poked her head in the door. "Okay. How many of you will also attend the hymn singing group?" No one raised their hand. "None of you?" *Silence.* "I will go up front and put a sign up noting that the hymn singing has been moved to the commons area at the front entry. Erma, why don't you receive them as they enter the building and direct them to the commons area? I will help the bingo game get started. A win-win for everybody."

"Yeah, Bertha, I mean Erma, go meet your hymn singers up front; we have this taken care of." Mr. Epstein whined and crossed his arms in front of his little abdominal paunch in defiance.

"Well, Ginger, I think that is a great idea. The hymn singers can greet the public with spiritual songs as visitors enter the building. That is even better than I had hoped."

Ginger took the microphone from Erma. "I think we have it from here."

Erma scanned across the room. "Carry on. I see you are in good hands." As she left, snickers and chatter escorted her out the door.

Ginger sat on the corner of a table up front. She turned off the microphone. "Don't need this."

As she clicked it off, James piped up, "Sure don't, Ginger, we can hear you into the next county, and most of us are deaf." The room laughed, half because it was funny and half because it was true.

"Okay, okay, I get it. So, I am not the most demure woman in the room, but I got your back and I think you are more than capable of playing bingo when and how you want to."

"How about offering prizes we *want,* too?" Mrs. Klinger interjected. Everyone turned around, because she usually remained quiet.

"What do you mean?" Ginger quizzed Mrs. Klinger.

"I am so tired of getting bubble gum and seasonal wall hangings. I have a drawer full of arts and crafts, bubble gum, and calendars. Bubble gum sticks to my dentures; arts and crafts make a mess of paper and glitter, and I really hate calendars. They remind me of how old I am, how many doctor's appointments I have, and how long it has been since I got a visitor. You will not see a single calendar within eyesight in my room."

Ginger listened and took in her words. "I never thought of that, Mrs. Klinger. You have a very good point. Okay. Let's do this. Let's play for ..." She found a sack full of Snickers and bananas on the table. This was not going to go over well. She opened the drawer and swept the sack into the desk's abyss. "Let's put something valuable out there. How about we play five games? The winner of each game gets to be first in line the next time the podiatrist comes to trim toenails. What do you think?"

"Now you're talkin'," James shouted out. "But *I* should only count for half of a winner on this one, since I only have one foot." James burst into laughter and the room followed.

"Ginger this is a wonderful idea." Mrs. Klinger held up both arms. "Let's get ready to RUM-BLE." She returned her hands to her lap.

"What did you say?" Ginger quickly glanced to make sure it was Mrs. Klinger who made the last comment.

"I don't know what that really means, but they say that before all those fake wrestling competitions. Sorry everyone, but I am going for blood; my toenails are hideous." Mrs. Klinger settled into her chair, ready to begin.

Mr. Epstein held up one finger and surprised everyone with the loud, whining volume of his voice. "Make room for me. I haven't seen a podiatrist since Bush was president. Old man Bush, not the son." His shoulders bounced with each chuckle.

"Okay, everyone. Here we go." Ginger spun the cage with the large, numbered plastic pills mixing inside. "B10. Mark B10 on your cards." Ginger had a list of other things she could be doing, but she was enjoying herself, so the rest could wait.

Chapter 24
1980s

Loretta sat with Harold in the waiting room. The neurologist was late, and their nerves were shot. Hopefully they would get answers. Loretta grabbed Harold's tremoring hand, keeping it softly in her safe touch.

"I wish I could make it stop." He stared at his hand as if it had a life separate from his body.

"The nurse opened a side door and read from the chart she was holding, "Harold Lyons?" She gave the full waiting room the once-over and made eye contact with Harold.

He nodded and in a quiet, monotone voice replied, "Here." Loretta raised her hand.

Harold stood, feeling as if everyone in the room was watching him. He stepped forward with slow, shuffling steps. The harder he tried to speed up, the more bound his legs felt, like they were made of concrete.

Loretta stayed by his side, refusing to go ahead of him.

"Right this way, Mr. Lyons." Recognizing his slow speed, the nurse slowed her pace to accommodate him.

Harold and Loretta sat in the treatment room and reviewed their notes. "Maybe this will be the time, Harold. We have prayed for answers. We have to believe we will get them."

The doctor came in with a confidence that seeped through his lab coat. "Hello, Mr. Lyons."

"Hello." Harold's voice trembled as he became nervous. No emotion was detected in his usually expressive voice.

"Can you speak any louder, Mr. Lyons?"

"No. That is part of the problem. I am a preacher and cannot control my voice."

"Hmm. Let me take a look here. Can you walk to the door and back to your seat?"

Harold stood and tried to take a step, but it was as if his feet were stuck to the ground and his legs were frozen. "When I get nervous, it gets worse. I am really nervous."

"Let's do some other things first. Let me see your arms." Harold held out his arm and the tremor was obvious. "Relax your arm the best you can." The doctor tried to move his arm quickly, bending it at the elbow, but Harold's elbow had catches in it, moving clunk by clunk like a cogwheel. The doctor handed Harold a piece of paper and a pen. "Write your name, address, and phone number on this paper." Harold's handwriting was small and bumpy. It continued to get smaller the more he wrote and it trailed off uphill on the paper. "Okay. Now that we are a bit further into the exam, can you walk to the door?"

Harold got up and shuffled slow steps to the door and back, embarrassed with the way he performed and the functional decline he showed.

"Thank you." He held out his hand to direct Harold back to his chair. The doctor pulled his stool up to talk with them face-to-face. "The preliminary things you just showed me reveal a neurological trend. We will have to do more testing, but many of your symptoms are consistent with Parkinson's Disease. Do you know if any of your family has similar problems?"

Harold and Loretta turned to each other. "Wow, this has a name, huh?" Harold cleared his throat, hoping it would improve his voice. "I don't know, but I have relatives on the east coast." The longer he spoke, his voice got softer and he began to stutter.

"The stutter is another symptom," the neurologist added.

Harold's fears were confirmed. His difficulty in the pulpit was becoming a problem. *What good is a preacher that no one can hear*? "I am having trouble preaching. They can't hear me."

"Parkinson's is a progressive disease of the brain. It will not kill you, but it will rob you of your bodily functions. The tremors, the small steps, the soft, stuttering voice are all a part of Parkinson's Disease."

Tears streaked down Loretta's face. She knew what this meant. His preaching days were numbered.

"There is limited treatment for Parkinson's, although we are learning more about it all the time. Stay active. This is one of the best things you can do. The longer you sit still, the stiffer you will become." This cut right to the heart of Harold. He sat hours upon end to prepare his sermons.

"Okay. I need to think about things." He squinted down at his trembling hand.

"Let me see you again in one month. Here is a prescription to take in the meantime. We will see if it has helped at your next visit."

The doctor wrote on a notepad, tore off the first page, and handed it to Loretta. Harold was still gazing downward.

As they left, Harold managed a brief smile and grabbed Loretta's hand for support, physically and emotionally.

"Thanks." Harold mustered, as they left the office, turning his attention away from the doctor and toward a new world that held new obstacles.

As they neared their car, Loretta tried to be encouraging. "We can do this, Harold. There will be new challenges, but there will also be new opportunities." Loretta spoke these words just as much for herself as she did for Harold. "We have spent our lives, day in and day out, watching others with challenges and praying for them, but *really* not understanding their plight. We will learn how to recognize blessings in the middle of struggles. God is big enough for all of our problems."

"My preaching." Harold's voice cracked in soft tones. "God called me to preach."

Silence flooded the air. Loretta had no answers and all she could offer was her presence and prayer. As they passed a park bench, Loretta turned to Harold. "Come here, honey." She saw her husband, heartbroken, and lost in spirit. Always so driven and motivated, he gave his heart to preaching the Word of God. Daily, he prayed with conviction that his preaching would be heard and God's will would be revealed.

Loretta turned to Harold and took his hands. "Do you want to pray for us?"

"I can't. I am lost. I have no words."

"Do you want me to?" Loretta was doing anything she could to encourage Harold.

Harold sat with his shoulders slumped and his trembling hands clasped and simply nodded *yes*.

Loretta quieted her soul, hoping the right words would flow like honey. She waited and felt a peace that calmed her spirit, but she had no miraculous words. She sat with her shattered husband, offering a questioning mind and a confident heart. "Lord, I sit with Harold asking you for answers and direction. We need you, Lord. We don't understand how you can achieve your purpose in Harold without his voice and with difficulties just stepping across the room. We question ourselves, but we do not question you. Give us new eyes for a vision we have not seen before; give us new motivation and direction for our lives, serving people and serving you. In Jesus' name we pray, Amen."

She squeezed Harold's hand and leaned in. "Just one foot in front of the other."

"Easy for you to say." Harold tried to break the tension with a laugh. He stood, hugged Loretta and took her hand in his. "Yes. We will put one foot in front of the other ...slowly, but we will always step forward." They strolled away with Harold shuffling a slow gait that drained his energy.

Chapter 25
Present Day

Wes grabbed his Bible and flipped to Titus. He dug into the secret recess created to conceal his vice. Oxy was a driving force in his life. He was drawn to it like a dog was drawn to its own vomit. *What the hell?* He got a paper clip and scraped the bottom of the secret compartment intended to hide his stash. Nothing. Empty. He tossed the Bible on his bed and rushed directly to the hiding place he made near the mirror in his bathroom. He knew there was a supply here, but it was limited. He only had enough to get him through another day or two. He grabbed a couple of pills, chewed and chased them with vodka. Once he swallowed, he closed his eyes in relief, knowing his sweats, pain, and shakes would be remedied for only a few hours. *Well, time for me to visit Skylar.*

###

Ginger stood in front of her first nursing aide class, a class she hoped would become a pipeline for future *good* nurses. "I want each of you to remember, although this class does not count toward your official nursing licensure for the State of Georgia, I can promise you that you will be the most prepared group in your class, if you have taken this preparation with me." She rubbed her hands together, like she couldn't wait to start. "So, you want to be a licensed nurse? Why? Let's go around the room and I want you to tell me what you think it will be like. Let's start over there."

The first student started off, "Well, I see myself helping people and saving lives. I want to change the world one patient at a time."

"Oh, that is beautiful. In fact, it belongs on a t-shirt." Ginger put her hand over her heart. "But what a crock of crap."

Hoping they heard Ginger's comment wrong, they gawked at each other, then studied Ginger's face in jaw dropping question.

"Really? Won't we help heal the world?" They were asking each other.

"Hello... nurses. You *will* make a difference in the world, one patient at a time. Occasionally, you will save someone from the pits of death, but mostly you will get peed and pooped on, cussed, work long hours, and make a decent living. But, if you were to compute the amount per hour you will be making, you would be better off at McDonalds. You will work Christmas and Independence Day and sneak out the back door for the smoke break you educate your patients will kill them." Ginger searched the eyes of one student after another. "Oh, and if you are doing it for the right reasons and you want to help people, you will spend countless hours, doing the right thing, on your own time, without getting paid."

Skylar sat on the front row. "I know there will be difficult days, but I think there couldn't be a better job than helping someone through the worst days of their life. How exciting."

Ginger scattered handouts about the room. "I like the way you think, Skylar. Class, today we are doing an experiential lab. The remainder of the afternoon will be spent in the dining room. Each one of you will go to the Fireside entryway, get one of the facility wheelchairs and meet me back in the dining room."

"Oh, how fun. This is going to be great." The class was chattering with excitement.

Ginger monitored her watch. "You have five minutes to get your wheelchair and be prepared for class in the dining room."

The class dispersed and they were electric with excitement. The first students out the door started running and Ginger shut them down. "Walk don't run. We represent professionals not hellions."

The students marched quickly but orderly to the entryway, where they kept the facility wheelchairs. Each grabbed a wheelchair and pushed them to the dining room. Several checked their watches but realized there was no time to go to the restroom, as five minutes passed quickly.

Ginger entered the classroom and announced there were release forms on the table. "These forms state you are voluntarily participating in this lab exercise. It will increase understanding of your patients. Read and sign the forms, then sit in your wheelchair till all have finished."

The students questioned, "Really? We have to sign a release form... for class?"

"Oh, just like when you are working on the job, you may get stuff on your clothes and you could be injured, using equipment for the first time. It is just for completeness." Skylar offered. "Right?" Skylar was the first to read and sign the form. "School is school; they never said it would be easy. Done." The others followed suit and they all sat back in their wheelchairs.

"I am going to give you all an opportunity to feel the impact of age today. Some will experience challenges of a stroke through hemiplegia, others will experience blindness or deafness, some will experience memory issues and others will be discounted just because of who they are."

Oh, this is gonna be fun, students were telling each other. Then one… then two… then three students stood and started to leave the dining room. One turned to Ginger. "We will be right back. Five minutes was not enough time to get a wheelchair *and* go to the bathroom."

"Sorry, class. That is not a part of the opportunity I am giving you."

"Opportunity? I am not asking for an opportunity. I need to pee."

"In a place like this, *that* can be considered a privilege for some people. Okay, listen up. There are ten of you. There are ten portable changing rooms over there, pointing to ten portable exam screens. Each of you go to a changing area and put on what I have prepared for you behind the screens."

"What have we agreed to?" One student whined. Another answered, "I don't know, but we better get moving. The longer we delay, the longer we will be here."

Ginger clapped her hands and rubbed them together. "Now that's the spirit."

Some of the students stood to go behind the exam screens and Ginger stopped them. "Whoa, whoa, guys. Nope. Use the wheelchairs you were assigned. For this section of the lab, all mobility will be done with wheelchairs."

"Ugh. Are you serious?" One student complained.

"Oh, C'mon, y'all," Skylar encouraged. "It will be fun." She was the first to push her wheelchair behind the curtain. When she saw what was waiting for her, she held in her reaction, but even *she* was surprised. She pushed her wheelchair back around the corner holding an adult diaper up for everyone to see. Along with a diaper, Skylar had a pair of goggles that had been sprayed with black paint to help mimic blindness. Another made her way around to show the rest of the class a diaper and an elastic Ace wrap bandage. Another had a diaper and noise-canceling headphones. This continued till they all stood speechless, looking at each other. They all had a replicated disability and they all had a diaper.

"I will help those who have elastic wraps, but the rest of you should be able to get ready for the exercise by yourself." Ginger checked out the room, proud of herself.

All the smiles in the room were starting to sour. "I thought we were going to sit in class and learn proper vital signs technique."

"Oh, you will. You'll sit in class, hear lectures, and prepare for a test."

"A test?" All ten students said in unison. Now all the fun was *completely* squeezed out of it. Diapers… now a test. Class couldn't get much worse. Ginger helped those who were given elastic Ace wraps. She wrapped the right arm and leg to prevent their use, providing the experience of someone who had a stroke.

"Okay, Great. Gather up class. Take a place at the table by the easel." Ginger was giddy with anticipation at the thought of what was to come. With everyone seated at the table, Ginger began, "This afternoon you will all get the opportunity to experience a fraction of what our patients go through every day, twenty-four hours a day. It's about to get real in here."

The students scrutinized the situation and it all made sense now. Ginger laid out the exercise to the class. "For this exercise, some of you can't see, some can't hear, and some won't be able to use half of their body. All of you should be wearing diapers, and all should need to go to the bathroom right about now. I have recruited some of our residents to help us out. Come on in, y'all." The class glanced at the classroom entrance to see a parade of elders entering the room with smiles from ear-to-ear. "To function, you will *have* to enlist the help of these elders. I have asked the elders to respond to your requests with the same reply they have commonly received from each of you." Ginger allowed a long pause and visually scanned the room to see the expressions on the students' faces. Many of the faces were easy to read ...*aw, shit.*

"Elders, please go find a partner to assist and sit next to them. You will be their lifeline. *They* must ask *you* for help. So, each student will eat a snack, and participate in the lecture. Everyone should take notes for future reference. You should make 100% if you fully participate in this exercise."

It was clear by viewing the elders' faces that they were relishing the opportunity. Residents ready to go included James Johnson, Mrs. Klinger, Mr. Epstein, and several others. The room was chattering with excitement and introductions.

"All right, let's get started." The elders fanned out across the room and waited for Ginger to give final instructions. "Okay, residents, you are not required to do one thing in this exercise. I am asking you to respond to your partner's requests for your help the same way *your* requests were received when you previously asked for help from these staff members. Students, you will not be able to complete this task without the help of the buddy sitting next to you."

A student on the front row pulled out her cell phone. Ginger came by with a sack and opened it for the student.

"What?" She saw the sack and glanced back at her phone. "No. I won't."

Ginger smiled. "Okay, I hate that you are leaving the program. Well, nursing is not for everybody." Ginger turned to return to the front of the room.

"I didn't quit," the student debated.

"Listen. You can participate or you can interrupt and stop the class. If you don't want to play by *my* rules, you aren't on the team. Remember, I am the one who picks the team. Yes ... you have to put your phone, the distraction magnet, in the bag. And ... if anyone else wants to go ahead and put your phone in the bag, do it now if you think you will be pulling it out in the middle of my class.

"Okay, let's get going with the vital signs lecture. Number one, you must sanitize your equipment between each patient. Use Clorox wipes to clean them before and after each use. Number two—"

"Hang on here. I didn't get that." One of the students with the noise-cancelling headphones could hear only mumbling as Ginger spoke but couldn't make out any of her words.

"Your assist is sitting right next to you." The student gave a side-eye to see an exuberant grandma. It was Mrs. Klinger. Seated in her wheelchair as she waited for instructions, Mrs. Klinger was tuned in to the assignment. The student shouted to Mrs. Klinger, "I can't hear what she is saying, can you help me with my notes?"

Mrs. Klinger flagged Ginger and waited a moment.

Ginger nodded at her, "Just tell her what she told you the last time you needed her help. The floor is yours."

Mrs. Klinger read her watch. "I have to go fold towels. I will come back and see what I can do for you on my way back. Okay, sweetie?"

"What? I didn't get that," the student shouted much louder than she usually talked. The headphones muted her world.

Mrs. Klinger increased her volume. "Oh, don't be so dramatic, I will be back in five minutes." She checked her watch, again.

The student wrinkled her brow and her face reddened. "I still can't hear—"

Mrs. Klinger increased her voice volume even more. "I... will... be... back." She turned her back and pushed her wheelchair out of the room.

The student held both palms up as if she was saying, *are you serious?*

Ginger stepped forward and continued her lecture on blood pressure. "Make sure the patient's legs are not crossed and they are breathing normally. Ask the patient if they have a preference of arm to be used for the blood pressure cuff." Ginger took the cuff in hand. "If they have no preference, you should use the left arm, as it is the standard testing position."

"Excuse me. I have to go to the bathroom." Another student turned to Ginger for permission.

"I am here to teach the class, it's not *my* job to help you." Ginger pointed to the resident next to him, Mr. Epstein, who was patiently waiting for his chance to turn the tables on the nursing aides. "As we continue, I am going to keep teaching. You have got to ask for help from those who have been assigned to help you."

"This guy can't get me to the bathroom. He is all shriveled up."

"As far as I am concerned, you can just use your diaper. 'An eye for an eye and a tooth for a tooth'," Mr. Epstein said without a flinch. He had been left without assistance more than once.

The student glared at Mr. Epstein in disbelief. "I can't believe it. This old man is ..."

Ginger stopped talking and turned toward the student. "He is what?"

"Yeah, I am what?" Mr. Epstein crossed his arms and leaned to get a full view of the student's face. "To the best of my memory, the last time I had to get ready for my colonoscopy, I didn't think I could get to the toilet in time and you told me that you were on your way to your break and that you would check on me when you were finished."

"Needless to say, I was 'finished' long before you returned. You don't even remember me, do you? Well, I will *never* forget *you*. Never." Mr. Epstein held up one finger. "This is written on my memory just like the Ten Commandments were written on the sacred tablets."

"*Please*, Mr. Eckstein. Please."

"Ep-stein," Mr. Epstein said, popping the "p", "The name is Epstein."

"Mr. Epstein, I understand more fully how this makes you feel. I will never—"

"Okay, don't go getting mushy. Hold on to the push handle of my wheelchair. I can pull you to the bathroom. Can you stand up to get on the toilet? If not, you will just have to use your diaper or I will have to go find someone else who is free."

"Oh, yes. I can stand and get on the toilet. I just have to get off this carpet; it makes it harder to push the wheelchair with one arm and one leg. If I get close by, I can do the rest."

"Okay. Ginger, is it okay if I take him to the bathroom?"

"Of course, if that is your decision."

Mr. Epstein inspected the student's face, enjoying the leverage he suddenly had gained over the boy. "We will be fine. Everyone needs help at some time in their life." Mr. Epstein gave a nod to Ginger. "Please excuse us. We will be right back." Mr. Epstein backed up for the boy to grab hold of the pushing hand grips, and they worked as a team to get to the bathroom.

James was seated with Skylar. As the lecture continued, she tried to keep all the facts straight in her head, but she started getting confused. Her frustration was palpable.

James leaned into her. "Can I help out? By the rules of this exercise, I am supposed to interact with you, the way you have treated me over my time here. You have been nothing but professional and helpful to me. Now, the way I see it, if we work together, you will ace this test and show your buddies what it is like to be a good teammate."

"Really? I hate to ask, but okay. I need help."

James took her tablet and pen and focused on Ginger. "I will take your notes. Let's kick some butt."

Ginger took notice of the interactions throughout the room. Most of the residents were enjoying their front-row view of karma, playing out in real time; they loved it.

Ginger scanned about the room and turned off the overhead projector. "That concludes my presentation on vital signs, but it was *really* an exercise in something more important. Stop. Quiet down. Look around you. Everyone, *look around you*. How limited were you functionally? Could you get along without help? Could you *thrive* without help?"

Mrs. Klinger pushed her wheelchair back in the room, holding up her watch. "There now. Where were we? Oh, yes. Have you found someone else to help you or do you still need *my* help?" She made eye contact with the girl she had been partnered with and gave a little half smile.

"Did you say something to me?" The girl turned her head toward Mrs. Klinger and then to Ginger. By now her hair seemed disguised as Medusa's head from running her fingers through it, her glasses were smudged due to fidgeting, and her temperament was edgy.

Ginger stepped back with her hands held up like Pontius Pilot, showing she had no blood on her hands. "This is totally between you and Mrs. Klinger."

"Sweetie, do you need my help?" Mrs. Klinger now felt she had proven her point and she transformed from the wicked witch of the West, back to Glenda the good witch. "You see, the way we talk to each other is so important, especially if you hold all the power. Although you are all, I'm sure, fine people; we are here because we need help. I don't want to sound harsh, but if you have a hard time doing that, maybe you should find another vocation."

Ginger stood and gave a slow clap applause. "That ... *that* is what this whole exercise was about. That small amount of degradation you felt over these last few minutes is felt by these residents every single time you make it sparkling clear that they are not a priority in your day. Let me make this perfectly clear. These residents *are* your day. They are the reason you are here. I learned a lot today. I learned that many of you have some soul searching to do. Skylar, you were the only one who had already fostered a great relationship with James. Good work. For that, you will make an "A" in the exercise. All the rest of you, when we meet again, you will have a ten-question multiple choice quiz over blood pressure. Relationships, people, we are in a profession that requires good manners and good people skills. You are dismissed."

As the class dispersed, their faces reflected a confused and exhausted expression. They filed out one by one, zombies with a lot to think about.

Wes sat down the hall with a good view of the now adjourning class, anxious to corner Skylar.

Wes wrung his hands and cleared his throat repeatedly as he waited. He had been reading the paper in a nearby wingback chair, ready for Skylar's class to adjourn. The other students were physically and mentally spent, but she was excited with all she learned and was walking with a purpose in her step and a smile on her face.

Wes saw her exit the classroom and recognized his opportunity. "Skylar, hi." He ran his hand through his mop of hair and drew on his acting experience to present an air of calm and control. "I was going to ask for you later, but I raise my head and here you are." He gave an over-jubilant, forced chuckle as he wiped his sweaty palms on his pants. He tried to make eye contact to see if he was connecting with her. "Can we talk for just a minute? I have some good news." He held out an arm directing her to a secluded nook with a couple of chairs and a small bookshelf.

"Oh, hi, Pastor Lyons. Do I need to come and check your temperature?"

Wes relaxed his posture as he heard the words he was hoping to hear, *check your temperature,* his code phrase for 'I need oxy.'

"Oh, that would be great. Yes, I am not feeling well." He touched the back of his hand to his forehead. "Yeah, I think I might have a fever. Thank you."

"Okay. Give me a few minutes. I will meet you in your room with my cart." Skylar had a heart of gold and a desire to help people.

###

Wes heard the firm knock at his door. He got his thoughts together and opened the door to greet her with a smile. "Skylar, thank you so much for stopping by to check me out. How is your grandma doing?"

"Oh, thank you for asking. She is as tough as an ole boot." She smiled with affection for her grandma.

"How is her pain?" He was working it, knowing the emotional empathy for her grandma's pain would transfer to him, even if it was slight, it was something he leaned into.

"Well, she is making do with what she has. No complaining. She is my hero."

Wes took his handkerchief from his pocket and wiped the sweat from his face. "I was wondering if you had any extra *help* for my pain?" He searched her eyes trying to connect to the love she had for her grandma.

"I know I haven't visited you for a while, Pastor Wes. I am starting to have second thoughts—"

"Oh, don't worry about me." He wiped his nose with the back of his hand and forced a smile.

Wes knew the best way to get and keep her help was through Skylar's heartstrings, not through guilting or harassing her into it. "I am just having a rough patch. The worst part about the pain is that it is relentless and slowly grows to a crescendo that you eventually can't ignore." Wes stepped closer to her and she was tuned in with her ears and her heart, listening to every word. "Perhaps the *worst* part is that the doctors got me hooked. They *told* me they were not habit-forming. The people I trusted the most, my doctors, put me in this position."

"What if we get caught? I am in this new class that will prepare me for nursing school. Ginger is teaching it. If we get caught that will be the end of me here at Fireside and my dreams of nursing will be out the door, more like down the toilet."

"But you are risking it for your grandma." Wes was leading her answers with a calm and understanding tone.

"Yes, for now, I have to. My goal is to find another way to help her. There is a new pain management doctor in town. I think we may try him."

"Oh, right..." Wes was thinking on his feet. "I saw a new guy not too long ago and I think he might be helpful." Pinky wasn't a doctor, but she didn't need to know that.

Skylar relaxed a bit. "That is great. Maybe my grandma could see him, too."

He quickly squelched the idea. "Oh, he is a rough ole guy in a nasty office. I can see past that stuff, but your grandma shouldn't have to do that." He was going in for the kill. He reached up to brush his hair out of his face.

The hand tremors were familiar to Skylar. "Grandma's hands do that when she is really hurting."

"Oh, don't mind that." he winced and then smiled. "I thank you for always being so kind to me and helping all these times that I had nowhere to turn. You are a true servant of God. May I pray over you?"

"Pray for me? No one ever asked me if they could pray over me."

"Then you must. It will be a way for me to thank you for all the help you have given me." He pulled his chair to the middle of the room and near the med cart. "Have a seat in this chair and close your eyes. When I feel the Spirit moving within me, I will place my hand on your head for a blessing, as I pray."

Skylar was a girl who blended in with the woodwork. She didn't draw attention to herself. She was never 'the squeaky wheel' so she seldom got the grease, or favors, or compliments, or encouragement. She wasn't going to let this pass by. She was going to have the famous Pastor Wes Lyons pray over her, something she would remember for the rest of her life. "Okay. I guess that would be okay."

He pulled out the chair for her, and she sat with her hands in her lap.

"Give me just a moment to prepare my heart. Why don't you close your eyes and prepare your heart to receive what the Lord is about to tell you?"

Wes scanned the room and came up with a plan. Skylar bowed her head, and he got busy. With her med cart nearby, he scanned the top of the cart and saw the key left in the narcotics push lock. *Bingo.*

"Okay. If you hear me shuffling papers and making noise, I have some of my favorite verses and thoughts in a notebook. You might hear me rustling paper or hear metal clasps click. Sorry about that if you do, but if the Lord moves me to find verses, I will do exactly that." Wes grabbed an old notebook and placed it on the cart.

Skylar was feeling special and taken care of, in a world that generally didn't even notice she was around. She was into it and trusted Pastor Wes implicitly. According to her grandma, if Jesus sat at the right hand of the Father, Wes sat at the right hand of Jesus.

Wes started praying, "Lord, we come to you with problems and needs that only you can fill..." he clicked a pen against the metal cart, desensitizing her to sounds. He saw meds on the top of the cart, but nothing of interest, blood pressure and constipation meds. He shuffled his feet across the linoleum floor, yielding a second texture of sound. "And Lord, I want to thank you for the tender and giving heart of Skylar. She is a true servant, and we are claiming your promises over her life..." He jumped up and down in praise a few times, and a flurry of sounds emerged, change jingling in his pocket, clothes jostling, and a bump into the med cart. As he bumped the cart, he knocked off a box of gloves and another set of keys for the linen closet. "Skylar, give me just a moment to clean up this mess. Just stay in an attitude of prayer, maybe sing "Amazing Grace" for a verse or two."

"Really? I don't know..."

"Oh, just sing like no one is listening, and focus on the words." He continued with random noises and worked on opening the narcotics lock and drawer with other noises.

She began by humming the melody and then followed with singing, "Amazing grace, how sweet the sound…"

"Beautiful. That song is a heartfelt prayer from the heart." The first narcotics bubble pill card Wes saw was for a resident who had just died. Bullseye. He slid his leather-soled shoes across the floor again and crumpled some note paper as he closed and locked the narcotics drawer lock. He kicked the bubble card under his bed and joined in with her rendition of "Amazing Grace." As they finished the verse, Wes spoke up. "So, Lord, I ask that you tuck this child under your wing and pray a hedge of protection about her." He then placed his hands lightly on her head. "Lord, give her insight to see your will and the courage to carry it through. I am so thankful for this young lady, God. Stay with us and lead us in your ways. For it's in Jesus' precious name we pray, Amen."

Skylar raised her head and blinked a few times. "Wow, I kinda feel tingly all over. Thank you for the prayer. I feel like I can take on the world …and win." She turned to face Wes. "Thank you." She gazed down, a bit embarrassed and not knowing exactly what to say. "Guess I better get back out there and save the world." She giggled and gave him a brief sideways hug. "Thanks, Pastor Wes. My grandma is not going to believe this."

That gave Wes an idea. "Maybe I should meet your grandma and pray over her someday."

"Oh my gosh. That would be amazing. I don't have much money; I can't give my grandma the things I would like to give her. To meet you *and* have you pray for her would be incredible."

"That sounds like a plan." he opened his door and said his goodbyes, "I'll be seeing you around."

As Skylar left feeling refreshed and equipped for the day, Wes got a knot in his stomach knowing he had just manipulated innocence. Although his body was repulsed by his actions, he still punched out a couple of pills and chewed them. He closed his eyes knowing a calming flow would soon be washing over his body. Wes now *felt* he had control over his life, although it was quite the contrary. This was a dangerous path, like a car with no brakes racing down a hill.

Chapter 26
1980s

Harold sat at his desk and stared at a blank page of paper with his favorite pen in hand. Watching the demon of his demise, he became disgusted at the rhythmic tremor of his hand, a curse to him and a symbol of decline.

Loretta's steps clicked on the wooden floor. As she neared, Harold spoke his heart, "My body is slipping away and my mind still has so much to give … so much to give." The volume of his speech trailed off as he considered the prospect of seeing his incomplete future bouncing away like his hand, lightly bouncing before him.

"You still have a bright mind. Maybe I could write your thoughts down and work with you." Loretta offered.

"Yeah, maybe we could. Better than nothing, I guess."

"Thanks, honey. You know how to make a girl feel good about herself."

"Oh, I'm sorry. I just don't want to need help."

"Yes, Harold, I know. We must remember that even in the midst of our affliction, we are blessed and loved. We have not been forgotten, Harold. We are being guided to a place we have never been, but it is God's direction. We need to find a way to truly be thankful."

"Who died and made you a preacher? Nothing like your wife preaching a better sermon in a few sentences than you do in an hour on Sunday. You are right, honey. It is just not how I saw my life—"

"Me either, Harold, but it *is* our life and I am grateful. Okay, Pastor Lyons. C'mon to the kitchen and I will pour you a steaming cup of coffee." She blew him a kiss and headed to the kitchen.

Harold scooted away from his desk and took a moment to unwind his stiff body. Bowing his head, he did the best he could. *God, look at me. I am a shadow of the man I used to be. I need you.*

Harold heard in his heart, *now we can work together, Harold. You are going to change a lot of lives.* Harold raised his head. *I'm ready, God.*

Walking took twice as much energy and twice as much time, but he enjoyed every labored step, as he knew there could be a day when he would no longer be able.

Loretta stood at the kitchen counter as her eyes welled up with tears. She listened to her brilliant husband struggle down the hall and lifted up her heart in prayer. *God give me the right words and actions. I know you have a plan, but I don't see it. You have to help me.*

Harold worked his way into the kitchen and managed a smile for his wife. "Thank you, honey. The coffee smells great."

"I made it just like you like it, coffee, cream, sugar … and hot."

"Great. What are you planning today?"

Loretta was in the middle of a long slurp of coffee. "Oh," she dribbled a little out the corner of her mouth, "I wasn't expecting that. You usually don't ask. You just get on with your day."

"Well ... I was hoping you might help me out with my sermon a bit. My writing is so slow and the longer I write, the smaller my writing becomes." He cowered in shame.

"Sure, I can help. I have a women's guild meeting this morning, then I go to get things together for children's church on Sunday. How about I meet you in your office about 3:00 p.m.?" She turned to Harold with a forced hopeful expression on her face.

"Sure." He checked his wristwatch, which read 7:30 a.m. "That will be great, thanks." He nodded and took a sip of his coffee, thankful he could drink it. He used a heavy ceramic mug, which tamed his hand tremors enough to drink it. Harold kept his thoughts to himself. *What will I do till she gets back here?*

Harold sat at his desk and poured out his heart. *Oh, God. Here I sit, a shell of a man ... a stiff and SLOW shell of a man. How could this bring glory to your name? A weak and struggling man shows none of your strength and glory to the world. I represent lack and weakness to the world. I am broken.* Harold waited on God to speak to him in his heart of hearts. Harold felt something rise up in him, a sense of power and direction. In the stillness of his heart, Harold felt God say, *in your weakness, I am strong. Follow me, Harold. I will take you where you couldn't go alone.*

Harold was not in a position to argue with God. God clearly had Harold's attention. Harold had little choice but to lean on God and those around him.

Harold startled as Wes whistled entering his dad's office. "Oh, hi. I didn't hear you come in."

"Didn't hear me come in? I was jamming to Jimi Hendrix and you couldn't hear my entrance? Wow, Dad, you okay?"

"No, I'm not okay. I am sitting here with a sermon on the brink of bursting from my brain and I can't write fast or well enough to get it properly on paper."

"Dang, Dad. You want me to help you?" Wes glanced at his watch. He had a few hours to help.

"Oh, son, I know you are—"

"*Not* busy." Wes interrupted. "I have time. How can I help."

"Really? Well, if I speak the text can you write it down?"

"Sure, Dad. Let's get going." Wes smiled with a warm love that told Harold he was not a burden.

"Thanks, Wes." Harold was humbled. Using the very son he frequently called a 'mess-up' to accomplish God's purpose in his own life.

Wes pulled up a chair and dabbed the pencil to his tongue like he was poised and ready to create a masterpiece with his dad. "Who knows, we may be an invincible, dynamic duo. The Wes and Harold Show."

"No. No. It will be the 'God Loves You Show," Harold mumbled.

"Okay, whatever you want to call it. Now, shoot. I'll try to keep up." Wes smiled at the potential to work with his dad in a cooperative way instead of an adversarial quest. "Let's change the world, Dad."

Harold cleared his throat and started pouring out his heart verbally, while Wes captured his words on paper. They both felt something special happening. Neither was complete on their own, but together, with the inspiration of God, they were a force to deal with.

Chapter 27
Present Day

Eric sat in his old-fashioned chrome and army green Naugahyde wheelchair, waiting on physical therapy in a line-up of other waiting patients. "Hi, I'm ready to roll." He pushed a few strokes on the wheelchair rims and introduced himself. "I'm Eric."

"Well, great, Mr. Harrison. Sounds like you are itching to work. We are burning daylight. Let's get going." His physical therapist sized him up.

"Great. I'm ready."

Eric followed the therapist who took off, expecting Eric to keep up. He hated people holding doors open for him and viewing him like he was unable. *We will get along just fine.*

The therapist sat on an elevated exercise mat and leaned forward with her elbows on her knees, waiting for Eric to park. "So... nice to meet you. My name is Rhonda. I will be your teammate for the next few days. I know a lot about your body already... reviewed your chart. What I am more interested in is your mind. What do you want to get out of this?" She straightened back up and awaited his response.

"Uh, hi, well, I wasn't expecting that question. I just thought you would tell me what to do and I would bust my ass to do it." He nervously gave an unexpected giggle.

"Oh, you *will* bust your butt, but every rep and every drop of sweat will be with a particular purpose in mind. What do you want?"

"I want to walk. I want to *run*." Quiet tears ran down his face. "I want to finish the police academy." His breaths started deepening and his speech became louder and louder. "I want to walk my fiancée down the aisle and I want to play baseball with my son." His volume resumed a normal level. "If I ever have a son." He connected with Rhonda's eyes and spirit.

"Good. Now that you have let yourself think about the uncertainty of life. I can guarantee you that I can show you the way to participate in all these activities."

"All right."

"But... it may not appear the same as it did when you had full use of your right leg. Remember this, Eric; there is always a way to get there."

"Will I walk, normally?"

"Dunno."

"Well, thanks for the vote of confidence."

"What you need to do, Eric, is find out exactly what you want to achieve. Then we will find a way to get there."

"Okay. The next thing I have to do is graduate from the police academy in Oklahoma City."

"Wow, okay. Most of my patients say something like, 'Get on the toilet by myself.' I like your drive. We don't know how much or *if* you will get more function out of that ole right leg. They got control of the infection, but not before significant soft tissue and nerve damage took hold. You are lucky they could save your leg at all. If we can, I will coach you to walk normally. If we can't, we do the next best thing."

Eric held out his hand. "Deal."

They shook on it. Eric quickly put himself in the role of athlete and Rhonda was his coach. They had a lot to accomplish and not a lot of time to achieve it.

Exasperated by another stoplight that delayed her arrival to visit Eric, Ginger pushed the clutch and the brake in her vintage Porsche and scratched the slightest rubber mark on the pavement as she stopped. It seemed it had been an eternity since she saw Eric. The light turned green and her destination was just a few blocks away. She cruised into the rehab parking lot, turned off the ignition, and pulled down her visor mirror to check for specks on her teeth. "Good as it's gonna get." She was so anxious to see Eric, she found herself half walking and half jogging into the building. As she entered and signed the visitors' register, the receptionist was preoccupied on a phone call. The receptionist held up a finger, asking Ginger to give her a second. "How may I help you?"

"I am here to see my fiancé, Eric Harrison."

The receptionist could read Ginger's face like a book. "Are you okay, ma'am? You seem pretty wound up?"

"Yes, I am fine. I am a nurse. I see this stuff all the time." Ginger shifted her weight from side to side, using a bit of the overflow of energy that was surging through her body.

"Oh, of course. I am sure you have." The receptionist followed Ginger's lead. "Just keep in mind that although you see this stuff all the time, it will hit you differently when it is a loved one."

Ginger raised her head to expose fresh tear tracks running down her face. "Yeah, I know." She brushed away the salty tears from her face and cleared her throat. "I'm okay."

"According to the treatment schedule, he is currently in the physical therapy gym." She leaned forward on her elbows and peered into the eyes of an anxious, overwhelmed Ginger. "Down the hall and on your right." She held out her arm like she was directing Ginger's attention to door number two on *Let's Make a Deal.*

Ginger stared down the hall for a moment, not moving a muscle. "Thanks." She gazed down at the ground and back toward the physical therapy gym.

"You okay?" The young girl probed again. She noticed Ginger's reluctance to go to the gym where Eric was working.

"No, not really. I am scared shitless, but it's not your problem. What is your name? You look like just a child."

"Bailey. My name is Bailey and I'm sorry about the misplaced interest." She held up a pink cane covered with sequins and rhinestones. "I had a car wreck a few years ago. I do okay, but since then, I use a cane. I know this place like the back of my hand. I was a patient here for quite some time. I know you are nervous and scared. It's okay. It is a lot to take in."

Preoccupied with her angst, Ginger turned to see down the long hall to the therapy gym. "Okay, Bailey, I need your independent advice. I don't know what to say to him." Ginger slid her hands into both back pockets on her jeans.

"I see this every day. You don't have to say anything. Just be there. "

"Yeah. I couldn't wait to get here and now I don't know how to be with him. Do I smile and try to raise his spirits with jokes? Do I let myself cry when I see him? Hug him?"

"You don't need to figure all that out. What he needs is *you*. Let him take the lead. Just being here lets him know you love him. They won't let you in the gym while he is working, so you can watch from the viewing window near the door."

"Viewing window? Sounds like an interrogation room at the police station."

"Nah, patients just act differently when their loved ones are with them. The therapist needs all of Eric's focus on the activity at hand. Watch from the window and when they are finished, you can surprise him. I am sure he will love seeing you."

"Okay. That will give me a chance to let it all sink in for me, too." Ginger wiped her sweaty palms on her jeans and started down the sterile, echoing hall. After a few steps, she turned around with a genuine, humble smile. "Thank you. This is harder than I thought it would be."

"Just know that he has never been through this before, either. Let him tell you what he needs. Be ready for anything." Bailey nodded in her solidarity with Ginger.

"I can do that." Ginger turned and with every strike of her boot heel on the linoleum, she readied her mind for what she would see.

The viewing window had a one-way glass allowing her to see Eric, but he couldn't see her. Ginger peeked through the window to see Eric standing in front of a full-mirrored wall. He had a canvas safety belt around his waist and his therapist was giving direction while she loosely held the belt. He watched his body move to certain commands. Some movements were better than others. His gray Braves T-shirt boasted of his effort, showing dark sweat rings across his back.

Tears ran across her cheeks and dripped from her chin. *Wow. Is this really happening?* Ginger dug deep. *God, in heaven, help me.*

The therapist checked the clock and then turned to Eric. "Well, great job today. Good work."

"It still doesn't move right." He pointed to his right foot, which was held in position with a brace.

"Not yet. We have to keep pressing. You know we have no guarantees. The only thing that guarantees no progress... is no work. You are putting in the work, so you have a chance. Just a chance. One day at a time, Eric."

"Yeah. Do I strike you as a patient guy?" He turned and sat in his wheelchair and put his feet on the footrests like an old man. "I am not patient, not when it comes to this.

It is great that I can walk for short distances with help, but I want to put that wheelchair in the trash."

"See you tomorrow, Eric. We will hit it again."

"Damn right." Eric spun the wheelchair in a full 360, letting off a little steam. "Gotta stop at the bathroom. See ya later." He pushed the wheelchair to the corner bathroom in the gym, and his therapist moved on to her office. Eric glanced over his shoulder and saw she left the area. A side door to the gym was beside the bathroom and Eric had a plan. He took a gum wrapper from the trash and slid it between the latch and the door frame to allow for secret entrance in the night. *The harder I work the more chance I have.* He spun around and pushed toward the gym entrance. As he drew near the door Ginger showed one leg with her jeans and dingo boots. Then she showed her sleeved out arm, teasing him bit-by-bit.

"My day just got a *whole* lot better. Come here."

Ginger slinked around the corner and immediately dropped her head to make eye contact with Eric. When standing, Eric was a tall man. This was one of the hardest things to get used to for Ginger.

"Man, are you a sight for sore eyes. This is the highlight of my day." Eric nervously pushed his wheelchair forward and back, in a playful rocking motion.

"This is the highlight of my day, too, babe. You are all mine right now. All mine ...all night."

"All night? Really?" He smiled with a confidence Ginger had not seen in a while.

Gazing in his eyes, all her doubts and questions melted away and all she saw was the heart, the love, and commitment of Eric. Nothing else mattered. "Let's get away. Ya want to?"

"Get away? Ginger, this is about as secure as a bank vault. We can't get away."

"Well, I'm moving in, then," she bantered.

"That sounds interesting." Eric pushed his wheelchair a little closer.

Ginger leaned in and slid her hand up his shirt as she gave him a slow, wet kiss.

Eric's head dropped back, and he held a satisfied grin on his face. "I really needed that, babe."

"Take me to your room." Ginger's words tickled as she whispered them into Eric's ear causing him to shiver in excitement.

"Are you crazy? It is time for them to pass out food trays and meds. We will get caught for sure."

"Well, we can figure this out." She lightly stroked his arm with the tips of her fingers, causing goose bumps of anticipation.

Eric motioned for her to lean down and whispered, "See that door by the stairs, I have it rigged so the door won't lock." He glanced at his watch and a mischievous grin crept across his face. "I will go up to my room, like I always do. They will pass out trays and meds and all that kind of thing… should be finished by 6:30. I have been sneaking back to the gym in the evenings to get in extra work. What else do I have to do, but work and get better? Then, about

6:45, come to that same door. I will have it fixed so you can get in. We will keep the lights dim and have a little workout of our own." He gave a wink and brought his lips together in a little kiss.

"That, Eric, is a perfect plan." She stepped back and looked him up and down, amazed at the scheme her straight-laced man devised for their long overdue rendezvous.

"I'll see you at 6:45. We haven't been together for months ... before you came back to sweep me off my feet at DJ's...right? Just to lie down with you will be amazing. See you shortly." She blew him a kiss and strode off in her boots like a rock star.

Ginger drove to the nearest liquor store, Tipsy Lips, and decided she would make this a party. She entered like she owned the place and perused the shelves.

"Can I help you, lady." The young girl didn't appear old enough to drink liquor and there she was selling it.

"Lady? Okay, call me anything but 'lady.' I am looking for something that will make a rendezvous memorable."

"Okay, sweetie—"

"Really? I'd rather be called lady."

"Okay, okay. I have just the right thing for you. Absinthe. Have you ever heard of it?"

Ginger screwed up her face in thought. "Yeah ... has a shady history, doesn't it?"

The salesclerk held up a bottle. "This is the stuff memories are made of."

"Great. I'll take it."

The young clerk gave directions she had obviously given many times, concise and clearly memorized, like the person on the other end of the speaker when you order at a drive-through. "Stop by the grocery store and get some sugar cubes. Google the recipe. It is a process, but not hard."

"Wow, okay. Sounds mysterious."

"An evening you won't forget." The clerk took Ginger's money and slid the bottle in a brown paper bag. "Have a good night."

"You, too." Ginger twisted the paper at the top of the bottle and scooted out the door as the bell announced her exit.

Ginger softly sang "Girls Just Want to Have Fun" as she drove away. She stopped at a grocery store and picked up other essentials such as glasses and sugar cubes. She would grab a fork for the absinthe process when she arrived at the rehab center. The dining hall was close to the entryway.

As she drove the last five minutes, her mind reflected through her memories. All the passion, the heartbreaks, the events at Fireside... and through it all, *Eric was there. Not only there, but he was always a part of the solution. He never stepped away in the middle of my struggles; he ran to me and helped save me.*

Ginger had done her share of primping in public bathrooms. As a common practice, she stashed makeup basics in her purse, in her desk at work, and also a few things in her car glove compartment. She was prepared for any situation. She dug through the glove compartment of her Porsche and stuffed a few things in her purse. *There, that should do it. I shouldn't need that much makeup. After all, it has been months since we have been together. After a few minutes, I hope he has shifted his attention to something other than my face.* Ginger's grin was infectious.

Chapter 28

Present Day

Ginger peered in the rehab center bathroom mirror and smacked her lips after applying lipstick. She smoothed her eyebrows with her pinky. She looked herself in the eye, and her words echoed in the room of porcelain and tile. "Eric, watch out, here I come." She threw her head forward and flung it back to provide a little needed lift to her hair. She blew a kiss to herself in the mirror and opened the door to what she knew would be a great night.

Ginger stepped into the hall and met a nurse pushing a med cart. She turned her head as if checking out a framed picture on the wall, trying not to be memorable.

"May I help you, ma'am?"

Ginger kept going.

"Ma'am, may I help you? Did you sign in the registry at the entry of the building?"

Ginger slowed to see if she was speaking to her. "Who? Me? Oh, I am here to see my fiancé. Just admiring the art."

"Yeah, we try to put inspiring stuff on the walls. I don't think you said. Did you check in at the front desk? It is just policy. Keeping track of those in our facility."

"Oh ...yeah, I signed in when I got here. I stepped out for just a minute." Ginger smiled a forced and disingenuous smile.

"Great. Who would you be here to see?"

Ginger put her hands in the pockets of her jeans and fidgeted, "Eric Harrison." It felt backward to be the one being asked these questions. She was usually the one checking strangers out in Fireside. Then another thought hit her. *I wonder how many people I have sneaking into Fireside for a little night-time lovin'.* She smiled at the thought of one of her elders sneaking their love into Fireside, to entertain their main squeeze.

The nurse gave a nod and welcomed Ginger. "Well, if you or your fiancé need anything, don't hesitate to ask. It is hard enough to just be here, trying to make it back to a normal life. Have a good night." As she pushed the cart farther down the hall, a squeaking wheel gave clear notice she was in the area.

As Ginger nodded, her thoughts made her smile. *I'm going to have a great night, but I'm going to give Eric a night he will never forget.* She slipped into the dining area across the hall and grabbed a fork to use in the absinthe preparation.

Ginger checked out the clock on the wall; it was 6:40 p.m. She was going to get ready for Eric. The door to the gym was just ahead and she wanted to be waiting for Eric when he got there. Ginger went inside and fixed the door with paper in the latch to ensure Eric could get in. She found a secluded exercise table and got busy setting up their romantic rendezvous.

Eric returned to his room after dinner and saw himself in the mirror. He felt as if he was half the man he used to be. Before he was beaten and left for dead, he was in the best shape of his life and had the love of his life by his side once more. He was on top of the world. Now, he was in a wheelchair with a gimp leg and a crushed spirit. He brushed his teeth, gargled with Scope and put product in his hair to make it more manageable, turning his head side-to-side as he checked out himself in the mirror. He sniffed his armpits and immediately reached for the antiperspirant and his favorite cologne, Versace Eros. *Well, Ginger ... here I come, ready or not.*

###

The elevator doors opened and Eric rolled out the doors like he was bored and searching for a change of scenery. He was totally alone in the hall and was thankful it would be fairly easy to get into the gym. After one more check of his surroundings, he grabbed the paper positioned at the door latch and stuffed it in his pocket as he rolled through to the gym. It was dark, but he saw a treatment room with the light on and the door slightly cracked. Music was softly floating from that direction. He gave a good push on the wheelchair rims and coasted toward the light. As he drew near, he could make out the song, "Come Away with Me," by Nora Jones.

He nudged the door and it slowly swung open. Ginger was waiting patiently inside. She had a urinal full of ice water and two glasses with an emerald green liquid in the bottom. The music was from her phone. Eric's whole demeanor softened, "Hi, baby. Nora Jones, Huh? Can I tell you how amazing you look, but I have to ask... is that a urinal full of ice water?"

Ginger's heart rate increased like it was a first date. "You look so good to me, honey. Well, yes, it is a urinal but let me explain first. It is washed and never been used."

Eric gave her the fish-eye. "Is that supposed to give me comfort?" He continued to slowly roll toward her.

"Have you heard of absinthe?" Ginger held up the bottle and smiled a mischievous smile.

"That's absinthe? The ecstasy of the 1920s?" Eric was intrigued.

"Well, it has made a comeback. I thought we would make some memories tonight." Ginger held up the urinal like displaying it at auction.

"Somehow it loses something when you hold that thing up." He pointed to the plastic urinal.

"Oh, it is just something to hold the ice water. We will drink out of the glasses." Ginger gave the air that she had it all figured out.

"Oh, well that makes it so much better." Eric laughed and checked his volume as he didn't want to be found out in the treatment room.

"Come here." Ginger held out one of the glasses for him to hold. She put a sugar cube on the fork and laid it across the rim of the glass.

"Now, I will pour the ice water across the sugar cube into the glass of absinthe until it is completely dissolved." Ginger was into it and couldn't wait to give it a spin.

"Babe, I think that is all great and everything, but what I am really into is *you*. I don't care about a fancy drink. Won't tequila do the same thing?"

Ginger blurted out a laugh. "Well, that may be true, but I have heard that it makes you freer."

"Freer than what?"

"Freer than tequila... freer than you have ever been... just saying... it is worth a try." Ginger gave a flash of a wink that was so sexy.

"Who am I to argue with a beautiful, smart, and sexy woman ... who is holding a glass of the world's greatest love potion." He held the glass while she poured. Then they fixed the other drink.

Eric transferred to the treatment table and sat next to Ginger. "Ginger. I have thought about you every day, every night. I can say that not only does absence make the heart grow fonder, but it makes my dreams hornier."

"Really?" Ginger was interested.

"Really. I don't think I am gonna need that absinthe, but I *am* curious."

"Well, Romeo. Here's to curiosity and orgasms. Cheers."

"Cheers," Eric tapped her glass, "chin chin." He took a deep drink and they lingered, peering into each other's eyes. "Ginger, I have heard people say what doesn't kill you makes you stronger. I am gonna come out of this a *better* man. I have had too much time to think. I *am* gonna be a police officer, and I *am* gonna walk you down the aisle, and I am gonna love you tonight like you have never been loved. Top to bottom, front to back, inside and out." His breaths started picking up pace and he looked at Ginger with eyes that longed for her touch.

Ginger took a long sip from her glass and placed it on a nearby table. "Who needs absinthe."

Eric gently touched her red, shining hair. She pulled his shirt over his head and kissed his lips that were aching for the sweet taste of her mouth. He returned the favor, unbuttoning her blouse slowly. As each button released, he opened her blouse a little more, lightly kissing the warm skin beneath. The tease of his progressive kisses drove Ginger crazy and she reached down to lower the waist of his shorts. As they continued to explore each other's body it was like the first time. It was new, it was more than a roll in the hay, it was expressing, without words, the depth of their love. It was a beautiful dance of commitment. As they laid there, completely fulfilled, they knew nothing could tear them apart.

Ginger gazed into Eric's eyes. "Eric, we will get through—"

SLAM. SQUEAK, SQUEAK, SQUEAK.

"Pull up your damn pants, Romeo. It's the night charge nurse."

"What? How do you—" Eric grabbed for his shorts.

"Who's in there?" A sharp female voice pierced the air.

"Sweet Jesus. We are found out. The night nurse has a squeaking med cart." Ginger got her blouse on and had two buttons closed when the door burst open.

"What is going on?" The nurse put her hands on her hips and saw the absinthe bottle. "Absinthe? You two have some explaining to do." She first directed her question to Ginger. "I ran into you in the hall. Let me guess... this must be Eric." She turned fully to Eric, waiting for a response.

"I can explain... uh—" Ginger was struggling to find the words as she continued to button her blouse and kept the sheet about her waist.

"Okay, you two. The party is over and you have to get back up to your room, Mr. Harrison. We will talk about this tomorrow." She cleared her throat again and closed the door.

As she left, her med cart squeaked along with her. Eric turned to Ginger. "Yep. We made memories all right."

Ginger picked up a pillow and hit him over the head. "It was worth every minute."

Chapter 29

Present Day

Erma's bloodshot eyes gazed at a computer screen of truth. Her desk was covered in Diet Coke dead soldiers and she played with her hair to the point that the side and front of her hair had softened, leaving the top and back of her head still stiff with hairspray, while the sides and front sprang out like a fringe of hay. Her hand along her jawline held up an exhausted brain. *Lies, lies, and more lies.* Erma was putting it all together. She found information on the internet concerning "Pastor" Wes Lyons. Financial failures and relationship failures documented right in front of her face. Anyone who wanted to see the truth could find it through public documents and online newspapers. *Wes Lyons was a shyster.*

Erma heard Ginger's boots approaching. She pushed away from her desk, ran to the door, and waited for her to draw near. At the right moment, she opened her door and almost hit Ginger in the face.

"Whoa there, Kemosabe, you about tagged me in the head." Ginger put her hand on the door frame.

"Get in here." Erma grabbed her by the arm and without another word, dragged her into her office. "I asked you weeks ago to find out more about Wes Lyons. What have you dug up?" She searched Ginger's face, hoping for a sign of success.

"First of all, Erma, don't go out in the hallway till you've seen yourself in the mirror. Not to be mean, but your hair looks like the mane of the cowardly lion in *The Wizard of Oz*."

Erma pulled out a mirror from her top desk drawer, held it up for a good view and threw it into the nearby wing-back chair. "Doesn't surprise me. I got *real* problems, Ginger." She leaned forward on her desk blotter from 2016 with random phone numbers and notes of importance written in no particular order. "Still no money from Mr. Lyons. His lies continue. By the time I figure out one deception, he has moved on to another believable story. I need one of these to be true, Ginger. I am in way over my head."

"Wow, Erma. You must be—"

"I am desperate. My ass is on the line. Not only am I at the cusp of losing my job, but it could go deeper."

"Deeper?" Ginger was amazed at the thought that Erma might lose her job. Initially, she felt a flicker of joy; life at Fireside without Erma would be a lot different, but Ginger suddenly felt an ounce of empathy for Erma, although she would not admit it out loud.

"That's all I can say." Erma wouldn't tell the whole truth, because she knew better than to let anyone else in on the whole truth, but she could go to prison for forgery and fraud, changing official bank documents.

"Erma, stop right there. I don't need to know your secrets. You have said enough. Let me get back with James. He is a true friend and knows how to keep his mouth shut when needed. All I need to do is ask what he has observed lately. Do you have a hat around here?"

"Well, I have that decorative piece over there. It was my mom's. I keep it on that table as a reminder of her."

"It is beautiful. You should put it on your head, go out of here and get some rest." Ginger reached over, grabbed the hat and handed it to Erma. "Go on. I will let you know what James has found out."

Erma took the hat and turned it a bit as if it were an old friend. "Well, Mamma, looks like you are helping me again, even from your grave." She tried to sweep her hair behind her ears and placed the hat on her head with a bit of a tilt. She turned to Ginger for a response, "Well, what do you think?"

"Looks like you are wearing your mother's hat, but ...it's beautiful and you don't have to answer anyone's questions. I say you grab your purse and your briefcase; you strut straight out the front door and don't pause for anyone. If anyone approaches you, just tell them you are late for a presentation at an antique club meeting and just keep stepping it off. It will work."

"Hey, I think you're right. I think it *will* work. Thanks, Ginger. Why are you being so nice to me? Why now?"

"Well, Erma. I don't like your ways. You are a money-forward administrator and, honestly, have little compassion for our residents. I also think the moment you showed a whisper of compassion for an elder, I took notice. Unfortunately, your first whisper of compassion was spoken in Wes Lyons's direction. Take this muted light of compassion you have shown to him and amplify it over your entire family of residents at Fireside."

"He snookered me and I am left holding the bag."

"Yes, he did. I will help you resolve this, but don't let it prevent you from viewing others through the eyes of compassion, Erma. We need a compassionate administrator."

"Help me get this resolved, Ginger and I will turn into Mother Teresa on Sunday." Erma dropped her head in shame.

Ginger stood and crossed her arms. "I have ways of finding things out. I will get to the bottom of it. Now get your things and go home. I will see you tomorrow."

Erma paused briefly at the mirror and gave a nod of approval. "You know, looking at myself in this hat, I briefly saw my mother's likeness in my reflection." She gave the flash of a forced smile. "Could I ever use you here now, Mamma." With that, she turned, held her head up high, and said nothing as she left her office and headed straight to the front door, with her briefcase in one hand and her purse draped over the other elbow. She pushed the heavy swinging front door open and let it catch on the air as it slowly closed behind her.

Ginger found James having a glass of iced tea in the dining room. *Great. James is alone. I can talk to him now.*

James stirred his tea while he watched Ginger approach. "Well, here comes trouble." He smiled with his tease, but knew full well that if you are not on the up and up, Ginger *could* certainly be "trouble" for someone.

"Okay, James—"

"I know what you want." He reached into his shirt pocket and pulled out his small spiral notebook. He dabbed the point of his pencil to his tongue and flipped the pages to find the proper place. "Wes Lyons. You want the dirt on him." He looked at Ginger and raised his eyebrows in question, without saying another word.

"Yes. Spill it." She wanted him to get to the point.

"Well, I have been keeping my eyes open. Some pretty shady people visit him. I started reading my books from a lighted corner chair in the sitting area right down the hall from Wes. His room is positioned in an area that many don't frequent."

"He is in that location on purpose," Ginger interjected, "to reduce any questions others may ask."

"Well, there are a few things that don't add up. He has had this young visitor, a heavy-set Latin fellow, who always wears an Astros ball cap. When he comes, he arrives with nothing in hand and doesn't stay long. Wes cracks the door and lets the guy in. He only stays a few moments and leaves. On occasion, I can hear raised voices, but only briefly. Then, usually only moments later, he squeezes out Wes's cracked door and leaves out the side entrance, near the kitchen."

"I don't think I have seen that guy." Ginger squinted in deep thought as if it would help her remember.

"Also, I have noticed Skylar, the meds pass nurse, goes there frequently. In between her usual routine. She always pushes the cart *into* his room. That is strange. I have noticed that she leaves her cart outside every other room when she visits ...but with Wes, she pushes it inside his room."

"That is interesting. Skylar is our prized hope for a future R.N. I am grooming her in my footsteps. She knows she is not allowed to push the cart in the resident's room." She searched James's eyes for answers.

"I don't know, what is going on, but I do believe *something* is going on. That's all I got, but I will keep reading from that chair over there." He pointed to the wing back chair within eye and earshot of Wes's room.

"Thanks, James. You are the best."

"Sure, Red. I know with a little time things will become clearer. Where you headed?"

"To find Skylar." She noted, as she turned to find the nurse who had a story to tell. She got up and took long strides down the hall with her Dingo boots giving alert to everyone in the area that the sheriff was in town.

Chapter 30
1980s

Harold struggled to write legibly. He sat at his home desk and glanced once more at the clock ticking on the wall. In the silence of the room, the ticking seemed to nudge out every other sound and became as loud as a drumstick hitting the rim of a snare drum, marking time; time needed to create a suitable sermon.

Harold picked up his half-filled mug of coffee for a relaxing sip to refocus his thoughts. *Back to the well, Harold. Back to the well.*

Wes wandered into his parents' house unnoticed. He went to his father's office door and stood there for a moment, secretly observing his dad in the silence. He cleared his throat and slowly stepped toward his dad. "Hi, Dad. How's it going?"

Harold flinched at the surprise. "Oh, it's you."

"I was supposed to be here at 2:00." He placed his hand on his dad's shoulder. "How about I give your coffee a warm up."

"Thanks, but I don't need a warm-up. I just got a fresh cup."

"It's only half full." Wes peered into the mug once more.

"Well, if I fill it all the way, my hand tremors will spill coffee all over the place—"

"So, you fill it halfway up and you have no spills. Smart. Let me get a little coffee for myself and I will be ready to start crackin'." He hustled to the kitchen, where an eternal pot of coffee waited for anyone who needed a little pick-me-up.

"I can see you missed the barber yesterday." Harold shook his head in disapproval as he shouted toward the kitchen. Wes wore his hair longer and in layers of flowing curls.

"No, I made it, Dad." He peeked over his shoulder and down the hall so his words would carry into his dad's office. Wes walked back into the office with his steaming coffee cup warming his hands.

"I got a haircut yesterday." His smile was briefly interrupted by a slurp of coffee.

"Well, not *my* barber." Harold voiced his disapproval.

"Actually, I used Mom's stylist."

"That is exactly what I thought, because it is a woman's hairstyle. If I didn't know better, I would think you were that woman, Farrah Fawcett, on the Charlie's Angels show."

"Thanks, Dad. She has beautiful hair." Wes shook out his loose curls.

"That wasn't a compliment."

"Well, I was thinking along the lines of Barry Gibb... or Jesus."

"Jesus? Jesus would be much more conservative." Harold put down his pen and turned his chair fully toward Wes.

"Well, he wasn't, Dad. He wasn't conservative... and he had beautiful hair." He nodded toward the picture of Jesus on the wall, reflecting a dark-skinned young man in a simple white tunic and flowing dark hair.

"Oh, you young people. That was then and this is now. If he were around today, he would have a respectable haircut and he would not have paid good money for a woman's haircut."

"I came over here to help you with your sermon. Can we do that? Can we just leave this other stuff alone and put together a meaningful sermon for our church members?"

"Okay, okay. Well, I was thinking that we could maybe do something on the Beatitudes.... You know, the 'Blessed are the...'"

"I am good with that. Do you have notes together, yet...with references? I will definitely need the references."

"Yes, I only have a bit more to add."

"Great." Wes grabbed the notes and tidied them up tapping the edges of the paper on the desk.

"Let me explain, son. It is one of the most important passages in the Bible." Harold settled in to preach the message to Wes.

"Okay, Dad. Give me the high points. I will prepare it and then pass it back by you for the details." He checked his watch, knowing how long-winded his dad could get when he had someone's attention.

"Oh, okay, do you have to be somewhere?" Harold searched in the notes for areas to underline that should have emphasis during the sermon.

"Well, I need to get to class. I have New Testament this semester, you know. In fact, this specific passage is a primary focus of this class. Guess it is kinda important, huh?"

"Important? *Important?* Son, this is a primary focus of the whole Jesus story. Let me show you something." Harold tried to scoot his chair beside Wes, but he was too stiff and with three attempts, his chair barely moved.

"I got this. I have read your notes for years now."

"You have?" Harold quizzed Wes's eyes, peering deep into them for a sign of sincerity.

"Well, yeah. When I was just a boy and you were at the church throughout the day, I would come in here and flip through your notes. I always knew what you were gonna preach before you preached it." He dropped his head while revealing this nugget of truth. When he finished, he slowly caught Harold's eyes to see his reaction.

His authoritative expression softened. "I never knew that."

"I was afraid I would get in trouble." Wes exhaled with the release of a life-long secret.

"Get in trouble for reading my work? Why would you get in trouble for that?"

"Why did I get in trouble for lots of stuff?" He grimaced at the thought of his discipline from the past. "I gave my sandwich to the new kid without a lunch ... I got a spanking. You caught me sitting on the curb talking to the black kid before I walked home. You gave me the 'you are known by the company you keep' talk."

"Well, Wes you *are* known by the company you keep and—"

"Dad, his mom taught Sunday school and his dad was killed in Vietnam. He was a great kid. No disgraces there."

"But others may not know them and you don't want people to think you hang out with people who are outcasts of society."

"Dad, Jesus hung out with prostitutes, tax collectors, politicians, and the undesirables ... *and* he had hair like mine." Wes stood up and gave his dad a tense sideways hug. "I will put it together and run it by you before Sunday. Promise."

"Okay, Wes," Harold remembered he was not in a position to be pushy, "thank you for helping your old man out. I really appreciate it. I just feel that I have so much more to give. I'm not through yet. My body is holding my calling captive, but with you, I can still make an impact. Thanks." Harold was showing a different personality now that he must work with others and depend on their goodness to achieve his purpose.

"You are welcome. You have always written great sermons." Wes jogged to his car and left in a cloud of dust.

Harold sat at his desk with an expression of surprise and contentment. *He read my sermons. He LIKED my sermons. Maybe there was more to Wes than met the eye.*

Wes sat in the sterile waiting room, surrounded by white tile, white linoleum, and nurses with white dresses and starched nurses' caps. The hyperactive acoustics were maddening. A simple cough or dropped pen could be heard all the way down the hall. Wes had rolled up the paper holding the final draft of his dad's sermon, and all of a sudden, it didn't seem that important anymore.

He turned and saw his mom walking toward him. He stood and started walking, then running, toward her. "How is he?"

"Your dad has pneumonia. You know that he has had some trouble swallowing. Well, he doesn't tell us when he always has trouble. He doesn't want to be viewed as weak. Some food went into his lungs, causing his pneumonia. He will be here for a while, and we will have to do a better job of giving him food that he can more easily swallow without aspirating it into his lungs."

"Oh, my gosh, Mom! That sounds serious. Is he gonna be okay? How are you?"

"He will most likely be here for several days, but recover. I am tired, but I am okay."

"Several days? This is Friday night, Mom. What about this sermon?" He held up the rolled papers holding his dad's sermon for Sunday. "Is he gonna make it to church on Sunday?"

"We should be prepared for anything."

Wes's spirit sank as if in quicksand. "Can I go see him?"

"Sure, but don't expect much, and don't upset him. He needs all his strength focused on recovery, not arguing."

"Thanks. I will not spend much time."

###

He knocked on the heavy swinging door and waited for an invitation.

"Come in." Harold spoke softly.

"I am so sorry you're sick, Dad. Is there anything I can do? I brought your sermon for review." Wes held up the twisted papers that had clearly been handled and fidgeted with while he was waiting in the waiting room.

"I might have to iron it before I can read it." Harold joked in a low volume.

Wes nudged his dad's shoulder, "C'mon, Dad, give me a break. I have been worried." He tried to interact with his dad in a jovial tone.

"Listen, son, I need your help. You think you could pinch-hit for me on Sunday?" He smoothed the sheets about his stomach and forced a small smile. "I won't be out of here by then, and I don't want the congregation to suffer for it."

"Oh, wow, Dad. I am not a preacher. I am a goofy guy who wants to make people feel better. I am a singer, not a preacher."

"I know… I am still the preacher. I just need your voice to deliver the message. You have a great voice and a way of connecting with people. I think it just might work." He bowed his head and then made eye contact with Wes.

"Okay. Don't worry. I'll fill in."

"Thank you. I know this is out of your comfort zone. I appreciate this gift."

The sanctuary was all abuzz with the sight of Wes sitting near the pulpit in a chair that resembled a throne.

Mumbles and murmurs wafted across the sanctuary, "Where is Harold?

Hearing the comments, he lightly stepped to the pulpit. "Good morning, everybody. No, you are not going crazy; Pastor Harold Lyons is still your pastor. I am just delivering his message today. Let's pray a simple prayer before starting." He bowed his head and prayed from the perspective of a servant. "God, take our focus right now and turn it to you … to your goodness, your protection, your love, and your provision. We come to you pointing to your perfection and goodness in the middle of our imperfect lives. May we live this week in a way that brings honor to you. Please be with my dad as he recovers. Heal him and guide him. We ask these things in Jesus' name, Amen."

Wes started the sermon Harold wrote only days ago, and it was clear that God was using Harold's words and his delivery to reach the people.

People shouted, "Bring it!" They stood and waved their hands and continued, "Hallelujah!" At the close of the service, people were standing just like at the end of a basketball game as the winning shot swooshed through the net.

Loretta approached him as he concluded the Sunday service. "What did you think?"

"I am still energized and feel this cool connection to God."

"Me, too, Wes, me, too. Sometimes we don't know God's direction till we are shoved into it. You were meant to preach."

He smiled with anticipation. "You know, Mom, I think you are right! Can you believe it? A long-haired, bell-bottom-wearing, rock 'n' roll-listening dude called to communicate the love of God? We are gonna make some noise, some good noise." He hugged his mom at the prospect. "He called me as I am. He will use me as I am."

Chapter 31
1990s

"Good morning, babe. Nothing like coffee in bed … in Paris." Jennifer stood beside her slumbering husband with a cup of French pressed coffee.

"Really? Oh, yeah, I forgot. Let me wake up a bit." He rubbed his eyes and then opened them wide, scooted his hips back in bed, and leaned against the wall. "That smells amazing."

"Come join me?" She enticed him with a smile.

"Oh, yeah. You kidding?" As she strolled by the window, she pulled the curtains open and quickly jumped into bed. "Look out there, Wes. Did you ever think we would be able to view out the window, drink coffee, and watch people milling about a French plaza?"

"Well. Never. Paris, France was never on my bucket list and I am craving an Egg McMuffin right now."

"Well, these croissants and macarons from the corner café will have to do." She handed him a classic white paper bag with heavenly pastries in the bottom.

"Okay, yeah, that will do." He reached in and pulled out a large buttery croissant.

"Amazing. Other people save money for years to have this experience, and you still hold Mickey Dee's as your gold standard for excellence." Jennifer snuggled into the bed and laid her head on his shoulder. "That is one of the many reasons I love you. You are not driven by money."

"Well," he took a bite of the croissant, "I think that McDonald's could maybe up their game, substituting the English muffin with a croissant." He kissed his fingertips in a symbol of culinary perfection.

"Uh, oh. Are you actually gaining an appreciation for the finer things in life?"

"Nope. I have a keen appreciation for butter. Period. I think that is a Southern thing, not a French thing." He shoved the rest of the croissant in his mouth and sprayed a little bit of croissant out in a blast of laughter.

"I love you, Wes Lyons. We better get moving. You have a service tonight."

"Jennifer, I don't know how this all happened so fast. Yesterday, we were in good ole U.S.A., and today we woke up in Paris, France, for our first leg of a worldwide tour. I know that as things started really exploding in our ministry, Dad and the church reorganized a lot of business and legal matters, so I am not really sure about the behind the scenes stuff."

"Speaking of your dad, you better call your dad this afternoon. Remember, they are seven hours behind us." Jennifer tipped her cup completely to catch every drop of delicious coffee.

"Yeah, I have that on the schedule. I'll review his notes and get my head around it first, then call him and get clarification of things. Thank God for Dad's knowledge of the Bible."

"Thank God for your ability to communicate with an audience in an intimate, inclusive way." Jennifer finished her thoughts while browsing through the suitcase for her outfit of the day.

"What's wrong, honey?" He saw her flipping back through the same clothes she passed by moments ago. "Did you forget something?"

"No. Just searching for something a bit different. I have worn the same thing for the last three services."

"Well," Wes licked his fingers after popping the last of a croissant in his mouth and wiped his lips with the back of his hand, "Never thought about that."

"Of course, you wouldn't think about it; you are a guy." She continued, as if she missed something the last time she looked.

"Really, is that a big deal?" Wes combed his hand through his '90210' hair," cut close along the back and sides and long, tipped, straight hair for bangs and along the top.

"No, not really a big thing. I just want to give the proper respect to your services that I should."

"Prepare your heart and mind for the people we are trying to serve. Your beauty will shine from the inside out and *then* our mission will be realized." Wes encouraged.

"You really believe that, don't you?" Jennifer searched the eyes of the man she loved.

"Yep. We are here to serve those who reach out to us. I believe that as long as God brings people to see us, he will give us the power and strength to serve them. People are tired of plastic impostors, and they can pick one out from a mile away."

KNOCK, KNOCK, KNOCK.

"Qui Est la?" Wes turned toward the hotel room door. His French was poor, but he still gave it a try.

"Monsieur, Raphael Est cue que je m'appelle. J'ai besoin de vous parler de vos recus."

Wes opened the door. "That's all I got, Monsieur." He smiled at his inability to converse in French. "Tu parles anglais?"

"Oui. Little bit." He held up two fingers measuring an inch and bowed, trying to show his willingness to help with the communication gap. "My name is Raphael. We talk money."

"Money? I shouldn't owe money."

"I no take money, I give." The Paris representative for this leg of the tour stepped forward.

"Excuse me?" Wes was clearly confused and concerned.

"I give you money." Raphael was using his hands in dramatic fashion while he spoke, as if it would make up for his poor English.

"You are giving me money? Why?" He was still unsure about this little exchange.

Raphael held out a paper with rows of numbers and totals at the bottom.

"10,000? 10,000 what?" Wes was afraid this was not going to be something he wanted to hear.

"Dollars, monsieur." His sincere smile was confusing.

If I owe him $10,000.00, why is he so happy?

"I *give* you $10,000.00."

"Oh, no. I don't want your money." He held his hands up like he was stopping someone's progress.

"Not my money. They give because they love you. I send someone to talk to you. Keep this." He handed Wes the paper with the notes of collected money listed.

"Okay. Merci." He was proud of using what little French he understood.

"De rien." The nice man excused himself and went back down the hall.

"Oh, my gosh, Jennifer, we are in big trouble. We don't have that kind of money. How does solitary confinement, breaking rocks in a French prison sound to you?" Wes was beside himself.

"Well, let's get our tour manager up here A.S.A.P. We will have someone who understands both languages here when they come to talk to us." Jennifer leaned into Wes.

"Yes. Great idea, babe. Let's get ready."

KNOCK. KNOCK. KNOCK.

Jennifer opened the door and a tall, muscular gentleman introduced himself, "Hello, I am Jacques. May we sit and discuss your financial situation."

"Nice to meet you. I just want to say that we didn't order anything and shouldn't owe more money—"

"Pay ME money, sir? No, no. Yesterday, after your prayer meeting, the congregation took up a love offering." He extended a fat envelope to Wes. "This money is YOUR money. $10,000.00."

"$10,000 for me ... for us... for the ministry?"

"Yes sir. This is yours."

He stood in awe. "Okay. Uh, thank you, Jacques. This is unexpected. Thank you so much."

He closed the door and turned to Jennifer in disbelief. "Babe, I don't get it. What are we gonna do? We have all this money and we travel to England tomorrow. I am not used to carrying even $100.00 in my pocket, but $10,00 0.00? And ... what if they search us at the airport? Do you think they will believe that I am a preacher and thousands of people 'gave' me the money because they like the way I preach? I am not carrying that around. Maybe we can get someone to help us deposit it in our account back in the states?" He paused briefly, "What do you think, babe?"

Jennifer smiled as if she had been let in on a secret. "I think your dad and the administration of the ministry knew this might happen. That is why they reorganized the structure of the ministry. However the ministry directs the funds, the more financially successful the ministry is ... the more financially successful *we* will be. So, what are we gonna do? I'll tell you what *I'm* gonna do. I am gonna contact our home office and ask for help getting this money deposited in Kingsridge Ministries account, thank God for blessing us above and beyond what we imagined ...then I am gonna go get a fantastic cup of coffee and one of those amazing pastries at the corner café." She tried her best to get him to smile. "We can learn how to be blessed beyond our wildest dreams, just like we learned how to be poor. Thank you, Lord."

Chapter 32
1990s

The tour bus's hydraulic brakes hissed as the bus came to a stop in the Griffin Observatory parking lot in Los Angeles. Built in the 1930's, the observatory was still one of the iconic Los Angeles landmarks with a breathtaking view. The driver, Wes's old friend, Thomas, threw the gear shift into park and peered in the rear-view mirror to see no sign of anyone awake in the luxury touring bus. *An Italian palace on wheels, and I am the only one awake to appreciate the beauty of it all.* The bus driver slurped the last of his Coca Cola from the bottom of his insulated "Wes Lyons Ministries" travel cup. One of the many marketing trinkets he got for free because he was the official driver for the Wes Lyons family. Times had really changed since he reconnected with Wes some twenty years ago, behind the A.C. units of the church.

He stood with his hands on his hips and scanned the horizon of lights and neon stretching from east to West. *Thank you, God. Who would have thought that some twenty years ago, Wes Lyons would change my life? From sneaking me into the gym behind old man Lyons's church, with only a sleeping bag and a few garbage sacks of belongings, to driving a yacht on wheels and living in luxury. My life has certainly changed. Wes never forgot his promise to me that night. He said he wouldn't forget me and he didn't. I wonder where I would—*

"Beautiful, isn't it?" Jennifer quietly stood beside him with her arms crossed and took in the beauty of the Los Angeles skyline and all that it represented.

Thomas startled. "Oh my gosh. I guess I zoned out for a minute. Beautiful is right." He quietly acknowledged Jennifer and returned his eyes to the nightscape scenery.

"Hey, I was wondering," she paused, choosing her words carefully, "would you have any of that sleeping medicine with you? Wes didn't sleep well and he needs to get some rest before the services tonight."

"Sure. We have such a crazy schedule; it is always tough gearing down to sleep."

"Aw, that would be great. Thanks." She pivoted to go back inside the bus.

"Give me just a minute." He smiled, gave a nod, and took his last glance at the lights, cars, glitz, and glamour of the valley below, then followed Jennifer into the bus.

Standing beside the bus cockpit, Thomas extended his hand. "Here ya go, ma'am, a few should do the trick for several nights." he dropped them into her hand, "guess I'll catch a few winks." Give me a shout if you need anything." He turned and stepped into his private compartment a few feet away and pulled the curtain shut.

Jennifer closed her hand, making sure she didn't lose the precious pills. A few feet down the way, "Here you go. Take one of these."

"One? How many did he give you?"

"A few," she peered into her hand to take inventory, "five to be exact."

"Give me two. Two won't hurt me, and I know it will put me to sleep. I want to be primed and ready for tonight." He winked as he smiled and extended his hand. His charisma dripped from every word.

"I am giving you *one,* Romeo. It will be *plenty.* And, may I remind you to call Jordan before you go on stage. He thinks his dad is the rockstar of all preachers and he can't wait for the next meeting when school is on break and he can join you with his guitar." Jennifer paused for a beat, then added. "Ya, know, I think he is right. You *are* the rockstar of all preachers, babe. Now, get some rest." Jennifer kissed him, dropped one pill in his hand, and stepped into the adjoining bathroom.

Wes leaned his head back and increased his volume, "Aye, aye, Captain." Reaching for his soda on the side table, he noticed a small, pink oval object against the brown carpeting below. As he reached for it, he recognized the pill before he even touched it. *Come to pappa.* He picked up the pill and washed both pills down with a swig of soda and settled in for a restful sleep.

###

Jennifer grabbed his soda at his bedside and poured it on his face. "Wes, wake up. You have to get ready for tonight. C'mon, honey, you are on in just an hour. Wake up."

Wes sat straight up like his back was spring loaded, sputtering, "What's going on?" As he coughed and choked, a drip of mucus slid out of his nose.

Thomas peeked around the corner, "Is everything okay?"

Jennifer spoke without taking her eyes off of Wes, "No, everything is *not* okay. He is sloppy drunk. I can't get him awake; I don't understand. I only gave him one pill, the same as always."

"Well, not really the *exact* same. The old pills were one mg Estazolam. What I gave you yesterday was two mg pills. The last time I went to the doctor, I asked him to increase it to two mg. That way when you ask for pills, I can just break them in two; you get one mg and I get one mg." He smiled with pride.

"So, he took double the dose he usually takes. I gave him a whole pill—"

"I took two." Wes slumped, battling to stay upright and slurred, "I took two." He flopped back into a full sleep.

"You took two?" she said, surprised at her husband who was supposed to conduct a prayer service for the stars in less than an hour." *Oh, heavenly Father, help us.* "Wes, you took four times your usual dose. No wonder."

The driver came back around the corner. "Here. Take this. It will wake you up. I use these when I am sleepy and need to keep driving to keep us on schedule. Don't worry, it is safe. Truck drivers all over the interstate use them regularly."

Jennifer saw Wes and couldn't help but be reminded of the many times when Wes was in college and she had to nurse him over a hangover; this time was different. He was a middle-aged man who was about to preach and pray over hundreds of people, while he was drunk. "Get up.

I am gonna fix you some coffee." She turned to Thomas. "*You*, sir, will stay with him and start getting him ready."

Jennifer was rattling pots in the small kitchen. "Help me, Lord."

KNOCK. KNOCK. The door opened slightly and an excited road crew member shouted, "Thirty minutes till showtime. Pastor Wes, there is standing room only. God is gonna move tonight in a big way. Praise the Lord." He shut the door just as quickly as he opened it.

Jennifer ran to the door, "Excuse me." The man spun around, "Pastor Lyons is still getting ready and has not yet come out of his prayer closet. This may be one of those times that we need to stretch the praise singers' time. Have them sing a little extra."

"Stretch the praise singers' time?"

"Yes, yes, sometimes, we ask the praise singers to sing a little extra to let him fully get in the flow of the spirit. I think this is going to be one of those times."

"Oh, wow. Okay. You got it, ma'am. We are here to make sure this goes well."

"Well, let's do this. You tell the ensemble from Upward with Jesus to just keep singing till we arrive on stage. That is what we need."

"I will make sure they understand. Let me know if you need anything else."

"That is all." She smiled and waved till he turned around.

She ran back in the bus and heard Wes's voice. "My scalp is tingly, and I feel like my heart is keeping time with "In-A-Godda-Da-Vida." I hope it doesn't last as long as the song does."

Jennifer studied his eyes. "Oh, my! Your pupils are weird, and you are sopping wet with sweat. What does the clock say?"

Wes turned toward the clock. "It is 6:00, showtime."

"*Your* showtime is when you are able to stand in front of that crowd with a heart dialed in to hear God speaking to you ... clear-minded and open-hearted. The Upward with Jesus ensemble will keep the crowd energized till you make it out there."

Wes stood up, stumbled to the mirror, and flashed one of his patented smiles. He inspected his own eyes. He saw a boy trying to do a Spartan's job, always an attractive guy in so many ways. Each decade brought a stage of stunning maturity to his undeniable good looks. Now in his forties, he resembled Paul Newman with piercing, trusting blue eyes, a square, rugged jawline, and dimples at his chin and each cheek. With a smile, he *looked* like Pastor Wes ... but could he pull it off? With his hands on the rim of the sink, he dropped his head in shame and spoke loud enough for Jennifer to hear. "It was a mistake. I just wanted to sleep. I glanced down and saw the second pill, orphaned on the carpet, and took it with the one you gave me. I was so tired and didn't want to let anyone down. We have prayer meetings several times a week, each in a different town, many of them are in a different country. I know there are a lot of people out there, waiting for a word from God. I wish I could talk to Dad."

Jennifer reached into her bag and retrieved a letter bearing evidence of being read and re-read many times. "Here, honey. Read it again. You're right; they will expect you to be impressive. You always are. I feel that this will somehow be one of your best meetings. You will *have* to lean on God and not on your own talents. Use your talents, Wes, but lean on God. Come out when you are ready. This is going to be a great night."

Wes took the letter and felt the wrinkles and texture changes from being folded and unfolded hundreds of times over the years, already knowing what was written inside. He sat, not taking his eyes off the letter, then blew into the previously opened end of the envelope and unfolded the letter written quite some time ago. "Wes, did I ever tell you that you were named after one of the greatest preachers of all time, John Wesley? Well, you were. What a great man of God. Here I lie in a hospital bed with pneumonia, unable to preach to my church. Thank you for pinch-hitting. Remember to pray, clear your mind to receive inspiration, and preach. Please tell me how it goes. Dad. *The first, and the best letter my dad ever wrote to me.*

Wes folded the paper, put it back in the envelope and slid it into the breast pocket of his suit. "It's show-time."

Wes knew this letter was written to get him through the hard times. This *was* one. He stood before the mirror. *God, here stands your 'David.' Breathe your life and courage into my lungs. With each breath, may I breathe in your courage and remove every doubt as I exhale. May my words give You the glory. Amen.*" Wes adjusted his tie, licked his thumb and combed his eyebrows. Then, spoke loud enough for Jennifer to hear him. "Jennifer, let's give them a service that will change their lives."

Jennifer got up from her knees, where she had been praying for Wes in the other room. "Okay, honey. I'm ready," she shouted, grabbed her things, and lifted her head to the heavens. *Thank you, God. Use us as you will.*

The praise singers had the crowd focused and prepared for the message that was coming. Wes stood in the wings of the stage and scanned the crowd, feeling smaller and less equipped the longer he stood there. People were standing, clapping, jumping and raising their hands. He took a deep breath, leaned in to kiss Jennifer on the cheek, and put his hands together asking her to pray.

Jennifer handed Wes a phone receiver. "I had the stage-hand call Jordan. Here, talk to him."

"How long is the cord?" He shrugged, took the receiver, and the whole phone, out to the stage.

"Babe, what are you doing?" Jennifer tried to grab his arm, but it was too late. *Oh, Lord, guide him to better judgment.*

"Hello everybody. So great to be here. Thought I would give God a call." Wes held up the phone to a crescendo of applause.

The crowd rumbled with interest and anticipation, wondering what he was doing.

"Well, before I do that, let me say hi to my son, and talented musician, Jordan."

The crowd hooted and hollered like they were at a sports event and the players were being introduced.

Wes held the receiver to his ear, "Jordan, hi, buddy. We wish you were here." The crowd went wild, trying to make sure Jordan could hear them. "Let me put the phone to the mic. Say hi to these beautiful people, son."

He held the phone receiver to the mic. "Dad, are you sure?"

The audience giggled at the humanization of the celebrity evangelist's family.

"Son, you are live. What do you want to tell the folks?"

"Uh. Hi, everybody. I wish I was there."

The audience's response grew to a crescendo, clapping and yelling, in efforts for Jordan to hear them. Someone from the back of the crowd shouted, "We wish you were here, too." The others laughed and agreed.

Jordan chuckled. "Okay, okay. I *will* be at the next one... *with* my guitar and will sing a song *just* for you guys." The crowd roared in applause. "I can't wait. Now... without further ado, everybody, give me a drum roll, please."

The crowd slapped their thighs and chair backs in a drum roll, drawing them into participation of the meeting.

Jordan cleared his throat, "Please welcome my dad, Pastor Wes Lyons, who will escort you into the presence of God. Dad, we are ready and waiting for God's Word today."

The crowd clapped into a frenzy of anticipation. Wes glanced at Jennifer, who was waiting off stage left. "C'mon out here, Jennifer. Say hi to the folks before we dive into the Word." He held out his arm in a live invitation.

Initially, Jennifer gave the universal symbol for 'kill it,' drawing a line across her neck with her thumb and shaking her head 'no.'

The audience increased their enthusiasm, trying to draw her out to the stage. She gave in to the response, just to get past the moment and move on.

Jennifer stepped just inside the view of the crowd and Wes motioned her out farther. "Everybody, this is Jennifer. Please welcome her. I would not be here with you right now if it weren't for her." *Truer words have never been spoken.*

Jennifer forced a smile, speaking softly away from the mic, "Okay. You knew exactly what you were doing with the phone. Next time leave me out of it," she winked, "I love you." She turned and waved as she exited the stage.

Wes applauded softly and turned toward her as she exited and blew her a kiss.

Then, returned his focus to the audience. "Now, please bow your heads and let's get ready for God." He waited for everyone to quiet their attitudes and voices, "Lord, please take this time as your own. I am just a simple man who wants to help people connect with you. Use me, a common man, to do extraordinary things in Your name. We need You like the air we breathe. God, be our air and sustenance. In Jesus' name, Amen."

The crowd raised their heads. "Amen."

Wes surveyed the crowd and took a deep breath. The introduction was in his wheelhouse. He owned it, relaxing in his strengths. Next came the hard part, the preaching. In fact, he never called it preaching. He called it 'sharing.' He felt capable of sharing, but did not feel capable of preaching. Thank God for all his dad's sermon manuscripts. Hundreds of sermons that had never been presented. Harold had a gift for the construction of a sermon. Wes had a gift for the delivery.

Wes scanned the crowd. Nestled in with the "regular ole Joes," he saw A-list celebrities from all sectors of entertainment. Sitting next to academy award winning actors, he saw New York Times best-selling authors, Grammy winning musicians, and professional athletes, many in their sunglasses and accompanied by an entourage or security. Overcome by seeing these movie stars in the audience, he decided to avoid specifically staring at their faces. *Oh, my gosh. What am I DOING here? C'mon, you can do this. When you scan the audience, gaze about a foot above their heads... grin... and nod a lot.*

He took in the sea of people and began. "The phone," he paused awaiting everyone's full attention, "I just had a brief conversation with my son, Jordan, on the phone. Just using a phone prompts us to do certain things. Just holding a phone signals your brain that you will soon be talking...*and listening.* Every day, we talk to friends, family, and colleagues. There will be words of expectation, explanation, conflict, and resolution. There will be tones of welcome, separation, anger, joy, and need. Whether we think of it or not, a phone whets the appetite for communication just like an appetizer prepares you for the steak.

"Let me get personal here. When was the last time you prayed? I mean really poured out your heart to God?" His confidence was improving and he scanned the crowd to see he had everyone's undivided attention... even the celebrities. "When was the last time you picked up the phone and poured out your heart to your best friend? We will all get closer to God, when we learn to include him in our lives, just like we do everyone else." The outdoor amphitheater was so quiet you could hear the distant traffic in the valley. Wes reached for the text written by his dad. "The scripture says, "Be joyful always. Pray continually, give thanks in all circumstances, for this is God's will for you in Christ Jesus. 1 Thessalonians 5:15-18. In other words, we all should continually communicate with God about our lives, pour out our feelings, and listen for His response, just like we do with the friends we trust the most. So, what am I getting at? Most of us spend much more time on the phone, telling our thoughts, feelings, hurts, and joys to our friends. I wonder what would happen if we gave the same time, energy, and devotion to talking to God about our lives. While you are talking to God, be prepared for His response. After all, a true conversation includes talking *and* listening. As you bear your soul to God, he will fill your heart with words of wisdom. So, this is my challenge to you today. The next time you pick up the phone to call your best friend, talk to God. Take His advice. The Bible tells us, 'For I know the plans I have for you, declares the Lord, plans to prosper you and not to harm you, plans to give you hope and a future.' Who better to talk to about your needs, your failures, and successes than the all-powerful God, who has a future planned for you beyond your wildest dreams? Sounds like a no-brainer, doesn't it? Talk to God. Sometime when you get home, pour yourself a cup of coffee, sit on the couch, literally put the phone to your ear, and talk to God about your life."

Wes connected with the sea of faces again. It was as if he saw into their homes. He saw into their hearts and into their lives. Wes understood them because he was just like them, human in his struggles and needing something bigger than himself.

"Praise singers, please come back to the stage and close out our services. Thank you, God, for another day to serve others and serve You."

Wes turned to leave the stage as his eyes scanned the wings for Jennifer. He grabbed her hand and with tears in his eyes, he poured out his feelings. "Why am I in this position? I am the least prepared to teach about God. I never went to seminary. I have not even read the Bible completely through." He hung his head. In his focus given to Jennifer, he accidentally knocked Jennifer's Bible out of her hand. When he bent over to pick it up, he noticed the pages fell gracefully open to a particular passage. Tears ran across his cheeks, "Wow, Jennifer read this." He handed the book to her.

Jennifer read the only underlined passage on the page, "Matthew 19:30; But many who are first will be last, and many who are last will be first." She lowered the book. "I guess God just gave you your answer."

Chapter 33

Present Day

Eric saw Ginger's Porsche from about a block away. Ginger pulled into the rehab center's circle drive, and there stood Eric, his duffel bag packed and seated with a nurse's aide on a nearby bench. He smiled, "Hi, babe. Man is it good to see you outside the walls of this fine establishment."

The nurse's assistant snapped her gum and stood. "Okay Mr. Harrison, you have your instructions in hand. I will let the charge nurse know your ride got here and you left."

Eric defended himself. "I didn't mean I was going A.W.O.L. I was going to peacefully and quietly wait for my—"

The nursing assistant glared at Eric in amazement. "Actually, sir, you said something like, 'I don't care what you people say, I am leaving this place right now. I will wait, however long it takes, outside on the benches.' So, here

I have been sitting with *you*, when I should be on my private smoke break." She turned to Ginger, "Every single one of us have had to take our cherished smoke break with *him*. That started about two hours ago." She crossed her arms and waited for his response.

"I didn't think it was any big deal. Why did it matter?" Eric thought he had a good case.

Ginger put a hand on her hip. "I would be so mad at you if you did that to me, Eric."

"What'd I do?" He turned both palms up.

"Eric, imagine this: You are working short-handed and are stressed out because a patient was sent out for chest pain, you just dug a pencil eraser out of another resident's ear and then spent ten minutes trying to explain to a deaf resident how to use their new remote control. You are struggling to maintain your composure and all that will get you through the shift is the thought of ten minutes of solace delivered in the form of a smoke break. At times, I have actually thought I heard angels singing when I rolled the wheel on my Zippo. Now, do you get it? They don't have enough time in the day to properly take care of the people who really need something. Then some self-absorbed, cocky guy announces that he is going to wait outside, all day, if need be, to wait on his ride. These folks are here to take care of you," she poked her finger in his chest, "until they have finished their job and handed you off to your caregiver, they can't leave you by yourself outside. If you were to get injured on rehab property, they would be liable."

"Uh, oh. I wondered why everybody who sat outside with me gave me the fish-eye and cold shoulder."

The nursing aide turned to Ginger and nodded. "Self-absorbed, that is it. I was trying to put my finger on it. Well, I gotta get back in there. I have a breathing treatment to start." She turned to return to the building.

"Really, Eric? I can't believe you."

"Well, you only got one side of the story, Ms. God's Gift to Nurses. I may have put a cramp in their style, but the minute I knew you were coming to get me today, I packed my duffel bag and could think of nothing else.

The food is terrible. No seasoning and no *real* meat. A lot of processed meat-like stuff and canned vegetables. The oatmeal could be used as a brick mason's mortar, the coffee is cheap and even the chicken surprise was weird. They tell you *when* you can go to meals, there is no sleeping-in, and the guy in the room next to me watches *Bonanza* every afternoon. Do you know how I know that? I know his whole television schedule by heart because I can hear every single word through the thin walls in there. The only way I could combat it was to put my television on the same station, or completely leave the area. I was going crazy in there, baby. I just had to get out of there. I didn't know I was creating a problem. Crazy because they were so controlling, and crazy because I was apart from you. Your little visits just weren't enough."

"Well, I guess it wasn't easy for you, either." She puckered her lips in a playful kiss. "Now that I am breaking you out of this joint," she glanced right and left as if she was really breaking him out of jail, "where do you want to go? How about a nice steak dinner? The food in a re-hab facility usually *does* suck. Now that I have you out of 'lock-down,' let's get you some really good food. No, I've got it," Ginger rubbed hands together, "let's grab a gourmet pizza, a six-pack of micro-brew, and listen to some Nora Jones at my place."

"That ... sounds ... amazing, but I want to make one stop first." Eric winked.

"Really? What?" Ginger thought it sounded pretty good, too. Plus, not to mention, the obvious innuendo that they would enjoy some long overdue private time.

"I want to go to D.J.'s and see our favorite bartender."

Ginger smiled in agreement. "Dixie would love that."

Eric pulled out his phone. "Did you know that she sent me a funny meme almost every day? The memes were funny, but it was more like she was telling me she was thinking of me. Other than you, babe, Dixie helped me get through those days in rehab more than anyone else."

"That is a great idea, Eric. Why don't we drop by for a few beers and good conversation, and then phone in our pizza order? It will be ready and we can just buzz by and get it."

"Now you're talking."

###

The door at D.J.'s bar swung open with a whoosh. Ginger stepped forward with both hands straight up over her head. "Look what the cat drug up."

"Ginger, hi." Dixie was excited to see her lifelong buddy.

Ginger then stepped to the side and directed Dixie's attention like Vanna White revealing another letter. "Not me … Eric."

He peeked his head around the corner with his pearly-white teeth glistening behind his smile.

"Eric, come over here. Long time, no see." She dropped her bar rag right then and there and ran toward him.

Eric stepped forward with the use of a cane, holding his free arm out for a long overdue hug.

Ginger started looking up the pizza joint on her phone while Eric and Dixie popped open 3 beers and waited until the order was placed. Ginger joined them at the bar and raised her bottle in a toast, "Here's to all of us. All three fighters … all three lovers … all three winners," They clinked their bottles, "chin chin."

This is one of the best days of my life, and I still haven't even got to the pizza and *other activities.*

"Activities?" Dixie baited. "You guys better have the most passionate, creative, sweaty sex you have ever had … TONIGHT. Now THAT will make it memorable.

Ginger added, "I'll drink to that!" and they all giggled while Eric and Ginger held hands till the beers were empty and they left for their much-awaited rendezvous.

Chapter 34
2000s

Sitting backward on the piano bench, Wes dabbed the sweat away from his forehead with a monogrammed handkerchief. He turned to see the empty stadium seating. With the hot stage lights turned off, he was alone for a moment and still basking in the warmth of the love exchanged within the walls of this hallowed, iconic arena, Madison Square Garden. *What a great show. Thank you, God.*

"Wes?" Jennifer could tell he was in deep thought. "Whatcha thinking?"

He turned with a smile before he even saw her. "Well, I am not really thinking ... just feeling, feeling the lingering warmth of love from the show. Wasn't it amazing, babe?"

"The connection between everyone was palpable ... and in Madison Square Garden? A memory we will never forget." She basked in the memory of the crowd.

Wes got up and gave Jennifer a sweet gentle kiss on her lips. "I had a childhood dream of playing Madison Square Garden. My dream was fronting a band with my long hair flowing and our amps blaring rock music."

"Crazy how things sometimes turn out even better than your dreams." Jennifer smiled.

"Well, speak for yourself, but I would still love to crank out a stellar rock anthem from this stage ... maybe next time I will do just that." He played air guitar and threw his head back like a rock star.

"Okay, Steven Tyler, let's get your feet firmly on the ground again," she gave him a playful shove, "earth to Wesley, come in Wesley."

"You made your point, can't blame an old rock musician for trying."

"Babe, I know you want to drive back to Atlanta, but I think I will fly back with the rest of the crew. I just want to get back to Jordan and wake up to his haystack hair sitting at the breakfast table and give him a big ole hug."

"That sounds like a plan. It will be good for me, too, probably. Give me time to think and pray ... and enjoy my new Jaguar XJS convertible." He smiled so big you could see the entire new set of pearly white teeth his dentist gave him last year.

"Okay, then, honey. If you don't mind, I am off with the crew. Please call home tonight when you stop at a hotel."

"Sounds great, I will be home before you know it. I can't wait to see Jordan, too." Wes embraced Jennifer. Holding her close, he whispered into her ear, "I am the luckiest man I know. Love you."

"Love you, too. Are you gonna start out in the morning?"

"No, babe, my mind is still alive with adrenaline. I won't be able to sleep for hours. I think I will go ahead and get on the road. I will get a room."

"Okay. Have fun on your way home. You deserve it. I had enough "fun" riding with you in the Jag all the way to New York. It was great, but remember to check the speed limits as you go down the highway. I will just leave it at that."

"Aye, aye, Captain." He clicked his heels and saluted Jennifer in a slapstick manner.

Wes saw his luxury ride waiting. The crew had it pulled alongside the back of the building, and all he had to do was hop in and scratch rubber as he left. His bags were already packed and he was good to go. "Thanks, Joe." Wes held out his hand for a high-five.

"She's gassed up and ready to go, boss."

"That's Wes. Please call me Wes. Did you test it out a little while you were out to get gas?"

"Oh, no sir. I just wanted..."

"Not even a little?"

"Well, there was that one time I had to pass another car." He winked at him with a grin of understanding. "Man, can she ever get down the road."

"Good, I am glad you enjoyed the ride. Thanks for all the prep work, Joe."

"Wes, I just want to thank you for being so kind. You don't treat me like a greasy roadie. You treat me like I am one of your buddies. I will always be around to help you."

"Thanks, man. You *are* one of my guys. Take care. See you again after the European leg of the tour. We head for Ireland in just a few days."

"I'll be ready. Always remember, there's no place like home."

"You got that right. I always love coming home." Wes gave a wave goodbye.

With Wes's wrist draped across the steering wheel, he jammed to Cream, one of his favorite bands from the past. He sang "White Room" at the top of his lungs.

Night pulled the shade, darkening the light on the horizon and Wes surveyed the stars in the sky. With the top down and his spirits high, he couldn't imagine a better drive, the wind in his hair and rock-n-roll playing in a magnificent car.

Wes started becoming a little drowsy, but he didn't want the evening to end. He reached in the console, trying to find his stash of speed, used to wake up from his sleeping pills. He chased the bottle with his hand to the left and right around other objects in the console. While he had one hand on the steering wheel and the other in the console, a skunk waddled into the highway. He jerked the wheel and the car careened off the road at a high rate of speed. He was thrown from his convertible and knocked unconscious.

The glistening stars and the full moon shined light on his motionless body. Travelers who saw the accident stopped and offered assistance. A woman pulled out his billfold to find identification. "Wes Lyons? *The* Wes Lyons. Guys, this is the famous preacher." She pulled out her cell phone and called for an ambulance.

Wes woke up in his hospital room to the beautiful sight of Jennifer by his side and holding his hand. "Oh, my shoulder, my neck ... what is this?" He reached up and touched a halo frame screwed into his skull that reminded him of Frankenstein.

"You rolled the convertible and amazingly survived, but you injured your shoulder, fractured your neck and ruptured your spleen. You have had surgery and the doctors say you will be sidelined while you recover. It is a miracle you are even breathing."

"Wow." He scanned the room like he was in a dream. "I better make some calls."

"I have made all the calls that need to be made. The press has also been very interested in your accident. We can deal with them later."

"Honey, I am really hurting. You think I could get something for pain?"

"Let me click the nurse's call light. No one wants you to hurt."

Chapter 35

2000s

Jordan's guitar was flipped upside down on his lap, and he was using it as a desk while he jotted down chords and lyrics to his new song. Then he flipped it back onto his knee and explored chord progressions. Just a teenager, he struggled with the spotlight pushed upon him by being the son of an American evangelical icon.

Isolated by the scrutiny of the public, he escaped to his small, trusted crew. His wounded heart struggled to heal following a recent breakup with his girlfriend, Madison. Young love had transitioned from hope and laughter to despair and tears.

Jennifer knocked on his bedroom door. "Time for supper." Her attempt to connect with him was met with silence. "Son, may I come in."

Jordan gave a huge exhale, "Okay, Mom, C'mon in." He set his guitar to the side and quickly made a few notes.

Jennifer stepped into his room and sniffed like she was trying to figure out the smell that accosted her olfactory nerve as she entered. "What *is* that smell? Oh my, Jordan." She covered her nose with her sleeve.

"What, Mom? I don't smell anything."

"It has been days since you have even left your room. I have supper ready; please come eat at the table." Jennifer was concerned about Jordan. He just wasn't himself.

"Okay, Mom, I'll do it for you." He ran his hand through his greasy, uncombed hair and gave her a hug before going to the kitchen.

He reached out his arms and the closer he got it was apparent that *he* was what exuded the pungent odor. Jennifer scrunched up her nose and turned her head. "Jordan, supper will keep. You have to take a shower first. You haven't taken a shower all weekend, have you?"

"Ah, Mom. C'mon." He threw his arms to his side in protest.

"Son, you smell like a teenage boy, with raging hormones and sweat glands that have been working overtime."

Jordan raised his arm to smell his armpit, "Whoa! Okay, I didn't know all that was going on."

"Did you even take a shower after soccer practice on Friday?"

He held up a finger like he was going to give his defense. "Uh ... well..."

Jennifer closed her eyes and turned her head in disgust. "Stop, just stop. Shower, son. This is one of the things that separates humans from beasts, a shower. Right now, you smell like the latter."

"Well, what is for supper?" Jordan weighed the cost of taking the shower against the benefit of dinner. If it was gonna be something gross, no way was it worth it to him.

Jennifer could tell he was weighing his options and she was dumbfounded. "What is the big deal about taking a shower? Madison will not be able to stay in the same room with you, much less hold your hand or kiss you."

His head dropped at her words. "She kicked me to the curb after soccer practice Friday. I can't believe it, Mom." His tears started to flow and he couldn't control his emotions any longer.

"Oh, Jordan, I am so sorry. What happened?" She reached to hug him and somehow her concern grew larger than his stench.

"I can't compete with the quarterback on the football team. He is already *shaving*. I may be a year older, but I could be his little brother."

"You know what, Jordan, if she will let her head be turned by every new boy that passes by, maybe she isn't the one for you."

"Oh, Mom, no. She was the one. She is beautiful, smart, funny—"

"And evidently a spoiled girl who is distracted by the lesser things in life. Someday a girl will come along and it won't be such hard work to be with her. You will find that person who just fits."

She opened his bedroom door to exit and looked back at him. "Shower first, then come on out for spaghetti; brownies for dessert."

"Okay. I will be there in a minute." He whined in a pathetic tone.

"I will keep it warm for you."

Jordan went to the mirror and saw nothing but a frail, little boy. His voice had not yet changed and neither had the rest of his body. He felt as if he was a little kid swimming in a sea of mature, cool and handsome guys. Jordan took a shower and after he got out, he was glad he did. *I hate it when Mom is right.*

When Jordan got to the supper table, Wes was telling Jennifer about his shoulder pain. "Yeah, so the doctor told me to take this new pain prescription. It has been out a few years, Oxycodone. It has really helped. I feel so lucky there is medication that can take away the pain. I just got a new prescription of it today." He then turned his attention to Jordan. "Son, your mom told me about Madison. There are a lot of fish in the sea." Wes reached for the salad tongs and served himself some greens.

Jordan winced as his dad's words cut straight to his bruised heart. "She *was* everything. She stole my heart and then stomped on it. I don't want to talk about it anymore." He took the large spaghetti bowl and then pushed it away, instead of serving himself a portion. "I can't eat. I'll be in my room."

"Just wait a minute, son. I'm sorry. I am just trying to say that you are young and will find another girl—"

"Dad, I loved her—"

Jennifer's head snapped around to Jordan's direction. "Loved?"

"I know you guys think I don't know what love is, but as far as I understand it... I loved her and she turned away from me without any care for my feelings. The minute someone else asked her out, she was out the door. I don't expect you to understand everything I am saying, I just need you to be here for me. I am going back to my room.

If I get hungry, I'll raid the fridge." He pushed his chair back from the table and left without another word.

Jennifer handed the spaghetti serving bowl to Wes. "That blind-sided me. How about you?"

Wes took a long sip of tea. "I knew he *liked* her a lot. Puppy love can be tough. I'll make more time to spend with him over the next few days. He will be fine."

On his way back to his room, Jordan passed by his mom and dad's bedroom and it triggered an idea. Dad just said he got a new prescription of pain pills. The guys in the locker room were talking about oxy. *I bet that is what they are talking about.* He checked left and right and scrambled into their bedroom with attached bathroom, where Wes kept his medications. There it was sitting on the side of his sink, begging Jordan to take it. He stuffed the dark green plastic bottle in his pocket and continued on to his room before his folks got up from the table. He could hear them laughing and teasing each other. He was in such pain; it was difficult to hear others who were happy.

Jordan sat on the edge of his bed and took the pill bottle in his hand, wondering what it was like to take them. The guys said you feel like you are floating away, no pain, no worries, no concerns... just floating. He went to his sink, gazed in the mirror and loathed the image in the mirror, the runt of his class, he was so tired of being overlooked. *It sure would be great to float away and feel numb, just for a while.* He opened the full bottle and poured out several in his hand. He didn't count them. He just took them ... all that he had in his hand.

It was about time to get ready for bed and they had not heard any more from Jordan. As they neared their bedroom, Wes decided to go check on him. He knocked on Jordan's door, but no response. "Hey, buddy, you want to jam a little? Bring your guitar and we can jam by the piano. You choose the music this time." He waited in silence. *Well, I'll try again tomorrow.*

Wes went on to bed and put his arm around the woman he loved. It made him ponder his son's feelings even more. *How would I feel if I suddenly lost Jennifer? Not just separated in body, but separated in emotion and commitment.* As he let his mind proceed down this path, he suddenly became quite thirsty. *I love those pain pills, but I hate the way they make me so thirsty.*

He tried to not awaken Jennifer and slid out of bed to get a drink. He reached for his water glass and noticed the green pill bottle was gone. He rummaged along the countertop. No sign of the pills. He searched the floor and saw nothing. His mind drifted back to Jordan and a chill went up his spine. He shouted aloud, "No! Not Jordan!"

Jennifer propped on her elbow in bed to see him running out the bedroom. She got up and heard him, shouting, "Jordan, Jordan, open the door." Wes grabbed the doorknob and it was locked. He rattled it, trying to open it. Then, with one smooth kick, he broke down the door. There lay his son, one hand on his guitar and the other with Madison's picture. He lay lifeless. "Jennifer, call 911."

Chapter 36

Present Day

Skylar sang and couldn't help but dance a little jig while she gathered stuff out of the fridge for omelets. She loved cooking like a boss. "Grandma, do you want cheese?"

"Of course. That is the best part of the omelet." Her grandma grinned.

"Did you sleep well?"

"I did pretty good for an old woman. Those eggs are smelling pretty good. Thanks." She re-arranged her place-setting in anticipation.

"Grandma, I will be a little later today. I have nursing prep class and we run late sometimes." She slid the spatula under the perfect omelet and served the eggs to the plate. "The grape jelly and butter are on the table."

"Thank you so much for the beautiful breakfast." She stirred the cream and sugar in her coffee.

Skylar grabbed her backpack and kissed her grandma on the cheek, "See you later."

"I am so proud of you, baby. You will be the first of our family to go to college." She took her toast and sopped up the last of the eggs on her plate.

###

James sat on post, down the hall from Wes's room, "reading" his detective novel and scanning the hall from his viewpoint, gathering answers to the mysterious Wes Lyons. He pulled his note pad from his pocket and dabbed the pencil tip to his tongue as he reviewed his notes. "*Tough, Hispanic young man visited. Astros cap and sunglasses.*" That was the last visitor James had seen. James returned his attention to his book and he heard the jostle of cups, papers, and pens while Skylar pushed the med cart down the hall.

James took casual notice of the young nurse's aide. Just another part of his regular day of repetition at Fireside.

She stopped with her cart outside a resident's room. She took a tiny cup from a stack on her cart and poured water into it. Then she found the resident's name on the flow-sheet notebook. She opened the top drawer and pulled out a couple of bubble-punch cards. She punched out pills from the bubble cards into a tiny cup and wrote in her notebook. Then, she unlocked the second drawer, popped out a pill, returned the card to the drawer, and locked it. She knocked on the door of the resident.

James decided to write her habits on paper; after all, he had been taking notes on every other Tom, Dick, and Harry roaming down the hall.

Skylar got to the next room, marked in her notebook, and went about the same process. She knocked on the next door and repeated the same process. James knew her routine and was beginning to get bored. Nothing happening here. James returned his attention to his book and returned the little notebook to his pocket.

He heard her move to the next resident. He was condi-tioned to investigate if he heard new activity. She went through her routine one more time. As she approached Wes's door, James decided to watch her again. She pulled the cart over to the wall.

Skylar took a drink from her insulated cup and checked out her surroundings. James kept his book in reading position, but he was really peeking over the top watching Skylar's every move. She unlocked the second drawer and walked across the tops of the cards with her fingers, reading names to the very back of the filed cards. She found the card she wanted, moved it to the front of the stack, and knocked on Wes's door.

Hmmm. This is interesting.

She knocked on the door, and a ragtag Wes answered the door, yawning. "Hi, Skylar, what's up?"

"Well, just making my rounds. Do you need your temperature checked?"

Odd question. James pulled out his notepad and started making his notes. He could make out some of their conversation.

"Thank you for dropping by. Come on in." He opened the door a little wider. As she pushed the cart through, he took a quick peek down the hall to see who was around.

James kept his book up in a reading position, the perfect cover for a man who read a lot and spoke very little. His mind was racing, and his heart was sinking. *This just didn't check out. Things are out of sequence.*

After a few minutes, Skylar emerged from Wes's room and pushed the cart right past James.

"Hi, Skylar. How's my favorite aide?"

"Oh, Hi, Mr. Johnson. I'm good." She flashed a smile and kept moving down the hall.

Guess it is time to talk to Ginger.

James transferred out of the comfy wingback chair to his wheelchair and cruised to Ginger's office. "Hey, Chief, you got a minute." He raised his notepad, "I got some things you may be interested in."

"Great. Step right in here, my friend."

"Really, Ginger? *Step* right in?"

"Oh, you know what I mean. Come on in. You are more able-bodied sitting in that wheelchair than most are on two legs."

"True." James gave a couple of pushes on the rims of his chair and coasted to Ginger's desk. "I don't think you are gonna want to hear what I have to say."

Ginger pushed away from her desk and stepped around to a chair near James.

"How do you know that?"

"I think Skylar is sneaking narcotics to Wes."

Ginger was in shock. "Whoa, here, James. Those are some pretty big accusations. She is the best aide we have."

"Well, here, consider my notes. I just noticed she had a very defined routine for all the residents as she passed out meds, but when she got to Wes's room, her routine changed."

Ginger pulled her eyes away from the notepad. "Tell me more."

James interlocked his fingers and assumed the posture of a relaxed witness under interrogation. "I watched her work her way down the hall. I figured out that the regular meds, like heart meds and stomach meds, are in the top drawer. Most people got six to eight pills from that drawer. If they got anything out of the locked drawer, it was only one or two pills, and she locked it back the instant she finished returning the card to its assigned position in the cart. Another interesting fact, if she gave one of the residents a pill from the locked drawer, she didn't have to dig very deep into the drawer to find their pill card. When she got to Wes's room, she checked out her surroundings, unlocked the drawer, dug to the back of the filed pill cards, and pulled one to the front. When Wes came to the door and I heard her ask, "Do you want me to check your temperature?"

Ginger's face sobered quickly as she followed James's story and was amazed at the deductive skills James showed.

Never raising up, Ginger sat with her elbows on her knees. "She is the best aide I have, James."

"Well, I may be wrong, but it seems to me that the best aide you have is dealing drugs. I'm sorry, Ginger. I hope I am wrong." James patted Ginger on her head and spun around to leave.

"Dang! Can I keep this notepad?"

"Sure, Red. Catch ya later."

Ginger knew what she had to do and she had to do it sooner than later.

Chapter 37

Present Day

Walking into the nursing aides' classroom, Ginger had one thing on her mind. She sat on the edge of a table and started the class with an unusual opening comment. "Honesty. Compassion. Integrity, and Perseverance. These four cornerstones of nursing are not what most think of when they consider the components of the exceptional nurse." She stood and distributed a handout with only these four words highlighted in the center of the sheet. "You can learn medications and reactions. You can study the parts of the body and the diseases that attack it. But listen to these next words, if you hear anything I have ever told you. You can be the best in the class when it comes to nursing knowledge, but if you don't possess these characteristics, you are not worth the price of the paper your diploma is printed on. Honesty. Compassion. Integrity and Perseverance. Never forget these four words. Your assignment for this class is to take this handout and give one example of using each of these attributes in nursing, then, one example of the lack of these attributes in nursing. You are dismissed if there are no questions."

The class was all a-buzz with the shock of being released from class the moment they got there. They searched each other's faces in disbelief. A response came from a girl on the back row, "No questions here, ma'am."

"Very well, don't half-ass this, guys. This is probably the most important exercise I have given you all year. Give it the kind of attention and effort it deserves."

As the nurse 'hopefuls" stood from their desks and start-ed filing out, she waited for Skylar. As Skylar exited the room, Ginger approached her, "Skylar, can I see you in my office ... now."

"Can I run to the break room—"

"Now, Skylar, this can't wait." Before the class started, Ginger did some research of her own and reviewed re-ports to see those patients who either recently died or moved out of Fireside. From that list, she knew those who used pain meds. The short list of pain med users who no longer lived at Fireside gave Ginger a roadmap to the answer.

###

Ginger was sitting at her desk and flipping through some papers when Skylar arrived. As her image darkened Ginger's office door, Ginger greeted her with a stoic expression. "Have a seat, Skylar."

"Is everything okay?" Skylar knocked on the door as a courtesy before entering.

"No, everything is not okay. I was reconciling ledgers from med pass. Something isn't adding up."

She swallowed, and it was like the tension squeezed off her air supply. "Oh, really? I didn't know you did that."

"Where is the med cart?"

Skylar wrung her hands. "I haven't seen it this morning, but it should be in the med room."

"Let's go get it."

"Oh, I can go get—"

"No. We will go together."

No pleasantries and smiles. Skylar ran her hand through her hair; this wasn't good. "Oh, okay. What is going on, Ginger?"

"I hope nothing."

They arrived at the cart, and Skylar grabbed the push bar. "Where are we going?"

"Back to my office."

The silence punished her, along the long hall back to Ginger's office. Skylar ravaged her brain, trying to think of what to say... what not to say, but her mind was a blur.

They approached Ginger's office, and emotions were at a crescendo.

They entered, and Rob, summoned as a witness, was already sitting in a desk-side chair. "I came as soon as I got word. What is going on, G?"

"I hope it is all a misunderstanding," Ginger reached for a patient list of those residents who were deceased or hospitalized from her desk and held it up. "I have reason to believe that you have been stealing narcotics, Skylar. We are here together, in front of a witness, to see what my inspection shows. You deserve to know of this suspicion before I inspect the med cart. Do you have anything to say?"

Skylar felt as if she were in a bad dream and her soul had been shattered the moment the words "stealing narcotics" pierced her ears. "I don't know what to say." Her head bowed in shame.

"Just say you didn't do it." Ginger closed her eyes in pain.

Skylar's face was wet with tears. The taste of salt saturated her taste buds as the tears washed across her face. A steady stream quietly seeped down her cheeks, dripping from her chin. "I can explain—"

"Oh my God, it is true?" Ginger had been hoping for the best. She picked up the receiver and watched Skylar's young life unravel before her eyes.

Skylar walked over and gently put her hand on the receiver and guided it back to the cradle. "I have never asked you for anything. Please, let me tell you what happened."

"Okay. Take your time and try to calm down. I want to make this work."

She took a deep breath. "It's my grandma. I am not taking them myself." Skylar couldn't make eye contact anymore, but continued with her confession. "She suffers with terrible back pain. She had multiple surgeries quite some time ago and they recently reduced her pain medicine, you know, new federal regulations." She stared at the floor, then took a deep breath as she raised her head with closed eyes.

"Who are *they*?" Ginger asked without emotion.

"Her pain management doctors." Skylar offered and continued, "I couldn't bear to watch her in excruciating pain. Day in and day out, like a clamp closing a little more each day, the pain was squeezing the very life out of her body. I noticed that when people go to the hospital or die, the narcotics bubble card is filed to the back of the cart. I never took meds from someone who needed them. I only took pills that would be thrown away anyway. I swear on a stack of Bibles."

Ginger connected eyes with Skylar for the first time during this conversation. "Who else did you sell them to?"

"I never sold them and I never used them. Test me. Test me right now."

"You mean to tell me you stole pain meds from dead people and never sold them or took them yourself?"

"That is exactly what I am saying."

Ginger picked up her phone and called the med room, "Bring me a urinalysis cup, please. Back to my previous question. You gave the pills only to your grandma?"

"Well, not exactly. Pastor Wes approached me one day. He was complaining about his excruciating pain. You know, he had a terrible car wreck about twenty years ago. He asked for some relief. I split my grandma's pills with him a few times."

"You gave drugs you stole from dead people to your grandmother and a preacher... and you never took one pill yourself?"

"That *is* it, in a nutshell. Yes."

"Why Pastor Lyons?"

"Well," Skylar reflected for a moment to make sure she got it right. "His doctors cut him off, too. We had a few conversations about my grandma and how concerned I was about her. He told me about his struggles with pain and we gave each other support."

About that time, there was a knock on the door frame. The urinalysis cup had been delivered.

"Okay. This is how it is going to go. There will be a witness for every interaction we have going forward. First, you will give me a urine sample, then you will write this entire story down on paper. We will ask employees if they have any first-hand knowledge of these occurrences. If they do, they too will write a narrative of what they know." Ginger gathered all her strength and looked her in the eye, "This is hard for me to say. You have shown so much potential. It is the policy of this facility that any employee caught stealing medications, especially opioids, is terminated immediately." Tears pooled at the corners of Ginger's eyes. "Today will be your last day at Fireside. Depending on the results of the urinalysis, there could be next steps taken."

"Next steps? What else is there?"

Still in a serious, yet kind tone, she said, "Skylar. You just confessed to stealing narcotics from a nursing facility. That is a felony."

"N-n-n-no. Wait. That's not me."

"Good intentions or bad intentions, the law calls it stealing opioids." Ginger turned to Rob. "Take notes on what you just heard. C'mon, Skylar. You have a urine sample to give me."

Once the sample gathering process was completed, Ginger escorted her to the door. "Skylar, I want you to know I still have your back and I want the best for you. Champions in life face the truth and in the midst of adversity, will themselves to a place of success, tied up in the wrappings of honesty, compassion, integrity, and perseverance. This valley of despair can lead to the true calling on your life. Don't miss it. Your life isn't over, but at least for now, your life at Fireside is."

Chapter 38

2000s

Wes dragged Jordan's body onto the floor and started C.P.R., keeping pace like the beat in the song, "Stayin' Alive." That was the only thing he remembered from health class in high school.

Jennifer ran back into Jordan's bedroom. "I left the front door open. I can hear their sirens, almost here." She ran to the front yard and flagged them in.

The ambulance parked and two young paramedics hopped out and asked basics as they came into the house.

Jennifer spoke quickly. "We found him unconscious in his bedroom with his dad's pill bottle near him. Almost half were gone."

The paramedics came through Jordan's bedroom door and waved Wes off his son's body.

"We'll take over now, sir." The paramedic turned back to his teammate. "Starting eighteen-gauge I.V. with saline. Get the A.E.D. ready."

"Are you going to use the paddles on him?" Jennifer asked.

The paramedic turned to her. "Yes ma'am, that is the A.E.D." Wasting no time, he peeled the film from the back of each adhesive pad and placed them on Jordan's unresponsive torso. The A.E.D. assessment gave the green light for an electrical shock. "Clear." They flipped the switch and a charge of electricity bolted through Jordan's flaccid body.

Jordan's back arched like a demon was being pulled from his chest. Flat-line. The paramedic operating the A.E.D. announced to the room, "Let's pack him up and keep working on him. We will be going to Emory Midtown."

"We will follow you." Wes grabbed Jennifer's hand.

"If we lose you at a stoplight, just come to the waiting area in the E.R."

As they loaded him in the back of the ambulance, one ran to the driver's side and the other uttered one word as he dashed past Wes, "Pray."

Wes and Jennifer prayed intently as they waited. A man walked toward them wearing a pastor's collar and khakis. "He must be the chaplain." Wes scanned all around them, selfishly hoping the chaplain was coming to counsel someone else. "You are coming to speak to us?"

The chaplain approached them with his hand out. "Mr. and Mrs. Lyons? Come with me." He stretched out his hand and directed them to a counseling room.

Jennifer suddenly started breathing rapidly. She felt as if she was in someone else's nightmare. "Babe, what do we do?"

"C'mon, Jen, we have to find out what is going on." They stood and followed the chaplain into a small, cold room with a table and six chairs randomly placed around the room.

"The doctor will be here directly. I will be right outside the room." The chaplain gave a slight bow of respect and excused himself for the moment.

A man in light blue scrubs with a stethoscope around his neck knocked on the door frame and entered. "My name is Dr. Bennett. Your son suffered anoxic brain trauma from lack of oxygen to his brain. We exhausted all our capabilities but were not able to save him. I am so sorry for your loss."

Silence. "Well, isn't there more?" Wes quizzed. "Surely there is more to say."

"No, sir. There is nothing else to say. He was probably gone for quite some time before the paramedics got the call. If it is any consolation, he would have lived on a ventilator the rest of his life, if we had been able to restart his heart. I am so sorry."

Jennifer was in shock. "I thought once, why don't you go in there and talk with him, but I was trying to give him space. I could have stopped it."

"Ma'am, would you like me to have the chaplain pray with you?"

"No. I would *like* you to give me my son back." She searched his eyes, but there was nothing else to say. "Oh... I am sorry. Please leave us alone."

"Very well, then. Someone from the emergency department will have some papers for you to sign."

Every reference to death was like a jolt of electricity shooting through their bodies. "We got it, we got it ... we lost our precious son and you guys have stuff you have to do to move on to the next patient."

"We are not in a hurry. You can certainly take your time. The chaplain will direct you when you are ready to proceed."

Jennifer felt her mind slipping away from reality, as if in a dream of all the wonderful memories of Jordan. His antics, his deep-thinking, and his love for music. He was so much like his dad. "Thank you, doctor. We would like to see him before the funeral home comes."

"That's fine. The chaplain will take you to his bedside. I will send him immediately."

"Follow me." The chaplain led them to Jordan's corpse.

They stood in stillness and saw the life of potential victories and dreams that were extinguished and why? *Why?*

Jennifer laid her head on Jordan's chest. She glanced up and stroked the smooth angle of his jaw. "He hasn't even started to shave yet."

Wes didn't touch him, couldn't look at him. He felt such guilt. They were *his* pills. "I am so sorry, son." He caved into a trembling shell of a man.

Jennifer on the other hand, couldn't let go. Other than the obvious attempts to save his life, with nearby tubes, cords and monitors, he seemed to be just sleeping. "I want to stay with him a while, Wes."

They found that they dealt with the tragedy differently. Jennifer couldn't let go of him because she was afraid that she would forget bits about her son. Wes couldn't allow himself to connect with Jordan's death and Jennifer's sorrow. He didn't think he could survive the torment.

Wes sat in a booth at the nearby burger joint and waited on the tour manager for his next Wes Lyons Ministries Tour. Wes inspected his phone to see if he had missed calls. Nothing. It had become a nervous habit since Jordan's death, always wanting to be responsive and ready for any dilemma.

In strolled a guy in his fifties, wearing his sunglasses indoors. Wes thought to himself, *yep, looks like a rock-n-roll tour manager to me.*

"Hi. Are you Wes?"

Wes stood to shake his hand. "Yes, thank you for meeting me on short notice. I just want to get prepared."

"I have to admit, I never have managed a ministry tour. I have only managed concert tours. Do you think we will be a good match?"

"The best match. I don't *want* it to feel like church. I want it to feel like a concert."

"Well, then, I am your guy."

"I want it to be up-beat, fun, and spiritually challenging. I want to integrate a light show, great music, and opportunities for the congregation to participate."

"Let me put some things together and we can meet again."

Wes smiled at the possibility of working with one of the best concert producers of all time. "Great. Here's my card. It has all my contact information. Talk to you soon." He reached out his hand and gave it a one beat handshake.

The producer turned to leave and Wes interjected, "I want to create a performance my son would be proud of."

The producer pulled down his shades so Wes could see his eyes. "I will do my very best."

Chapter 39

2000s

Wes sat at his desk, staring for hours at the same phone number scratched on his calendar. *How can I go teach a multitude of people about the goodness of God, when I feel abandoned, lost, and so inadequate? I should have seen Jordan's heartbreak. I should have been there for him.*

He picked up his phone again and pondered the phone number written on the date of his next show, in his calendar. He had circled it; drawn a star to mark it, and underlined the phone number three times. He just couldn't make himself dial the call.

Jennifer came down the hall drying her hands on her apron. "Honey, what are ya doing?"

Wes closed the calendar, knowing she was coming in his office. As she entered, he gave her his full attention. "Trying to get organized." He grinned briefly, not wanting to bring her down. His skin stretched tightly around the corners of his mouth reminding him of how long it had been since he smiled.

"Let's get out of the house, babe. How about we get in the car and go to the drive-in? I think a chocolate sundae would really hit the spot and it would get us out of the house." She started untying her apron around her waist.

Wes held his arms out, inviting her to come closer. As Jennifer drew near, she sat on his lap and draped her arms around his neck.

"Yes? You were saying?" He held her around the waist.

"Well, I think we should go to the drive-in and get out of this morbid, gloomy house. I think both of us are breaking inside, but we don't want to let each other down, so we aren't talking ... about *anything*, but especially not talking about Jordan."

"Wow, Jen, you are right. I don't want to bring you down, but I can't get my mind on anything else *but* Jordan. I was just considering canceling the next show, in Seattle. I was about to call when you came in the room."

Jennifer took Wes's hand and brought it to her mouth for a heartfelt kiss. "I love you. How can we get through this if we are not talking?"

"I don't think I can... I mean my emotions are so intense, it is hard to name them or voice my feelings. I... I feel like the biggest loser in the—" He then let out a guttural noise like an animal in pain. Tears the size of raindrops trailed down his face and fell to the floor, as he leaned forward with his elbows on his knees. Jennifer knelt down in front of him, and embraced him, trying to shoulder some of his pain.

He leaned on her and she softly prayed. "God, here we are and we need your help. We are drowning in sorrow and feel as though we are going underwater. It is as if Jordan went under water in a sea of despair, and we saw him slip away. Now, we feel as if we are going underwater, too. Save us, God. Lead us to the place where we can serve you again as your servants to the masses, an example of strength and love. People look to us as an example and I'm ashamed to say I haven't talked with you lately, God, as I should have. We need you now more than ever. Amen."

"Amen. What a powerful prayer, honey. It does help to talk about it. I just didn't want to show my weakness." Wes stood and reached for the hand of the one person he knew really had his back. "Let's go to the drive-in. I'm getting a banana split."

"Of course, you are. You always get the biggest and the best."

Wes smiled a genuine smile. The first true smile he had given in a very long time.

###

They pulled up to the drive-in stall in Wes's classically restored 1976 Corvette Stingray. It was flawless. Collectors would say it was a "time capsule" because it was kept in such pristine original condition. He pulled in. "Hot fudge sundae, babe?"

"Of course. Extra fudge." She looked at him with the most mischievous smile.

"Oh, really. Well, I'll see your double hot fudge and raise you a banana split with extra nuts." They both died laughing.

"Okay, banana split guy, I need to slip out to the bathroom. They have one inside. Would you go ahead and order for me?"

"Sure, babe." Wes hit the glowing red button and waited to order.

Jennifer got out feeling more like herself and it was encouraging.

The car hop made her way to the Stingray. She looked to be in high school or college and for a brief moment, he thought to himself *I wonder if Jordan knew her.* He shook his head, trying to get some sense into his brain.

"I have a hot fudge, extra fudge and a banana split, extra nuts?"

"Yes, that's right."

"All this for you?" she teased.

"Oh, no. My—"

"Please don't tell me you have a girlfriend. All the hot guys already have girlfriends."

"Oh, no. You got me wrong, my—"

"That will be $5.25," The car hop continued as she saw Jennifer get nearer.

He paid and took the ice cream. "Keep the change."

The car hop spoke as she left, "Maybe I'll see you again sometime."

Jennifer flopped down in the low sitting sports car and was salivating at the thought of the hot fudge masterpiece. "Give me that sundae."

Wes couldn't get his mind off the car hop that seemed interested in him. He startled when he realized Jennifer was waiting. "Okay, here ya go."

They dove into the ice cream like it was an eating contest. Both of them laughing and gobbling up the sweet, cold confections. Wes felt a bit of steam was released from his soul. He was still lost and his heart still cramped with the pain of separation from his son, but he knew he couldn't keep all this bottled up inside. He had to talk it out.

Wes ran the chamois over the sparkling Stingray, polishing for a perfect shine. He had a stable of sports cars and the ride to the drive-in reminded him of how fun the classic Corvette was to drive. He glanced at his watch. "Oh my gosh, I have to get going." He had to drop off some documents to his tax guy and thought, *might as well take the Stingray again. She's shined and ready to go.* Wes got his briefcase and dropped into the Corvette and started it up. A classic Corvette had a unique sound, like a boat's motor under water, *lub-lub-lub.* Then he revved it like he was at the starting line and took off.

After dropping off the papers to his accountant, he drove past the drive-in, again. He thought, *why not.* He whipped the wheel and got a bit of rubber as he turned into the drive-in. He pulled up to a stall and ordered a Diet Coke.

The same car hop brought out his order. She smiled and said, that will be $1.28... then she pulled it back, "Or I'll buy your Coke... and you can buy me a spaghetti dinner sometime."

"Oh, I can't do that, I'm married. Have you ever seen me before?"

"Yeah, silly. You drove in a few days ago and got a hot fudge and banana split."

"No. I mean, uh, have you ever seen me before we came in for the sundae and banana split?"

A slow, sexy smile crept across her face. "Nope. Our recent meeting was enough." She smiled and reached in to hand him the drink. As he handed her the money, she touched his hand and dragged her fingers slowly down to his fingertips. "Maybe I'll see you again." She turned with a lingering look that gave Wes the shivers.

He was speechless and felt his heart pounding from the young girl's flirting. "Get a hold of yourself, Wes. What the heck are you doing? Get your head on straight." It was exhilarating to imagine the young girl was interested in him. After he pondered the situation a moment, he knew he better get home.

Wes started to frequent the drive-in and the hot car hop was always ready to strike up a conversation. Time passed and he became more comfortable with her, till one day, early afternoon, she gave him his drink, "That will be $1.28." She didn't make any small talk this time. Wes searched her eyes while she took the money. Then, she gave him a napkin, with something inside and left. He unfolded the napkin and inside was a note and a key wrapped inside.

She wrote, "This is a key to my apartment. I have got to see you. Tomorrow, I am off. Come to my apartment at 2:30 and I'll give you some dessert."

Wes was shocked. He was conflicted. In a strange way, it gave him a real charge, which surprised him, and in another way, he felt he had to shut down her advances.

He drove home and Jennifer was unloading groceries from the car. He parked the Corvette and hustled over to Jennifer's car. "Here, let me get that." He grabbed the sacks from her arms.

"Thanks, babe." She lightly scratched her nails across his shoulders, as she knew that he loved his back scratched.

"I would follow those nails anywhere." They both giggled because they both knew he would.

As they got the bags in the kitchen, Jennifer turned to Wes. "Now, let me put them away. You don't know where anything goes."

"Suit yourself. I'll go get washed up. Maybe we should grab a pizza and watch a movie or something.

"Sounds great."

"Okay. I will order the pizza for delivery and change my clothes." Wes started pulling things out of his pocket before he reached the bedroom. Keys, money, Chapstick, and the note. He had almost forgotten about the note. *Oh, geez, what will I do with this?* He decided to put it inside his Motor Trend magazine at his bedside. *She won't*

*look in here. I'll get this all cleared up tomorrow. I need to
shut that down.*

Knock, knock, knock! Wes stood at apartment 201 in the
Metropolitan apartment complex. It was down the street
from the drive in.

She opened the door just enough to see his face. "I didn't
think you would make it. Come on in."

"Well, I am not going to stay long. You see, I am married
and I love my wife. I just want you to send your affections
to some other guy."

"Is that what you really want?"

"Yeah, I came here so this would stop—"

"I haven't even given my name. My name is Heather."
She made no eye contact and walked around him, lightly
dragging her hand around his waist and then across his
shoulders. She reached around and started to unbutton
his shirt from behind. "Is this okay?"

"Uh, what are you doing? I told you that this had to stop."

"Your words said to stop, but your cologne, your tight shirt, and your eyes tell me something different." She slid her hand inside his shirt and he tightened his chest against her touch. "Oh, you like that, do you?"

Wes dropped his head backward and he was lost in her touch. He and Jennifer had walled themselves off from feeling and expressing feelings. They had not been intimate in quite a while. They were doing good to just make it through the day. They were exhausted.

The rush of feelings and hormones were a tidal wave of sensation. He turned around and kissed Heather without thinking. He felt good for once. He didn't feel like a loser and actually craved the touch of another. It had been a very long time.

They had sex right there in the living room. No words were spoken. It was exhilarating and horrifying for Wes. While they put their clothes back on Heather teased, "Not bad." She handed him his shirt as she gathered his pants and belt.

"This was a mistake. I can't do this again." He now felt even lower than he did before he came to the apartment.

"You'll be back. Keep the key."

Heather was right. He did come back. Later she also introduced him to other vices like oxies, and weed. Her apartment door led him straight into a cascade of loss: loss of his wife, loss of his home, his ministry, and left him ultimately on the streets, addicted and looking for food and shelter.

Chapter 40

Present Day

Standing in front of the wall of mirrors at physical therapy, Eric gave all he had. Stretching his will and his body to go further. Re-sculpted, he had his eyes on the prize. All of his body was a new and improved version of his original self, except for his right foot. It had several problems that just had not improved. Eric hoped to return to the police academy in Oklahoma City, and everything boasted high potential except that darn foot. It just didn't move normally and that meant he didn't run, or even walk normally. He worked like a man possessed for the last six months. His body transformed into a physique like an Italian statue, but he was not able to participate in all conditioning drills because of his right foot.

Ginger knew he was fighting for his dreams and sometimes got up early to peek through the plate-glass window at the local gym, just to see him work out and chase his dream. Today, she sat in her Porsche and sipped on her coffee as she cried. *Oh, God, bless him and his hard work. Please open the door to his dreams.* It was difficult to watch. Ginger came to have coffee with him before she went to work.

Eric gathered his gym bag, grabbed his water bottle, and limped out of the gym. Her Porsche caught his eye, so he went over. "What's a nice girl like you, doing in a place like this?" He leaned on her car door and tried to appear seductive.

"I am here to give my fiancé a little fire."

"Fire?"

"Yes, fire. What are you saying?"

"Well, there are a lot of different kinds of 'fire'." Eric grinned.

"I am here because I needed to see you. I needed to see how you were doing."

Eric dropped his eyes to the ground and backed up. "I am wondering that myself. How *am* I doing?"

Ginger reached across her little roadster and opened the door from inside. "C'mon … let's take a ride." She winked.

Eric smiled at the notion of a cruise in the Porsche with the top down and nothing else he had to do. "Okay, that is the best thing I have heard all day." He hopped in the car and slumped in his seat with his gym bag on the floorboard.

"Anywhere special you want to go?"

"Let's just drive."

"Okay. That is my kind of relaxation." Ginger wanted to see how Eric was *really doing*. His leg had improved with continued work, but his foot progress was slowing. The foot and ankle trauma from the brick attack may have changed his life forever.

"I am a bit concerned. My foot just isn't changing like the rest of my body. My deadline is coming up."

"I am so proud of you, Eric. There are plenty of things you can do. Police work isn't the only thing you can do."

"No. I will be a policeman, period. This is not over. I heard from the academy and they will let me take the physical portion of the exam, whenever I am ready. Well, they will give me till the end of the year. After that, I must re-apply from the beginning like every other applicant.

###

Ginger turned the tumblers in the door lock with her key and stepped inside her place. Hannah was sitting on the couch listening to music on her phone and trying to not notice her mom.

"Shouldn't you be doing your homework, Hannah?"

"Huh? I can't hear you." She bounced her head to Coldplay playing in her air pods.

"Honey, Mom's gonna take a nice long bath." Ginger paused briefly, then continued down the hall.

"What's wrong, Mom?" Hannah took out her air pods.

"Nothing's wrong. I just want to soak in the tub a bit."

"Not true." Hannah turned off the music on her phone and tossed it on the other end of the couch.

"Back up a minute, my young psychiatrist. Aren't you a little young to tell me about my motives and emotional needs?"

"Well, not when I am right." She flipped her hair behind her shoulder. "You 'soak in the tub' a lot when you are stressed-to-the-max and want to chill-out."

"Okay, okay, I am too tired to debate. Like Burger King, have it *your* way." Ginger kissed the top of Hannah's head.

Ginger stripped as she neared the bathroom. She flung off one shoe at a time and kept going, leaving each where it landed. She pulled her t-shirt over her head, and kept going, released the hooks on her bra without missing a beat and it, too, went in the floor. As she rounded the bathroom door, she unbuttoned her jeans and walked straight to the tub and turned the faucet on full blast with one hand and grabbed the bath salts with the other.

As the bath salts melted and gave forth an intoxicating scent, Ginger slowly let her guard down and allowed her brain to wander. She tested the water with her toe and proceeded to lower herself in the water.

Just as she let out a long exhale there was a rap on the door. *Knock, Knock.* "Mom, I got something for you."

"What is it?" Ginger asked, a bit perturbed.

Hannah entered carrying proof that she knew her mom. "I thought you might like a cold beer."

"Hannah. What are you doing?" Ginger sat up in the tub surprised and a little upset.

"Mom, it is okay. I know you had a bad day." She handed Ginger a cold beer with lime, her cigarettes and Zippo.

"You are just a kid and have no business playing bar maid to your mother." Ginger's voice increased in volume.

"Mom, you are still the mom and I am still the kid, but there is nothing wrong with me showing some compassion for you. We have had beer in the fridge since I can remember. I don't care. I don't drink it. I don't actually want to drink it, but I know it helps you unwind. Just take it and say, thank you." She cracked the beer top and squeezed the lime straight in the can. "I've seen that in the movies." She then handed Ginger the cigarettes and lighter. "These, on the other hand... we need to talk about these at some point."

Ginger sat in the tub, anxious to experience her version of Nirvana.

"We learned about all the health issues of cigarettes in third grade health class. Not a pretty picture, Mom. I know you have a had a rough day. Unwind and give me a shout if you need anything."

"First of all, thank you, you know your mother very well. Secondly, you better not get into those beers or cigarettes. You are still way too young, and thirdly, I seriously need to save more money for your education. You are more mature and smarter than I was at your age. Thank you, sweetie."

"Welcome, Mom. I'm gonna go listen to more music." Hannah flashed her patented smile.

Ginger chugged the beer and lime, soothing her nerves and relaxing in the moment, holding the beer in one hand and a cigarette in the other. *More mature than me when I was her age? No... she's more mature than me now.* Ginger slumped shoulder-deep into the tub. *Not gonna think about that now. Ginger Mahoney's third grade daughter, in training to be a psychologist or lawyer, at the age of eight. Who would have ever thought?*

Chapter 41

Present Day

Ginger sat across the corner of the table with one leg on the table and the other on the floor. The nursing preparation class filed in and as more arrived, she could hear the chatter. *Did you hear? Skylar was dealing drugs... Skylar got caught stealing narcotics... such a sweet girl... You never really know somebody.* The comments were predictable and hurtful to hear as a matter of gossip.

"Have a seat, class, and listen up. My, my, my... word travels fast, especially if it deals with someone failing or falling along life's highway." The room became so quiet, you could hear ceramic dishes clicking and crashing together as they were handled for the lunch service in the nearby kitchen. "Well, I think it is wise to remind ourselves that rumor is not fact and should never be taken as fact. For example, take Simone over there." Ginger pointed to one of the girls on the back row that was enjoying the Skylar gossip a bit too much. "Last week I heard she spent several *extended* breaks in her car, listening to music and talking on her phone. Anyone else hear that? Oh, what's wrong? Nobody wants to talk gossip when the object of that gossip is sitting amongst you?" Silence choked out any remnant of excitement and laughter. "It is true, she spent some extra time in her car. Simone, would you like to tell the others what you were doing?"

"Well, now that it is out there, I guess so. My grandmother has been very sick and we are really close. She has always been a fighter and has been a source of strength for my whole family. She went through a rough patch and had lost her will to live, asking 'What good is this used up, wrinkled old lady to anyone?' Well, she is the purest form of love I have ever experienced. Her love has anchored me through rough times. I wanted to be *her* anchor. Those of you who really know me well, know she is really more of a mother to me than a grandma. I was in my car playing her favorite music, The Happy Goodman Family, on my phone and talking to her. Several times I was late returning from my break, but I couldn't bear to get off the phone with her."

"Did I know about all this?" Ginger questioned her in front of the class.

"You are the one who told me to do it." Simone quickly offered, adding, "I will never forget your generosity and understanding at that time."

"How is your grandma, now?"

"Oh, she is back to her old self. I think loneliness is a thief. She just needed to feel connected to someone; she needed to feel she belonged."

"See guys, we all have a different perspective and *none* of us have the whole story. Give your friends grace. Trust in the character of your friends first, before you judge what you have heard. Yes, we all know Skylar is no longer an employee at Fireside. Many of you have written statements relating to this situation, as the investigation is still ongoing and we need all the information we can get to have an accurate picture of the problem. I want to be perfectly clear, because it is important for everyone to understand my next statement. She has been fired because she stole narcotics from the med cart. Period. I want to back up that statement with this. Skylar is one of the most caring and smartest aides I have worked alongside. She made a huge mistake that will cost her employment at this facility and could cost her in bigger ways in upcoming days. Even I have not heard the full story, yet. I am taking a hard stand, people. No thievery of any sort, especially stealing narcotics, will be tolerated at this facility. But I also want to make it crystal clear that I will do everything in my power to help Skylar. We all have struggles and we all would fall without the extension of grace. There is a story behind Skylar's trouble, just like there was a story behind Simone's trouble. Do any of you have questions, or a statement regarding Skylar's situation?" Stillness fell on the room, "Okay then, let's move on." She smiled and grabbed her glucose tester kit. "Now, who wants to tell me the proper steps to checking a resident's blood glucose level." Just like that, she changed gears and focused on the faces before her.

###

Knock, knock. Ginger glanced at her watch. *Right on time.* Ginger pulled out a box of cookies from her credenza and sat it squarely in the middle of her desk. "Come in, Erma."

Erma opened the door and peeked in, "Are you ready?" Her hose swished as she strode over to the chair in front of Ginger's desk.

"I am glad you brought your coffee," Ginger acknowledged. "I brought some of your favorite cookies."

"Really? Why?" Erma reached for a cookie with a smile.

Ginger waited for Erma to choose first and then got a cookie for herself. "Well, it just so happens that these are some of Hannah's favorite cookies as well, so when I got her some, I picked up some for us to share this morning."

Erma slowly raised the cookie to her mouth and checked the room in distrust. "That kinda sounds flaky, but I will take it.... and the cookies." She smiled. "Let's get to it, what do you know about Wesley Lyons, the celebrity with no money." She sat like Grasshopper in front of the Master, waiting to be enlightened.

Ginger tidied papers that were scattered in disarray on her desk. She reviewed her notes, although she knew it by heart. "Wes has a drug problem. He has been getting drugs from some hoodlum... and from Skylar." She kept her gaze fixed on her notes, waiting for Erma's response.

"Drugs? Skylar? No wonder you brought me cookies." She pushed away the box. "Tell me more."

"I don't have much more that has been verified, just rumors. I am gonna get to the bottom of it, though." Ginger offered a serious tone.

"The hell you will." Erma bristled with an emotional response.

Ginger took a double take, as Erma usually presented with a fake facade of sweetness. "I am close—"

"Hand me your phone. *Hand me your phone.*" Erma stood and started grabbing for it herself.

"Erma, get a hold of yourself! Take a beat and listen. The staff has started the protocol of writing statements of knowledge concerning the situation. The investigation started just now and we should know more in upcoming days.”

“Well, okay.” She flounced about the room, perturbed and nervous. The box of cookies came back into her view. She scooted it back in front of her coffee and took out two. “You know I am chin-deep in trouble. The Big Boss, Mr. Miles, has a meeting with me in only a few weeks to discuss cash flow and occupancy rates. Our occupancy is slightly up, but our cash flow is slightly down. This is a problem, and I will have to explain. Did you hear that? I will have to explain and I *have* no explanation. I have been played like a fiddle at a hoedown, and Pastor Wesley Lyons is the only one dancing.” She put down her cookie in disgust and huffed as she threw her head back in desperation.

“There is nothing that has to happen this instant. It is best to act in measured steps of reality, not reactive punches of emotion.” Ginger paused and took notice if her words were sinking in.

“Yes, well, of course. What are you saying?”

"There is value in not regurgitating everything you know to everyone around. We don't have to tell everyone *everything* we know. I am actively gathering facts and will report back to you by the end of business tomorrow." Ginger kept her composure neatly in check.

"Okay, Ginger. You better have some answers tomorrow," Erma warned.

"C'mon, we don't work together on projects very often, but I won't let you down. See you tomorrow."

Erma stood. Before she pivoted to leave the room, she snatched the cookies and tucked them under her arm, like a running back with a football. "See you tomorrow. Thanks for the cookies."

Ginger closed the door behind Erma and went back to her desk. Sitting in her chair, she leaned back and put her feet on her desk. *I'm counting on you, James.* She sat back up and picked up her phone. "Hi, James. I need to talk to you. Can I talk with you in your room after lunch? Great. See you then." She hung up the phone and took her pen in hand to make notes for her meeting with James.

\#\#\#

Knock, knock. "Hey, James, it's Ginger."

"C'mon in, Red." James reached into his fridge and grabbed a diet soda for Ginger.

"Thanks, James. Hey, I need your help again. This is just to help me get some footing, some perspective from which I can work."

"Okay. Sounds covert. How can I help you?" He leaned in toward Ginger with his elbows on his knees, focused on her eyes.

"You know, Wes Lyons, the guy Skylar was giving the drugs to? Do you know who he is?"

James paused. "Well, I don't guess I do. I feel sorry for him. He's a sad man with no north star."

"Yes, he is. Let me show you something." She pulled out her phone and pulled up a newspaper article from the '90s. Wes was showcased in a picture with the Eiffel Tower in the background. "Conquering The World in the Name of Jesus," read the title of the article.

James took the phone and inspected the article. "Yep, that's him, cleaned up and without the scars of life."

"I need you to help me connect with Wes. How did he get here? Why did he come here? Where is his family?" She took back her phone. Ginger needed to get to the bottom of his financial demise, but that was not something she felt comfortable asking James to tackle. If he could get her the stated information, she could take it from there.

"I'll start right away. May take a few days."

"Thanks, ole friend." Ginger gave James a hug from the side and marched with a purpose feeling the breath of fresh hope she just encountered. *If anyone can figure it out, it's James.*

Chapter 42

Present Day

James rolled down the hall with his book and a little cooler lunch bag in his lap. He sat in the familiar wingback chair and read, waiting for Wes to exit his door. Keeping an eye on his watch, he remembered that Wes usually exited his door, mid-afternoon. He should be leaving anytime. James could hear metal upon metal as Wes slid the key into his lock and turned it to lock the door.

James sat up a little taller in the chair and waited for the right moment to talk. "I love this little spot for reading."

He turned to see if someone was addressing him. "You talking to me?"

"Oh, yeah, well, I was about to go outside and have a beer or two. I thought I'd ask if you want to join me. A good cold beer is good anywhere, but always best if it is shared with someone."

"And even better yet if it is free." He smiled and turned to address James. "I think I have seen you around here."

"I am sure you have. These wingback chairs always have a good lamp. I read in the halls because my world gets too small if I stay in my room... and I love to read."

Wes held out his hand with a genuine smile. "Wesley Lyons. You can call me Wes."

"That sounds so familiar... Wes Lyons, Wes Lyons. Where do I know that name from?" He snapped his fingers as if that would make his brain work faster.

"Awe, a while ago we had a gig preaching on the road. You could have been remembering that. It was years ago and actually feels like another *life* ago." He chuckled at the truth in what he had just said. It truly felt like another life, like someone *else's* life. At one time, he couldn't wait to see what the future held. Now, he tried to find a way to hide from the future.

"That's it. I saw you on TV, man. You were in Hawaii, preaching the Word, as my mamma would say."

"That was me." He smiled at the memory of their trips to Hawaii. *The poi, fresh fish, the sun, the ocean... ah, those were the days.*

James closed his book. "Well, how about that beer."

Wes liked James. He seemed down to earth and not hung up on his prior celebrity status. "You bet. Let's go." He held out his arm, inviting James to go in front and lead their trek to an early happy hour.

James opened his small lunch bag cooler and pulled out a couple of beers and two insulated cups.

"Oh, so nice of you to bring insulated cups. A good beer has to be ice cold."

"Yes, ice cold, *and hidden* at a facility that doesn't allow beer outside of events." James looked around the court-yard for curious residents.

Wes tilted his cup to reduce the foamy head as he poured the beer into the cup. "Well, I guess so. We are not hurting a single soul and to be honest, you have no idea how much

I am anticipating this beer. Cheers! Here's to beautiful days and decent pilsners."

James raised his insulated cup. "I'll drink to that. How do you like it here? I haven't seen you around very much. I don't stay in my room, and I never see you around at the gatherings or parties."

"I stay in my room mostly. I just don't have the desire to mingle."

"That is odd for a preacher; they are usually mixing it up and challenging my beliefs, but I can respect that. Just don't ever try to push me into believing a certain way. I believe what I believe and I will let you know when I change my mind."

They both laughed.

"You know, that has never been my bag anyway. I have always told people what my experience is, how God has changed my life. I have found that most people are not against God; they are against self-righteous, pious demagogues." He took a long tip of his cup and let the beer roll across his tongue.

"You know what? You are exactly right. I refuse to go hear a guy preach about the evils of drink, and gambling only to see them at an odd hour in the grocery store with a six pack in their shopping cart. I can't stand two-faced people."

Wes enjoyed the good conversation and beer. He slumped in his metal lawn chair with his wrists limply dangling from the armrests. "So, what about you, James? Tell me a bit about yourself." He killed the can of beer and shook it side to side, drawing attention to the fact that he was empty.

"Oh, here ya go. I brought a few."

"Really? Well, it does taste good, and it has been so long since I sat down in a lawn chair and shot the breeze with a buddy. Back to you, tell me a bit about yourself." He tilted his head back to get a good swig.

Surprised a bit about Wes's response, calling him a buddy, when they had barely met, but James felt it probably just showed the isolation he had been experiencing. "Tell you something about myself, huh? Well, I grew up at a time when schools were desegregating, and I was the first black boy on our high school football team. I never had anything given to me; worked hard all my life. I have always been proud of the fact that I worked my way up to a great position at the tire company and retired with full retirement. This is a picture of my beautiful wife, Estelle. She died from breast cancer. Then I moved here. I did really well by finding this place. I feel like it is home now."

Wes was awe-struck. "Wow, James, your wife was beautiful. I bet you have some amazing stories about your life together."

"Yep, well maybe another time." James now finished his first can and reached into the bag for another. "Tell me about your family. Do you have any pictures?" James was trying to deflect focus back to Wes.

"Well, yes... let me see here." Pulling out his billfold, he shuffled through it and pulled a couple of pictures. "This was my wife, Jennifer. We split only a few years ago. We both suffered tremendously after the death of our son. I don't blame her for leaving me. I didn't handle it very well. Well, guess I still don't." When Jordan died it was hard for me to find a good argument to carry on. He was a beautiful boy. When he died, a piece of me died, too." A track of tears silently ran down his face.

"So, your ministry on the road? What happened to that? You are still young enough, you could still be preachin' and teachin', movin' and a groovin'." James, relaxed by the beer and honest conversation, was truly interested in his newly found friend. He had to keep reminding himself that he was on a mission.

Wes glanced down at the picture of Jordan once more. "I lost it all. The preaching tour, the house, my wife, my health... all gone. I felt like I was sucked under the water by grief and never really came back up to the surface. I exist day to day, but my drive, my love, and my ambition were buried with Jordan when he died."

"What happened to your son?"

Wes was visibly shaken, even after all this time since his death. "Oh, man, look at the time. I need to get going.

Been good talking to you, though. Think I'll get my supper to go. I eat most meals in my room."

James started gathering his things. "Maybe we can have happy hour again, some other time. It is nice to talk to an intelligent man that is not full of himself. I expected a man who had traveled the world in his own jet would be full of himself, but somehow you escaped all that. You are all right, Wes."

"I didn't escape the trappings of fame. It was ripped from my grasp when Jordan took his last breath. I am a changed man, James. No one should take the path I've traveled. I am a disgusting, shell of a man. In fact, I would imagine most people here watched me on TV at some point, but they don't recognize the man I have become. I am pretty glad about that. I would just as soon they didn't know who I was. That's why I hide in my room a lot. I would like to get together again sometime. It was nice to talk to someone who didn't know me from before and didn't judge me for who I became."

"Sounds like a deal. I'll bring the beer and you bring some stories about your travels." James zipped his small cooler with the dead soldiers inside.

"It's a deal, friend. Give me a shout next time you are ready." He gave a flicker of a smile and went to get a sandwich.

James knew he was sent to get dirt on him, but he connected with Wes's humanity and felt he knew Wes.

James knew enough to help Ginger solve her mystery. Wes's life fell apart in the midst of life's tragedies. Everyone had them. Wes just had further to fall than most.

Chapter 43

Present Day

The lump in Skylar's throat made it hard to swallow her warm soda. She had been sitting in her car, curbside, near her grandma's house for over an hour. Like a movie trailer running through her brain, she kept seeing the disappointment on her grandma's face if she told her she was fired for stealing drugs at work. *How do I tell her? Can I get away with NOT telling her? No, that would be just more lies. I just need to get my head straight and remember she loves me.*

She glanced at her watch and knew she had to get the show on the road. *I just need to calm down a bit. Hmmm. Any food in the glove box?* She rummaged through the papers, maps, sunglasses, a bag of peanuts, and a familiar scrap of folded paper. *What's that doing in here?* Skylar knew the familiar fold to the scrap of paper. *Oxy stash.*

Must have been in the glove box for months. She unfolded the paper and rolled the pills loosely in her hand. All that time... she stole hundreds of pills for her grandma and Wes; she had never experienced one herself. She sensed her hope and future was crumbling before her very eyes.

She took her warm soda can and checked to see how much was in there. Without another thought she slammed the pills in her mouth and washed them down with her remaining soda. *I am hurting all right. My soul is hurting. Maybe this will help me relax before I go in to face Grandma.* She closed her eyes and prayed till her mind drifted away from reality.

###

Skylar slowly felt herself coming awake. Not totally aware of her surroundings, she startled and remembered she had taken the pills to relax. She quickly became acutely aware of a sour stench in the car, followed by gagging and forcefully trying to swallow the vomit trying to spew like a geyser out of her mouth. Gazing to the left, her vision blurred in streaks. When she corrected her head position to the right, the whole process streaked again in reverse. With her head spinning and a new forceful spasm of her stomach, trying to expel any contents that might remain, she opened her car door in a flash, leaning her body heavily out of the car in an effort to vomit on the street.

Immediately, she heard tires squealing and smelled the burning rubber of tires trying to stop, but they failed. The burned rubber was followed by sounds of crashing and twisting metal amplified as vehicles crunched and smashed as they slammed one into the next. As she instantly gazed over her shoulder, there was no way out. The pile-up slammed directly into Skylar, pinning her between her car door and the cars that couldn't stop. The other drivers climbed out of their vehicles and immediately called 911, racing to see if they could help.

The commotion caused Skylar's already worried grandma to survey out her porch window. She instantly recognized Skylar's car and melted into her wheelchair. Unable to physically get to her, she opened her front screen door and screamed to the onlookers. "That is my baby in that car. Is she okay?" Between the screams and cries she continued to call out, "Help my baby... my baby."

A woman in scrubs ran over to her. "Ma'am, she is unconscious. We have called the ambulance."

"Push me out there. *Push me out there!* Skylar, I am coming."

"Okay, ma'am, but I can't get you too close." The woman in scrubs promised.

As the nurse carefully helped Skylar's grandma down the front porch ramp, the ambulance arrived and took control of the situation. The police were close behind, forming a complete cluster for several city blocks. Skylar's grandma couldn't get close enough to see her, much less touch her. Her sobs could be heard by all the neighbors. Her heart, torn out from sorrow, was raw and exposed for all to see.

A paramedic hustled over to Skylar's grandma. "You are her family?"

"Yes, her grandma. Is she going to make it?"

"Ma'am, I don't know, but we got her heart started again. We will do our best. We are taking her to Emory." He turned and ran back to the waiting ambulance, and they sped off with lights and sirens blaring.

Skylar's grandma watched all the disinterested people peel off and return to their boring lives, while hers had just been changed forever. She shouted, "Hey, you, yes you… young lady in the scrubs, please take me to the hospital. Please. My baby needs me."

"Ma'am, excuse me for interrupting, but I work in the Emory maintenance department. I am on my way there now. Do you have family or friends that can pick you up?" The tall man in a mechanic's uniform stepped closer.

"Yes, I have people I can call."

He pushed her to his car and helped her in the passenger side. "I am working a double tonight. You will need another ride home. God bless your granddaughter, and God bless you."

"Thank you."

###

The tall maintenance man pushed her near the information desk and said goodbye. Skylar's grandma found herself in a sea of people who all seemed to know where they were going. Bumping into her wheelchair, passersby scanned right over her like she was not even there. She pushed her wheelchair, the best she could, toward the information desk. All the while, asking anyone who noticed her, "Where is the emergency room?" Voiced through her tears.

A young volunteer quickly noticed her. "Here, ma'am. I'll push you."

"Thank you, child. My granddaughter was hit by a car, and I have to get to her side. Thank you, Lord, for sending this young lady."

"Leave it all to me. We will roll right past the nurse's station, as if we have a meeting to attend."

"We do. My granddaughter's meeting." Skylar's grandma held onto the armrests as they raced toward the emergency room.

"Your granddaughter's name?"

"Skylar. Skylar Jennings."

The volunteer scanned the emergency room cubicles as they passed with curtains pulled open and a variety of patients being treated. She peered at the end of the hall and noted an array of bloody linens, dressing packages, and bandages littering the floor. "I bet she is in here." She pushed the wheelchair near the curtains that were pulled closed. The volunteer announced herself and pulled the curtain back to see a bruised and broken girl, Skylar.

For the moment, she was only attended by one nurse, who was monitoring wires and tubes.

Skylar's grandma quietly pushed her wheelchair to Skylar's bedside. Not only her grand daughter but her champion, her provider, her counselor, and her inspiration. She cleared her throat. "Ma'am, this is my granddaughter. May I see her a minute."

"We are waiting to check the placement on the tracheostomy. We were able to secure a steady heartbeat.

She has not responded to any questions. She will go for imaging of her brain as soon as they come to get her."

"Honey, I don't understand everything you just said, but I am going to come over there and hold my baby's hand and tell her how much I love her."

"Yes, ma'am."

"Skylar. I am here, baby. I love you, sugar. You are the smartest, kindest, most hard-working girl in Atlanta... maybe all of Georgia." She saw the vomit still on her face, not to mention the blood in her hair and pieces of rubber car-trim tangled in her hair. "Nurse? Would you please get me a warm washcloth? I want to wash my baby's face. I would keep my eyes shut, too, if I had vomit and blood all over the place."

"Certainly." She handed Skylar's grandma a warm, wet washcloth and turned back to study the monitors.

"Skylar, I am gonna get you all cleaned up, honey. You know you can't keep me away." She gently held her young bloody fingers, taking notice of every crease and every freckle. "I love you. I want to thank you for your giving spirit and the love you have freely given to me."

Skylar moaned.

"Nurse, she is trying to say something." She never took her eyes off of Skylar.

The nurse came to her bedside. "Can you open your eyes. *Open your eyes, Skylar.*" The nurse gave her a brisk sternal rub, which elicited no response.

"She did make a noise. Skylar, Skylar, I love you, baby."

Skylar uttered strange guttural sounds, no true words, but it was becoming clear that she was trying to communicate in some way with her grandma.

The nurse backed up a bit observing the interaction between them. "Sometimes families can connect when no one else can. Do what you can."

She took Skylar's hand in hers. "Squeeze my hand, baby, if you can hear me, squeeze my hand."

The monitors began to alarm with frequent loud sounds, Skylar squeezed her hand and her eyes bolted open in an expression of shock, or pain. It was hard to discern the difference. Then just as quickly as her hand squeezed and eyes opened, her body became limp and her heart monitor showed a flatline, blaring an annoying, single, prolonged tone. The room was instantly filled with a Code Blue Team and Skylar's grandma was rushed out of the room.

She was rolled to the waiting room packed with others waiting for word on their loved ones. A wall phone delivered updates on some. With others, they called the family into a counseling room. After a few moments, the same nurse that had been with her in the emergency room came to the waiting room and asked her to follow her to a counseling room. "Honey, please, say she is okay. Don't take me in there. The people who go in there all leave crying. Oh, Lord, help us."

"The physician taking care of Skylar will be right in." The nurse turned and left with no more said.

She sat in her wheelchair with her elbows on the arm-rests, fingers interlocked and hands lying on her large abdomen. Her head was hanging low as huge tears dropped from her eyes and splashed on her lap one-by-one.

A doctor in scrubs rounded the corner as he rubbed hand sanitizer into his hands. His stained scrubs of blood and body fluids spoke volumes before he ever opened his mouth. Sweat rings about his arms, neck, and belly spoke of the valiant command he gave while working on Skylar. "Hello, I am Dr. Jones. I have been caring for your granddaughter. She sustained severe damage to her left arm, leg, brain, and, multiple injuries throughout her spine, spleen and liver. We revived her, but we chose to put her in an induced coma, to allow her brain swelling time to reduce. Are you here by yourself?"

"Yes. A kind stranger brought me here."

"Your granddaughter is touch-and-go and will need all the mental, emotional, and physical help her loved ones can offer. That is if she makes it. I believe in telling it like it is. Her chances are slim, but she is young and healthy and I will take her on like she was my own. I will have the chaplain help you call family or friends to come to the hospital. He will also give you the number to the nursing desk in your granddaughter's area. You can call to check on Skylar. If they are too busy, they will call you back." He stood and touched her shoulder as he turned away. "Oh, one more thing. Your granddaughter was in her scrubs. I have attended many people wearing scrubs. Your daughter is the only one I have ever seen that had a prayer list taped to the back of her name tag. You and Pastor Wes Lyons were at the top of her list. She clearly loves you deeply."

Chapter 44

Present Day

Skylar's brother, Jason, sat in his car in the Fireside parking lot. He held a family photo from years ago. Two kids at a summer picnic, eating watermelon and spitting seeds. He ran his finger across the picture, as if it could take him back to those days of laughter. He flipped over the pic to find 'Skylar 7, Jason 5, written on the back in their mom's handwriting. *How did we get here? You were my example, my proof that we could be somebody in this world. Now, I am holding this stupid picture and working up the courage to go inside and clean out your work locker. You told me there is a God. You told me He would make a way for me when I was in trouble. Well, sis, where is He now?* Jason kissed her picture and returned the precious photo to his wallet.

###

Jason dragged his feet up to the heavy wooden door and took a deep breath as he stepped through. Immediately, he was met with the sight and smells of a well-maintained, ornate vestibule. Large vases of cut flowers welcomed all visitors with the sight and the scent of beautiful flowers, directing attention to the sign-in table and receptionist waiting to be of service. Along with the flowers, the entry was staged with leather wing back chairs and cream colored, tapestry sofas book-ended with coffee tables. Jason took a minute to survey around the room. It was the first time he had been in Fireside. It made him proud to know his sister worked in an upscale place like this.

The receptionist put the phone on hold and addressed young Jason like he was a CEO. "Hello, sir. How may I help you?"

Jason stepped to the side and checked over his shoulder, as if she was talking to another man, but he was the only one in the area. "Oh, me? Yes, uh, I need to talk to the supervisor of the nurses, I guess."

"Is there a problem? May I tell her the reason for your visit today?"

"Uh, sure. I am here to pick up any leftover stuff from my sister's locker."

"Who is your sister? She should pick up her own things. We don't let friends and family in our employees' lockers. I am sorry."

Jason began weeping. "My sister is Skylar Jennings. I don't want to be here any more than you guys want me here, but my grandma sent me after her things."

About that time, Jason heard the loud clomping of boots on linoleum. Ginger strode around the corner in her Dingo boots, lab jacket, and jeans.

"What's the trouble?" Ginger extended her hand with her best professional persona.

"Oh, no trouble, I was just explaining that I couldn't let him into Skylar's locker."

He clenched his fists to summon all the strength he could muster. "She is fighting for her life at Emory Hospital...

she was hit by a pile-up of cars. I am here to get anything that she may have left behind. I know she was fired and should be cleaning out her own locker, but she may not even survive."

"Skylar is in *intensive care?*" Ginger leaned in as the news seemed to suck all the oxygen out of the room. "I just saw her yesterday. It was her last day of work." In a daze, Ginger looked at a young boy who had clearly lost his way. "Please come into my office and tell me more." She stepped up beside Jason and briefly put her arm around his shoulder in sympathy as she led him to her office down the hall. "I'm Ginger, Skylar's boss. Would you like a Coke? You must be thirsty."

"How about a Mountain Dew?" He crossed his arms and scuffed his shoe on the floor.

Ginger turned her head back to the receptionist as they continued down the hall. "Please get us two Mountain Dews from the dining room."

The receptionist shouted, "You got it, Ginger."

As they nervously awaited the drinks, Ginger offered him a chair. "Please tell me what happened."

The receptionist knocked on the door frame as she entered. She placed the drinks on Ginger's desk and left just as quickly. She excused herself and closed the door behind her.

"I don't know, exactly. Grandma called me last night, crying. I came over to her house and she was a mess. She still had blood stains and smelled like vomit from holding Skylar at the hospital. Sis was parked at the curb. She fell asleep in the driver's seat. She leaned out of her car and into traffic... and was hit by a pile up of cars."

Ginger closed her eyes, as if it would make the mental images go away. "I am so sorry."

"My sister is the nicest person I know."

"Me too, Jason."

"She is always thinking of others first." His lower eyelids were brimmed full of tears and with his next blink, tears started to roll again.

"Yes, I can say that she was a great nursing aide. Did they give any other information?"

Ginger put two and two together and felt deep sadness and a twinge of responsibility in the whole matter. She felt fairly certain, if Skylar had not been fired yesterday, Skylar would still be fine. Ginger knew she had to fire her, but even the best decisions sometimes come with surprising and difficult outcomes.

Ginger stood. "Come with me. We'll go open her locker and med cart. She spent much of her day pushing that cart around. There may be a small trinket of hers locked down in the cart." Ginger fought to maintain her composure and lend strength to Jason. She pulled out a credenza drawer and opened the locker file. She shuffled through the stack and paused at the sight of Skylar's name written at the top. "We will use this check list to identify those things that were Skylar's and those things that were the property of Fireside. C'mon, let's get her stuff."

"Cool. Thanks. Let's just get it over with." Jason sniffed back mucous in his nose and grabbed a tissue on her desk. "Can I have one?"

"Of course, take several. In fact, get a few for me."

Jason flashed a glimmer of a smile, thinking of Skylar's boss caring for his sister.

###

Ginger slid a master key in the lock hanging on Skylar's locker. "Here, you want to do it?"

"Sure, if that's okay."

"You bet. Why don't you take the things out one-by-one and I will check the list for Fireside property."

"All right." Jason stood still for a moment. As he swung open the metal locker door, a soft, squeaking hinge added to the suspense. The back wall was totally covered in photos. Jason's knees weakened at the sight, buckling initially. He steadied himself and continued scanning the locker and all the photos lining the locker, photos of family, friends, residents, and laughter. Front and center was a picture of Skylar, Jason, and their mom huddled around a homemade birthday cake with thirteen candles on the top. "That is one of the few pictures we have with Mamma. She was sick a lot and we really lived with Grandma most of the time." Skylar wore a crown made of red construction paper and Jason held rabbit ears behind her head, as only a little brother would do. "That was the best birthday party. We had pizza and birthday cake." Extending from this center photo were scads of people Skylar held dear--her grandma, friends and co-workers... Wes Lyons... and *Ginger*.

"Let's pull down the photos first. These are obviously not the property of Fireside." With care, one-by-one, they both gently pulled the photos from the metal locker and removed the tape from the back of each. Ginger removed the photo of herself, teaching the nursing class. "I never knew she took this."

"Oh, she is tricky with her cell phone. We have very few pictures of her, 'cause she was always the one taking the pictures.'"

Ginger paused and was moved to her soul, as she read the handwritten words on the bottom of the photo *Someday, I will...* "She said that a lot in class...someday I will help older patients; someday I will start a killer I.V.; someday I will be like Ginger."

"She thought you were a superhero. I got tired of hearing about how perfect you were." Jason continued pulling down photos, "Someday... I will be Ginger. Nothing would make her happier."

Ginger saw the picture of herself in front of the class and nodded the slightest nod. "She would be the best nurse, Jason. I hate to ask, but would it be okay if I kept this pic."

"Sure." Jason started reaching the contents in the bottom of the locker--breath mints, notebooks, pens, tampons, chocolate... a stethoscope. "Is this her stethoscope? Wow, it is all official and everything." He focused on the stethoscope and inspected it like it was a treasure.

Ginger examined her checklist and found 'stethoscope' listed as Fireside equipment. "Oh, yeah, well, actually that stethoscope was assigned to her—"

"This is *Skylar's*. Skylar wore it around her neck every day. Wow." Jason was mesmerized.

Ginger checked off the stethoscope from the list as if it had been returned. "Jason, how would you like to hold her stethoscope for safe keeping?"

"Really? Well, that would be great."

Ginger peeked in the locker once more and found it empty. "Seems like we are finished with the locker. Let's look in the med cart." The med room was adjacent to the employee lockers. She slid the key in the spring-loaded lock and as she turned it, the lock popped out and the drawers became visible. She had cleared out a place for her favorite thermal cup. There it laid to the front, right side of the top drawer. "Here ya go. She kept this thing full and cold. She might use it again when she gets over this. We must think positively."

Jason looked her in the eye, "You think she will make it?"

"I would never bet against Skylar. Never! Let's go back up front."

Jason nodded. "Yeah, I am ready to be done."

As they approached the front door, Ginger knew hard days were ahead for Jason. "May I give you a hug?"

"Sure... I guess." A bit embarrassed, he held out one arm.

Ginger bent over slightly and gave him a brief, but heart-felt hug. She felt Jason hug back, and that squeezed her heart in a swell of emotion. "Jason, I would appreciate any news you can give us as time passes and her condition changes. Skylar is a remarkable young woman. My money is on her to beat this thing! We still care a lot for her." Ginger gave him her card as she opened the door and waved as he turned to leave. As she saw him go down the sidewalk with Skylar's stethoscope around his neck, she knew if there was a chance, Skylar would come through it.

Ginger spun around at her desk with the phone receiver in her hand. "I am gonna be out of the office for a bit, just wanted you guys at the front desk to know. If anything pops up and you need me, just call my cell phone. I have to go get another stethoscope."

"Ginger, you lost yours again? How many times does that make?"

"I am not sure...too many, but this time it was worth it." Ginger hung up the phone and took off her lab coat. With her tattoos shining and a cigarette poised between her fingers to light on her way to the car, Ginger gave her time with Jason some thought. *You know, everybody is a hero to someone. I was Skylar's hero and she was Jason's hero. Ginger, it is time you start living your life like someone is watching you... 'cause they are.* She dropped into the low seat of her Porsche, flicked the ashes from her cigarette and scratched rubber as she left. *I won't be getting my usual black, Littmann stethoscope. This one will be purple, your favorite color, Skylar.* Angels, do your job. Protect Skylar and guide her healthcare staff.

Chapter 45
2010s

Wes exhaled, releasing the valve a bit on his pressure cooker life. He sat in a clean, white button-down business shirt, skinny jeans, and white Stan Smith sneakers. His full beard suffered, in need of grooming, and he sported modern horn-rimmed glasses. "Do you have anything a little smaller, or perhaps a bit cheaper due to the inconvenience of third floor locations, construction noise outside the windows, or something like that?" Wes flashed a hopeful smile.

The apartment manager pulled back the information packet from Wes's hand. "Surely a man who has a prominent position in distribution for *The Atlanta Journal Constitution* doesn't have trouble coughing up rent at a low-level apartment building like Magnolia Gardens."

"Well, it's not that I don't have the money." He fidgeted in his seat. "I'm just using this for nights I leave work late and don't want to drive the distance to my home in Haynes Manor." He looked out of the corner of his eye for a reaction from the apartment manager.

"Haynes Manor?" The manager quizzed showing interest.

"Yes, we've had a place there for several years." Wes sat quietly reading the manager's face. "How do you think rich people stay rich? We negotiate *everything*." He forced a chuckle.

The manager was looking for good renters, not just anybody. "Yeah, I've heard that somewhere before. Okay, Here's the deal. Just last week I was offering first month for fifty percent off. I can wiggle that much, that's it."

Now, it was Wes's turn to make a move. "All I want is your best deal. Thanks." He stood to shake hands, but noticed black ink smudges on his fingertips and palms. He nervously shoved his hands in his pockets. *Are you crazy? You didn't wash your hands?*

"You can take the paperwork and return at your leisure."

Wes needed it yesterday. "I will just sit out front, fill it out, and leave it with your secretary. That is, if that is okay with you."

"Really? Okay, suit yourself. I'll get back with you once I have gone over it. If it all pans out, do you want the unit you walked through?"

"Uh, maybe the same floor plan on the back of the complex. I like things quiet."

"All right, quiet it will be. You should receive my call within a few days."

He smiled with the energy of success. "Thanks. This should work out fine."

He filled out the application, stepped outside, and walked directly down the street to the trucking dock at *The Atlanta Journal Constitution*, only ten-minutes away. As he approached, Wes waved down a dock worker, "Do you have time to go ahead and swap out?"

"Yeah," his buddy, Al, took a long draw on his cigarette. "My smoke break is about over, anyway." He dropped the cigarette nub on the concrete and Wes stepped on it as he made his way to the men's locker room.

Wes thanked Al for helping out with his interview. "Al, I really owe ya one. That interview would not have gone so well if I showed up in my greasy Amy Grant t-shirt and jeans. The same clothes I walked out of my house in, two weeks ago. In fact, if you meet me in the park, about 4:20, I will share my treat with you. What do you say? I will go change clothes in the locker room and hang your clothes on your locker handle when I am done."

"That sounds great to me." Al smiled at his good fortune.

"Cool. See you there at 4:20." Wes turned toward the men's locker room.

"I am just lucky we planned this yesterday." He slapped Al's back in camaraderie.

"Yeah, I guess so. I will clean my work station and then I'll change myself. Meet you at the park."

"Works for me." Wes spoke a little louder as he pushed the heavy locker room door open.

As he changed back into his own clothes, it was almost like the dirty, grease-covered Amy Grant t-shirt and jeans, reminded him of who he really was. A respectable man who loved music was now wallowing in squalor. But, today was a good day. He did find a job recently, loading newspapers into trucks for delivery and now, not only did he have a paycheck, but he and his new girlfriend would have a place to stay by the end of the week.

Wes sat on top of a concrete picnic table, made by the WPA in 1938. It was nestled at the back edge of the park and turned toward the street. He saw Al walking toward him. They waved in recognition of each other. Once Al drew closer, Wes got up and they sat on the benches facing each other. They usually did this so that they could both see if anyone was stepping toward them. Wes sparked a joint, with a deep breath and then exhaled. "It was nice wearing your clean, stylish clothes for a change. I almost felt like myself again. I have some really nice clothes still at Jennifer's place. Once I have an apartment, I'll go clear my stuff out of her house and I will have my new start. Divorce brings you to your knees. Here you go." He offered Al a drag on his prime stash.

"Too bad that you and your wife are splitting for good. I hate that," Al held his breath momentarily, then exhaled. "So, what from here?" Al turned the joint sideways, getting a good look at his elixir.

"Guess the next thing is to get my stuff back from Jennifer. Oh... I just had a great thought."

"Yeah? What?" Al was holding the smoke in his lungs for a strong hit.

"If I spot you another smoke, could I borrow those clothes, again? I don't want to show up to get my stuff in the old t-shirt and jeans I was wearing when I left a couple weeks ago. What do you say?"

"Sure, I guess. This is some pretty good stuff. Some more of *this*?" He held up the doobie.

"Yep. More of that."

"Okay, deal. Just let me know ahead of time and I will bring them in a sack for the next adventure."

They both laughed, even though it wasn't really funny.

Wes wiped a dribble of vodka from his mouth with the back of his hand. He looked into the bottle. After clearly seeing none at the bottom, he tossed the pint and paper sack in the trash as he strolled by a nearby convenience store. Wes was quite a different person since moving out of his and Jennifer's house. He drank to forget. He "used" to forget. After finishing off the vodka, he felt confident enough to pull it off. He stepped up to the intercom on the automated gate and pushed the button. "Hello?"

"Yes?" Her voice sounded so fresh.

"Jennifer? It's Wes. It's been a long time."

"Wes? What are you doing here?" she said, speaking in a much less energetic tone.

"I need to talk to you. Can I come in?"

"Why didn't you call?"

"My phone is on the blink. I'm sorry."

"Okay. That's fine. I'll meet you back by the pool."

"Thanks."

The large, black metal gate hung on stucco pillars that matched the house. Jennifer pushed the button to open the property gate and he felt as if he didn't belong there.

Wes walked the front property and peeked around the corner of the house to see Jennifer. It seemed like he was a visitor in his own life. Her hair that once was blonde, long and parted down the middle as young lovers, was now a short, blonde, bob. Her skin was kissed by the sun and she looked refreshed and healthy in a floral sundress and barefooted. He was standing there, looking at his beautiful wife and he was homesick. The way she sat back in the patio chair and crossed her legs at the knee, shook loose her blonde hair, and glanced at her watch, it was "Jennifer perfection" and he still loved her. Wes got his thoughts together and came around the corner as she poured two glasses of iced tea.

"Thank you for meeting me." He nervously cleared his throat.

"Look at you and all that facial hair. I never thought you'd grow a beard. Well, anyway, why are you visiting me?"

He instinctively reached up to touch his beard. "I just wanted to arrange a time to pick up my clothes and a few things." Turning away, he couldn't bear to look her in the face. "I have made arrangements for a truck next Friday, but I wanted to ask if it would be okay."

"That would be fine. If I am not here, I will have the maid let you in and answer any questions."

"That would be great. Thanks." Wes was still unable to make eye contact with her. "How are you doing?" He was unconsciously wringing his hands.

"I still cry, but I don't cry as much as I did when you were still here. At least now I know that you aren't coming home, ever. I am not waiting up, crying all hours of the night, only to find you in the morning passed out in the driver's seat of your Audi, with vomit all over the seat. I am still lonely, but I am not as lonely as I was sitting in the same room with you, while I ask questions about your day with you zombied out, just watching the television, never answering a single question I asked. I still have trouble sleeping alone, but it is better somehow now, because I am praying that you are getting help and are okay somewhere, somehow. I am a whisper of the confident, smart, funny woman I used to be, but I will rise above all this. I have started my journey to find the me I was meant to be. The ministry managed to find an position for me, so I have a job lined up, which I think will help a lot. God made us to reflect joy to the world, but I have to find it first. You look pretty good. I like your new jeans and tennis shoes. I guess that shows something. It wasn't long ago that I literally hated everything associated with you."

The more Jennifer talked, the smaller he felt. He knew it was hard living with him; this was a brutal reminder of the truth. He really *wasn't* the same man. He looked at his watch and knew he needed to be leaving. The vodka did its job, but time was running out and he would soon turn back into the dirty, intoxicated, unreliable man she filed divorce papers against.

"Thanks. I will be here next Friday afternoon. It shouldn't take long." Wes faked a face of confidence.

"Okay. You will have access to your clothes and all that is yours."

Wes knew he wouldn't be taking a lot. A few boxes of his dad's work, clothes, and other personal items, and hopefully, another picture of Jordan. He was riding along with a delivery guy next Friday and they were making deliveries on her side of town. They would stop long enough for him to grab his things and then he would be dropped off at his new apartment. Next Friday was move-in day. "I still have a long way to go, but I am trying to salvage my life and morph it into something positive. Thanks for letting me come in. I'll let myself out the gate."

"Oh, I changed the code. I will punch you through when I go back inside. Bye." She stood, took a swig of tea and twitched the slightest smile as she turned for the patio door.

"Sure, I understand. What was I thinking? Thanks again." He squeezed the words out just as she closed the door behind her. Wes left and as he viewed mansions to his right and left in his old neighborhood, he reflected on the life that was behind him and what was before him. "God, please protect Jennifer from all harm, including me. After I get those clothes, I know I never will be back."

Several years passed and Wes had become comfortable with his new life, his life filled with girls who came and went like the wind and apartment buildings he left in the middle of the night to avoid paying the rent. As time ticked away, his need for alcohol, weed, and pills escalated. What used to get him high just wasn't doing the trick anymore. As his appearance declined, he rarely was recognized as the mega preacher from days gone by.

Wes lost his job at *The Atlanta Journal Constitution*. His buddy, Al, warned him about random drug tests. It was a must, especially in departments where intoxication could cause one to injure themselves or someone else. Wes was promoted to fork-lift driver and accidentally clipped a rack of pallets, causing them to tip and demolish the entire stack of product. Every accident of this sort flagged the employee for a drug test. He flunked the drug test, showing cannabis in his system from a while back. They also gave him a breathalyzer test, and he lit it up like a Christmas tree. He was drunk on the job and driving a forklift, which resulted in immediate termination. Wes already knew that, but he immediately went to his boss's office. *Knock.*

"Come on in," a gruff voice rang out, somewhat irritated.

"Hi, Mr. Wood—"

"You have a lot of cajónes coming in here after screwing up my productivity today. What do you want? Who are you?"

"My name is Wes." He already had to scrounge up every bit of courage to talk to his boss and his boss didn't even remember his name. Wes was trembling.

"Whatever. What do you want?"

"Sir, please give me another chance. I will do anything." He glanced around the room and thought he recognized an adjoining bathroom. "Is that your private bathroom, sir?"

"Yeah, What's it to ya?"

"I will clean your private bathroom every single day. I know how to shine shoes. I'll shine your shoes every week. I will bring the morning paper to your office every morning with a cup of coffee. Most of all, I will stay clean. I really—"

"You can stop right there. I have been in this position a long time. You had enough booze in your body that it wasn't a near miss! I am surprised you weren't driving the damn forklift with a lamp shade on your head. Did you really think you wouldn't get caught?"

"I just didn't *think*." Wes dropped his head.

His boss showed a breath of compassion. "Get yourself together, man. All the guys around here really like you.

You are personable and a hard worker. You can have a good life, but you gotta get straight."

"Thanks for seeing me." Crushed by the words spoken and the reality setting in that he would soon be homeless with no way to pay next month's rent. Wes turned and shuffled out of the building.

So, Wes resorted to an encampment of homeless people that lived behind the convenience store he frequented. Hidden in the thickly wooded, green space between two housing additions, he had noticed homeless folks walking into the trees with loaded shopping carts always nearby. *How bad can it be? I guess I will see this afternoon. Better get all my stuff packed.*

###

Wes had his possessions literally tied up in a sheet from the apartment. All he needed was a long stick to slide through the knot and he would look like the hobos he read about in books as a child. An unexpected problem, how would he "fit-in"? How do you check out joining a homeless encampment? It wasn't like checking into a five-star hotel.

No one saw them, no one missed or looked for them. There was an old abandoned car near the convenience store and woods. Wes used the interior of the car as his locker to store things he didn't want to get stolen, such as his dad's box of sermons and a bag of personal items. Wes was at the end of his rope and he needed another plan for the future. If he didn't find another answer, he would die in that encampment. He made a great contact with the girl who opened the convenience store each morning. Most of the homeless population was not allowed to use the restrooms there. However, Wes offered to carry the trash out if she would allow him to use the restroom early in the morning, before most people got out. That way he could make himself presentable for any possible job interviews.

Wes was a gifted man and he knew he just needed the right opportunity. With an unclouded mind, he could think more clearly, but he was sweating now and had a huge headache. He started thinking. *What can I do?*

About that time, he looked across the street and saw a nice facility. *I wonder what that is.* Wes went across the street to check it out. *Fireside ... Hmmm... Assisted Living Center. What if I could get something going there? Everything a man needs, food, a bed, shelter. Okay, Wes, time to make a plan.*

Chapter 46

Present Day

Ginger and Rob basked in the quiet solace of the back door 'office.' Leaning against the building near the soured dumpster hiding trash and decaying food, they sat on old milk crates. Both struggled in a funk, trying to make sense of the latest happenings.

Rob put out his cigarette and kept rubbing it back and forth on the concrete, shredding the remaining tobacco till the white filter was exposed.

"You are not at risk of setting anything on fire, dude. The filter is obliterated."

"Oh, well, better safe than sorry. So, what now?"

"Well, Erma and I have to talk to Wes. He won't know what hit him. He doesn't know Skylar was caught and he doesn't know she is critical. He spent more time with her than anybody else. Of course, now we know why, but it will still be difficult for him to deal with... not only did he lose his dealer, he could lose his friend."

"It would be different if she was a sordid low life." Rob played with the remains of the cigarette filter, again.

"Would it, Rob? She is only twenty-something. She hasn't been on this earth long enough to become her true self; however, the time she was on this earth, she was a giving, young woman with amazing potential. *That* is what is tragic."

Knock, knock. The exit door opened and James leaned forward. "Ginger, Erma is looking for you."

"Grrr-eat. Thanks, James. I'll find her and get this over with." Ginger stood and wiped her hands on the back pockets of her jeans. "Here goes nothing. Say a prayer for me and rub Buddha's belly."

Erma could hear Ginger's boots clomping down the hall. She quickly pulled out her mirror from her desk drawer and gave her hair and nose a quick check. *Good, no strag-glers.* "Come on in, Ginger." Erma raised her voice.

Ginger came straight in her office without pausing, "How—"

"Your boots preceded you. With those boots on, you are not going to sneak up on *anybody*."

"Good morning to you, too, Erma." Ginger flopped down into the chair alongside Erma's desk. "I am heart broken."

"So where do we stand with Wes." Erma peeked at her calendar.

"Well, he knows nothing. If that is what you are asking. You have got to be involved in this, Erma."

"Why?" Erma blatantly questioned.

"Because you are the boss. That's what bosses do."

"Well, bosses also delegate." She picked up her cup and slurped hot coffee as she maintained eye contact with Ginger.

"Really, Erma? No way. I know you have a heart beating beneath all the crust."

"Crust?" Erma furrowed her brow.

"Erma, I will do most of the talking, but I need you to be there and show solidarity."

"Oh, okay," Erma pulled out a face powder compact and opened it, checking to see if she needed to address a shiny nose. She dabbed an obligatory pat of the powder puff on her nose and snapped it shut. "So, we need to inform Wes that Skylar has been fired and that she will no longer be giving him any 'perks.'"

Ginger flinched at the callousness of Erma's words. "And that she is fighting for her life, Erma. His friend is critical."

"*And* that he is drastically behind on his rent. I have drafted a letter of promised eviction proceedings if he doesn't produce a miracle... I mean money. I realize this is tragic, but I didn't really know her that well. I hate it for her family and friends, but my responsibility is about the money, Ginger. Show... me... the money."

"Why does this not surprise me? Okay, Erma, let's nail down the high points and I will drive this train. I think it would be best." Ginger held up one finger, "I think we deal with the money first. He won't even hear the point about rent if we discuss Skylar's death first."

"However, you want to do it, is fine with me." Erma glimpsed at her watch and nodded. "You take care of that part, Erma. I will take care of the more sensitive topic of Skylar."

"Okay, I can do that, let's go. I have a hair appointment at lunch and I don't want to be late."

"Of course, you don't." Ginger stood, not ready for this discussion emotionally, but she knew it had to be done, and she didn't want Erma handling anything that was emotionally sensitive." Just stand there with me, after you handle the money talk."

"Whatever. C'mon let's go." Erma got up and brushed off her vivid, floral, rayon pleated skirt.

"Take off, Erma, my long legs and boots will catch up." Ginger took a moment to get her focus.

"Suit yourself. Close the door when you leave." Erma took off for Wes's corner room.

Ginger caught up to Erma in just a couple of minutes. "Remember, you go first."

"Sounds good." Erma nodded. She and Ginger made an odd-looking team, walking with a purpose to a show down. Erma sported her lace-up, rubber soled oxfords, hose, and loud floral skirt. Her hair stank, plastered with enough hairspray to choke a horse. Ginger strode out with one step for every two of Erma's. Ginger's boots were polished, her jeans were tight, and her lab coat caught on the air and floated away from her body as she marched down the hall. Even so, Ginger was clearly the professional between the two. They neared Wes's room and their pace naturally slowed.

Chapter 47

Present Day

KNOCK, KNOCK, KNOCK. Wes opened the door with a questioning startle on his face. "Erma? Ginger?" He was trying to think quickly, but for him, nothing happened quickly in the mornings.

"Mr. Lyons—"

"That's Pastor Lyons, right, Sister Erma?" He tucked in his messy shirt and combed his straggly hair, trying to appear more presentable.

Wes was not fully awake, but there was nothing like a pissed off administrator you have been fleecing, to sober you up quickly. "Please come in, ladies. He pulled out the folding chairs he kept for visitors. "To what do I owe this pleasure."

"You owe me money, Mr. Lyons."

"What? There must be some mistake."

Erma handed him the letter of notice. "I will give you two weeks before putting this plan into action. You get me the money and we can find a way to move forward. If I don't have the money within these two weeks. I will formally go through the process of having you evicted."

Wes's mouth gaped open and his mind raced. "Uh, wow. I will have to do some research."

"Don't research too long, the clock is ticking. Don't mess with me, Mr. Lyons. I will not be the loser in this situation."

"I will make some calls and get back to you in the next few days." Wes got a softness in his eyes that Erma had never seen. His usual snap of confidence had been reduced to a soul requesting mercy.

Ginger then stepped a little closer. "There's more, Wes."

"Oh, what else?"

"We need to talk to you about Skylar." Ginger searched his eyes.

"Skylar is such a caring young girl. She is the brightest part of my day." Wes paused for more information.

Ginger scooted her chair near Wes. "We know that Skylar was supplying your opioids."

He gazed down at the floor and clenched his eyes tightly, causing the crevices in his face to deepen. "N-n-no. Don't get her in trouble. She is an angel trying to help all who suffer. Please, listen to me."

Ginger interlaced her fingers and gathered all the courage she could muster. "Wes, there is more. When she arrived home from being fired, she took some opioids and napped in her car before getting out. She must have been trying to relax and figure out what she was going to tell her grandma."

He looked from Ginger's face to Erma's and he knew something was drastically wrong. Even Erma had a face of sadness and emotion.

"When she woke up, we think she must have gotten sick. She opened the door to throw up and was hit by oncoming traffic. They are doing all they can. She is in intensive care at Emory with life threatening injuries."

He searched Ginger's and Erma's faces. "She is a strong kid, she can—"

"Yes, she is strong and she is fighting, but we have no guarantees." Ginger was direct and empathetic as she reached to touch Wes's shoulder.

Wes dropped to his knees and covered his face with his hands. "N-no! No. It can't be true." He raised his face to search Ginger's eyes, which were red and glistening with tears that ran down her face and dripped to the floor.

"I know you are her friend, Wes. I am so sorry."

"She is probably my *only* friend." His guttural sobs amplified the anguish of his heart.

"Okay, I will leave you with this." Erma handed him the letter promising eviction. "You can talk about the contents of the letter with Ginger or myself."

"Letter?" Wes held the letter in his hand, yet asked, "What letter?"

Ginger leaned over to Erma. "I got this, Erma, give me a little time with him."

"Good idea, Ginger. I have to be somewhere in fifteen minutes." Erma stepped toward Wes and gave him three sharp pats on his shoulder. "I am sorry about Skylar's untimely accident, but you have to get real, here. You have to make things right to stay here. You have two weeks. Ginger will help you if you need it."

"Ginger, I want to be kept abreast of this situation. Got it?" She gave a fleeting nod as she exited Wes's room.

Wes remained on the floor as his emotions continued to flow with anguished thoughts and memories, his world crushed in the span of five minutes.

Ginger lowered herself to the floor and sat cross-legged leaning shoulder-to-shoulder with Wes. Her shoulders shook as she wept with no reservation. She gathered her composure. "Okay, you gotta level with me. I am sorry to dump all this on you right now, but damn it, Wes, something *good* has got to come out of this. Start talking, man. We have all made mistakes. Level with me."

Wes trembled with heartache. "Next to my ex-wife, Jennifer, Skylar is the kindest person I ever met. I sought her out, hoping she would hook me up with some oxy. One day I noticed she stashed a scrap of paper in her pocket and that led me to ask her. When she told me that her grandma was a huge fan of my ministry, I knew I had her. Just so you know, I was prescribed opioids after my wreck that was plastered all over the newspapers. They told me it was safe. I believed them. I lost my son to an overdose. He overdosed on *my* opioid prescription after his girlfriend broke up with him. That is what *really* pushed me off the cliff. It was just a long fall to the bottom. I kept asking for re-fills and they kept giving them to me. I had a problem. I was a preacher with a multi-million-dollar empire and a habit I couldn't shake. I lost it all. When I started probing the streets for the bane of my existence, I lost all respect for myself and my ministry. I disappeared after my divorce and wanted to fade away into nothingness. I was broken in spirit and body, living on the streets. I decided to see if I could con Erma into staying here a while. She was easier to manipulate than I expected. Once I got settled in and found a way to stay apart from most of the people, all I had to do was find a supplier. That's where Skylar came in." He made a quick unexpected inhale, then began blubbering uncontrollable sobs. His cries almost didn't sound human. His suffering was palpable.

Ginger moved in front of Wes and took his hands. "Look at me. Is this the first emotion you have allowed your heart to feel? If you have been numbing yourself with Oxycodone, you have probably been hiding from anything that was difficult emotionally, but this... you can't hide from and you can't justify."

"She was so kind and told me once she had to stop helping me, because she wanted to be a nurse. She wanted to be like you, Ginger." Ginger closed her eyes as if it could make it all go away. "I talked her into a continued, occasional tap. That was only last week."

Ginger took a huge breath of air and blew it out her mouth. "I am gonna leave you to your thoughts. All this peaks with the eviction notice. Read the letter and let me know what you think."

"I can tell you already what I think. I have no money and I have nobody. I will be moving. Thanks. Now, if you don't mind, I would like to be by myself."

"Sure, Wes. Even though I don't agree with what you have done, you are still one of my residents. I will do anything I can to help you. That is my job and you can still count on me."

"Thanks, Ginger. Give me some time."

Ginger leaned in and gave him a hug. "We all need love, Wes. We have all fallen short and we have all been saved from ourselves. You will be given a way out. That is just how the Man Upstairs works. I am not the most religious person, but I believe in God and I believe he loves all of us. Get back to me in the next couple of days. We will talk about the money."

"Okay. Talk to you soon." As Ginger left, Wes thought about Ginger's words, *we have all been saved from ourselves.* Wes laid face-down on the floor in humility and repentance. *God, make a way where there seems to be no way. I will change, God. I will change.*

Wes had to get out of his room. He paced the halls and searched his soul for any flicker of hope or life changing inspiration. He felt like it was time for another hit of "help," but the thought of taking another oxy was not an option. *I am gonna really quit this time, for Skylar.* Sweat poured from his skin as he combed his hand through his greasy hair. As he paced the halls, he decided to drop by the cafeteria and get a cup of coffee. As he got closer to the dining room, he heard a sweet melody coming from the parlor, near the facility entry. Like the Pied Piper, the music was leading him. The closer he got to the front, the more the melody swelled. It had been years since he had given his attention to his first love, music. He had to get closer. It was balm for his wounded soul. As he turned the corner to the parlor door, he stepped into a powerful sight. The baby grand piano was positioned near the window and the sun, breaking through clouds, was streaming across the face of a young man that could have been Wes in his college days. The song, "I Don't Know How to Love Him" flowed over him like sweet oil poured on the wounds of his heart. It was like he was watching himself decades ago, singing to his dad's church in the early days.

Wes couldn't take his eyes off the young man and sang along with him under his breath. Wes began to weep, washing the dirt, the lies, the craving, and disappointment free from his spirit. He sat quietly as God dealt with him in the most personal way. *God, I really* don't *know how to love you. I have offended you while I have made a mockery of the gifts you have given me and wasted the treasures you showered upon me. Please give me a second chance, God, please.*

The young man suddenly realized he was not alone. With a start, he stopped playing and wiped his sweaty palms. "Oh hi, mister. I thought I was by myself. I am just practicing for a play. We have dress rehearsals in a few days. I am a little nervous." He avoided eye contact with Wes.

"What is your name, young man?" Wes managed the words without sobbing.

"Jordan." The boy smiled an innocent grin.

His words sent shivers up Wes's spine. *Jordan. What are the chances that I would find a boy who looked like me as a boy, and is named Jordan, singing the very song I sang in my dad's church? The song that literally changed my life.*

"I know it is supposed to be sung by a girl, but I just love this song. I think it is for everybody." He spun around on the piano bench to see Wes face-to-face. He wasn't as threatened now that they had spoken a little bit.

"I sang that song fifty years ago, Jordan." He was taking in the spitting image of himself and chills moved across his body as the hairs stood at attention on his arms. He was speaking to the boy, but he was also speaking to himself. "You know, it is a simple expression, stating I don't know God the way I should and I want to know him better. It is a song about getting real with God, honestly and wholeheartedly. Where can a guy watch this play you are in, Jordan?"

"Uh, at my school, Jefferson High School, a week from Friday at 7:00 p.m." Jordan spun about to see if anyone else was around.

"I will be there, Jordan. Thank you for taking me back in time. I needed to hear that song in the worst way. In fact, God used you today. Thanks."

"Really? God *used* me? Huh... that's wild. Well, see you around, mister, I gotta go."

Wes watched the mirror image of himself at eighteen leave Fireside. He sat in the silence and knew God had not given up on him. God called out to him in the only voice Wes recognized, a voice from his past...his own. Wes sat and cried tears of joy. He still had a purpose. In fact, he was now able to see, hear, and understand much better, the full depth of God's love. He now better understood those who struggle and long to feel God's touch. *God, thank you for being God. I never knew the full depth of your love till you lifted me from the pit I threw my life into. I get it now, God. I get it, and I am going to get my life together and make up for lost time.* He felt a warmth and a closeness to God he had not felt in quite a while. A burning... a yearning... a new calling to speak of God's love.

Wes's detox was difficult. Compared to most who detox, this was one of the worst he had seen in his circle of addicted friends. The shakes, the sweats, the nausea, the horrific pain, and this creepy-crawling, sensation that his insides were going to come through his skin. During this most difficult time, it was his thoughts of Skylar and his prayers with God, which included just as much listening as talking, that got him through it. He swore at times that it would kill him, but each time he thought of back-sliding, a vivid picture of Skylar in his mind kept him on the right path.

###

Ginger rested with her back against the brick wall, her burning cigarette draped over her knee while her mind decompressed by the dumpsters. Drawing in a harsh drag of cigarette smoke, Ginger turned to see the last person she expected to see peeking out the security door by the dumpster. "What are you doing out here, Wes?" She tilted her head to the sky and blew a stream of smoke.

"Uh, if I could just have a moment of your time?" He shifted from foot-to-foot with his hands in his pockets.

"Sure, man. Shoot. Whatcha got?" Ginger was clearly surprised he would have the balls to address her. She flicked her ash and waited for his response.

"I just thought I would let you know, I will be making plans to move out, but I would like to ask you a favor, though."

"Really? Shoot. What is it?" Ginger was surprised and anxious for his reply.

"I want to give a prayer meeting for Skylar, here at Fireside. We can have it in the chapel, and I will keep it short so that hopefully everyone who wants to pray can attend."

"Wes, do you think you are the one to give poems and prayers for Skylar?" She waited to hear his response.

"I know, I know. I am not much. I have thrown my life in the gutter, but I love her and was a direct recipient of her care and love. She loves me, too. At least she cared for me while she was here. We were friends. I want to do it, Ginger, please."

"I doubt that anyone will want to hear you speak, but I will ask Erma to okay it and I will back you, mainly because I sense a change of heart with you. Everyone deserves a second chance." Ginger stood and brushed off her jeans, "I will tell Erma you are going to move out. That will make her happy and possibly push your wishes over the goal line."

"Thanks. Anything you can do would be great."

"Oh, and Wes... you better be sober for the services, or I will shut it down faster than you can say Oxycodone."

"Got it. You won't have to worry. I won't forget it, Ginger. Thank you for giving me a chance. I won't let you down."

Chapter 48

Present Day

Mr. Epstein and Ruth sat at the entryway of Fireside, greeting anyone who might be stopping in for Skylar's prayer service. Dressed up in their temple-attending best, Mr. Epstein and Ruth greeted the guests as they entered, "Welcome to Fireside. Are you here for the prayer meeting for our dear friend Skylar? Have a program." He nodded to Ruth who would hold out a leaflet with Skylar on the front. In the picture on the cover, she was laughing while she took a classmate's blood pressure in the pre-nurses' training course. "Thank you for coming. The chapel is down the hall and to the right." Ruth would point down the hall, where James waited to further direct the crowd to the correct area.

A lot of interest was shown in this service to pray for and celebrate Skylar. She was loved by her co-workers, family, and friends, and even though she made some bad decisions, she was also someone's daughter... someone's friend.... someone's classmate... someone's sister. Regardless of her failures, she made a positive impact on those she met.

Everyone who knew Skylar had a story of how she had helped them in one way or another. The services were needed... supporting and praying for her, but also so that those who were hurting could heal. The chapel was crowded. In fact, Ginger had to open the collapsible divider to increase the room size. As people filed into the chapel with silent reverence, a poster-sized portrait of Skylar was at the front. The chapel décor was tasteful and respectful. Soft music played and all walks of life were present to show their respect for young Skylar. No one knew who was presiding over the services. It was a moot point to most in the room. The important person was Skylar.

As the hour drew near to 5:00 people started checking their watches, anxious to start the service.

###

Wes waited down the hall, also keeping a good watch on the time, knowing he would likely be entering a less than accepting crowd. Wes held his Bible in one hand and the service program in the other. *God, give me the words to give proper honor to Skylar and proper praise to You. I will follow You, one step at a time. Amen.* Wes stood and opened his Bible to Titus 1:15-16, an old habit, and read his favorite passage, "Everything is pure to those whose hearts are pure. But nothing is pure to those who are corrupt and unbelieving, because their minds and consciences are corrupt. Such people say they know God, but they deny Him by the way they live." There was nothing in his deceptive cut-out stash. He closed his eyes and then closed the Bible, holding true to his promise. *I* will *change.*

###

Wes stood at the chapel entrance and scanned the unique crowd. Employees, co-workers, residents, and even some family and friends came to lift up Skylar, and her doctors. Erma stood waiting near the door at the rear. She did not want to celebrate a thief. Skylar put a smudge on the reputation of her staff. She would not prevent others, but she would have no part of it. Ginger and Rob were poised and ready, on the back row.

Wes took a deep breath and held his shoulders back. *Thy will, not mine.* He slowly stepped to the front of the chapel, laid his Bible on the pulpit, and made eye contact with several people. "Good afternoon, all. We are here to lift up the life of our friend, our co-worker, Skylar."

"Uh-Hmmm." Erma cleared her throat, standing at the rear of the chapel in disgust, seeing a con artist who was about to celebrate the life of a thief. The entire room turned to find a fuming Erma. "Mr. Lyons, what are you doing?"

Wes's heart rate quickened, and he instantly stepped from behind the pulpit. "Although I am a pastor and have led services for thousands, I understand that many of you feel that I am the least qualified to preside over *any* service of respectable intent. In fact, *I* would say that I am among those who feel I am not qualified. I have been a disappointment to my family, my friends, and most importantly, I let God down. Please allow me to continue, not to bring attention to myself, but to bring attention to Skylar's need for prayer and to give thanks for her example and servant's heart. True, sacrificial love comes from the Father. Skylar loved all of us with a pure and giving love, unmarked by selfishness or greed. So, friends, if you would like to participate in this prayer meeting for Skylar's life, please stay in your seat. If you can't pray for her life with me, feel free to go with Erma. Perhaps she will pray with you in another room." Wes paused for a few moments.

Surprised, Erma responded, "Well, if you folks want to stay... stay. I will have no part in this situation. I will be in my office."

Wes scanned the chapel and felt his spirit settle into the familiarity of the past. "Let me do something, folks." Wes picked up the pulpit and moved it to the side. "Let me just be perfectly transparent. I *am* the least among you. Over recent years, I lived a life of illicit drugs, lies, and deception."

Ruth turned toward Mr. Epstein in shock. "Is that true?"

Wes overheard Ruth. "Yes, I will tell you it *is* true. It is disgraceful and with God's help, I have been clean since Skylar's accident and with God's help, I will remain sober."

Ruth stood and looked Wes in the eye. "Well, Pastor Wes, I cannot speak for anyone else in this room, but I am happy to listen to what you have to say. No one else in this room has had the guts to give a confessional of our worst selves before a crowd of fifty, much less commit before the same crowd and God to transform into a better person. It takes a person of conviction to confess his sins before many and proclaim his desire and efforts to become a better person. Go ahead, Pastor Lyons, I want to hear what you have to say."

"Me, too," added Mr. Epstein, "At temple last week, we were reminded that we are not called to judge our neighbors. We are called to love our neighbors. Skylar was the single kindest, most compassionate employee in this place, and for that, we should recognize the service and love she gave to all of us daily and join in a common prayer for her healing." The rest of the people nodded or spoke aloud in agreement with Ruth and Mr. Epstein.

Ginger stood. "Well, I may not support the road that led us here, but we are broken, and I certainly can support a road that can lead us to a better place. You have my attention, Wes, please continue."

Wes stood without the prop of the pulpit, feeling it was not right. "I have a passage to mention as we reflect on the life lived by Skylar. 1 Corinthians 13:4-8. 'Love is patient, love is kind. It does not envy; it does not boast; it is not proud. It does not dishonor others; it is not self-seeking; it is not easily angered; it keeps no record of wrongs. Love does not delight in evil, but rejoices with the truth. It always protects, always trusts, always perseveres.' I always smile when I think of the young girl named Skylar, who always had a smile on her face and took her break time to check on me and others. Did she make mistakes? Of course." Wes put his hands in his pockets and slowly paced the front of the room. He stopped and fully faced the crowd. "He among you without sin, cast the first stone." Wes became overcome with emotion and bowed his head for a few moments, trying to regain his composure, because he certainly had no room to pick up a stone. "May I say that even her poor choices were made in the name of trying to help someone who needed it. She was a true follower of God. The scripture tells us that others will know we are Christians by our riches? No. By our underlined Bible? No. By the way we boast of all the things we do for others? No. They will know we are Christians by the way we unselfishly and secretly give love to others, with no concern for selfish gain. This is what Skylar did for me daily, just by showing she cared. I bet she did the same for you." He searched the eyes of those in the pews, many of whom were nodding their heads. "I lured Skylar into a situation that satisfied my unscrupulous weakness while putting her at risk. This is for God to judge, but she put herself in jeopardy to ease the extreme pain of others. So, how do we move forward from a catastrophe like this? We pray for Skylar, that she be healed and lifted above this tragedy. Pray that this doesn't only change Skylar, but that we all pray to give to others as selflessly as she did on the daily. Love others... even when you might think they don't deserve it. Carry on Skylar's legacy by showing kindness and love to all you meet. Look around you. We have all been placed in a position to see others who could use a positive word or an act of love. Seek those you can touch. Be *God's* hands and *His* love, to help a hurting world.

"I am going to give you a challenge today. Live like you are a special agent for God. Today, I am a better man because of the life Skylar lived. I am determined to not let her hardships be in vain." By now, the chapel was so quiet the crowd could hear Mr. Epstein's Timex watch ticking. Every mind and every ear were fixed on the words of Wes Lyons as he was inspired by God. "Skylar was no saint, neither are we. But... she *intentionally* walked in the light of God's love every day, trying to help people one-by-one as she saw their need. She loved people in spite of their humanness and because of God's goodness. Tomorrow, if you see someone who seems torn inside, help them knit themselves back together. Now, I am going to pray for Skylar, my own unique prayer. Rather than me praying for all of you as a group, I ask that you do the same. Spread out across this room and make yourself comfortable to say your own prayer silently to God. Now, God forgive us all of our shortcomings as we fan out to lift our friend Skylar. Touch her as only you can. Send your pure healing light to penetrate every cell and give her a second chance. Now feel free to spread out over the room as I sing a song offering to inspire you as you lift our friend in prayer." Wes sang "He Ain't Heavy; He's, My Brother." He invited all to pray in their own wonderful and unique ways.

"This concludes our service. If you would like to write a note to Skylar's family, there is a notebook at the back of the room. Also, I want everyone here to know that each morning, the chapel will be open for prayer, 7:00 to 7:30, if anyone feels inspired to come and pray for Skylar through the workweek." Wes turned his attention to the back of the chapel, and Erma stood in the doorway with teardrops staining the front of her dress as she quietly sobbed. Wes turned to avoid creating an obvious conflict.

Erma stepped forward a few steps. "Wes, I heard most of your talk. I must say, it was not what I expected. Would you please stop by my office after you have dismissed the service?"

"Sure, Erma. I will be there shortly. Thank you." He turned his attention back to the crowd and finished, "Go in peace and serve your neighbor, like Skylar did."

Wes knocked on Erma's door and waited for her invitation to enter.

"Good. C'mon in here, Wes. Do you remember the first time we spoke in my office?"

"Yes, I do." Then he thought to himself, *how could I forget, I was focused in on you like a used car salesman trying to reach my quota at the end of the month.*

"Yesterday, I was so angry with you, because of all the destruction caused in my facility. You were the lowest of the low during your stay here. But Skylar's tragedy has made an impact on you." Erma studied the sober, clean-shaven face and saw a changed man. "Let me change the subject. I know you are going to move in a few days. What will you be doing? Where are you going to go?"

"Uh, I don't know yet. I was on the streets before I found Fireside. I can live on the streets again—"

"No."

"What do you mean, no?"

"I can't believe I am doing this. Read this letter." Erma handed him a letter on Fireside Corporation letter head stationary.

Wes read it and glanced back at Erma. "You have been awarded a grant for a pastor placement. That is nice, but why did you want me to read this?"

"Our corporate office is putting out an initiative to improve the community within Fireside and all of their properties. One of the initiatives is to start a church onsite, not just someone who, as an outreach, comes in on Thursday to give a sermon after they have already preached for their regular church. I am talking about a church that is located in our building with a preacher that lives *in* our building. The preacher will preach, visit the sick, teach the Bible, and everything else that a preacher does. The pay is not that great, though.

"Wes, how about you? Would you be interested?" Tears rimmed along her lower eyelids. As she blinked, tears dripped onto her cheeks, making shiny trails down her face. "Listening to you speak in that chapel, I saw and heard the Wes I remembered. The old Pastor Lyons, who got real with the congregation and spread hope and love to *everyone*. I think you made mistakes, but I also think that you are what we need at Fireside to rekindle the community we want here. The position is a residency, meaning that most of your pay is room and board, with a small stipend for spending money. That's the best offer I can make. What do you say?"

"What do I say? Thank you... and *yes*." He stood and held out his hand. "Deal. I am a little unorthodox at times, but I will seek to serve God and those living here at Fireside. Thank you for this opportunity. I won't let you down."

Wes opened his Bible and turned to Titus. He dug deep into his stash and dug out two Tic Tacs and popped them into his mouth. It was his first official service at Fireside.

A new routine for Pastor Lyons. Wes closed his Bible, Wes and stepped out to greet his congregation. Not only did he see the regular ones he expected, like Mr. Epstein, Ruth, James, and Ms. Klinger, but sitting next to Ginger was Eric, Hannah, Rose, Dixie, old friend Celeste with Hope, and Rob. They wanted to hear a preacher who had fought some of the battles of life...and won. It took a young, everyday nursing aide, with a heart full of love, to show Wes that a successful preacher wasn't confirmed with world tours, jammed concert stages, and celebrities clamoring over his latest book. No, the success of a pastor is proven by his ability to live a life reaching for others in love and his ability to keep pointing to the light.

Wes stepped to the front of the room and moved the pulpit to the side. "Thank you for coming. Listen and hear the Word of the Lord. 'I waited patiently on the Lord. He turned to me and heard my cry. He lifted me out of the slimy pit, out of the mud and mire. He set my feet on a rock and gave me a firm place to stand. He put a new song in my mouth, a hymn of praise to our God. Many will see and fear and put their trust in Him.'" He scanned the chapel, readying himself for his first full service at Fireside, and he took a double take. It was Jennifer, his ex-wife standing in the back of the chapel. Quietly smiling and nodding her approval. She put her hand over her heart, showing her care for him. Overcome with her obvious forgiveness, Wes let a reflexive noise escape the depth of his being, his uncontrollable reaction to her amazing gift. He took a deep breath and proceeded with a much-warranted comment. "Everyone, please welcome my ex-wife, Jennifer. She is truly a saint and the last person I would expect to see here today. Thank you from the bottom of my heart."

"I took the 'Left Cheek Challenge,' didn't I? I will see it through."

The congregation was mumbling, "Left cheek challenge? What's the left cheek challenge?"

"The Left Cheek Challenge is an inside joke from college." Wes grinned with the memory of their college days.

"Don't let me interrupt. I saw the little article on you and Fireside in the community section of the paper and wouldn't have missed this for the world. I'll be on the back row over here. Please continue."

Wes continued with a huge smile and a pep in spirit. "As we continue in an attitude of prayer, we will start our service with prayer requests. Remember to include Skylar in your thoughts and prayers, as she continues to improve and fight for recovery from her accident. She continues to fight every day to regain her strength and cognitive ability. Who else has a request?"

"My brother is getting a pacemaker," Ruth noted, "please pray for him."

Ginger raised her hand. "Please say a word for me. Next week I take a wound care certification class," Ginger noted, "I may need divine intervention, if ya know what I mean." The crowd chuckled softly.

"Okay, everyone, bow your heads and talk to God, with these and your own silent prayer requests."

###TWO YEARS LATER###

Wes stood at the Fireside entrance, holding a stack of programs, ready to welcome anyone coming to attend his Sunday service, starting in ten minutes. "Hello, welcome to the Fireside Sunday Services." He gave the mom of three young kids a program. "If you want to take your kids to children's church, you will find Mrs. Klinger down this hall in the parlor."

"Oh, great. There is children's church? I might actually get to hear you speak," she said with a smile.

Wes saw another group coming down the sidewalk, a group of college kids with pink hair and piercings in places Wes didn't know was possible, and some girls holding hands.

"Hi, you guys. There is a youth gathering down the hall. It celebrates diversity and welcomes all of you and your friends. A guy named Rob is waiting for you with doughnuts, soda, and coffee. After you guys socialize a bit, he will bring you down to the chapel for the service. There is a sign-in list if you have any problems or questions. We are happy to help if we can."

"Cool." A young man, who seemed familiar to Wes, stepped up and peeked into the chapel down the hall. "Are those electric guitars and drums? What is going on in there?"

"You were in *Jesus Christ Super Star* a couple years ago... Jordan, right?" Wes remembered.

He stared at Wes suspiciously. "Yeah...how did you know?"

"You practiced on that piano right over there. I came to see your performance at the school. You were very good."

He smiled. "Thanks."

Wes told the group of kids, "Anyone who wants to sing in our services will be welcomed. There is a sign-up sheet. We can get you signed-up and ready to perform."

A young girl with pink hair, holding the hand of her girlfriend, spoke up, "Even me?"

Wes stepped closer to her, "Especially you. We are a gathering that celebrates an awesome God. All are welcome to celebrate our loving and welcoming God. Period."

"Sweet. I will be finding that sign-up list." She smiled and nudged her girlfriend in the side.

"Great, kids, keep moving down the hall. We have some folks right behind you. Come visit me anytime. I live here at Fireside. All you have to do is ask the receptionist, she will find me." Wes held out his watch. "Wow, I need to get to the chapel. Come in everybody. Church starts in a few minutes."

Wes moved the pulpit to the side. He made this a part of his service intentionally. He wanted it to be perfectly clear that he was not preaching at them, but *sharing* his own experience of following God. "James, will you please give the folks our announcements for the day."

James stood and commanded everyone's attention with his confident, baritone voice.

"Thanks, James. Mr. Epstein, would you please offer a prayer of thanks as we start."

Mr. Epstein stood, with Ruth's help. "Shalom. Let us pray." Mr. Epstein gave a short, heartfelt prayer. Never before at Fireside, had Mr. Epstein been given the opportunity to publicly share his Jewish faith with others who believed. He cherished this opportunity. It gave him, and his beliefs, a place at the table.

Wes scanned the congregation that held the hopes, disappointments, dreams, and hardships of a diverse people. "Welcome to Fireside Chapel. All are welcome. I would like to remind everyone that my ex-wife, Jennifer, will be speaking next week, as I will be sharing at one of our sister Fireside chapels." He turned and saw Ginger leaning on the door frame with her arms crossed in front.

"Come in, Ginger. There is a place there on the back row, right by Skylar." He pointed to the chair within her reach, right next to Skylar and her grandma, Skylar with a cane and her grandma in a wheelchair.

"Nah, Wes. I am doing my nursing thing. Just wanted to drop by for a second. Maybe I will catch the next one."

"I would like that." He waved as she left. Wes gave his attention back to the congregation. "Regardless of what we look like, sound like, think like; regardless of our mistakes, our successes, or failures; God loves us ALL the same. He reaches out to ALL of us; and calls us ALL by name—"

"Amen, Wes, amen!" Mr. Epstein shouted with enthusiasm.

James added, "Bring it, brother!"

Rob sneaked in on the back row just in time to shout, "Never thought I'd be doing this but… Amen, Wes, I got you!"

Everyone chuckled and mumbled in agreement. They *all* fit in, and for some it was a first.

Wes spoke from the heart, and it felt good. It felt right. He was back in his element, using his gifts for the benefit of others and the glory of God. After he closed his Bible, turned out the lights to the chapel, and returned to his room, he sat on his bed and reflected on the day. He should have felt tired and ready for bed. He had a long day but he was motivated like he had never been before. *I'll get a head start on the next sermon.*

He went to the closet and dragged out the old box that held all his dad's sermons, the ones he left to Wes when his illness worsened. Over the time of moving and home-lessness, he found a way to keep the sermons with him, stowed away in the abandoned car near the homeless en-campment. Wes protected them the best he could. Wes developed the system of taking a sermon from the original box and putting it in another box after he used it, keeping the 'used' separated from the 'not used.'

Wes opened the box and dug down to the bottom. His hand searched left to right and found a thin stack of pages. *Hmmm... guess I'm down to the last one.* Peering into the box, he pulled out the stack of papers and some-thing at the very bottom caught his eye. It was a single piece of paper that had been folded and twisted over years of sloshing papers in a box too big for the remaining sheets. Taking out the last sermon, he was anxious to see the title, "In Humility, Value Others Above Yourself.' Ephesians 4:2. *Cool, a sermon based on humility. Love it.* He reached in to take out the orphaned, messed-up page. He pulled it out and smoothed the paper so it would fit the stack like the others. As he ran his hand over the paper to smooth it flat, he realized it was not the last page to the sermon. It was a letter from his father. *Oh my gosh! This letter was here all this time?*

His heartbeat was like a bass drum, the beating getting louder as it progressed.

"Wes, if you are reading this, you have reached the bottom of the 'sermon box.' I am so proud of you for sticking with this and running the course all these years. I am sure you have lived an exciting life! You don't know how to do it any other way. I want to apologize for the lack of understanding, well, the lack of *desire* to understand your heart and your life. I was hard on you and that was wrong. I knew that God had his hand on my life, and I was supposed to write these sermons for the world. I never understood that my long-haired, rock-n-roll son would be the one to deliver those messages. God used *you* to complete *my* life's calling. Remember this above everything else in this letter, Wes, I love you, and always did. I should have said it more. I should have considered your ideas and encouraged your creativity more. My calling was made complete when you took these sermons and gave them life. God used your talents to complete my calling; He used my knowledge to complete yours. No one reaches their purpose without the talents of others. If you try to do it all on your own, the road will get bumpy, and it will be too difficult to travel alone. Embrace the talent in those around you, and they will embrace you, walking with you to the finish line. I realized, at the end of my days, you were not sent to lift me up and support my ministry, but rather I was sent to this earth to elevate yours. Know this, I will always be with you, and I am so incredibly proud of you.

I love you, Dad

Wes sat alone in his tiny room. Holding a crumpled piece of paper, without cheering crowds and celebrity receptions, he finally felt he had arrived. He was good enough;

he was accepted and complete. *Thanks, Dad... just thanks. I will see you on the other side.*

THE END

About the Author

We hope you enjoyed this book. Please consider writing a review to help other readers enjoy FIRESIDE: The Wes Lyons Story.

Dee Britt

Dee Britt grew up in the small town of Anadarko, Oklahoma. As a young adult, Dee fronted several bands. Her songwriting revealed a love for storytelling, and it eventually led to the Fireside fiction series. The book's medical setting and love for elders arose from her "day job" as a physical therapist, where she provided function-saving treatments to elders in assisted living centers. Although none of the characters are biographical, all the characters are inspired by patients and clinicians Dee worked with over her years as a physical therapist. Her books are an effort to give back and give a voice to those whose history is often overlooked simply because they are old or infirm. To her patients who have taught her about the important things in life, Dee sends a big thank you!

www.ingramcontent.com/pod-product-compliance
Lightning Source LLC
Chambersburg PA
CBHW050953180726
48291CB00006B/1809